# CRITICAL ...
# RUTH AXT...

## LILAC SPRING

"*Lilac Spring* blooms with heartfelt yearning and genuine
conflict as Cherish and Silas seek God's will for their
lives. Fascinating details about nineteenth-century
shipbuilding are planted here and there, bringing an
historical feel to this faith-filled romance."
—Liz Curtis Higgs, bestselling author of
*Whence Came a Prince*

## WILD ROSE

"...the charm of the story lies in Morren's ability to
portray real passion between her characters. *Wild Rose* is
not so much a romance as an old-fashioned love story."
—*Booklist*

"...a beautiful, believable love relationship...
Richly defined characters and settings
enhance this meaningful novel."
—*Romantic Times*

## WINTER IS PAST

"...inspires readers toward a deeper trust
in the transforming power of God....
[Readers] will find in *Winter Is Past* a novel
not to be put down and a new favorite author."
—*Christian Retailing*

"Ruth Axtell Morren writes with skill, sensitivity and
great heart about the things that matter most....
Make room on your keeper shelf for a new favorite."
—Susan Wiggs, *New York Times* bestselling author

"...faith journeys are so realistic all readers can benefit
from the story. Highly recommended."
—*CBA Marketplace*

# RUTH AXTELL MORREN

# LILAC SPRING

Steeple
Hill®

Published by Steeple Hill Books™

STEEPLE HILL BOOKS

Steeple
Hill®

ISBN 0-373-78550-X

LILAC SPRING

Copyright © 2005 by Ruth Axtell

This edition published by arrangement with Steeple Hill Books.

® and TM are trademarks of Steeple Hill Books, used under license.
Trademarks indicated with ® are registered in the United States Patent
and Trademark Office, the Canadian Trade Marks Office and in other
countries.

www.SteepleHill.com

**Printed in U.S.A.**

For the town of Cutler,
from where I drew my inspiration for *Lilac Spring*.

My thanks also to the guys at *The Boat School* of
Washington County Technical College in Eastport,
who allowed me to ask many questions and observe them
as they worked on their wooden boats.

# ✢ Prologue ✢

*Haven's End*
*Maine, 1861*

"You're the new 'prentice, aren't you?" Cherish asked the boy hunched over one of Papa's drafting tables.

He twisted around, a startled look on his thin face, as if she'd caught him doing something wrong.

Cherish stepped through the doorway of the boat shop and approached the table, her rag doll, Annie, swinging back and forth from one hand.

The boy swiped the edge of his palm against the corner of his eye, watching her silently as she neared.

"Aren't you?"

Staring at her through disconcertingly gray eyes, he finally answered, "Yes."

"Why're you crying?"

"I'm *not* crying!"

"Yes, you are. I can tell. Your eyes are all red." It suddenly occurred to her that maybe, being a big boy, he didn't want to admit to crying. She never minded crying; it usually made her feel better afterward. The only problem was it usually followed a spanking.

"Whatcha' doin'?" she asked curiously, peering beyond him to the drafting table.

"Nothin'. Just looking."

"That's Papa's model." She stood on tiptoe at the edge of the table, eyeing the wooden half-hull sliced in sections like a loaf of bread cut lengthwise.

She dragged another stool over to the table and climbed up on it. "I waited till Papa was down at the yard 'fore I came over this morning. It was a long time! Then I was 'fraid Mama wouldn't let me walk over." She smiled. "She thinks I'm outside playing with my kitty-cat."

The boy said nothing.

"I cried yesterday," she told him, settling Annie on her lap. "Mama sent me to my room."

He continued eyeing her as if deciding whether she was friend or foe. He had nice eyes, she decided. Green-tinged gray, like a choppy sea. "What did you do?" he asked.

"I pulled kitty's tail. I was trying to tie her to my dolly's stroller, but she wouldn't 'bey me."

She could see the beginnings of a smile tugging at the corners of his lips, and that made her glad.

"Kitty scratched me. See?" She pushed up her sleeve and showed him the bright red line running up her forearm.

"Papa never sends me to my room or spanks me. Mama says I'll be spoiled if someone don't spank me. Papa says I'm his little lady and should never be spanked."

The two sat quietly for a few moments. The boy's attention, she could see, had returned to the pieces of carved wood on the table. "Are you from far away?" she asked, shifting on the hard stool.

"Real far," he murmured.

"Where?" she asked, finding it hard to picture anything beyond Haven's End.

"Swan's Island."

"Swan's Island," she repeated in awe. Her mama had just read her a story about a swan the night before. She imagined a beautiful island full of snowy-white swans.

"Do you have a mama and papa?" she asked when he said nothing more.

"Just a mama. Papa was lost at sea," he added in a fierce tone, as if proud of the fact.

"That's too bad."

He sniffed, rubbing the back of his hand against his nose. His thick golden hair fell over his forehead as he bent over the smooth pieces of wood that fitted together in descending order.

"Are you your mama's little gent'man now your papa's gone to heaven?"

He scoffed. "I'm too big to be a little gentleman."

"Are you going to be a gent'man when you grow up?" Papa said she was going to marry a gent'man when she grew up.

"Naw! I'm going to build boats."

She smiled. "I am, too!"

He turned his head toward her as if seeing her for the first time. Instead of laughing at her the way Papa did whenever she told him, he looked interested. "You like boats?"

"I love boats!"

"Your father is going to teach me how to build boats."

She nodded. She'd heard Papa talking about the 'prentice.

He focused on the model again, running his forefinger down the sheer of the gunwale. "Some day I'm going to design them, too," he said softly, reverently. He seemed not to be talking to her, but to himself.

"Me, too," she replied at once, wanting to bring his attention back to her, although she wasn't quite sure what "design" meant. That was okay. If the new boy could do it, so could she.

"What's your name?" she asked, taking a liking to him despite his aloofness. He was nice, not like those big bullies at the schoolhouse.

"Silas."

"I'm Cherish."

"Cherish." He turned his gray eyes on her again. "That's a funny name."

"It is not!"

He grinned, revealing even white teeth against the honey-hued skin of his face. "Do people call you Cherry?"

"No! My name is Cherish 'lizabeth Winslow."

"Cherish Elizabeth Winslow," he repeated. "That sounds too grown-up for you. How old are you, Cherry?"

"*Cherish,*" she corrected, and held up her fingers. "I'm five and a half."

He nodded.

"How old are you?"

His thin chest puffed out. "I'm twelve."

She remembered his red-rimmed eyes. He hadn't seemed so grown-up then. She looked down at her doll. "Here. You can have Annie. She's good for wiping tears. See?" She picked up a limp rag arm and wiped her eyelid in pretend fashion. "I use her a lot."

He frowned, forced to take the doll she'd thrust at him. Before he had a chance to do anything with it, they were interrupted by her father's voice.

"Silas! What are you up to?"

Silas jumped down from the stool he'd been straddling. "Nothing, sir."

"You're not here to loaf but to learn a trade. Now, go stow your gear upstairs and report down at the yard."

"Hello, Papa." Cherish climbed down more slowly from the stool. "I was talking with Silas."

Her father gave her cheek a soft pinch when she reached him. "Cherish, sweetheart, haven't I told you more than once to stay out of Papa's boat shop? This is a place for men."

"I'm going to 'sign boats," she told him, ignoring the scolding.

He chuckled, taking her by the hand and leading her toward the door. "You're going to learn to be a lady and marry a handsome gentleman. Run on home now to Mama. Papa'll see you at dinner."

As he walked her to the door, she realized her other hand was empty and she remembered she'd given Annie away. She gave one last, longing look toward the drafting table, but there was no sign of her doll. She remembered Silas's hunched back and the sight of red-rimmed eyes and she shrugged away her sense of loss. He needed Annie more than she right now.

# ✑ *Chapter One* ✑

*May 1875*

Cherish paused on the threshold of the boat shop. The smell of cedar wood tickled her nostrils. She breathed deeply of its lemony, spicy fragrance and smiled. Home.

The rays of the late-afternoon sun pierced the tops of the ancient fir trees across the inlet and shone through the windows of the boat shop, picking up the dust motes and bringing a golden gleam to the wooden frames of the boat hulls laid upside down in various stages of construction. Her eyes didn't linger on these; there'd be time enough to examine the works in progress. She was interested only in the shop's lone occupant.

Silas stood at a worktable. Intent on his task, he leaned his wiry frame against a plane as he pushed it against a plank of wood. A curling cedar shaving emerged from the tool and dropped to the floor, a floor littered with a hundred others.

"Hello, Silas," she said softly.

His eyelids rose and she was the focus of those gray eyes—the turbulent green-hued gray of a stormy sea.

"Cherish!" A smile broke out on his face, transforming it from a frown of intense concentration to an expression of boyish delight.

Cherish felt a slight easing of the tension that had been building with each mile she'd traveled closer to Haven's End. After days across the Atlantic and a night up the coast from Boston, she'd finally arrived back at her home port.

She stood motionless a moment longer, wanting him to take a good look at her. The golden afternoon light shone on her. She knew the slate-blue of her gown complemented her complexion and eyes. She was glad she'd had the outfit made in Paris, just before her departure.

Every item was in place. She'd brushed and redressed her hair just before disembarking. She knew how to read men's appreciation—she'd learned in the countless European capitals she'd visited in the past year. Now she wanted to read it in the only eyes that mattered.

He laid down his plane and took a step toward her. "We didn't expect you until tomorrow. I would have come to meet you, but I knew your father would want to have you all to himself."

"That's all right. I'd rather say hello to you right here." How she wanted to run to her childhood companion and throw herself into his arms. But suddenly she felt shy. She was no longer a girl in pigtails but a young lady he hadn't seen in over two years. Oh, how desperately she wanted him to see the changes in her.

So with deliberate steps, those years of balancing a heavy tome on her head at the young ladies' academy paying off, Cherish walked toward Silas. Her skirt rustled, from its ruched panels down to its pleated hem. She carried a small parasol in one hand, swinging it lightly to and fro as she neared him.

When they stood face-to-face, she stretched out her hands to him, still seeking that appreciation in his eyes. It was there…yet, was it?

"How did you get here?" he asked, smiling at her, his hands clasping hers. "Your father said you were sailing in tomorrow. Does he even know you're here?"

She shook her head slowly from side to side, smiling all the while. Did he see how ladylike she'd become since he'd last seen her? Did he notice her hair swept up under the stylish little hat perched atop the ringlets cascading behind her head?

"I took a steamer out of Boston a day early and caught a ride with Captain Stanley on the schooner *Emerald* out of Eastport. I just arrived. My trunks are still down on the wharf," she added, unable to restrain the laughter bubbling out of her.

His gray eyes were alight with amusement. How she'd missed that look! "Your father's planning a big homecoming tomorrow."

"I *know*. That's precisely why I came a day early. I wanted to settle in quietly. Tomorrow I'll be the dutiful daughter, but today…" Her glance strayed across the cluttered boat shop. "Today I want to savor just being home."

He nodded, and she knew he understood. "Are you glad to see me?" she asked, her eyes searching his once again.

"Of course I'm glad. The place isn't the same without Cherry underfoot. But you must have had a grand time—a tour of the Continent. I'm surprised you wanted to come back."

She frowned. "Of course I wanted to come back. This is home." *This is where you are.*

"And you've come back quite the lady."

How she'd dreamed of this moment, when at last he'd see her as a woman.

"Last time I saw you, you were still running around like a hoyden, banging up your fingers with hammer and nails, trailing after Henry to teach you everything about drafting."

"Do I look like a hoyden now?" She let go of his hands and turned around slowly as she'd seen the mannequins do in the House of Worth off the rue de la Paix.

"You're looking so grown-up I hardly recognized you."

Cherish experienced a moment of disappointment at his tone. There was admiration, certainly, but nothing more.

Never mind, she thought, there was plenty of time. She was home for good this time.

"Your father will have a fit when he knows you traveled unaccompanied from Eastport." He frowned. "Did you come up by yourself all the way from Boston?"

She put a finger to her lips. "Shh! There was an acquaintance of ours on board, so I was properly chaperoned. Anyway, I'm back, and that's all that's important. I wanted to say hello to you first, right here, just as when we first met."

He grinned. "You came nosing around to meet the new apprentice and caught him sniveling with homesickness and trying his best to act grown-up."

"You had a right to be homesick. You were only a boy." She took her time examining him, looking for any changes during her two-year absence. His build was still slim and compact, but the lean frame was deceptive. Her glance strayed to his bare forearms. She remembered their corded muscles when they had pulled on a pair of oars across the harbor.

He was in a vest and rolled-up shirtsleeves, his collar undone. His deep blond hair, thick and straight, was pushed away from his face, a face tanned from his hours down below in the yard. He'd always been a serious boy, but now his face showed a deepened maturity.

"Do I pass inspection, Cherry?"

She rolled her eyes. "Haven't I finally outgrown that silly nickname?"

He smiled wickedly. "What's the matter? Remind you too much of the pesky brat you were?"

Before she could take offense, he said, "Europe seems to have agreed with you."

It was about time he noticed. "It was wonderful. Are you glad to have me back?"

"Sure, though I expect you're too refined for the boat shop."

"Not at all." She laid her parasol on a table, fighting the sense of letdown. Something was missing in his welcome. Stifling a sigh, Cherish turned her attention to the boat frames in the large room. "What are you working on?"

"Oh, just finishing up these dories for a Gloucester schooner. We've laid the keel on a schooner down in the yard, now the good weather's come."

She touched the wood he'd been planing. "I *am* going to be coming to the boat shop, you know."

He eyed her sidelong. "Is your father aware of this?"

"Not yet. Not that I've ever hidden my intentions."

Silas brought her a stool and got one for himself. "Why don't you tell old Silas all about it."

She felt on surer ground now. Silas was the only one who truly understood her yearning to be equally involved in the work at her father's boat shop.

"Silas, I need your help."

His mouth turned up on one side. "Already?"

She didn't return his smile. "I didn't come back to Haven's End just to be courted by some gentleman from Hatsfield and get married." She could feel her face coloring at the steady and attentive way he was listening to her. "I know that's what Papa expects. I could have stayed in Boston with Cousin Penelope, if that were the case. Or even in Europe," she added, thinking of the marriage proposals she'd refused.

"Your father would have been sorry to lose you to Boston or the Continent. Ever since your mother passed away, you've been the apple of his eye."

She nodded, remembering that awful time when her mother had fallen ill. "Papa needn't have worried that he'd lose me," she continued more briskly. "I always meant to come back to Haven's End, because I want to work here. In the business. I want to build boats, Silas, just like you. Has…has Papa done anything to replace Henry?" she asked, referring to her cousin, whom her father had hired around the time she'd been sent away to boarding school.

Silas shook his head.

"Is Papa giving you more to do now that Henry has left?" As soon as Henry had reached his majority, he had accepted a job at a larger shipyard in Boston.

"My job's the same as it's always been."

She frowned. "Papa doesn't need to replace Cousin Henry. He has you. You're much more talented than Henry ever could be. I'm sure that's why Papa hasn't found a replacement for him."

When he made no comment, she went on. "My time wasn't completely wasted those years at the young ladies' academy in Massachusetts." She smiled at him conspiratorially. "All that pin money Papa sent me—most of it went for lessons. I learned as much as I could pay for about naval architecture."

She leaned forward eagerly, placing a hand on his forearm. "I'll teach you everything I know. But I'll need your help, Silas. Papa will fight me on this. Do you believe I can work with you here?"

She held her breath as he remained silent. Would he laugh at her ambitions the way her father did?

"I don't think my opinion holds much weight with your father, but for whatever it's worth, I'm on your side."

"But will you think I'm just a nuisance hanging around here in the shop? Or do you think I can earn an honest day's pay?"

"After the time you spent with Henry, I know you're just as capable as he of drawing up a floor mold."

"Thank you, Silas." Slowly she removed her hand from his arm and offered it to him. He took it in his and they shook on it as if they'd just come to a momentous agreement.

Silas scraped at his jaw with the razor's edge. He would have preferred many times over to have stayed down at the yard working on the schooner in the stocks, but he knew Cherish would be hurt if he didn't attend her homecoming party. She'd made him promise to be there.

He bent over the basin and washed the shaving soap off his face, wetting the front part of his hair in the process. He patted his face dry before taking up a comb and doing his best to flatten the damp hair as he looked at himself in the small square of mirror hung on the wall above his washbasin.

His blond hair looked dark and slicked back now, but he knew it would fall back against his forehead as soon as he was out the door. He turned away from the mirror and took up the clean white shirt folded in the chest of drawers. Mrs. Sullivan, Cherish's aunt, insisted on doing his laundry, ironing and mending his clothes—"keeping him in clothes"—as she called it, the way she'd done since he'd first come to the Winslows as a boy. She said he was family to her and she wouldn't do less for him than for her own boy, Henry.

As he unbuttoned the starched shirt and slipped it on, he marveled at how grown-up Cherish had become in the time she'd been away. She'd been away before—off to boarding school during her secondary school years, but home during holidays and summers, always coming around to the shop as soon as she arrived. But he hadn't seen her in over two years, between the year at an exclusive girls' academy near Boston, followed by another year on the Continent accompanying a wealthy distant cousin.

Silas hadn't expected her to come straight to the boat shop. It must be a testimony to her dedication to boatbuilding that a year in Europe had not diminished it.

He put on his gray trousers, his only good pair, and knotted a string tie under the collar of his shirt. Last of all, he pulled on the dark blue sack coat, which had seen quite a few summers already. Glancing into the small mirror one last time, with another unsuccessful attempt at smoothing back the wave that fell forward, he headed toward the door.

A short walk brought him to the Winslow residence, a large Victorian house set high on a bluff. A veranda ran all along the front, with turrets at each end. The house overlooked the inlet, and from its height one could catch a glimpse of the village farther down the road at the mouth of the harbor.

Arriving at the house, Silas ignored the invitation of the wide-open front door and headed on up the drive to the kitchen entrance he'd been using since he was a lad.

The screen door banged shut behind him as he left the sunshine and entered the dimmer kitchen. Celia, the kitchen maid, greeted him and sent him toward the front, telling him that Cherish had been asking for him.

He walked down the corridor, the noise of people having a good time growing louder with each step. The party was in full swing in the large front room overlooking the veranda. He clearly distinguished Cherish's voice among the crowd of people.

He stood still, watching her. Once again he had to gaze in wonder at the transformation in her. Not that she hadn't always been a pretty girl, but now she looked so much like a lady. She wore— He searched for an adequate word. *Frock* didn't seem to describe the concoction she wore. It was nothing like the simple schoolgirl dresses and pinafores he'd been accustomed to seeing her in. This gown sported bright blue polka dots on a white background. The skirt was all gathered up in the back and cascaded down in folds like a waterfall. A wide blue sash draped over one side. The rest of the skirt seemed to be all ruffles and pleats. The bodice was the complete opposite, molded tightly to reveal a tiny waist and hourglass figure.

As soon as she spotted him, she headed straight toward him.

"Silas, there you are!" Cherish reached out both her hands to his and gave him a wide, welcoming smile. Her dark brown hair was also dressed very differently from the pigtails or ponytail she used to favor. Now it was pulled back, showing a wide creamy forehead, and fell from the top of her head in ringlets. Little dangling earrings shook each time she moved, bringing his attention to her soft pearly earlobes.

Her eyes gazed up at him now with laughter in their smoky-blue depths.

"What kept you so long?"

He shrugged. "I figured you'd have enough folks wanting to welcome you back to keep you busy all evening."

She looked around in amusement. "Yes, I suppose I do. It's wonderful being back home. Come on, let's go outside. You know everyone, although there are a few acquaintances Papa is expecting from Hatsfield whom he wants me to meet."

She linked her arm in his and drew him toward the veranda. They were stopped every few moments by guests wishing to talk to Cherish. Everyone wanted to hear about her European tour. Silas admired how deftly she turned the conversation around, asking instead about the local happenings in her absence.

They finally reached the veranda.

"Cherish!" Tom Winslow, a handsome, dark-haired man, hailed his daughter from the drive where he walked alongside a tall young man with a young lady at his side.

Before Silas could disengage himself, Cherish tugged at his arm, pulling him along with her as she descended the porch steps, where the trio reached them.

Her father said, "I want you to meet Mr. Warren Townsend from Hatsfield and his sister, Annalise. They've driven all the way over especially to welcome you back."

Cherish held out her hand first to the sister, a pretty, brown-haired girl, who wore spectacles.

"Pleased, I'm sure," Cherish said before turning to the young gentleman. He was at least half a head taller than either Silas or her father and wore a well-cut tweed suit. "Mr. Townsend, welcome to our home."

"Annalise and I have heard so much about you from your father that we wanted to make the acquaintance mutual as soon as you came home."

Cherish smiled at her father. "Papa has probably exaggerated half the details, but I am grateful for the chance to present myself in person so you may separate fact from fantasy." She turned to Silas, including him in the group. "This is Silas van der Zee, Papa's most gifted shipwright." After shaking hands all around, Silas was content to let Cherish do the talking.

He marveled to see how the year of finishing school had "finished" her, and the year on the Continent had given her an unmistakable presence. Gone were any remnants of the girl he remembered. He doubted she would be the same Cherish who would be content to get her hands dirty in the boat shop.

"Well, I'll let you young people get acquainted," Mr. Winslow said with a chuckle before moving away from the group.

"You have just returned from the Continent?" Mr. Townsend asked Cherish.

"Yes. My year abroad," she said in a laughing tone that disparaged the event.

"I was there a few years ago."

Cherish's eyes widened in delight. "Truly? Where did you travel?"

"London, Paris, Vienna—all the capitals. We also had a wonderful time touring the Black Forest, the Swiss Alps and down the coast of Italy."

"Oh, yes, aren't those regions beautiful? I was so charmed by the scenery. I remember a perfect afternoon boating on Lac Léman. I must try to paint it some day from my sketches."

"Yes, I was there, too. Château de Chillon."

"Couldn't you just picture Byron's words?"

As the two continued chatting about mutual experiences in Europe, Silas glanced over at Annalise Townsend, who looked mutely from her brother's face to Cherish's. He judged her to be about Cherish's age—nineteen.

"Have you been to the Continent as well, Miss Townsend?" he asked, wondering if she felt as out of place as he did. Although she, too, was fashionably dressed in a gown with a bustle, her outfit was somber in comparison to Cherish's.

She shook her head silently. After a moment, as if realizing it was her turn to contribute to the conversation, she asked, "Have you?"

Silas had to bend forward to hear her soft tone. "No, I haven't." Then he grinned. "Would you like me to get you some refreshment? There is a delicious assortment of food inside."

She looked hesitatingly at her brother. Cherish, having heard his question, turned to them. "Why don't we all have something? The gentlemen can get us each a plate—how about that?" Before anyone could counter the suggestion, she took Annalise by the arm and led her toward the veranda.

About an hour later Cherish leaned against the veranda railing, eyeing the guests on the lawn. Several couples were ranged about croquet wickets set in the grass.

After eating with her and the Townsends in the parlor, Silas had excused himself and wandered off. She spotted him now, down on the lawn in conversation with a couple of men.

She was only half-sorry. If he'd stayed with her any longer, how much better acquainted would he have become with Miss Townsend? He certainly had a knack with the shy young lady, even getting her to smile now and again.

Cherish stifled a yawn, glancing to her side. Mr. Townsend still stood there, as if awaiting her next move. He reminded her so much of the dozens of young men she'd met in Europe—so proper, so "Yes, Miss Winslow. No, Miss Winslow. Here, let me get that for you, Miss Winslow." She sometimes felt she'd drown in a sea of politeness.

She smiled at him, conscious of her duties as hostess. "Why don't we play a round of croquet? Would you and your sister like that?"

At his ready assent, she led them both down to the yard, heading toward Silas to invite him along. If he thought he was going to spend the afternoon talking with a bunch of men he saw practically every day when she'd been deprived of his company for over two years, he could think again. And she'd make sure he'd be *her* partner! Mr. Townsend could assist his sister.

She and Silas had a lot of catching up to do.

# ❧ Chapter Two ❧

The next morning Cherish entered her father's office and breathed a sigh of relief to see him alone.

"Good morning, Papa. I'm sorry I missed you at breakfast. I was lazy this morning."

"Hello, Cherish! As well you should be, only your second full day back. What are you doing down here? Your aunt want something?"

"No, nothing. Only to have me stay inside cooking and cleaning, but I escaped her."

He chuckled. "Well, I suppose it's not a bad idea to have her teach you a few things. I know she's been after you, and I've been pretty indulgent with you since your mother passed away."

Cherish patted his hand. Although it had been four years since her dear mama had succumbed to influenza, they both still felt the void she'd left behind. Even though his sister had taken over the housekeeping, things had never been the same.

Her father sighed. "Well, no matter. I want you to enjoy your summer. There's plenty of time to think of other things."

Cherish brought a chair over, to sit across the table from her father. Relieved, she looked at the plan he had been reviewing. "A new boat?"

"Yes, a forty-five-foot pinky." He tapped the end of his pencil against the paper. "Charles Whitcomb's commissioned it. He'll use it up and down the coast for the herring trade and cod fishing. It's not much of a boat, but I'm glad to have the job." He sighed. "Business has slowed a bit lately. It's not like the old days."

Cherish studied the three profiles of the hull: side view, plan view and forward-and-aft view. "When will you lay the keel?"

"In a few weeks. I need to order the wood and draw up the loft mold." He sat back, a smile creasing his face. At fifty-two, her father was still a good-looking man. His dark brown hair was thick, interspersed with only a few strands of gray. "I thought I'd go see what Townsend has in his lumberyard. You met his son yesterday. What did you think of him?"

"Nice enough, I suppose."

"You don't sound too enthusiastic."

Cherish interlaced her fingers and extended her arms in front of her. "To be honest, he seemed a duplicate of most of the young gentlemen I've met since I've been away."

"What do you find so wrong with today's young gentlemen?" her father asked in amusement.

She made a face. "They're so bland, like milksops."

"Oh, come," her father chided. "I wouldn't call young Townsend a milksop. He seems a fine, strapping gentleman with a good head on his shoulders, and a good future, I might add. I'd be proud to have someone like him for a son-in-law."

"Oh, Papa, I'm only nineteen and just returned home. Are you marrying me off already?"

"Of course not. You're right. You have plenty of time for courting." He looked down at the lines drawing and made a notation on the table of offsets. Then his dark eyes pierced hers. "Your mother was your age when she married me. I suppose people married younger back then.

"Girls are too modern nowadays. Wearing bloomers, wanting the same higher education as men…"

"As we should be entitled to," she countered.

"Oh, well, I'm not going to debate that with you this morning. It's too fine a day and I'm too happy to have you back home again." He coughed. "I just want you to promise me you'll give young Townsend a second look. You've hardly known the man long enough to form an opinion."

"That's true," she conceded. "I promise to withhold judgment on 'young Warren Townsend the Third' until further acquaintance."

Ignoring her teasing tone, he said, "Good girl. I can't ask for more than that. Now, why don't you sail over with me to Hatsfield tomorrow? You can meet the Townsends again. Their daughter was about your age, wasn't she?"

Cherish stopped herself from making a face as she thought of the insipid girl who could hardly get two words out without blushing and stammering. "Yes."

"They're a very nice family. They bought out McKinley's Sawmill. They own a lot of timberland up-country. Townsend has plans for a few schooners to ship the lumber to Boston and farther on down the coast."

Cherish's interest perked up. "Maybe he'd contract us to build the schooners…although there are shipyards he could go to in Hatsfield."

"Precisely." Her father looked pleased at her acumen. "So far, I've managed only a nodding acquaintance with him. That should change now you're here."

"How so?"

"Well, Townsend's offspring are about your age. Perhaps you could cultivate the friendship by planning a few parties and outings, now it's summer weather, and invite them along."

"Certainly, Papa, if you think it would help." Cherish clasped her hands before her on the table. "Papa?"

"Yes, my dear?" He eyed her fondly.

"I'd like to help you out here in the shop."

"Why, you've just helped. If you play hostess for me, you can't imagine the benefits that could result."

"I'd enjoy that. But Papa, what I mean by helping is that I want to work here, as I've done in the past, but now that I'm finished with school, I want you to consider me a permanent helper—the way you did with Cousin Henry."

Her father's face soured. "Don't talk to me about that ungrateful boy! After all the training I gave him, to up and leave me. Thinks he's found greener pastures down in Boston. He'll find out soon enough," warned Winslow.

"You can't blame him for wanting to work in a large shipyard where they're building steamships. He sees the future there, and perhaps he's right."

"Those tramp steamers can't compete over long distances with our three-masted schooners. They've got to fill half their hulls with coal. Think of the expense. And when their coal runs out, they're dead in the water."

"Yes, I know, Papa. I think there'll always be a place for the sailing ship, but you can't fault Henry for his ambition."

Her father stared gloomily past her. "I groomed him to take over the shipyard, and now where am I? Certainly not getting any younger. He was the only family member left, the only one showing any promise for the business."

"You have Silas."

"What's that?" He turned startled eyes toward her.

"I said, you have Silas. He can do anything Henry did. You know he can go beyond Henry. He can be more than a shipwright. You know he could design his own vessels given half the chance. He probably has half a dozen designs in his head."

"Whoa, Cherish, you slow down. Silas works down in the yard. He's a fine worker with a good understanding of ship's carpentry, but don't expect me to hand this shipyard over to him." He turned back to his drawing.

Stifling her desire to argue further, she said instead, "Anyway, we were talking about me—about my working here."

Her father sat back and folded his hands on the desk. "As to you, my dear, I know you've always had a hankering for boats and hanging around the shipyard, and I've indulged you in a good many ways, but you're no longer a little girl. You're a young lady. I've given you the best education money can buy just so you could go out in polite society and hold your head high, knowing you're as good as—better than—most ladies around here."

"I appreciate all you've given me, but Papa, what I really want is to work with you."

"Don't be silly. A shipyard is no place for a lady."

Cherish felt her temper rise, and she prayed for composure. "In that case, I relinquish my claims to the title 'lady.'"

"It's a little late for that," he said dryly. "Do you honestly think I've invested all the time and money in your education and travels just to have you working in a boat shop?"

No doubt seeing the outrage in her eyes, he chuckled and patted her hand. "You're too young to know what you want. I suggest you run along home and do what your aunt bids. You still have your watercoloring, don't you? Why don't you walk down to the harbor and paint some of the ships? Then tomorrow we'll sail over to Hatsfield and you can do some shopping, visit some acquaintances and get to know the Townsends better. We'll make a full day of it."

"Papa," she said quietly, swallowing her frustration with an effort, knowing it would do no good to vent it before her father, "what *are* you going to do about replacing Henry?"

Her father ran a hand through his hair in a gesture of impatience. "I haven't figured that out yet. At this point, I don't need any extra hands."

"Then let me help you out a while, until you do decide!" She stood and came around the table to her father and put her arms around his shoulders. "Please, Papa! I've learned much about draftsmanship over the years. It's true I haven't been here full-time as Henry was, or—or—Silas, but I made Henry teach me everything you taught him. I can help with the lofting. I can keep the books. They didn't only teach us to be ladies at school. I learned solid geometry. I learned enough arithmetic to keep track of your bills and expenses.

"Oh, Papa, please, *please,* say yes!" Annoyed with herself even as she gave him her most persuasive smile, and wondering why, with all her new maturity, she still had to resort to little-girl tactics, she held her breath, awaiting his reply.

"Oh, I suppose it wouldn't do any harm for you to putter around a bit here in the office." He gave her a stern look. "But only up here. I don't want you down on the yard. And get these silly notions of Silas out of your head. I know *whom* to put in charge of *what* in my shipyard. I know my men better than anyone else.

"Now, you spend some time with Phoebe, doing as she tells you, paint me some nice sailing pictures and play hostess for me the way I asked."

He turned to the shelf behind him. "If you do all I tell you, you can have this." He handed her a wooden half-hull model of a boat, about a foot and a half in length.

She took the smooth wooden boat, which was attached to a plank of wood. Above it was labeled in neat print "13' Whitehall."

"It's a model for Ernest Mitchell. Let's see how much you do know. You loft it, and I'll judge what you're capable of."

Her eyes widened in delight. She'd gotten what she'd come for! "Really, Papa?"

He smiled at his daughter's delight. "Get along with you. Go make yourself useful somehow so I can get back to my work."

Deciding she'd better table her arguments in Silas's favor for the present, she gave her father a quick hug, "Oh, yes, Papa! I'll be the best hostess! I'll become the best cook and housekeeper Haven's End has ever seen! *Thank you, Papa!*"

She bent and gave him a kiss on his whiskered cheek, then fairly flew out of the office, headed for the workshop.

She was halfway out the office door, her mind spinning with ideas, when her father's voice stopped her. "Remember, we'll go to Hatsfield tomorrow. I want you to be especially nice to young Townsend and his sister."

"Of course, Papa. I'll put on my best company manners and play the lady to the hilt."

Silas came into the boat shop after working the morning down in the yard, hewing timbers with an ax for the frames and planks for the schooner keel that sat on the stocks down on the beach. Although the spring day was still fresh, he felt hot and thirsty from his labors.

He stopped short at the sight of Cherish at the worktable.

He glanced down at his sweat- and tar-stained work shirt. "Hello, Cherish. What are you doing here?" He felt suddenly awkward before her dainty femininity. He wasn't used to the new, grown-up Cherish. At least she looked more like her old self in a cotton frock and apron, her hair tied back with a bow.

She gave him a frown. "Not you, too! Didn't you think I'd be here?"

He wiped his shirtsleeve against his forehead as he approached her. "Not quite so soon. You've only just arrived home." He raised a brow skeptically. "Did you miss this place so much?"

Her eyes chided him. "This place *and* its people."

He could feel himself flushing under her intent slate-blue gaze. For a second it seemed she was referring to him alone. Shaking aside the foolish notion, he observed, "At least I have less trouble recognizing you today."

She glanced down at herself. "Yes, my gowns are all put away for the moment, though I suppose I'll be diverting you tomorrow with a latest Parisian creation."

"Don't tell me—another party?"

She shook her head, but didn't say anything more. Her tone turned brisk. "Papa has given me this half-hull for a thirteen-foot Whitehall. He doesn't think I'll be able to loft it." She grinned, suddenly transformed into the little girl he remembered, always out to prove she was as capable as the men around her.

He neared the table and reached for the model. As he did so, an elusive fragrance reached his nostrils. It reminded him of dew-sprinkled lilacs in June. He didn't remember ever smelling perfume on Cherish before.

He cleared his throat and turned his mind back to the boat in front of him.

"Well, you certainly tagged after Henry enough to know everything he knew. But it's been two years since you've stepped into a boat shop. Aren't you afraid you've forgotten a few things?"

She touched the model with a fingertip. "I think it's one of those things that isn't easily forgotten. Just looking at this hull brings back all sorts of recollections."

She gave him a sidelong glance, mischief lighting the blue depths of her eyes. "Anyway, we are going to loft this together."

"We?" He quirked an eyebrow up. "Since when am I a draftsman?"

"Since Henry left…and Papa has no immediate plans to replace him."

Silas was surprised. "He doesn't?"

She shook her head, sending the little dangling earrings with their minute turquoise stones shaking. Then she frowned. "He says at present he doesn't need anyone else. He told me it has been slow around here. Has it?"

Silas looked out the square-paned window that overlooked the shipyard below. The tide was out, leaving smooth mudflats visible, with rivulets of water running between them in crooked lines down toward the sea.

"Yes, I suppose it has, this past year especially. We used to average three good-sized vessels a year, up to seven-hundred-ton ships, in addition to the smaller craft." He nodded down at the stocks. "That's a fifty-ton schooner—small for us—and it's the only sizable order this spring. Everything else is like this." He motioned toward the model on the table.

"Do you think things will pick up?" she asked.

"Hard to say. There's still a lot of building going on farther down the coast."

"Do you think Henry was right to head south?"

He shrugged. "Some say the days of sail are numbered. The opening of the Suez Canal in '69 spelled the beginning of the end for the clipper trade."

"But what about us here down east? Apart from the passenger steamer service from Boston and Portland, we don't see much use for steam. All the fishermen sail, even out to the Grand Banks."

"Yes, I think there's still a demand for the smaller fishing schooners and those used in the coastal trade. But eventually I see even those supplementing their vessels with steam." He shrugged. "And more and more of the larger schooners are being built with steel hulls. I don't know if they'll prove more successful than wood, but the fact is, shipping companies look at cost. The steel hull will probably last longer than the wood. Most of the larger ships' hulls are now steel reinforced."

Cherish turned back to the model. "Oh, well, let's hope these changes don't come too quickly. Right now we have a loft to lay out and a mold to build."

He looked down at her indulgently, encouraged as always by her optimism. "There's that word 'we' again. Do you propose to help me build the mold?"

"If you're agreeable."

He didn't say anything, not wanting to dash her hopes. He realized as he watched her that it was good to have her back—even an adult version of the girl who'd seek him out every chance she got and "discuss" things with him, from every aspect of boats to the latest storybook character she had read about.

"Your father has agreed to this?" he asked finally, his arms folded in front of him.

"Don't worry about Papa. I'll take care of him."

"You've been taking care of him quite some years now. I wonder if he'll ever discover it."

"Papa doesn't know the talent he has right under his roof. So it looks as if, now that I'm back, I shall have to show him." When he didn't reply, she continued. "You ought to be Papa's successor. If he can't see that, well, he will, if I have anything to say about it."

He turned away his gaze, not reminding her of his own dream—she probably didn't even remember it. "I still have to be down on the yard," he reminded her instead.

"So spend your mornings there." She stood and went to the window. "There are more than enough men down there. You said yourself things were slow. There's no reason you can't spend your afternoons up here." She turned to him, making a face. "I have agreed to spend my mornings with Aunt Phoebe, learning to run a house. But after that, I'm free. Papa said I could help out here."

"You have it all worked out."

She gave him a secret smile. "Papa will be convinced, you'll see. He'll realize your talent, and he'll see I have a head for business. He's already taking me with him to Hatsfield tomorrow to visit the Townsends' operation."

So that's what she'd meant about her fashionable attire.

"Apropos, do you know anything of the Townsends? They were at the party yesterday."

"Not much. Townsend's a lumber baron. They're important in Hatsfield—that's about all I know."

"I shall charm them with my European polish, and they will order a fleet of coastal schooners from our yard."

He frowned at the sudden picture of Cherish laughing and batting her thick, dark lashes at the tall, handsome, impeccably groomed Warren Townsend.

The next morning Cherish took extra care with her toilette, wearing a deep rose gown with white ruffle collar and cuffs. She stuck in a pair of coral earrings and pulled her hair back in a thick coil, knowing the sail would play havoc with anything fancier. She pinned on a pert straw hat with ribbons that matched the gown and pulled back the short net veil. Then, she clipped on a matching pair of gold bracelets she'd purchased in Florence.

She and her father rode in their buggy along the road down to the harbor. From the top of a slope they could see the village of Haven's End set snug against a hilly curve of land. White houses nestled along its edges and up the surrounding hills. Three long wharves jutted out from the land into the protected harbor, which was filled with moored boats. Beyond, at its mouth, lay a wooded island.

Her father dropped her off at the harbor and went to stable the horse and buggy. Silas was waiting on the wharf, dressed in a creamy, cabled sweater and pea jacket. Although the May day promised to warm up, Cherish knew it would be cold on the water. She had brought along a duffel coat, which she carried on one arm.

"Good morning," she greeted him.

"Good morning," he replied, his gray eyes taking in her appearance. "You're looking smart."

If the compliment wasn't all she'd hoped for, at least it *was* a compliment. Her efforts had been worth it. "Thank you," she answered demurely.

He took her coat and parasol, and she climbed down the catwalk after him to the awaiting skiff. Silas held out his hand to her as she stepped into the bobbing boat. Her father returned and loosened the painter before joining them.

She settled aft and waited for her father to descend. He coiled the line and gave a nod to Silas to shove off.

Silas sat forward and pulled at the oars, heading toward her father's pinky schooner moored amidst the other fishing boats in the harbor.

As soon as they arrived, Silas jumped aboard the schooner, and her father threw him the line. When the skiff lay alongside the pinky, her father climbed in and turned to help Cherish in. She took the line from her father. "I'll secure it," she told him.

He loosed the pinky's mooring line as Silas ran the foresail up the mast. Cherish went immediately and helped him with the lines. Her father took the tiller while Silas and Cherish trimmed the sail, and they maneuvered the vessel out of the crowded harbor.

They left behind the briny smells of the harbor and the shriek of gulls and headed out to sea. Silas hoisted the mainsail and jib. The cloth caught and filled with the wind, sending the vessel skimming over the inky-blue water.

Cherish went to sit beside Silas when he took over the tiller from her father. They sailed past the rocky, evergreen-wooded coast. Farmhouses were visible above the bays, but the tips of the peninsulas were woodland, the thickly growing spruce and balsam fir black against the rising sun. They navigated through narrows and channels between the coastal islands, some

wooded, others bare, rocky fortresses withstanding the relentless battering of waves.

Cherish breathed deeply of the crisp breeze. Her glance met
Silas's and she smiled. He smiled back and she knew they
needed no words to express the enjoyment of being in a well-
built craft upon the sea. She closed her eyes and lifted her head
heavenward, feeling the sun on her face, the wind whipping at
her cheeks. It was good to be alive. She praised God for all she'd
seen and done, but most of all that she was home at last, close
to the man she loved, within reach of her dream.

All too soon they arrived in the tidal river leading up to the
town of Hatsfield. Hatsfield was larger than Haven's End, and
Cherish eagerly noted the number of schooners, brigs and
barks arrived from different ports.

Silas lowered the sails and dropped anchor. She and her father climbed aboard the skiff once again as Silas stayed to secure the sails and leave everything shipshape.

"I'll send someone back with the skiff," her father told him.
With a final wave, they left him. Cherish looked back at him,
wishing he were going with them.

She turned her attention to the busy port. Stacks of logs lined
the quay. Loads of shingles and shooks and freshly sawn lumber waited to be loaded onto the ships that brought barrels of
molasses, dry goods, salt and grain from places afar.

"Winslow!" called a voice from farther down the wharf.

"Morning, Townsend," her father answered as he advanced
to meet Townsend senior and his son.

Warren Townsend and his father presented an imposing pair
of gentlemen, Cherish noted as the two men approached them.
Warren was dressed in the manner of the young men in Boston, in contrast to the young farmers and fishermen down east.
He wore a fine gray frock coat and matching vest and trousers,
his boots polished to a shine. He was clean shaven, his hair, a
rich brown, cut short.

Mr. Townsend sent his son to escort Cherish to their home.

"Mrs. Townsend and Annalise are awaiting you," Townsend
senior told her.

"We'll be up for dinner," her father added.

"I shall see you and Silas then," she said, giving him a peck on the cheek.

They rode along the river, past stately homes. Just before entering the main town of Hatsfield, they turned into a tree-lined drive before a white-columned portico fronting a Greek revival house.

"Welcome to our home," Mrs. Townsend told her. She was a handsome-looking woman, with light brown hair and a stylish dress. "Annalise has been telling me what a nice visit she had with you and what a good hostess you were to her."

Cherish turned to smile at the bespectacled girl, surprised that she had made such a favorable comment. If the girl had enjoyed herself at all, it was thanks to Silas. She couldn't remember Annalise having said more than two words to her. "I'm glad you enjoyed yourself, Miss Townsend."

"Come, let us go inside, shall we?" Mrs. Townsend said.

They chatted amiably for a while in a back parlor, although Cherish realized she and Mrs. Townsend did most of the talking.

"Warren, why don't you escort the young ladies around the gardens? I think the day is warm enough for a walk."

"I'm sure I should enjoy that, Mrs. Townsend." She rose as soon as Warren stood, relieved to leave the overstuffed parlor for a while. Annalise followed suit.

"Annalise, put on your wrap."

"Yes, Mama," she murmured.

They walked onto the slate porch that ran the length of the rear of the house. Warren offered them both an arm and proceeded down wide flagstone steps.

They walked all the way down to the water's edge, where the Townsends had a small dock. After a few moments of contemplating the river, they strode back up to a cedar bench amidst the flower beds.

Cherish racked her brain for a conversation starter. She didn't feel she had done anything for her father yet.

"Did you truly enjoy yourself at my house the other day?" she asked Annalise.

"Oh, yes," she answered softly.

"I would have been overwhelmed, having to meet so many strangers all at once."

"Perhaps she was a bit," Warren answered for her. "But you stayed by her side. The young man who was with us—I don't recall his name—was also very attentive."

"That was Silas van der Zee. He's been with our family since he was twelve. He works with Papa in the boat shop."

"We must have him come back with you the next time, then."

"Oh, you'll surely meet him today. He sailed over with us. He'll be by with Papa."

"That's fine," Warren said with a smile at his sister.

"I do hope the two of you can come back to Haven's End again," Cherish said after a bit. She thought quickly. "I'd like to give another party. Perhaps with a little dancing and games this time."

"We would look forward to that."

Cherish breathed a sigh of relief when the dinner hour approached and they decided to head back to the house. Her father would have returned.

When she saw he was alone, she asked him, "Where's Silas?"

"Oh, he'll get something to eat down at the wharf."

Cherish tightened her lips, not saying anything. How could he have Silas come along and then treat him like nothing but a hired hand?

She would make it up to Silas, she promised herself.

# ❧ Chapter Three ❧

After breakfast the next day, Cherish reported to her aunt in the kitchen. "I am yours to command, Auntie."

"We'll be baking, so get on a big apron if you don't want to be covered in flour," the woman replied without looking up.

"I'm going for a picnic this noon with Silas. Do you think the bread will be ready by then?"

Aunt Phoebe gave her a sharp glance from behind her wire-rimmed spectacles. "You're not still thinking the sun and moon sets on Silas, after traipsing over the Continent, meeting who knows how many young gentlemen?"

"Silas is the finest man I know."

Aunt Phoebe placed a large earthenware bowl in front of Cherish on the worktable. "Set the cake of yeast in here with the sugar and put about a cup of milk on the stove to warm.

"Well, perhaps it's more than a schoolgirl's fancy if it's lasted this long," her aunt conceded. "If it is, you've got more sense than I credited you with."

She brought a large crock of flour out of the pantry. "We're making four loaves, so we'll need a good bit of flour. That milk should be about ready. Test it on the inside of your arm. It should feel just warm enough to stand."

"Yes, that's what it feels like."

"All right, bring it over and pour it over the yeast." After she'd done so and let the yeast work a few minutes, her aunt dumped in some cupfuls of flour.

"Still, I hope you won't be disappointed in Silas. I've known him since he was a lad. He's grown to be such a nice young man, but sometimes I wonder what's going on behind those gray eyes. He's never given me any trouble, not like my Henry," she added with a shake of her head. "He's never gotten drunk to my knowledge, never uttered a profanity, nor gambled away his money. I admire those things about him—but as I said, I wonder sometimes…"

"Whatever do you mean?" Cherish asked, never having heard her aunt voice a concern about Silas.

She sighed. "Sometimes it seems as if something's hurt him so deep, he's buried all his natural feelings. I wouldn't want you getting hurt by a want of feeling on his part. You're a sensitive girl, a giving soul. I don't know…some people can't give what they don't have."

"I don't believe that of Silas," Cherish answered, emphasizing her remark with a decisive punch at the gooey dough, which succeeded only in stirring up the flour Aunt Phoebe had just emptied into the bowl. Cherish waved away the cloud of flour threatening to go up her nostrils. "I think Silas is a very sensitive person."

"Well, you never can tell about people," her aunt answered philosophically. "Sometimes no matter how long you live with someone, you still have no idea what lies beneath the surface, what—or *who*—it'll take to awaken 'em."

She poured in some more flour.

"How am I supposed to mix this? It's so heavy and dry!"

"You just work it in good with your hands—you'll see how smooth it gets. The more you knead it, the softer the bread'll be." Her aunt went to get the bread pans and began to grease them.

"I've always treated Silas like my own Henry. Your father didn't hold with that, but I put my foot down, and I'm glad to say your mother, God rest her soul, did, too. We always sat him down with us at the table with the rest of the family. Your father wanted Silas to sit in here in the kitchen and take his meals with Celia and Jacob.

"'Oh, no,' I said, 'Silas is going to sit at the table with us, where I can keep my eye on him and teach him his manners.' His mother entrusted him to us. I was going to do right by him."

"This dough feels good now. Like a big pillow, but my arms are aching."

Her aunt prodded the dough. "It's coming, but you're not through. Sprinkle some flour on the table and turn the dough onto it and begin kneading it." Her aunt stood beside her until satisfied she was doing it right. "Keep that up a good ten minutes and you'll have the softest, lightest bread you've ever bit into."

"Ten minutes!" This was worse than sanding a plank of wood.

"Just think how good those sandwiches are going to taste on that picnic," her aunt said placidly as she began gathering up the used utensils.

Picturing Silas biting into a slice of her freshly baked bread, his eyes lighting up in pleasure, Cherish leaned into the dough with a new will.

"That's my girl."

Aunt Phoebe poured hot water from the stove into the dishpan. "I don't know why your father has never given Silas the credit he deserves. According to what you've told me over the years, he has more talent in one little finger than Henry ever had—and that's my son I'm talking about."

"I've wondered that myself. I love Papa dearly, but sometimes I could just shake him the way he treats Silas. Take yesterday. Can you believe he didn't take him along to have dinner with the Townsends? He left him to fend for himself on the docks as if he were just an ordinary deckhand."

Aunt Phoebe stopped in her act of wiping off the table. "Is that the reason for the picnic today?" Her knowing blue eyes looked deep into Cherish's.

Cherish could feel her cheeks warming. "Partially. It's also a beautiful day for a picnic, and I haven't had a chance to have a good chat with Silas since I've been back."

Her aunt smiled in understanding, her face softening. "You go and have a good time. I'll take care of your father." She sighed. "Sometimes I've thought Tom resented Silas's talent, resented the fact it's in a stranger, come out of nowhere, and not in the son he wishes he'd had."

Two dainty booted feet beneath a ruffled white gown sprigged with lavender flowers appeared at the edge of Silas's vision.

He gave one last whack with the adze against the timber. Curls of wood chips went flying. Resting the metal head of the tool lightly against the plank he was forming out of a long piece of lumber, he straightened. Wiping the back of his arm against his forehead, he shoved aside the hair that kept falling forward. "Hello, there. What are you doing down here?"

"Come to fetch you." Cherish was like a breath of cool sea breeze on the hot beach. She carried a picnic hamper in one hand and twirled a white parasol over her shoulder with the other.

"Where?" He laid down the adze on the pebbly beach and took a handkerchief from his shirt pocket to wipe his face.

"You and I are going on a picnic."

"Oh?"

"Yes, so put away your things. I want to sail over to the meadow on Allison's Bay."

The idea was tempting. Then he looked at the pile of lumber still to be shaped into planks for the schooner standing over him like a giant elephant carcass, its ribs held together by scaffolding. "I don't think I can leave right now."

She followed his line of vision to the hull. "Nonsense. It's almost dinnertime anyway. I've already told Aunt Phoebe not to expect us. Besides, you promised to spend the afternoons with me up in the workshop. We're already a day behind."

"I'd better tell your father," he began, rolling down his shirt-sleeves and buttoning the cuffs.

"Already taken care of."

He eyed her, wondering what wiles she'd used on old man Winslow. The only one who could soften that man was his daughter. "Let me get cleaned up. I won't be but a minute," Silas told her, and headed toward the boat shop. Quickly he put on a clean shirt. Whistling, he came back down the stairs.

The day was indeed beautiful. Although spring didn't come down east until May, once it came, it arrived in full force. Silas rowed them out to his own boat, a twenty-seven-foot yawl he'd built himself from stem post to stern. The name *Sea Princess* was painted along its bow.

He loved this boat, its sleek wooden lines, its full white sails, the way it handled under his guidance.

"We've got a strong northwest wind. We'll be able to run her pretty clear," he told her as he sheeted the mainsail close. It filled with the wind, making great clapping noises as he tugged on the sheets.

Once clear of the harbor, he worked the tiller and line, Cherish seated beside him.

She smiled. "May I?"

He gave a brief nod, relinquishing the tiller to her. She knew these waters as well as he.

"How do you like her?"

"She's wonderful."

Silas glanced at Cherish. The wind whipped at her ponytail. She brought a hand up to her forehead to keep the strands of hair out of her face. A smile played along her mouth. She looked as if she were enjoying herself to the full.

"I remember you were still working on her the last time I was here."

"Mmm-hmm," he answered.

"Why haven't you named her after someone? *Sea Princess,* that could be anybody."

He shrugged. "There's no one to name her after."

She gazed at him under her brows. "How unromantic of you."

He looked away, not having given it much thought until then. "I guess my romance is with the sea," he said after a moment.

They didn't have far to sail, the site suggested by Cherish being only the next bay over. They passed Ferguson Point, with its pebbly cove and beautiful house far above it overlooking the ocean, before heading into the bay. As they reached the spot Cherish indicated, he began reefing in the sail. After dropping the anchor, they rowed the short distance to shore in the skiff.

He jumped out into the shallow water to pull the boat up onto the beach. Cherish stood to get out.

"Hey, don't get your feet wet," he cautioned. He hesitated an instant, wondering at the same moment why he did so. But one glance at her delicate-looking white kid boots settled it. He leaned forward to pick her up. He'd done the same thing a hundred times when she'd been younger—why did he vacillate now? She was the same girl—only bigger.

She immediately put her arms around his neck and laughed, a sound of sheer delight. His arms held her under her arms and knees, his fingers feeling the soft fabric of her gown, his nostrils catching the same soft fragrance of perfume. He strode the few steps to dry ground and let her down as quickly as possible, wondering at the change in him. Assisting her should not have had such an effect on him.

She slid her hands down from his neck to his chest before letting go completely. "Thank you, Silas," she said, her voice breathless, her blue eyes alight with amusement, as if she were conscious of the queer sensations running through him.

The awareness passed as soon as she stepped away from him, and he shoved the incident from his mind. He concentrated on securing the line, then going back to get the hamper.

Cherish had already walked on ahead, heading up the disused path that led from the beach to a meadow above on higher ground.

The grass of the field was just beginning to turn green, and it was covered in a carpet of white.

"Oh, the bluets!" Cherish stooped to examine the tiny flowers, which up close weren't white, but pale blue four-pointed stars.

Silas found a spot sheltered from the breeze but still in sight of the bay. Cherish came back with a tiny bouquet, which she tucked into her neckline. Silas turned away, willing himself not to notice the narrow wedge of pale skin where her gown came together. Unfortunately, the sprig of flowers only served to call attention to it.

She knelt by the basket and opened the lid. "We can spread this out," she said, taking out a red-checked cloth. He grabbed two corners, glad to have something constructive to do. The bright cloth billowed in the air as they held it.

Silas went to retrieve some stones with which to anchor it. When he returned, Cherish had placed the food in an inviting display on the cloth, and he realized how hungry he was.

"Here." She handed him a thick sandwich. "Bread baked this morning. My first culinary endeavor since I've been back, I shall have you know."

The sandwich looked inviting, spread thick with butter and stuffed with slices of ham and cheese. She took out a mason jar and removed the lid. "Sweet tea. I didn't bring any glasses, so we shall have to share this between us." She set it down against the basket.

"Everything looks delicious," he said, wanting to make her feel good about her efforts in the kitchen with her aunt.

When she had served herself, she sat across from him and smiled. "This is my private homecoming." She looked out across the bay. "I thank God for the privilege of seeing a bit of this great, vast world, but I'm even more thankful to be back home to my small corner of it." She took a deep breath, her eyes half-closed, her chest rising and falling, drawing Silas's gaze once more to the flowers tucked there.

"This is one of those 'moments of azure hue' Thoreau wrote about, don't you think? How I missed this smell—sea, sun, a hint of sweetgrass and an indefinable something else." She opened her eyes and focused on him once again. "Perhaps its essence is the company I longed for, the faces I grew up with."

Once again he had the sensation she was referring specifically to him. Before he could think about it further, she bowed her head and gave thanks for the food. She peeped up at him again as she said "amen."

"I hope you like it. My arms are still sore from kneading dough!"

He found it hard to think beyond the fact of Cherish's womanhood and how it was affecting him.

He bit into the bread—soft and wholesome tasting, the ham smoky and salty, the homemade cheese sharp, the mustard gracing it all adding just the right amount of tangy spice.

"Well, you haven't spit it out or choked on it, so I suppose it will pass."

"It's very good," he hastened to say.

They ate in silence some moments. When she took the jar of cold tea and put her head back to drink from it, Silas couldn't help noticing her neck, long and graceful as she took deep drafts from the jar.

Then she lowered her head and handed it to him. He reached out his arm and took it slowly. How many times had they done similar things years back? He held the cold glass jar and looked at it, hesitating, the act suddenly taking on intimate proportions. He tilted his head back and sipped from the same liquid she'd drunk from.

She rummaged in the basket again and brought out something in a napkin. "*La pièce de résistance,* or should I say the final test?" She unveiled the item, revealing golden tarts. "Strawberry preserve tarts, also baked this morning."

She offered the napkin-wrapped tarts and he took one. "You had quite a morning," he commented.

"I'm exhausted. I could lie down and sleep an hour here."

"It's delicious," he was quick to tell her this time after the first bite, and he didn't exaggerate. The pastry was light, the filling just the right degree of sweet and tart.

"Well, I can't take all the credit. Aunt Phoebe was hovering around me like a hummingbird, telling me exactly what to do and how long to do it. Next time I prepare you a meal, I shall do it unsupervised."

Again the words conjured up something exclusively for him. Silas shook away the thought. In an effort to dispel the unfamiliar sensations she was awakening in him, he said, "Tell me about Europe."

She tilted her head to one side, a small smile playing at her lips. "Europe...what a vast topic. Actually that brings another thought to mind."

Her smile turned to a frown. "I've been meaning to ask you, why were you such a poor correspondent while I was away? Let me see..." She held up her fingers, counting. "One, two, three...yes. Only a few short scrawls during my entire year abroad. I sent you dozens of postcards, and all I got in return was 'Dear Cherish, I trust this finds you in health. Your travels sound interesting. Nothing much new around here. All is well, Yours sincerely, Silas van der Zee.'"

He felt his face warm as she quoted his meager correspondence back to him. "I guess there just wasn't much to tell. Everything was about the same." How could he write about the joys of seeing trunks of trees being formed into ships and boats, when every postcard and letter of hers presented a vivid image of a new city, a new experience, new faces?

"That's nonsense. You know how much I love to know what's going on at the shipyard."

"I'm sorry," he answered. "I just didn't think it would interest you." He looked across the meadow to the bay. "The happenings at Winslow's Shipyard, much less the life of one Silas van der Zee, seemed inconsequential in comparison to the adventures you were having."

"You were so wrong," she said quietly. Before he could analyze her serious tone, she began to gather up their things.

"You must have met a lot of interesting people over there," he said as he helped her, wanting somehow to make up for his delinquent correspondence efforts.

She glanced at him. "Do you really want to know?"

Remembering how she used to tell him everything about her school life, he nodded. "Of course I do."

"Well, Cousin Penelope must know everyone there is to know on the Continent," she began, her enthusiasm returning.

He reclosed the jar of tea and handed it to her.

"If Cousin Penelope didn't know a person she felt worth knowing, she found someone who did and wangled an introduction," she continued, placing the jar of tea back into the hamper. "Society is very formal across the Atlantic. You can't just present yourself to someone. An introduction must be arranged."

She stooped to gather up the tablecloth. Silas stood and took it from her and shook it out away from them.

"Take for example at a dance—excuse me, I mean a ball or an assembly—you can't just dance with anyone who asks you. You must first be formally introduced."

She giggled suddenly. "When we were in Vienna, I was requested by a third party to dance a waltz with a certain titled gentleman. He wouldn't be so bold as to force himself upon the young 'American demoiselle.' No, that would be most improper, so he sent an emissary, a female relative—titled, of course. Once I gave her my consent—to an introduction only— he approached and the formal presentation was carried out."

She took the folded cloth from Silas and laid it atop the picnic basket before facing him and assuming a very straight stance, her hands clasped behind her back. "So, having navigated the appropriate channels, Prince Leopold Christian Otto von Braunschweiger von Black Forest von Wiener Schnitzel von something or other—" the longer she spoke, the thicker grew her false German accent and she bowed low, clicking her heels as she did so "—was presented to me in all the glory of his many family names. I was most impressed, and I gave him my lowest curtsy, like so."

Silas was laughing at her antics by this time, relaxed once more. She was, after all, the young girl he'd always known. He watched her maneuver an exaggerated curtsy.

"I was afraid my knees would creak, and I almost toppled over—oh goodness!" Here she miscalculated and began to fall forward. Silas stepped into the gap and caught her just in time. She laughed up at him, her hands resting lightly on his shoulders. "Thank you, Silas. I don't think Prince von Leopold could have been any more agile." She frowned. "He wore a monocle, you know. It might have popped out if he'd been forced to exert himself so."

Silas could feel his heart begin to thump heavily as she kept her hands on his shoulders and did not step back.

"Anyway, we are now correctly placed for the waltz. You know it was invented in Vienna? I needn't summarize the prince's—or was he a count?—well, anyway, I needn't go on with his flattering speech. The introduction alone took a good half minute. It was a few more minutes before I realized he was asking me to dance. His accent was so heavy, his circumlocution so flowery, it was quite some time before I realized all he wanted was a waltz."

Cherish laughed to hide her nervousness. She felt she hadn't stopped for breath in the past minute, terrified lest Silas disengage himself from her. Now as she looked into his smiling face, she wished she could have an inkling of what he was feeling. Was it anything remotely akin to the way her heart was skittering about in her chest?

She gazed into his gray eyes, her aunt's words coming back to her. What was going on behind them? They regarded her with that same fond amusement they always had. Was there never to be anything more?

"Come on." She tugged at his shoulder and took one of his hands from her waist into her own. "I'll show you the Viennese waltz."

Then he did react, as she had already begun taking the first step. "I'm not much good at waltzing."

"It's simple. I'm planning another party—did I tell you?— and I intend to have dancing this time. But you must lead. One, two, three…one, two, three…" She continued looking into his eyes as she counted. "It's fatal to look down at your feet. You're sure to trip then. It's just a box step, as simple as counting one, two, three. This way—one, then two here, and then one long step, three." They turned together.

"Yes, you're doing it." She began humming a Strauss waltz. "One, two, three. One, two, three. Imagine a hundred chandeliers, sparkling upon the ladies' ball gowns, and you in a black jacket and starched white shirt with stiff points and white or black tie." She continued humming, wanting this dance to go on forever.

She laughed when he tripped on a tussock of grass. "You can't stop, but must find your place once again, or someone might step on my train. The ballroom is packed with dozens of couples...."

Cherish kept up a steady flow of talk, as if by sheer will she could make Silas fall in love with her, feel what she was feeling for him, sense the enchantment of this moment under the cloudless sky in the midst of a field of bluets more glorious than the most radiant Viennese ballroom.

At the noonday dinner Tom Winslow turned to Phoebe when she sat down across the table from him. "Where is Cherish?"

"Out on a picnic with Silas," she answered him, reaching for a dish of potatoes and taking a helping.

"Out on a picnic?"

"That's what I said. They went for a sail and a picnic. Now, would you care to serve yourself a slice or two of the corned beef and pass me the platter?"

"What? Oh, yes." He stabbed the red slices and put them on his plate, then passed the dish to his sister. They finished serving their plates and bowed their heads to say grace. After taking his first bite, Tom chewed thoughtfully. "I don't know if I like her hanging around with Silas so much. First down at the boat shop and now picnicking together."

"Silas is a good boy."

"She's tagged after him since she was a little girl, always defending him whenever she's so much as thought I wasn't treating him right. Now—" here he gave a grunt of incredulous laughter "—she wants me to think of Silas as my successor."

"You could do a lot worse," she answered shortly.

Their cutlery clattered against the china as they ate in silence for a while.

"Still, now that Cherish is home, I want her to start meeting some of the men of her own class. Take that young Townsend. I like that fellow. A real gentleman."

"The question is, does *she* like him?" Phoebe asked pointedly, prying open her biscuit with the tip of her knife, the steam escaping in a sheer vapor.

That night Cherish knelt by her bed and prayed. *Lord, You know how much I've always loved Silas. Only You know. Only You know how long I've waited for him. I've done everything that was expected of me.*

*Oh, please, Father, make Silas love me back. Let him love me as I love him. I want him so badly. I feel I shall burst with love for him.*

# ❧ Chapter Four ❧

After the Sunday-morning church service, the congregation filed through the entryway, greeting the minister.

"Well, if it isn't little Cherish Winslow!" Pastor McDuffie took her hand in a hearty handshake. "What a fashionable lady she has become. What do you say, Carrie?" He turned to his wife.

Mrs. McDuffie turned to Cherish with a warm smile. "Welcome back, Cherish. Please forgive us for missing your homecoming. We had to be away that day. We are so happy to have you back in our midst."

"Thank you. No one is gladder than I am," she answered.

"Now that you're back, can we look forward to seeing you with us on Tuesday nights for choir practice? Carrie can certainly use another good singing voice."

"I would love to come." She turned to Silas. "You'll join me, won't you? We could walk over and back together."

He fingered his tie. "I'm not much of a singer."

"Nonsense," McDuffie contradicted. "You have a fine baritone. I could hear you from the pulpit."

Cherish smiled at the color creeping up his cheeks. "I hope it didn't hurt your ears," he said.

McDuffie laughed. "*Au contraire*. I was heartened to hear such a good, strong male voice. Just what we need in our choir." He leaned over to whisper conspiratorially, "We have a surplus of little old ladies, dear souls, whose voices are becoming a mite quavery. We need some new blood." He gave them both a last firm handshake. "It's settled, then, come out Tuesday evenings at seven. Good to have you back, Cherish."

Silas walked home from church with the Winslows as usual for Sunday dinner. Though he had deliberately slowed his steps to avoid walking with Cherish, he found her at his side.

She was a vision of loveliness. In fact, she had been every day he'd seen her since her return. He was beginning to realize he was looking forward to her appearance each day. Today she wore a yellow dress, with flounces and ruches up and down its skirts. A wide yellow sash, tied low on her hips, swayed in the breeze. The tight sleeves of the gown came down to her elbows and her hands were covered with dainty white gloves.

Silas wondered whether it was perhaps because he'd been around men too long, down on the shipyard, that one prettily dressed girl could stir his senses so.

Cherish was chatting away merrily with old Jacob, the Winslows' handyman and gardener. "I look forward to hearing you fiddling away at the party."

Silas realized none of the girls of Haven's End could hold a candle to Cherish. Was it the city polish? Was it that every detail in her appearance was pleasing to the eye? Did women achieve that deliberately, or did it come about naturally?

Cherish's deep brown hair cascaded down her shoulders in ringlets beneath a little straw bonnet trimmed in yellow ribbons and bows. He remembered her hair caught up in a simple wide ribbon the day they had danced in the meadow, how it had swung around as they'd played at waltzing in a ballroom. She'd been just as beautiful then in her simple frock and hairstyle.

He smiled inwardly at the image. Cherish pretending he and she had been in some elegant Viennese ballroom. Noth-

ing could be sillier. He glanced down at his hands. They were
marred by scars of cuts old and new from carpenter's tools and
burns from hot tar, and they felt as rough as the sandpaper he
used to make the boats he worked on as smooth as silk.

How did they compare to Prince Leopold's? *Like sandpaper
to silk* beat a refrain in his mind.

They reached the Winslow house and turned up the drive.
Aside from the hotel down by the harbor and the few summer
residences, this was the grandest house in Haven's End.

"I hope you're hungry," Cherish told him, her blue eyes
laughing up at him. "I was in the kitchen since dawn with Aunt
Phoebe until it was time to get ready for church."

"That right, Miss Cherish?" Jacob piped up. "What goodies
you ladies been preparing for us starvin' menfolk?"

She turned to him. "Roast chicken, mashed potatoes, pick-
led beets and biscuits."

"Well, bring it on and we'll do it proud," he exclaimed.

After a delicious dinner, in which they all complimented
Cherish on her cooking skills, Cherish made Silas promise
that he would meet her out on the veranda later.

He usually walked back down to the shipyard after Sunday
dinner, but he sat a while making desultory conversation with
Mr. Winslow. When the older man took up the paper to read,
Silas made his way out to the front porch.

He glanced around and decided to lounge on the two-
person swing set at one end of the porch. He swung lazily on
the seat, pushing back and forth with the heel of his boot, un-
accustomed to idleness. In his free time he was usually whit-
tling away on a ship model or cleaning out his boat.

Just as he felt himself dozing, he heard the front door swing
open and footsteps walking toward him. He shook aside the
drowsiness and stood to help Cherish with the tray she carried.

"I brought us some lemonade, in case we get thirsty." She
indicated where he should set the small tray down.

"Everything done?"

"All shipshape to Aunt Phoebe's satisfaction," she answered,
settling herself beside him on the swing with a small leather-

bound book beside her. A barn cat, which had come onto the veranda from around the house, jumped onto her lap.

"Hello, puss, where've you been all morning? Out hunting mice?" The cat purred smoothly as Cherish stroked its gray fur.

To hide the feelings Cherish's proximity was creating in him, Silas pushed his feet against the wooden floor, bringing the swing back into motion. They rocked in silence for a few moments, listening to the creak of the swing.

He was just managing to ignore her nearness, his eyes closed, his back resting against the seat, when Cherish asked him, "Do you have a sweetheart these days?"

His eyes snapped open. Cherish sat observing him as her hand caressed the cat's fur.

"What?" Why was she asking such a question? Simple curiosity—or something more?

"You heard me. Is there anyone occupying a special place in your heart?"

He took his time in answering, unused to such personal inquiries. The men on the yard talked about the ships they were working on, the latest cargo in port, the price of lumber. Mrs. Sullivan made sure he was well fed and clothed and noted if he was looking "peaked." Mr. Winslow cared only that he reported to work every day and carried out his duties. And all he, Silas, ever thought about was the feel of wood under his hands and the goal he was working toward.

No one had ever asked about his heart. Finally he shook his head. "No." Why had the answer been so difficult?

"No one since Emma?" she asked softly, referring to his childhood sweetheart from back home.

"I guess I'm married to my boats now."

"That's silly. You can't be married to boats."

He continued rocking the swing gently, looking down at the toes of his boots. "I haven't thought about things like getting married, starting a family, or getting a place of my own since Emma passed away." He spoke the next words slowly, articulating them for the first time. "I guess I decided then that marriage was not for me."

"That's nonsense, Silas." The chiding words were spoken gently.

He shrugged. "I'm content with things as they are. I have my dream, and that's enough for now."

"You have a wonderful dream, and I know it will be fulfilled, but that doesn't mean you can't want more."

He glanced at her again, surprised for the second time in the space of a few moments. She *did* remember his dream.

But she continued speaking, not noticing his reaction. "Love is the highest thing you can experience."

He said nothing, the word making him uncomfortable.

"You loved Emma."

"I was just a boy." His fingers tugged at his collar, trying to think of another topic to distract Cherish.

"Age has nothing to do with it. Just think, you were a boy of twelve and you promised yourself to a girl you'd known all your life, and you loved her faithfully all the years you were here. That's not childish sentiment. It's a beautiful, noble thing."

He turned away from her earnest gaze. "You've just become a romantic since seeing all those old castles."

"Love has nothing to do with seeing castles! I've always believed in love. I've just become old enough to express my views better now. And there is One Who agrees with me." She tapped the cover of the book between them. "God. He has a lot to say about love."

"Yes, I know all about that kind of love…doing unto others…."

She looked away from him. "That sounds like doing your duty. It's so much more than that. It's about loving one's Savior. It's an all-consuming love He has for us."

"You sound like Pastor McDuffie."

Her lips curved slightly. "He's the one who began making me see that being a Christian was more than just going to church on Sunday or following the Golden Rule. Do you know what I discovered through him?" Her slate-blue irises were rimmed in a deeper hue that was almost black. "How wonderful it is to fall in love with God."

Silas turned away, her words leaving him feeling inadequate, as if he were missing some vital component in his makeup. The cat had climbed onto his lap, and he touched its fur, feeling the throb of its purr under his fingertips.

"When one realizes the love Jesus poured out for us on that cross, it becomes easy to love Him back with every particle of one's being, to hold nothing back, to say 'Yes, Lord,' when He asks something of us." She picked up the Bible and hugged it to her breast. "Don't tell me this is just romanticism. Love is our whole purpose for existing."

He wasn't ready to concede any such thing. His mind went to the feel of a boat taking shape under his hands. That was life to him. He pushed the swing back with a jerk.

The cat, disturbed by the motion, got up and jumped to the floor. It stretched its back and sauntered off.

They swung in silence for a while.

Cherish sighed. "God gave us the love between a man and a woman as an—" her hand fluttered out in search of the correct word "—extension of His love for us."

Again he didn't know how to answer. "Someone will love you some day, Cherish, with the kind of love you yearn for."

She tipped her head to one side, regarding him steadily. "Do you think so?"

"I'm sure of it," he replied, wondering who that man would be and realizing he couldn't conjure up any image of the man who would be good enough for her.

"I hope you're right," she answered him, and set the book on her lap. "Don't you want to be loved again? The way Emma loved you?"

Her eyes searched his, and he had a fleeting sense of how much more wrenching and painful the death of a loved one would be to a man than to a boy. He turned away from Cherish and looked down the lawn toward the inlet beyond. The tide had filled it, just as Cherish's words had filled his mind without any conscious resistance on his part.

"I never think about it," he answered honestly. "I was awfully young—we both were—when Emmy and I 'pledged our troth.'

Then we just kept the promise, although we didn't see each other but just once a year after I came up here for my apprenticeship.

"When I turned nineteen, I asked your father for permission to get married. Although I'd already fulfilled the terms of my apprenticeship and didn't really need his consent, he counseled me to wait until I was at least twenty-one, with more money saved up."

He looked straight ahead to some indefinite point in the center of the painted porch floor. "His advice made sense. At that age you don't expect to lose someone younger than yourself, just like that, even though we go through it all the time. I'd already lost an older brother and sister, and my father never came back from the Grand Banks."

He cleared his throat, the recollection of those days coming back to him as he spoke about them. "Then she got rheumatic fever and died, just a month shy of my twenty-first birthday." He'd felt bitter about it for a long time. Just when it had faded, he didn't know.

"Do you still miss Emma after all these years?"

He shook his head slowly. "It's as I said—I guess I'm married to boats now."

"You know I love you, Silas."

He lifted his gaze to hers, her words arresting him.

Before he could figure out what she meant, she asked softly, "Don't you love me?"

Her big blue eyes waited for his answer. He could feel himself redden. He rubbed the back of his neck, at a loss for an answer. How was he supposed to answer such a question? Was she talking about their old familiar affection for each other, developed over the years? Or that sublime sentiment she had been describing to him? He managed to tear his gaze away.

"Well...uh...yes."

"You don't have to say it as if you're going to choke on it!"

His face grew warmer. "I'm not! Of course I love you. I've known you since you were a little girl. You're like a sister to me."

When he looked at her again, she was gazing away from him.

He felt the weight of responsibility. Cherish trusted him. Winslow trusted him. How could he live up to that trust when he found himself yearning to kiss those sweet lips inches from him?

Silas lay on his bed, hearing the lap of the waves below boxing him in. He could no longer push aside Cherish's question. *Don't you love me?*

She'd said *I love you* in her frank, childlike way. She loved the boy who'd come to Haven's End fourteen years earlier. But it was a naive, girlish emotion that would soon pass once she'd been back a while and realized Silas van der Zee was the same uneducated man she'd left two years ago, who'd never been beyond this coast, who never could come anywhere near the kind of gentlemen she'd met in her travels. Soon she'd outgrow her childish fancy and turn admiring woman's eyes on someone like Warren Townsend.

But what about Silas himself? *Don't you love me?* Why did the question make him squirm like a pale grub dug out of the dark, damp earth and exposed to the unfamiliar light and air?

What did he know of love? Did he even know *how* to love?

He loved boats. He could hold on to that one fact. He loved the feel of smooth wood emerging from the sanding, knowing it was something tangible, something he could force and shape and tame. He loved the look of a rift-sawn timber with its straight grain, knowing its superior strength, its unlikeliness to cup or warp in the water. He loved the smell of cedar and oak and pine that permeated the boat shop even up to his room, the only home he'd known for the past fourteen years.

He loved the challenge of taking straight, strong, unbending logs and cutting and shaping them into a buoyant craft. He loved the triumph of seeing that craft ply through the waters, daring that depthless expanse of waves, defying nature itself when it brought even the wind to do its bidding through that mathematical precision of setting sails at a certain angle to move forward.

He loved the challenge, the speed, the feel of that maiden, the sailing vessel.

But loving a woman—a real, flesh-and-blood woman? Silas sat up, his elbows on his knees, his chin on his fists, too uncomfortable with the question to lie still. Again he felt unable to respond, as if he were untaught or immature in this aspect of the organ called the heart. It seemed to him it had stopped developing when he was twelve and had left home.

He still remembered waving goodbye as his boat pulled away from the harbor. Little Emma, come to see him off, holding his mother's hand. His mother, still looking lost, as she had since she'd received the news that his father wasn't coming back from his fishing expedition. And his older sister with her harsh, Nordic looks prematurely middle-aged although she was only in her twenties, since she'd had to take over the running of the household.

Silas had been one of the last of the siblings to leave home. Almost all the others, older, had already found employment elsewhere.

So Silas had arrived at Winslow's Shipyard and his heart had given itself over to boats. He'd lived among men and boats ever since. The only women he'd had contact with had been Cherish's mother, a kindly, beautiful woman, and the plainer, more acerbic Mrs. Sullivan. With both, their conversation had been limited to *Wash your hands, Silas. Wash your face. Don't forget to scrub behind your ears. Clean your plate, Silas. Get your elbows off the table.*

And then there had been Winslow's cherished daughter, radiant and outgoing and sensitive to his every mood.

He didn't know how to cope with these strange new feelings she was stirring in him. He felt stunted like a gnarled apple tree, beaten down by the salt-laden winter winds, standing squat and twisted beside the tall, majestic firs surrounding it.

Cherish talked about that high-flown sentiment called "love." Was Silas's heart even capable of housing such a noble-sounding emotion?

Tonight was the night she would find herself once again in Silas's arms.

He might not realize what a wonder true love was, but Cherish Winslow was going to show him. She'd make herself irresistible to him.

After taking a sponge bath, careful not to touch her curls, Cherish donned clean underclothes, stockings, corset, coiled wire bustle and petticoats. Then she turned to her wardrobe.

Her dress already hung on the door, pressed that morning. Every ruffle stood up, every pleat lay perfectly flat. She lovingly took the pale blue dress off its hanger. An original Worth creation. Cousin Penelope had presented her to Mr. Worth himself in Paris, and he'd designed the gown for her, allowing her to see it modeled on one of the young French mannequins.

She buttoned the tiny row of buttons up her front and smoothed down the formfitting bodice. The upper skirt was formed *en tablier,* like a puffed-up apron draped across the front in loose folds and gathered in the rear to fall gracefully from the bustle. The underskirt was a shade of deeper blue and trimmed in a wide pleated hem.

With a glance of satisfaction in her full-length mirror, Cherish turned her attention to the details of hair and face. She rummaged in her jewelry box and brought out a black velvet choker with its amethyst pendant.

After placing it around her neck, she brushed her hair carefully, curling each ringlet around her fingers. Now she brought them up high on her head and fastened them with a tortoise clasp, and arranged the cascade of curls down her back and around her shoulders. Her amethyst earrings dangled from her ears. She frowned at her reflection, wishing she could use rouge the way the ladies in France did, but Aunt Phoebe would be liable to make a public spectacle of her, sending her upstairs to scrub it off her face. Instead she contented herself with putting a little rice powder on her face and pinching her cheeks to bring out the color. Finally she dabbed a little eau de toilette on her temples and behind her ears.

She stood and gave herself a final inspection in the glass. It was not a ball gown by any means; she knew enough not to wear anything too fancy for Haven's End. What would Silas think? That was the only thing that really concerned her.

Sending a prayer heavenward, asking the Lord to bless her endeavors, she straightened the articles in her room, then left to see whether her first guests had arrived.

The corridor was crowded with young people. Cherish could feel Annalise's hand clutch her arm in resistance, but she ignored it and blithely sallied forth into the crowd, greeting her friends and presenting Annalise to everyone she spoke to.

Her eyes scanned the hallway for Silas, but she didn't see him. Disappointed, she entered the parlor with Annalise. Warren, taller than most of the people present, walked over to them immediately.

"There you are." He turned his gaze from Cherish to his sister, and she could see the question in his eyes.

"Yes, here we are. I promised Annalise to stay with her until she is better acquainted with my friends." She didn't explain to him how reluctant his sister had been to come into the parlor at all. "Would you be so kind as to get us each a glass of punch?"

"Certainly."

After that, Cherish was swamped with friends stopping to chat with her. The music started up in the opposite parlor and she wished she could loosen Annalise's hold on her and seek out Silas. She had seen him come in. He had given them a brief greeting and left again, and she hadn't seen him since. He was probably out on the veranda chatting with the menfolk.

Finally, feeling she was being released from an ordeal, Cherish left Annalise sitting with Aunt Phoebe and one of her friends and headed for the doorway. There Warren accosted her.

"Where's Annalise?" he asked her.

Biting back a retort, she answered sweetly, "See, there? I left her with Aunt Phoebe and Mrs. Drummond."

"I wanted to thank you for being so patient with her. She's—" he hesitated, looking down at the cup in his hand "—very shy."

Cherish felt her impatience evaporate, and her heart warmed to the man who showed such concern for his sister.

"Yes, I noticed. I think she'll be all right. Perhaps we can ask one of the young men to dance with her."

He smiled in enthusiasm. "Yes, that would be grand. Now, how about you? Can I interest you in a dance?"

Cherish swallowed her frustration. Perhaps she should dance with him and get it over with. That way she could reserve a waltz for Silas later. She'd gone over the waltzes with her piano-playing friend Alice, who would play when Jacob and his fiddler friends took a break.

She nodded her acceptance, and the two of them entered the other parlor, where furniture and carpets had been cleared from the center of the room. Cherish allowed Warren to swing her around in the spirited dance amidst the other dancers. One dance led to another. About halfway through the second, she spotted Silas in the doorway. She lifted an arm in greeting and he nodded to her with a smile.

As the music ended, she and Warren moved off the dance floor. "You dance very well," he told her as he led her toward the doorway. "Let me get you some refreshment before the musicians start up again. I'll bring Annalise back with me."

"Yes, do." Maybe he could dance with his sister.

She turned to Silas with a smile. "Where have you been keeping yourself all evening?"

"Around," he answered with a lazy grin. His thick hair was swept back from his forehead. Darker sideburns contrasted with the burnished gold of the rest of his hair. His gray eyes were alight with humor. "You are looking quite the fashion plate."

"I trust that is a compliment."

He tilted his head in acknowledgment. "Most certainly. Another Paris creation?" he asked with a nod at her gown.

"Yes, monsieur. I've been looking for you," she said after a moment.

"What for? To foist some young lady on me to dance with?"

She laughed, thinking that was precisely what she intended. "Why aren't you dancing, anyway?"

"I told you, I'm not much of a dancer."

"You never will be if you don't practice."

At that moment Warren returned with Annalise.

"Silas, you remember Warren Townsend and his sister, Annalise."

"Yes, of course. Pleased to see you both again," he said, giving Warren his hand and smiling kindly at Annalise.

"It's good to see you, too," Warren replied.

They exchanged pleasantries as Cherish sipped the cold fruit punch. She heard the first notes of the piano and looked for a place to set down her cup.

Her arm, stretched toward a low table, stopped, paralyzed, when she heard Warren's low, friendly tone behind her. "Would you mind escorting Annalise onto the dance floor? I'd like to dance with Cherish and don't want to leave my sister unescorted. Although she'll deny it, she's a wonderful dancer."

"Uh, of course," Silas said after a second's hesitation. "Miss Townsend? Would you care to dance this waltz with me?"

Cherish turned, seeing the look of fright on Annalise's face. For a moment she felt relief, certain Annalise would turn Silas down.

But her brother pushed her gently toward Silas, urging, "Please say yes. Otherwise everyone will think Silas was turned down by the prettiest girl in the room."

Annalise's eyes widened in concern. Silas stood by, saying nothing. The girl hesitated between the two men.

Finally Silas held out his arm, smiling encouragement. "They'll understand once they see me waltz."

Annalise returned his smile and put her hand on his arm.

Everything faded out for Cherish—the sounds of the waltz, the babble of voices around her—as she watched Silas, arm in arm with Annalise, walk toward the dance floor. The distance between him and Cherish increased with each step, making it a reality she could do nothing to alter.

As if coming back to the present, she heard Warren's voice. "So, may I have the honor of this dance?"

She licked her lips, tempted to give him the set-down of his life. *How dare he? He and his stupid little sister with her shy, childish ways!* Cherish swallowed the words that roiled through her mind, knowing how unfair they were, but unable to stop from feeling hurt and humiliated even as she nodded her assent.

She followed the dance steps like an automaton while her heart ached with the feeling of betrayal. The warm smile she thought reserved for her, the encouraging words she'd always received from Silas, the gentle teasing were not for her alone. They were for any young lady that came along.

Obviously, he'd felt sympathy for Annalise. Was that all Silas felt for Cherish, as well?

He'd always been her big brother, pal, confidant…hero. But now she wanted something more from Silas.

As the strains of the waltz played on, Cherish refused to believe her years of waiting for Silas had been in vain. There was no other man for her. Didn't Silas see that?

# Chapter Five

Silas held Annalise gingerly. Heaven knew, he wasn't used to dancing the waltz, and his partner looked as if she was ready to expire at any moment. He glanced helplessly across the room, but relief was not forthcoming.

Cherish was in Townsend's arms, smiling up at something he was saying as they moved in time to the music. They both looked as if they belonged in a ballroom in Boston rather than in a front parlor in Haven's End.

He turned back to Miss Townsend as the two moved awkwardly among the circling dancers. "Smile, or everyone'll think I'm stepping on your feet."

The look of fright in the girl's large green eyes gave way to a slight relaxing of her facial features.

"That's better. Even if you can't manage a smile, at least it doesn't look as if you're being tortured."

A tiny, tentative smile appeared on her pink lips.

"Getting better and better. I admit I'm not much of a dancer, but I don't want to pass myself off as a worse clodhopper than I already know myself to be. I was convinced I couldn't waltz, but I have it on the best authority that it's as easy as counting one, two, three. Of course, having left school young, I don't know as I'm too capable in that area either."

Her smile grew, and he took a deep breath of relief. He couldn't abide the thought that the girl was here by force, only to please her brother. "Thatta girl."

Silas kept up a flow of conversation as they danced. It occurred to him he was chattering. It reminded him of the day Cherish had been waltzing with him in the meadow. He wondered now whether she had been as nervous as he felt right now.

No—he dismissed the notion as soon as it was formed. Cherish was the most poised girl he knew. He glanced at her again across the dancers, remembering her as a little lady even at the age of five when she'd come to make his acquaintance on his first day at the boat shop.

"—so many years."

He glanced back at Miss Townsend. "Excuse me?"

"I said you've been in Haven's End so many years."

"That's right. I always knew I wanted to build boats, so I was glad to find a place to apprentice."

His gaze roved over Cherish and Townsend once again.

She certainly seemed to be at ease, speaking with Warren as they glided across the dance floor, and it seemed to Silas that she was as graceful in a meadow as in a ballroom.

He, himself, was finding it hard to keep up a flow of conversation and at the same time mind the placement of his feet. Deciding to concentrate on his steps, he stopped talking.

When the song ended and another started up, he wished for a moment that it was Cherish in his arms on the dance floor. But after that brief tuneless waltz in the meadow, he had resolved to avoid dancing with her. Holding her in his arms, however innocently, put too many crazy thoughts into his head.

Cherish awoke the next morning late. Turning from the window, its shade unsuccessfully hiding the beautiful spring day and sound of birdsong, she burrowed farther into her pillow.

How she wished she could stay out of sight all day.

She groaned, remembering her unwanted guests. Like her Worth creation, which now lay in a crumpled heap on the floor in her line of vision, they intruded where they were not wanted. Warren and Annalise Townsend were still under her roof, and she was their hostess.

She stared at the wallpaper before her, reliving the fiasco of last night. *Oh, Lord, why do I have to go down and pretend everything is all right? They ruined everything last night. It was my party and I had everything planned. I've waited so long for Silas. All I wanted was to dance with him!*

Her lips trembled and her eyes welled up with tears, the way they had all night as she'd tossed and turned.

It was almost as if Silas had deliberately avoided her. She'd never seen him so elusive. If he wasn't talking in such a chummy manner to little miss whey-faced Townsend, he was nowhere to be seen. She couldn't understand it.

She'd had to swallow her anger and disappointment and pretend everything was just fine. When they'd finished eating and gone back inside as another waltz started up, she'd turned to him and there he was, taking Annalise out onto the dance floor again, as if they were the best of friends.

After that she'd seen Annalise dancing with another man— a friend of Silas's—and Silas vanished. She'd had to exercise every ounce of self-control to keep smiling and chatting with Warren and later with Annalise when she'd wanted nothing better than to tell her to stay away from Silas.

She swiped at her eyes now. It would do no good to go getting them all swollen. Then everyone would know she'd been crying. She wouldn't give Silas the satisfaction!

She had guests to see to. Thankfully, they were leaving this morning. Cherish threw off the bedclothes, resolved to brave the day. First a repair job on her face, she decided, peering at the red-rimmed eyes in the mirror. Then to play the charming hostess to the Townsends as she'd promised her father. Then, finally, down to the boat shop to comfort Silas and discover why he couldn't have spared one dance for her!

* * *

In the afternoon Silas headed up to the shop after spending the morning working in the stocks scarfing together lengths of wood. They had been cut and shaped to fit together like puzzle pieces, forming the vertical ribs of the schooner's hull.

He hadn't been up to the house for dinner, but had brought a lunch pail down with him.

Now he welcomed a break from the tiring work in the sun. Try as he would to deny it, he also looked forward to seeing Cherish again. Why, when he'd managed to live without her for months, even years on end, did his eyes now long for a glimpse of her daily, his soul for some moments of communion? These were questions he chose to ignore for the moment as he pushed open the back door to the boat shop.

He spied Cherish down on her knees before a large board.

"Hi, there. At work already?" he asked in a friendly voice. In her simple cotton dress and pinafore apron she appeared so different from last night, yet just as captivating.

She did not look up at him, but continued drawing a straight line down from top to bottom of the board. "Yes."

Feeling slightly put out that she'd started without him, he squatted down beside her. "Sorry I couldn't get here sooner. I had to finish framing a section of the hull."

She finished the line. "That's quite all right. Excuse me." She indicated she wanted him to move and he complied, wondering why she was behaving as if he'd done something wrong.

"Sure. Need some help?"

She finally sat back on her heels and addressed him directly. "I'm marking out a grid on this board. I've figured out the scale of the half-hull model measurements, which I've plotted on this chart. See, 'two inches equals one foot, zero inches.' So we'll divide the board into a grid of one-foot spaces. Here, you can do the next one."

He took the yardstick and pencil from her and followed her directions. In the meantime, she began measuring out the horizontal lines on the board, explaining how she'd calculated those spaces. The two of them worked silently, crisscrossing paths every once in a while.

The flowery scent of her hair came under his nostrils when this happened. She seemed completely unaware of him, her focus intent on the pencil and yardstick in her hand. He noticed how slim and attractive her hand looked, splayed against the white board. Its only adornment was a thin silver ring with a small amethyst stone set in a filigreed mount.

"Tired after last night?" he asked.

"A little," she replied, her back to him.

"It was a nice party," he offered, hoping to make her feel better if she were upset about something.

"Thank you."

"Miss Townsend seemed to flounder a bit there, not knowing anyone but you."

"Thank goodness you were there to rescue her."

He eyed her back. Did he detect a trace of sarcasm? What had he done? "She's all right, once you get to know her. We spoke about you," he said humorously.

That caused her to crane around to look at him. "What about me?" she asked with a frown.

He grinned, hoping to get a rise from her. "Oh, I just told her she'd better follow you around if she wanted to learn how to socialize."

"What does that mean?" She didn't sound pleased.

"Just that. You know how to talk to people, dance, put on the charm—"

"Is *that* what you think I do?"

He cleared his throat, wondering why she was so touchy. "Anyway, she was a bit shy, and I thought you could help her."

"Is that so?" She drew another line across the wood. "What else did you talk about?"

"She admires you. Maybe you could befriend her, you know, take her under your wing. She seems to be in mortal fear of strangers. I felt kind of sorry for her last night. I told Charlie he'd better dance with her and treat her nicely if he wanted me to help him with his next boat."

Cherish turned his way and began to measure the next line. "I thought I treated her rather graciously last night. What more do you want me to do—bring her along to the boat shop?"

Now he was certain she was upset about something. She never brought her girlfriends to the shop. "No-o, but you could, oh, you know, have her over, be her friend, talk about whatever it is girls talk about when they're together."

She didn't reply, but continued working.

He drew another line. "What's up?"

She glanced at him. "What do you mean?"

"I know when something's bothering you."

"Nothing's wrong." She took up the chart and began studying it intently.

"Come on. You can tell ol' Silas."

"You're imagining things."

"What is it, Cherry?" he asked in a cajoling tone, using his childhood nickname for her.

"Don't call me that! You know I can't abide it!"

He thought of something. "Is it Townsend? He stuck by you most of the evening. Did he say anything to offend you?"

"No. He was the perfect gentleman."

Silas frowned, remembering how good the two had looked dancing together, each one so elegantly attired. "Your father seems to think highly of him."

"Perhaps justly so."

"Yes, I'm sure," he answered dryly. Seeing his questions were getting him nowhere, he gave up, telling himself Cherish was just in a mood. He'd heard women got into funny humors, although Cherish had never done so before she'd gone away. Maybe that was something she'd picked up on her travels.

But Cherish wasn't ready to let the topic end. "I noticed you had no trouble dancing last night," she said, and again Silas noticed the edge to her tone.

"Well, I couldn't very well refuse Townsend's request to dance with his sister."

"You were very gracious to take her out onto the dance floor so many times. It's a pity you couldn't spare one dance for your hostess."

Silas stared at Cherish. He read hurt in her unblinking gaze, and he finally understood. She had wanted him to dance with her.

He swallowed hard and turned away. How could he tell her he had deliberately avoided holding her in his arms?

He cleared his throat, his fingers fiddling with his pencil. She deserved an explanation, but he didn't think she'd accept the only one he had.

"You were pretty busy on the dance floor all evening. I didn't think you needed me to fill up your dance card."

She turned away from him and resumed her work. He couldn't tell whether she'd accepted his explanation or not.

"You're right, Silas. I didn't *need* you as a partner. I would have *liked* you as a partner."

He had no reply to that. How much he would have liked her as a partner he knew only too well. And the less she knew of it, the better.

On the night of choir practice Cherish put on her hat and grabbed up her shawl to walk to the church. As she walked out the door after supper, she saw Silas walking up the front walk.

"You ready to go?" he asked her.

"You didn't have to come all the way here to fetch me." She had deliberately not reminded him of choir practice when they'd worked together in the boat shop earlier in the day.

He looked unbearably handsome, his dark golden hair brushed back from his forehead, his skin bronze against the collar of his white shirt. He wore no jacket, only a vest.

"Of course I was going to fetch you. Come on." Not waiting for her reply, he turned back on the path.

They were quiet on the walk there. Halfway to the church they were joined by another couple going in the same direction.

"Evenin', Cherish, Silas," said the man, the woman beside him nodding with a smile.

"Evening, Billy," Silas replied. "Going to choir practice?"

"Yep. Fine evening, ain't it?"

"Sure is."

"When you gonna launch that schooner?" Billy asked, indicating the ship in the stocks as they passed the boatyard.

"By summer's end, we expect, or early in the autumn."

"Don't see any more keels being laid. Don't you have any new orders for the summer?"

"We're working on some dories in the workshop right now. Charles Whitcomb may commission a sloop."

The man nodded. "Not like the old days when the yard was littered with hulls."

The two men continued chatting as they neared the white clapboard church.

During the practice, Cherish stood with the women. The pastor wasn't present—only his wife, Carrie, who played the piano. Another gentleman from the congregation directed them.

"Let's turn to hymn number eighty," he told them. They sang a rousing "All Hail the Power of Jesus' Name" about half a dozen times before the man was satisfied.

By the time they left, Cherish thought the words to the hymns would be revolving in her head all evening. Several people walked along with her and Silas as they turned homeward.

"You don't have to go with me. I'll walk along with this group until I reach home," she told him.

"I agreed to accompany you there and back, and that's what I'm going to do," he insisted.

She sighed. How nice it would have been if he'd said he would walk with her because he *wanted* to and not because he felt obliged to. Hugging the shawl around her, she contemplated the night sky, which was just turning a deep blue, its edges still pale and edged by a wash of orange where the sun had set.

"Chilly?" Silas asked softly.

She shook her head.

"I'll be settin' out my onions and taters tomorrow," Billy said to them. "Too early for the squash and corn. We could still get a frost."

"We have peas, radishes and lettuce coming up nicely," Cherish told him. "Aunt Phoebe and I will probably be planting more seeds tomorrow."

"'Spect we'll have some rain in another day or two, so it's the time to get some seed in the ground."

They waved goodbye to the other couples when they reached Cherish's gate. Silas followed her up the walk to the veranda. When they approached it, Cherish climbed up the first step before turning to bid him good-night.

He stood on the ground at eye level with her. "For the past few days you've been looking as if you've lost your best friend," he said jokingly. "Don't be sad. You've still got me." His lips crooked upward in the dim light.

Her throat tightened at his words. He didn't realize what he was saying. She *had* lost her best friend, who wasn't even aware of it. She could feel the tears welling up in her eyes.

Not able to speak, she leaned forward to kiss him on the cheek, wanting somehow to express what she felt for him.

At the same instant Silas turned his head to hers and began saying "Good night."

He never finished the words, as her pursed lips touched his half-open mouth. She could see his eyes widen with the shock of the contact.

She didn't dare move, didn't dare breathe. All that she could think was she never wanted the moment to end.

A second later he jerked back.

"Well," she said, too awed by the contact to say anything more.

His eyes stared into hers, and his Adam's apple bobbed as he swallowed. "I—I'm sorry about that," he stuttered, taking a step away from her. "I'll say good-night. I'll—I'll see you tomorrow." Already he was hurrying down the path.

"Good night," she called after him, laughter in her voice, her high spirits returning. He had kissed her and it had not left him unaffected! If it hadn't actually been a kiss, it had been close enough! If he was going to act shy about that, well, she'd make him see it was all right. More than all right!

*Thank You, Lord, oh, thank You, Lord!*

She stayed on the veranda until Silas was out of sight over the rise in the road. She brought the shawl up over her mouth, hugging herself with it, reliving the feel of his lips against her mouth, their softness and warmth.

It was a sign, a definite sign, that she and Silas were meant for each other.

Silas strode away from the Winslow house as if his rapid pace could outstrip his thoughts. He didn't slow down until he arrived at the boat shop.

How could it have happened! He'd been going to say goodnight and the next thing he knew his mouth was touching hers!

Cherish was his employer's daughter. He'd never...it had never occurred to him— Horror filled him at the reality of the brief touching of her lips.

How could this—this intimate act have happened? The more he tried to puzzle out the madness of that moment, the more he remembered the feel of her soft lips against his, her warm breath brushing his.

He recoiled at having violated some unwritten code that put Cherish beyond his reach. But even as he tried to erase the memory of her mouth, he felt a yearning for more.

When he entered the silent boat shop, the smell of wood permeating the cavernous room, he could feel the fingers of loneliness creeping out from every corner of the room, seeking him out, and laying hold of him.

This room contained all he had lived for for as long as he could remember. There was no room for loneliness in his life; he'd come to terms with his solitary existence long ago.

He climbed the stairs to his room under the eaves of the workshop. Everything was as he'd left it, bare and neat. He fell on the narrow cot, thinking even as he did so that he should hang up his good trousers and take off his starched shirt before it became wrinkled, but he didn't move. The walls pressed in around him, the sensation magnified by the lapping of the waves at high tide down below against the concrete foundation of the boathouse, pushing against the defenses he'd erected over the years.

They had crumbled like a sand castle before the tide in the space of a few seconds in an accidental encounter of one girl's lips with his. He wiped the back of his hand against his mouth as if with the action he could wipe away the memory of her lips. But the gesture was futile—he could still taste the sweetness of those lips.

## ❧ Chapter Six ❧

Cherish rose early. Ever since she was fifteen and had first given her heart to the Lord, she'd made a practice of having a quiet time with Him before beginning her day. She'd slacked off in recent days, but now felt she needed to get back to that firm foundation of God's Word and prayer. She opened a book of devotions and turned to the day's scripture reading.

"Be not wise in your own conceits," she read in the portion of Romans. She went over the explanatory passage, then got down by her bed to pray.

She asked for the Lord's guidance that day. She prayed for her family members and those she knew who had need of a special touch from God. She prayed for the missionaries taking God's Word to far-off lands.

Lastly, she brought up the need that was most pressing on her heart. "Father, You know my feelings for Silas. You know all things. Oh, God, I want to do Your will. But…but—" her heart swelled again with hope "—with what happened last night, I feel as if I've received your blessing. I don't want to be wise in my own conceits, but I know he feels something for me, too! Oh, God, grant me to follow the right course. Let me see a sign in his eyes that he cares for me—oh, even an inkling of what I feel for him! I pray in Your dear Son Jesus' name."

She ended her prayer, then stood to wash and dress, ready to face the day, hope restored.

Her hope was strengthened when she saw that Silas was still at the breakfast table with her father. Had he waited for her?

"Good morning," she said brightly.

Silas was standing at the table, removing a spoon from the sugar bowl. His hand jerked, spilling sugar onto the white tablecloth. His glance dropped from Cherish to the spoon.

"Good morning," her father replied. She kissed the top of his head before approaching Silas at the other end of the table.

She smiled at his clumsy attempts to sweep up the spilled sugar. "Here, let me help you," she said, coming to stand close to him. He immediately moved away about a foot. She took up a knife and used its edge to collect the sugar and bring it to the edge of the table, where she scraped it into her other palm.

"See? No harm done."

He pushed his coffee cup forward. "Uh, you can put it in here," he said, his voice sounding strange.

She let the sugar crystals fall from her hand into the awaiting cup. Then she brushed her hands off over the table. "So what is planned down at the yard for today?"

Her father answered, "We're continuing to build the frame for the schooner. We'll probably start some of the crossbeams in preparation for laying the decks." He folded his newspaper as Cherish sat down. "Silas tells me he'll be readying the lumber for the Whitehall mold in the shop this afternoon."

"He?" She turned to Silas as Aunt Phoebe came in with a stack of pancakes. "You mean 'we,' don't you, Silas?"

He didn't meet her gaze. "If it's all right with your father."

She looked at him openmouthed. *All right with her father?*

"Flapjacks hot off the griddle," Aunt Phoebe said, setting down the steaming platter. "Help yourselves." She stuck the serving fork into Silas's hand.

"Papa, I shall be working with Silas on the Whitehall. I told you about that last week."

"On lofting it, not building it," he reminded her as he helped himself to pancakes from the platter Silas held for him. He then passed them to Cherish. She served herself absently.

"Well, Silas and I agreed we'd spend afternoons in the shop after he's had his morning down on the yard and I've had mine helping Aunt Phoebe." She gave her aunt a smile. "Speaking of which, can I prepare a special dessert for dinner today?" She tried to think what Silas would like.

"Certainly. We'll be baking this morning. You can help me fry up some doughnuts after we've set the bread to rise."

"Mmm!" her father said. "Nothing like some hot doughnuts and coffee. Bring some down to the shop when you come, Cherish. Speaking of which, I'd prefer to have Silas work down in the yard today and the next few days to finish the framing. We need to get started with the planking."

Cherish frowned. "You mean he can't work on the lofting for the next few days?" she began, dismay in her voice.

"Before you start in, I'd better tell you the rest."

"The rest?" she asked, her mind gearing up to argue against whatever new obstacle her father threw into her plans.

"Don't give me that look, dear. It's good news."

"What is it, Papa?" Cherish laid down the maple syrup.

"You two must have made such a good impression on the Townsends that they've invited both of you for the weekend."

Cherish's eyes lit up and she turned to Silas, who was looking at her father as if his mouthful of pancakes had just turned to pig slop.

"Oh, what fun! Silas and I, both, to go over to Hatsfield and spend the weekend with them?"

"That's right, dear," he answered, wiping his mouth and throwing down the napkin. "They have all kinds of activities planned with some other young people, a boat outing on Whittier's Lake, games and dancing, church on Sunday and then you can sail back that afternoon." He rose.

"So I need Silas down on the yard working on the stocks if he hopes for time off this weekend."

"I don't need to go over to Hatsfield, Mr. Winslow…" Silas began as soon as he'd swallowed his food.

Mr. Winslow contemplated him silently a few seconds. "I appreciate your attitude, Silas. However, in this case, you would also be serving the shipyard with your weekend at the Townsends'. Don't forget, we need their business."

The two men looked at each other an instant longer. Finally Silas's gaze fell to his plate. "Very well, sir."

"I appreciate your loyalty." Winslow took a final sip of coffee. "Ready to go? Otherwise, I'll see you down on the yard." He took up his folded newspaper and headed for the door. "Don't forget to bring us some doughnuts, Cherish."

"I won't, Papa. I'll be down later," she answered as she took up a forkful of pancake, wondering why Silas had appeared reluctant to go to Hatsfield this weekend. Perhaps he didn't care so much about Annalise Townsend after all?

She glanced at Silas, who seemed intent on finishing his breakfast in record time. Before she could engage him in conversation, he stood.

Aunt Phoebe said to him, "Don't forget to collect your clean laundry on the way out."

"Yes, thank you," he answered, already heading for the kitchen.

"I've put everything in a satchel by the door," she said to his departing back. "Mercy, he seemed in an awful hurry all of a sudden. Wonder if it was that invitation your father just mentioned. Though I'd think he'd like an outing. He doesn't get together with enough young folks his age. Hangs about all day with those rough men down on the yard.

"Now, we are going to try your hand at dinner rolls today," she said, turning her attention to the morning's baking.

"That sounds interesting," Cherish answered, her mind on the coming weekend. Two whole days in Silas's company. Her thoughts flitted briefly to Annalise, but she decided she would do as Silas had asked her and befriend the girl. She would show Silas what a good friend she could be.

She wondered vaguely if the invitation had been Warren

Townsend's idea. He was a very good-looking and personable young man. She ought to be swept off her feet. Instead, she wondered how she would endure two days in his company. And how was she going to prevent being paired off with him again?

She pondered the situation as she ate her breakfast. She'd need to come up with a strategy before the weekend.

Cherish came down the wooden stairs that led from the boat shop to the beach. She picked her way through the rubble, stepping over piles of lumber stacked above the high-water line.

"Hey there, Cherish, need somethin'?" one of the shipwrights called down to her. He was standing above her on the scaffolding against the schooner hull, a mallet in his hand.

"Good morning, William. I thought you men might like some freshly made doughnuts." She removed the gingham cloth from the basket she carried and showed him. "See?"

"Oh, they look mighty good," he replied. "Why don't you come on up here so we can sample 'em?"

He met her on the ramp that led up to the scaffolding platform and escorted her the rest of the way. Wiping his sweaty forehead with a handkerchief, he took a sugary doughnut from the basket. "Thank you kindly." After the first bite, he wiped his mouth with the back of his forearm and said, "Mmm. That is some good. You make them all by yourself?"

"Well, Aunt Phoebe helped."

"That woman can bake a stone and make it come out tasting good."

"Let me offer Ezra some." She moved toward the other man farther down the platform. "Where's Silas?" she asked him after he'd taken a doughnut.

Ezra pointed with his doughnut down into the skeletal hull. "Down fitting the 'knees' between the crossbeams."

Cherish chatted a few moments with the two men. They were both middle-aged with grizzled hair and skin as brown and cracked as baked mud, from years working in the sun.

They'd known her since she was a babe and she treated them as uncles.

She wrapped a few of the doughnuts in a separate napkin and left the basket with the men with a parting encouragement to eat them while they were still warm.

She climbed back down the wooden ramp laid diagonally alongside the hull. Once back on the beach, she hiked up her skirt and climbed into the cavernous hull. It was still only a structure of vertical ribs, the sunlight coming through in bands. Spying Silas down near the stern, she made her way there, carefully stepping along the keelson.

Silas was standing on a ladder set against the ribbing. He didn't hear her approach over the banging of his mallet against the wood above his head. She watched him pounding trunnels into the holes that had been bored into the wood.

When he stopped a moment, Cherish welcomed the stillness.

"Ahoy, mate," she said.

He swiveled around on the ladder. "What are you doing here?" Before she could answer, he added, "How did you get in?"

"I walked."

"You could have tripped or fallen."

"Well, I didn't. Don't scold so."

He began descending the ladder. "You didn't answer my question. What are you doing here?"

"You didn't give me a chance to." She swung the gingham napkin in front of him. "I brought you this, but if that's the way you're going to greet someone who's brought you a tasty morsel, I may reconsider. I've already been told by both Ezra and Will that they are delicious," she added as she watched him shove the mallet through the belt at his waist and eye the doughnuts she held out on the napkin.

"What's the matter? Think I put sawdust in them?"

He shook his head as if waking up. "No, of course not."

He wiped his hands down the sides of his pant legs and asked in a friendlier tone, "So, how is the baking coming?"

"You might say I'm excelling in the culinary arts," she replied, handing him a doughnut. "But you be the judge."

Their fingers touched as he took hold of the doughnut. As he took his first bite, she brought her fingertips up to her lips and licked off the sugar crystals that clung to them. He watched her as he chewed. Abruptly he looked away.

He finished the doughnut.

"Here," she said, handing him her handkerchief from her pocket.

"Thanks." He took it and wiped his mouth.

"You missed a spot." She took the handkerchief from him and rubbed it against his chin. "There." She stepped back and looked around for a place to sit between the ribs.

"Careful you don't get your skirt soiled," he warned her, his eyes watching her every move. She arranged her skirts, feeling a curious thrill inside her.

"Don't worry. It's an old skirt."

"Saving all your finery for the big weekend?"

She cocked her head at him, considering his tone. Could he perhaps be jealous of Warren Townsend? She propped her chin in her hand. "I haven't yet decided on my wardrobe for the weekend. You didn't seem too anxious this morning to be pulled away from here to enjoy the Townsends' hospitality."

"I've got a lot of work to do."

"All work and no play makes Silas a dull boy," she commented, picking up one of the doughnuts from the napkin in her lap and eyeing it. It had come out perfect, round and plump, its little hole almost closed up in the middle. She took a small bite. Delicious. Light and slightly sweet with a hint of nutmeg. Aunt Phoebe had been right in her exacting attitude toward cooking.

"Am I a dull boy?"

"Hmm?" She brought her mind back to the conversation. She tilted her head at Silas as she held the doughnut near her lips. He was examining the drill bit on the end of the drill with what appeared to be the utmost concentration.

"Let's just say you're in danger of becoming one." She set the doughnut back down on the napkin and brushed off her fingertips. "But don't worry. Cherish has arrived and will save you."

Instead of replying, he climbed back up the ladder and positioned the drill against a timber.

"How is it coming?" she asked, standing up and approaching the base of the ladder.

"Fine."

"So I see. Where were we? Oh yes, saving Silas van der Zee from becoming dull as dishwater—or should I say, in this case, bilgewater?"

He stopped drilling and eyed her from his perch. "What's the remedy, Dr. Winslow?"

"For starters, you will enjoy fun and relaxation this weekend in Hatsfield."

"Is that an order?"

"Yes. Consider it so. Part of the regimen."

"From you or from your father?"

She looked at him nonplussed. "Are you upset with Papa for wanting you to go to Hatsfield this weekend?"

"No." His tone didn't sound convincing.

"He only wants you to have some fun."

"He only wants us to ingratiate ourselves with the Townsends."

"What's wrong with cultivating their friendship along with their business?"

"Nothing, as long as you enjoy their company in the process."

She pondered his meaning. "Don't you enjoy their company?" she asked with a sly smile. "I thought you liked Annalise."

He shrugged. "I do. I feel sorry for her mostly."

His answer annoyed her. She wasn't sure why. "What is there to feel sorry for? She's pretty, she's well educated, she has a dear brother, her family is well-off."

"She's also morbidly shy."

"That can be overcome."

He glanced down at her. "That might be easy for you to say, not suffering from shyness."

"How do you know I think it's so easy?" Here she'd come with the best of intentions, bringing him a gift, and she was made to feel as if she were the one lacking in charity. *Charity.* Ugh! That word, which conjured up other words like patience and kindness… "I promised you I'd befriend her. What more do you want?"

"Nothing." He turned back to his work, giving Cherish the sense that she was dismissed.

"I just want for us to have a good time," she said in her most coaxing tone. "Is anything so wrong with that?"

She couldn't see his face anymore. "No, I suppose not," he answered shortly.

"Well, I don't know what you're so grumpy about. I just came by so you could sample a doughnut or two. Excuse me for interrupting your important work." She set the remainder of the doughnuts on a plank of wood and brushed her skirts off. "I think I'll continue with the lofting at the boat shop. You can join me when you find the time," she added, as if his involvement were the least of her concerns.

Silas didn't come home for dinner, preferring to finish his job on the hull, but told Winslow to make his excuses to Mrs. Sullivan. He ate the remaining doughnuts, including the one Cherish had taken one bite out of.

He knew he was acting churlish and as skittish as a colt around Cherish, but he couldn't help it. He felt as if he must salvage a remnant of control over a situation that was fast unraveling.

Cherish didn't know what she was playing with. He didn't blame her. She was just a young girl used to having fun. She didn't have a clue what she was doing to him. She was probably doing the same thing to Townsend.

It would be interesting—but it would certainly not be "fun"—to see events unfold at the Townsend weekend.

He pounded the trunnels into the wood savagely, his arm aching, knowing he couldn't avoid Cherish forever. He'd better develop a pretty tough skin.

## ❧ Chapter Seven ❧

"Warren plays the piano beautifully," Mrs. Townsend told Cherish as the serving maid cleared the first course from the table. "Do you play, Miss Winslow?"

"Only indifferently," she replied, sitting back to let the girl brush the crumbs from the cloth.

"Miss Winslow is quite an accomplished artist," Warren told his mother from across the table.

Cherish gave him a brief smile before her glance strayed to the other end of the table. The senior Mr. Townsend was talking with Silas, who sat at his right. Annalise sat across from Silas, her gaze riveted on his face.

Cherish gave her attention to Mrs. Townsend, though she strained to hear the conversation between Mr. Townsend and Silas.

"Oh, do you sketch, my dear?" Mrs. Townsend asked her.

"Now, what's the tonnage..." she caught from Mr. Townsend.

"Yes, ma'am, and watercolor. I like to paint each ship that's built at the shipyard."

"Oh, how lovely," Mrs. Townsend said. "I imagine you saw many fine monuments to paint on your European tour?"

"I believe if we increase the length overall and deepen the draft…" came Silas's voice.

"Yes, indeed. I filled a portfolio with sketches. I even tried my hand at oils."

"You must show me some day."

"Now, you take the three-masted coastal schooners. They've proven their worth up against the steamers."

"You certainly can't find any vessel more weatherly," Silas agreed.

"I've tried to get Annalise to paint my garden, but she hasn't shown an inclination."

"But the question I have is which is superior—the deep-draft keel model or the shoaler centerboard?"

"Well, sir, I've given it a lot of thought, and…"

Cherish's tongue itched to contribute to the conversation between the two men at the far end of the table, but she smiled at her hostess and tried to infuse some enthusiasm in her replies.

She glanced at Silas and saw him take up his silver knife and delineate something for Mr. Townsend along the tablecloth, his face alight with eagerness. The older man listened intently.

Cherish finally gave up trying to listen in on two conversations and reply to only one of them. She turned to the crystal bowl of sorbet placed in front of her. If dinner were any indication, it was going to prove nigh on impossible to find time alone with Silas.

Cherish and Silas spent the next day out on Whittier's Lake with a party of young people the Townsends had invited. The clouds had broken and the sun shone bright and warm over the dew-damp landscape.

To her chagrin, Cherish was not able to maneuver a place in the skiff with Silas. Warren had deposited Annalise in it. Cherish's smile was becoming strained as she was helped aboard a second boat by Warren.

Pleading the excuse that she was going to sketch the lovely scenery, she was spared from making polite conversation. As the others fished, she drew desultorily.

They rowed toward the middle of the immense lake. Cherish, despite her growing frustration, finally settled on sketching the boat Silas sat in. She concentrated on drawing both its occupants so it would not be obvious which one drew her attention, but she took special care in drawing his features.

He had a classic profile and lean cheeks. Although he was usually serious, she could always tell when something sparked his humor. The amusement was evident in the deep-set gray eyes long before it reached his lips.

He was smiling now as he faced Annalise in the boat. Cherish could just imagine his teasing tone as he coaxed a response from her. His arms bent forward and back as he rowed them far out into the lake. What solicitude when he helped her bait her hook and cast her line! Cherish's pencil lead snapped against her tablet.

"Did it break?" Warren's soft voice intruded. She glanced up to see him looking at her in concern.

"Yes. Careless of me. I pushed it too hard," she replied tersely.

"Here, let me whittle a new point for you," he offered.

"No, thank you. I have a spare pencil." She set down her sketching pad. "I don't think I'll do any more right now."

"May I?" Warren asked, reaching for her pad. "That's very good."

"It's just a rough sketch," she answered hastily.

A sudden shout of laughter drew her attention back to one of the other skiffs. She saw it jostling back and forth as one of the occupants landed a fish.

"They seem to be having a good time," she said.

"What did you catch there?" Warren called over. "An old boot?"

"Don't you wish!" a voice shouted back as the fisherman held up a good-sized trout from his line.

"We'll have to redouble our efforts," Warren told the other boaters. "They're one ahead of us now."

After that Cherish decided to try her hand at fishing, as well. When she landed a trout, she felt vindicated. She held it up to Silas across the water when he caught one, too. They used to go fishing together, long ago.

By midafternoon they had beached their craft on the crescent of sandy beach where the Townsends had a "camp," the name for their sizable summer cottage.

Warren grasped Cherish briefly by the waist and swung her ashore to prevent her getting her feet wet. She turned in time to see Silas rendering the same service to Annalise.

"I shall put you in charge of the ladies," Warren told her with a smile. "You can collect some kindling."

Cherish gathered her skirts, saying over her shoulder, "Come, ladies, let's get this task under way. Annalise, why don't you show us the way? Are there any footpaths?"

"Yes, over here."

When they returned with armloads of fallen sticks, the men had the trout cleaned. "That's just what we need." Warren walked over to Cherish and relieved her of the wood.

Soon they had a fire going. Cherish, hoping to show off her new culinary skills, joined Warren to cook the trout, but he refused her help. "This is a man's affair," he told her with a chuckle. "Fishing, cleaning our catch, cooking over an open fire on the beach."

"Oh-ho, is that so?" she answered with a laugh. He really was a nice person, she thought, looking up at his smiling face. Some woman would be blessed to have his affections. "And what are we supposed to do in the meantime? I warn you, we've developed quite a hunger all morning." She glanced at Silas, who was crouched by the fire, feeding it twigs.

"You have nothing to fear. I've done this many times. You'll have the crispiest trout you've ever tasted."

"Crisp, I hope, doesn't mean burned."

"Oh, Cherish, you wound me," he said. As he spoke he was busy setting a frying pan on the fire and sticking a hunk of lard in it. He had taken off his jacket and rolled up his shirtsleeves. He left Silas in charge of the fire and took one of his friends with him to unpack the hamper they had brought.

As they set the table, Cherish made an effort to get to know the other young ladies. She stole another look at Silas, who hadn't addressed her once during their outing. He stood talking with Warren and another gentleman as they watched Warren roll the fish in flour and place it in the hot fat.

Cherish felt tears prick her eyes. What had happened to her closeness with Silas? Didn't he care at all about her anymore? *Oh, Lord, help me to understand. I know I must trust You in this, but…but…it just seems…*

"Your father has a lot of plans for the lumber mill," Silas said to Warren. The aroma of the frying trout filled the air.

Warren smiled at him over the smoke from the hot fire. "Yes, he no sooner completes one venture than he comes up with a new one."

He flipped a trout expertly with the spatula. The fish sizzled and spattered as the flour hit the grease. "The latest is to build some schooners to handle the lumber we anticipate coming through the mill. He seemed pretty impressed with some of your ideas last night. You were explaining something about using a deeper centerboard."

"Yes, I think it would have the stability of the keel and yet carry more cargo than the current centerboard models."

"If what you're saying proves true, it would be ideal for the coastal trade the three-masted schooners now handle. It would be just what Father needs for the trade he envisions."

Silas didn't say anything. He knew his idea would work, but he wasn't used to selling his ideas to anyone. His glance strayed to Cherish, who was making herself useful as usual with a cheery demeanor among the women she'd just met. He marveled how at home she always seemed in any new situation. Completely unlike Annalise, who viewed her with awe.

He could understand that feeling.

He turned his attention back to Townsend. If he knew anything about Thomas Winslow, Cherish's father had this man earmarked as a suitable candidate for his only daughter's hand.

Was that why Silas had made a deliberate effort to get to know the man to see what he was made of? To see if he was worthy of Cherish? Try as he might, Silas could find no fault with Warren Townsend. None at all.

Why did that conclusion give him no satisfaction?

It only left a bitter taste in his mouth, curdling the appetizing smell of frying trout to an acrid stench of smoke in his nostrils.

The trout indeed proved delicious. Mrs. Townsend had sent along loaves of bread, pickles and salads. Seated far down the picnic table from Silas, Cherish did her best to join in the laughter and teasing of the company around her.

After they had cleared up, one of the men, Ted, said, "Can you hike up to Dexter's Summit from here?"

"Yes, there's a trail," Warren told him, and pointed toward the woods. "It's about an hour's hike up."

"Who's game?" Ted asked, looking around the company.

"Oh, it sounds like what we need after all that trout," Cherish answered immediately.

"I don't know," Warren began. "It's a rugged path, all uphill. Are you sure you ladies are up to it?"

"Of course we are!" She looked at the other three women. All except Annalise quickly seconded her.

Warren pulled out his pocket watch. "I don't want to head back to Hatsfield too late. What do you think, Annalise?"

"It *is* rather far," she began.

"Perhaps one of us could stay down here, to accompany the ladies who don't feel up to the hike," the other gentleman, Andrew, offered.

The other ladies quickly scoffed at such a suggestion.

Cherish watched Silas shift from one foot to the other. Afraid that he would volunteer to stay with Annalise, or that Warren would volunteer him, Cherish said, "Oh, come, we're not so fainthearted, are we?" She deliberately addressed her question to Annalise. "The gentlemen didn't let us prove our skill in the preparation of our meal. We must prove our worth in keeping up with them on the trail." She gave the girl a sweet smile.

She could see Annalise hesitating, glancing at her brother and back to Cherish.

"We'll help carry you back, Miss Townsend, if you weary," Andrew offered, with Ted agreeing.

Cherish saw the look in her eye, like that of someone who knows she's trapped and has no recourse but to put the bravest face on circumstances and carry on with good grace. Cherish's conscience fought with her desire to thwart Annalise's will.

"Very well," Annalise said quietly.

As Warren oversaw stowing the hampers away in the wagons, Silas wandered over to Cherish.

"Do you really think it's such a good idea to take a long hike after that meal, and with so many ladies present? I know *you* can do it, but what about the others? They're probably not used to the activity you are."

"Oh, Silas, don't be such a ninny. What's an hour's walk?"

He shook his head at her, his face unsmiling. "What happens if one of these ladies twists her ankle? It's all very well to say we'll carry her down, but reality is quite a different matter from some fool's romantic notion—"

Before she had time to do more than make a face at his concerns, Warren was calling them to the hiking trail.

Cherish breathed in the spicy scent of balsam and spruce as they trudged over the floor of dried fir needles. She tried to convince herself the day wasn't a complete fiasco, but she had a hard time ignoring the sting of Silas's words. He hadn't spoken two words to her the entire time, and when he finally did, it was only to reprimand her as if she were a child.

For the second time that day, tears threatened to spill over, and she brushed at her eyes impatiently. Why was he so concerned about Annalise's welfare, anyway? For that was what it boiled down to, didn't it? He didn't care two pins for any of the rest of them. It was precious, shy Annalise Townsend who concerned him. It used to be Cherish who held that place.

She grabbed a tree branch to help her up the path. What had begun as easy and wide soon became narrow and steep, so they had to walk in single file.

By the time they reached the summit, the group was quiet for the most part, tired and footsore. The mid-May temperature was not yet too high, but the day was sunny and the climb had them feeling warm.

"Oh, how breathtaking!" Cherish gazed down at the lake from the bare rock promontory Warren led her to. Down below was the lake—a flat, shiny mirror, only a portion of the vast body of water visible through the heavy forest surrounding it.

"This was worth the climb, wouldn't you say?" She turned to Ted, who stood on her other side.

"I should say so! And we're none the worse for it, are we?" He turned to the ones straggling up the trail. Last came Annalise, leaning heavily on Silas's arm.

"Annalise! Are you all right?" Warren asked, walking quickly toward his sister.

"Yes, quite all right," she answered. "It's just that I wore these new boots."

Silas led her to a large rock.

"Oh, it feels good to sit down," she said with a sigh.

"Why don't you take the boots off?" Warren asked, crouching at his sister's feet. "I can pour cool water over your feet from my canteen."

She shook her head. "I'm afraid if I take them off I'll never get them back on again. Let me just sit here a moment."

Cherish's feelings warred between irritation and compassion. This time the latter won out. She walked over to Annalise and perched on the seat beside her. "I'm awfully sorry. I didn't realize you weren't wearing comfortable shoes."

Annalise gave her a wan smile. "It's not your fault."

Silas went off to stand at the edge of the promontory. Why was it every time she came near Annalise, he walked away, and every time Cherish walked away, Silas was at Annalise's side?

"Well, why don't you rest them a bit and perhaps we can take the walk down more slowly?"

"Yes, I should be fine."

Cherish gave her a final smile and rose. Smoothing her skirts, she walked toward the edge and came to stand near Silas.

When he didn't say anything, not even an "I told you so," Cherish remained silent, as well. The last thing she wanted was to admit to him she'd been wrong. So she surveyed the scenery. After a while she was lost in it, seeing it from a painter's eye. The camp down below was no longer visible, hidden by the dense forest, nor were any of the others she knew nestled among the trees at intervals along the lake's edge.

Silas's voice interrupted her observation. "Are you satisfied with the view?"

She couldn't escape the sarcasm that tinged the soft tone. She ignored it. "It is lovely, isn't it?"

"It's a long trek downward, nevertheless."

"Since when have you become so concerned with such practicalities of life?"

"Since I have become so closely associated with someone else's pain."

"Well, perhaps you can allow another gentleman to take over from you for the second shift."

"You've become awfully callous since your return. Is that part of the European polish you gained overseas?"

"Perhaps I learned not to need a man to prop me up in every circumstance."

They didn't look at each other during the short exchange and spoke in soft tones, contemplating the tranquil scene.

"It seems to me you've become very intolerant of those weaker than you."

"It seems to me you've become quite the champion of the underdog. Is that because you've learned to play the role to perfection yourself?"

"You are perhaps the best judge of that." Even though her words had meant to sting, his tone revealed nothing but calm.

"I can only judge by what I see." After a moment she said, "If you'll excuse me, I believe I can better use my European polish elsewhere."

When she left, Silas kept his eyes on the view below him, not revealing by a flicker of an eyelash that Cherish's words had meant more to him than the hovering of a pesky blackfly.

The lake's tranquillity mocked him. He was feeling anything but tranquil inside.

He was seething. If he had an ax in his hand right now, he would be hewing down a tree. If he had an adze, he'd be hollowing out timber. If he had but a simple chisel, he'd be hacking away at a block of wood.

But he had nothing in his hands. He could only clench and unclench them.

He was in polite company after all. He must control every word, every impulse until he was alone again, working with the wood.

He only hoped his temper cooled by the time he had to turn around and face the company again, the misters and misses Townsends and Bradshaws and Belvederes, all the polite society of the town of Hatsfield, or—as Cherish would probably put it—the crème de la crème of this down east town. Weren't these the people Winslow wanted to impress? Wasn't that why he'd been sent on this dismal weekend in the first place?

That evening at the Townsends' mansion, Silas sat beside Annalise on a narrow settee as a hired band played tune after tune. He watched Cherish being twirled around by Warren and wondered how he could get so worked up over one girl he used to see as a kid sister and who clearly saw him as nothing but her father's lackey, there to do her father's bidding and then scorning him for it.

He glanced over at Annalise. And here was this new girl, in whom he wasn't the least bit interested, making cow eyes at him, as if he were some sort of hero.

A hero was the last thing he felt like. The image of a downtrodden, servile hireling kept dancing around in his mind. Is that what he'd become in all these years of doing Mr. Winslow's bidding, saving every penny he earned, waiting for that day when he would have enough to strike out on his own?

*Oh, God, when can I have my dream?*

Would he just grow old like Ezra and Will—mere laborers on the yard, put out to pasture the day he got too old to lift the heavy timbers?

Had he been fooling himself all these years?

# ❧ Chapter Eight ❧

Cherish felt the weight of remorse beat down on her like a caulker's mallet with each passing hour.

Aunt Phoebe set a wicker basket at Cherish's feet with a thump. "There you go."

Cherish groaned as she glanced at the pile of tightly rolled white linens. After a weekend of pleasure, the realities of housekeeping duties had awaited her at Haven's End. She'd spent the day before bending over a hot washtub and hanging things out on the line. Today it was over a hot stove, heating flatirons and taking them over to the ironing board to press everything that had been washed.

"All that?" Would she get to the boat shop today at all?

She sighed as she bent to retrieve a garment from the basket and shook it out. A man's white shirt.

Could it be Silas's? She draped the damp garment over the narrow end of the ironing board and began to press the shoulders. The steam rising up from the white cotton smelled fresh and clean, embodying all the outdoor air the cloth had received the day before.

Cherish flipped the shirt over and began pressing the broad

expanse of back. Her thoughts couldn't help going back to the weekend. By their return to Haven's End, neither she nor Silas was speaking much to each other.

Things hadn't improved in the interim. She'd seen him only at dinner and supper the day before, when he'd come in and silently eaten his food, merely nodding in greeting to her.

A scorched smell reached her nostrils.

"You better watch what you're doing there," Celia commented, looking up from the pile of clothes she was folding.

"Oh—what?" Cherish lifted the iron and looked with dismay at the singed area on the otherwise pristine white garment. She set the iron down and touched the brown part, hoping it might rub off. But no. It was burned through. Part of the cloth began to fray under her fingernail.

"What am I going to do?" she said in dismay, feeling doubly worse for the damage she'd done. First the taunting insult and now this? Was she ever going to do anything right?

Aunt Phoebe walked over to the table. "Learn to keep your mind on your work, for one thing." She took the shirt up from the ironing board and eyed it critically. "It'll have to go in the ragbag. Pity. That was one of Silas's good shirts."

Cherish bit her lip, her self-assurance dropping another few notches. "I'm sorry." Why couldn't she say those two simple words to Silas?

Her aunt thrust the shirt at her. "No use moping about it. You'll just have to sew him a new one."

Cherish took the garment back from her, seeing it in a whole new light. "Yes, I shall, shan't I?" She smiled at it. She would make him a new shirt and with it, apologize for that awful remark she had made. Although he hadn't referred to it, she felt it lying between them like a leaded keel.

"Can you show me how to use your new sewing machine?" she asked her aunt.

"Certainly. You'll have it sewn up in a jiffy with that."

Nodding, Cherish picked up another shirt and went to the stove to grab a hot iron.

\* \* \*

After a week of steady work in the boat shop, Cherish and Silas had cut out the mold, a temporary structure made up of pine boards, over which the hull would take shape. Unlike the schooner down below on the stocks, this smaller boat was built upside down. They were now shaping the frame around the keel, stem and sternpost they had built over the mold.

Silas straightened from the cedar rib he was planing down to the correct width and rubbed the back of his neck. He expelled a gust of breath as his glance went over to Cherish, who crouched over their original loft, the full-sized working drawing of the hull. It was a network of complicated lines, curves, initials and numbers.

He wondered how much a man was supposed to take and still keep his distance. Everywhere he turned, Cherish was there. It seemed a dozen times in the afternoon, at least, her hand would touch his, or her arm reached across his, and always that innocent look in her eye, which made him wonder whether she was aware at all of the havoc she was causing with his senses.

"I think some of those ribs are ready now," he said when she stood from the loft. "They've been sitting in the steam oven a good while. They should be soft enough to bend."

"All right. Let's get them out."

He put on some mitts and opened the specially built oven to extract the narrow wooden strips that would become the vertical rib frames of the hull.

It was hot work, keeping the stove under it going at full blast, to supply the steam necessary for the metal box where the wood strips were set.

"Watch out for the steam when you first open the door. It can be very hot."

"The planks seem just right, as soft as putty," Cherish said as the two laid the strip over the mold, bending it to conform to its curve and clamping it down.

"We'll let it dry and harden before taking it off again to plane. Come on, let's get another one."

After she had assisted him with two of them, she told him she could do one by herself.

He went back to planing one of the dry ones he'd shaped to the frame the day before.

He had to admit that Cherish was the best worker he'd ever had. He'd decided from the outset he'd treat her just like any man who worked alongside him, and she'd proved her worth. She did everything he did, everything he asked. She'd even made some good suggestions.

But how much of her proximity was he supposed to endure before he did something foolish?

"Ouch!"

He swiveled at the sound of her voice. She was standing at the oven door, holding her fingers up to her mouth. Silas hurried over to her.

"What happened?"

She smiled ruefully from around her fingers. "Burned myself on the steam."

"I warned you about it."

"So you did."

"Come on, let's pour some cold water on those fingers."

He led her outside to the hand pump. He began pumping on the handle, and as soon as the water began to flow out, he took her hand and held it under the stream of icy water.

"Feel better?"

"Much," she said with a smile.

He looked down at her slim hand lying in his. It was turning red with the cold. He glanced back to see her watching him gratefully. When she looked at him like that, he wanted nothing more than to kiss her.

Why couldn't he forget that night? Why couldn't he forget the feel of her mouth under his?

"You're always patching me up."

He shrugged, letting go of the pump handle and her hand at the same time.

"I'm sorry for what I said to you at the lake."

He pretended he didn't understand. "What was that?" he asked casually, already beginning to turn away toward the door.

She cleared her throat. "Calling you an underdog."

Slowly he turned around, his hand on the doorknob. She hadn't moved from the pump. When he said nothing, she continued. "It was mean. I don't know what got into me."

"Forget it," he answered lightly. "It was the truth, wasn't it?"

He opened the door and motioned for her to go ahead of him. She stood her ground. "Of course it wasn't!"

"I *am* nothing but your father's hired hand."

"You are *not*! You're the finest worker he has, the best shipwright in all Haven's End and Hatsfield and—and—beyond."

Not wanting to let her praise move him, he reentered the boat shop. He walked to the oven, hearing Cherish quickly walking after him. He removed the soft wood strip Cherish had been about to get when she'd gotten burned. He took it over to the mold and began laying it down over it.

Cherish came to stand beside him, holding the bottom end in place while he bent the rib to the contours of the mold.

"How do your fingers feel? Are you up to this?" he asked, glancing down at her.

"They're fine. Just a dull smoldering. It'll pass soon enough. My fingers should be used to this, after all the ironing and baking I've done this week."

"Got burned?"

"I'll say."

"You should have told me. I'd have taken the frame out."

They worked silently some minutes more before Cherish spoke again. "Are you still saving for your own shipyard?"

His eyes met hers. What did she think, that he would be her father's lackey forever?

As if reading his thoughts, she asked, "How long do you think before you'll…you'll have enough?"

He surveyed the bent wood critically. "Hard to say. It'll be one of these days."

"We'd miss you," she said softly.

"Maybe you could come work for me," he quipped. "Try being my lackey for a change."

Her laughter gurgled up at him, touching his nerve endings like a teasing feather.

"I'd like to come work for you."

He looked at her, not expecting such a ready reply.

Then she smiled impishly. "But only if you make me a full and equal partner."

"Oh, yeah?" He turned away and began walking to the oven again. "Well, I won't have to make any decision right away. At the rate I'm going, it'll be a long time before I have enough to tell your father goodbye."

"I'm glad. I mean, I'm glad we can still work together."

Her words made him stop midway to the oven. But he refused to acknowledge their effect. Her words at the lake still rankled. He continued walking.

Cherish was at her wit's end. What more must she do for Silas to see her as a full-grown woman? Although he was polite and helpful, she sensed a widening gap between the two of them. Working in the boat shop, going to choir practice, sitting together in church, instead of drawing them closer, only seemed to increase the distance.

She couldn't believe the rift had been caused merely by a few careless remarks, which she'd apologized for. She knew Silas; he wasn't one to hold a grudge this way. He certainly didn't seem angry or hurt, just aloof. Friendly but aloof. What was wrong with him? she asked herself for the hundredth time.

She craned her neck around, easing the ache that was forming from bending over the plane on the workbench. She brushed aside the curls of wood in its wake.

She brought Silas treats she baked. She had finished his shirt, but had ended up stacking it in with the rest of his laundry instead of presenting it to him. She'd decided it would be more fun to be a secret giver.

Even though it was a plain white shirt like all his others, she'd placed her own sign upon it by monogramming his initials on the corner of the front pocket. That was how she knew he was wearing it today.

She hid a smile as she carried over the bent frame, hardened to its original firmness over the mold. The mold and emerging hull sat over a ladderback, a horizontal wood foundation upon which everything rested, insuring a perfectly level surface for the upside-down hull.

She laid the bent frame over the mold at its proper position. The boat was beginning to look like a skeleton, with the cedar frames descending vertically from the keel.

Silas helped her clamp the frame back on the mold.

She observed the lock of thick golden hair that fell across his forehead as he bent forward.

"Only three more to go," she said. "Then we begin planking, right?"

"Uh-huh," he answered without looking up. The shirt stretched taut across his shoulders. She was proud of that shirt. It couldn't have been better made if it had been sewn in a factory or by a skilled seamstress.

She had decided that morning she'd try a bolder approach. Now her heart hammered against her chest as she wondered whether this was the moment to begin.

She wet her lips. "Silas?"

"Hmm?"

"Did you ever think what it would be like to kiss me?"

He said nothing at first, but his motion on the clamp stopped. He straightened, but continued looking at the wood rib. "What do you mean?" he asked slowly.

"Remember that night? How your lips touched mine?" *Could he have forgotten?*

She was beginning to regret her boldness, when he finally said "Yes" in a low tone.

She swallowed, determined to say her piece. "Hasn't that made you think what it would be like if we really kissed?"

His fingers fiddled with the clamp screw.

Deciding she had gone too far to back away, she admitted, "It has made *me* think of it."

She was standing so close to him she could trace the outline of his jaw if she but raised her hand. "I liked the feel of your lips. They were soft and warm."

"Cherish!" His gray eyes registered shock at her words.

"What?"

"Your father!"

"What about him?"

"What would he think about this conversation?"

"He's not here. Besides, what is so wrong with our kissing each other? We've known each other forever."

He made a strangling sort of laugh and jabbed a hand through his hair, pushing away the golden thatch. "You think your father would consider those good reasons to kiss you?"

She touched the monogram on his chest pocket. She outlined the letters with her fingertip. *SvdZ*

Then she flattened her hand and felt the pumping of his heart through the thin material.

"Don't!" His voice was lower now, like a whispered supplication.

"What?" she asked, not understanding his reaction. "You act as if you're scared of me."

He stepped away from her without replying.

Had she been too daring? she wondered as he walked away.

"Cherish." He stood at the worktable all the way across the room.

"Yes?" she asked hopefully.

"I—" He cleared his throat and began again. "I hope you don't behave like this with all the young men of your acquaintance."

Her mouth fell open.

"Others might misunderstand. You're used to being pretty independent. No doubt you've gotten a lot of other ideas, having traveled, and all that. But you know, people here in Haven's End are still pretty conventional."

"Of course I don't behave like this with anyone else!" She could feel her face redden with shame that he should even think such a thing.

"I'm glad to hear it. I just want to caution you. You're a young girl. I'm a bit older and I know…I know how men are. I just don't want you to find yourself in a situation where the man might not be as honorable—"

"There's nothing wrong with how I spoke to you. You're my best friend."

"But that doesn't mean we can—can— Maybe where you've been young ladies are permitted to flirt—"

"You think I was flirting with you just now?"

He picked up a screwdriver from the workbench and turned it around and around in his hands. "Well, I don't know. I don't know what girls do when they flirt."

She began to laugh, relieved that he had misunderstood her.

He frowned at her. "What is so funny?"

"You! You thought I was flirting."

"Well, weren't you?"

She just laughed some more. "Poor Silas. What would you do outside Haven's End, where young ladies *do* practice the art of flirting?"

"The 'art' of flirting?"

"Mmm-hmm," she answered airily, feeling on surer ground. "It's quite an art form."

"Tell me," he answered, his frown deepening.

"Well, I heard a lot of talk from other young ladies. Some of them have even stolen kisses from young gentlemen—at dances, behind the potted plants, or on a darkened balcony."

"And you've followed suit?"

"Certainly not! I never flirt!"

"What would you call what went on just now?"

"I just told you. There's nothing wrong with our kissing."

He let out a frustrated breath. "You can't just go around talking like that to a man. He'll take it the wrong way, think you're a flirt or a—a loose woman or something."

"Silas van der Zee, I don't understand you!" She put her hands on her hips. "Ever since that night, I've sensed something between the two of us. I thought you felt it, too. But instead you've been acting so—so strange. What is wrong with you?"

He stood still, his face set, giving away nothing.

"Ohh! I give up! You're insufferable. I have never seen such an unfeeling, conceited, pompous…" Before he could hear the rest, she marched to the door and slammed it behind her.

t him steadily now until his gaze shifted away
ell you one thing I *don't* need, Silas," she said

?"

flirting with young gentlemen."
nt after that, and Silas addressed her only about
d.

th Annalise Townsend was not nearly as tedi-
had anticipated. She realized much of it had to
n attitude. She'd taken Annalise to visit some
l friends in the village the first day, and this
ad spent snipping dandelion greens and fiddle-
e forest.

g, Cherish's father spoke across the supper ta-
you drive the girls over to the grange tonight
I don't like their going over alone, and I'm feel-
l."

right, Papa? We can stay home."
e. Nothing that putting my feet up and reading
won't cure."

father awaited Silas's reply, Cherish intervened.
ght. We can go on our own. It's only a mile down
village. It's a beautiful evening."
them, Mr. Townsend. It won't be any trouble

red at him. He wasn't looking at her, but back
late. She glanced over at Annalise, who looked
h. In fact, there was a radiant glow to her

bered the verse about charity seeking "not her
ed, taking up her fork once again.
last tack. "We can walk over to Julie's and ride
family."
ake you," Silas repeated, still not looking at her.
t understand Silas. Unless… She gazed at the girl
s it because of Annalise? Cherish speared the last

# ⨳ Chapter Nine ⨳

"Be not deceived; God is not mocked: for whatsoever a man soweth, that shall he also reap.

For he that soweth to his flesh shall of the flesh reap corruption; but he that soweth to the Spirit shall of the Spirit reap life everlasting."

Cherish read the verses prescribed by her daily devotional and frowned. They made her uneasy as she thought of the previous day's scene in the boathouse with Silas.

"Flesh" came too uncomfortably close to describing what she'd been feeling standing so near Silas, feeling his heartbeat under the palm of her hand.

The verses sounded rather harsh and uncompromising. *God is not mocked.* The words had a finality to them, and she felt as if God had been looking at her antics around Silas for the past few weeks, every time she'd deliberately come close to him, let her hand or arm or body brush his "accidentally."

Cherish knelt beside her bed and asked the Lord to help her receive His Word. *Am I wrong to love Silas the way I do? It seems I'm so in love with him one moment and about as angry as one person can be toward another the next.*

She flipped her Bible back to First Corinthians and read the chapter on charity. "Charity vaunteth not itself, is not puffed up, doth not behave itself unseemly, seeketh not her own, is not easily provoked…beareth all things, believeth all things, hopeth all things, endureth all things."

Her behavior seemed all the more shameful in light of God's love.

As she knelt quietly, waiting for direction, she thought of how far her life had come from those early days of fervor when she'd first asked the Lord into her heart.

Somewhere, somehow she'd become dry and hadn't really known it until now. Was it because she'd been too busy living life to notice?

She searched through her Bible some more. "And let us not be weary in well doing: for in due season we shall reap, if we faint not." Those words made her feel better. They encouraged her to believe in her love for Silas.

"As we have therefore opportunity, let us do good unto all men…."

She pondered the exhortation. Maybe in the past few years she'd forgotten about the Lord's work. Well, perhaps she could begin again.

A timid face came to her mind. Maybe she should make a real effort this time to befriend the girl.

She reclasped her hands and bowed her head. *Dear Lord, help me to be a friend to Annalise. Help me to show her Your love….*

Making good on her promise, she asked her father if she could invite Annalise for a few days, this time by herself without Warren.

"Are you sure you don't want her brother along?" he asked. "He's a very nice young man."

"I'm sure, Papa. Don't fret. There'll be other opportunities to socialize with Mr. Townsend. I'd like to get to know Annalise better."

"Very well. I'm going into Hatsfield later, so I'll be sure to extend your invitation."

Now Cherish stood in the boat shop, waiting for Silas, not

sure how to behave around
cided she'd better rein in h
to think of her as anything

She sighed and took up t
boat frame.

The door banged open.
lumber planks.

At the sight of them she
the boat.

"We're going to begin th
sandpaper and approaching

He glanced at her sharply
the floor. "Yes. This is som
drying all winter. We'll start
garboard strake."

Silas didn't indicate by ei
remembered their conversat
noyed and embarrassed Ch
her, when his very proximit
body tingle?

They worked quietly for
planks called battens along
permanent planks that wou

As they clamped on a bat
Silas suddenly said, "Cheris
about yesterday, about how

She bristled at the patro
thought she went around a
needed to learn a thing or tv
ish's own state of mind was n
as she worked by his side. Fr
ened to get the upper hand,
tried to recall the Scriptures
that soweth to the Spirit sha
ing."

Small comfort when Silas
glance crossed his, and they

She look
from her. "
sweetly.

"What's t
"A lesson
They fell
the task at h

The time
ous as Cher
do with her
of her girlh
morning the
head ferns i

That eve
ble. "Silas,
for the danc
ing a little t

"Are you
"Oh, I'm
the newspa

Now as h
"It's quite al
the road to

"I can dr
at all."

Cherish
down at his
happy eno
cheeks.

She reme
own" and s

She tried
over with h

"No, I ca
She coul
beside her.

chunk of codfish cake onto her fork and rubbed it around her plate. She would certainly not expect him to dance with her this time. She swallowed the piece of codfish and felt it stick in her throat.

*Lord, help me to put myself out of the way.*

She gulped down the lump of fish, and although her eyes swam with a sudden wash of tears, she felt the comfort of God's spirit. It brought a sudden spurt of joy in the midst of her heartache.

When they arrived at the grange building, Cherish was ready to descend the wagon by herself, thinking she'd let Silas assist Annalise, but he stood there in front of her before she could do more than rise from her seat. He placed his hands around her waist and swung her down. She looked at him briefly, but he wasn't looking at her, his eyes gazing somewhere above her head.

Her skirts swished out of his way and she began walking toward the grange, not bothering to wait for him and Annalise.

From the entrance she watched him and Annalise. The two made a nice-looking couple. The admission cut her deeply, and she turned away. She had to control her feelings and not ruin the evening for Annalise. *Grant me Your grace, Lord, to do Your will.*

She purposely stayed away from Silas and greeted all her old friends, reintroducing them to Annalise. When they had a circle around them, she looked around to find Silas gone. Searching the dance hall, she spied him across the room, standing chatting with some young men.

The music started up, and she had no more chance to think about Silas. She grabbed Annalise by the hand and led her to the set forming for square dancing.

Later in the evening, when the caller had taken a break and the musicians began playing a waltz, Cherish and Annalise suddenly found themselves partnerless. Now she looked around and realized no young man was going to ask either of them. She laughed. Such a situation hadn't happened to her in years.

She'd always had a superfluity of partners, young gentlemen begging to put their names on her dance card.

There were no dance cards here. Just a bunch of people who had grown up together, whose families knew each other and who had a good time together. She smiled at the dancing couples, as if to say, "Well, it's good to sit one out. I don't know about you, but my feet are sore!" She glanced down at the toes of her slippers.

Then, casually, as if it was the most natural thing in the world for Cherish Winslow to sit out a dance, she observed the dancers, all childhood friends. A curious nostalgia swept over her. All the time she had been away, being educated, seeing so many new sights, time had not stopped for them, either. They, too, had gotten on with the business of living, in a different rhythm from her own.

There was Julie with Matt, and Rachel with Jed, and Alice with Douglas. They'd known each other their whole lives, and without her noticing, they had begun pairing off. Cherish had no doubts, watching them now, and remembering other signs she'd seen in the few weeks she'd been home, that soon engagements would be announced.

For the first time, Cherish felt like an outsider in her own hometown. What had happened? Had she grown up too much for them? For her own good?

Silas stood across the dance floor with his friend Charlie. The two sipped at their cups of cider, eyeing the couples gracefully moving around the scuffed wooden floor.

"Do me a favor, will you?" he asked his friend.

Charlie took a sip and wiped his mouth with the back of his hand. "What's that?"

"Ask Miss Townsend to dance."

"The one you asked me to dance with at Cherish's homecoming?"

"Yes."

Charlie gave him a questioning look. "You sure you don't mind? You don't want to ask her yourself?"

"No, of course not."

"Well, I thought…the other night at Cherish's party…then you went and spent the weekend at her parents' house, didn't you?"

"I was just being nice to her, as a favor to Cherish," he said, annoyed at having to explain himself. "They invited me to Hatsfield just to round out the numbers."

"Oh, well, if you don't mind. She's a pretty girl. She just don't talk much."

"Well, you do the talking," Silas suggested calmly, hiding the growing impatience he felt. Was the piece going to end before he convinced his friend? "She'll talk back if you talk to her."

"Okay," his friend replied with a grin. After a few more seconds' rumination, he added, "You're not sweet on Cherish, are you?"

"What makes you think that?" he asked more sharply than he had intended.

"Oh, I dunno. You two sure are together an awful lot."

"Well, we practically grew up together. That doesn't mean we're sweet on each other."

"No, course not," Charlie replied with a sly grin. His smile widened. "And ol' Winslow, if he ever sniffed such a thing, whoo-ee, he wouldn't let you within ten feet of her. You sure you don't want to go after Miss Townsend yourself? Old Mr. Townsend makes Winslow look like small fry. You could probably have your own shipyard or two!"

"Yes, I'm sure."

"You play your cards right, Townsend could set you up for life if he takes a fancy to you."

Silas smiled slightly at the image. "I'm sure," he repeated.

"Oh-kay," Charlie drawled as he set down his cup and sauntered around the dance floor toward Annalise Townsend.

Silas knew even as he deposited his own cup and began skirting the edge of the dance floor in Charlie's wake that this was the reason he'd come tonight. Even as he'd agreed with Tom Winslow's request, even as he'd shaved and dressed and gone to hitch the wagon, this was why he'd come.

Ever since the last dance at Cherish's house, when he'd deliberately kept himself away from her, the reason had been there, simmering down deep below his conscious thoughts, waiting to be put into action.

Charlie sidled up to Annalise before the waltz ended and asked her for the dance as Cherish looked on in amusement. "Go on, Annalise," she urged. "I'll be fine. My feet need the rest."

She watched the dancers, her toes keeping time to the music. The waltz ended and another started up.

So she, Cherish Winslow, whom Annalise had said made every social gathering sparkle, was left sitting out not one, but two dances. If it weren't so bittersweet, it would be amusing. Her lips already felt chapped with the strain of keeping them stretched in a smiling line.

She refused to look to see where Silas was. She followed Annalise and Charlie's progress around the floor.

"Need a partner?"

Her composure almost broke at the sound of that low, familiar voice above her ear. Then she remembered his censorious attitude, and she was tempted to turn him down. Finally she looked at him, and her breath caught. He looked so handsome, his lean features softened, his gray eyes tender.

"I don't *need* a partner," she reminded him with quiet dignity. "But if you are proposing yourself, I would graciously accept your offer."

He held out his hand, and she placed hers in it.

Determined to keep her emotions in check, she assumed the most proper stance for a waltz—arm's length apart, her hand just resting lightly on his coat sleeve, the other lying in his hand. They came together on the dance floor amidst the other couples and began to move in time to the music.

"I'm still not the best waltzer," he said above her head.

She bit back a rejoinder concerning his efforts with Annalise. "You dance fine," she said instead.

They moved about the dance floor and Cherish began to lower her guard and enjoy the feel of his arm about her waist, her hand in his. She was afraid to look at him, afraid of what she would find there—that same older-brother superiority, or worse, pity that she had been without a partner, or worst of all, indifference.

Instead she kept her gaze fixed over his shoulder, watching the other dancers whirling by her. She smiled, catching a glimpse of Charlie talking earnestly with Annalise, and wondered what he was saying to her. She'd tease Annalise about it tonight.

On an impulse she looked up at Silas to tell him about Charlie, and the words died on her lips.

Silas was looking at her in a way she had never seen before. It was as if for a split second the shutters had been lifted from his gray eyes and she could peer all the way down to his soul. It made him look vulnerable, needy.

She smiled tentatively, but the next instant he averted his gaze. She wondered whether she'd imagined that look. Had it been real?

"What were you going to say?" he asked, looking over her head.

"Uh—oh, just that it seems Charlie and Annalise are having a good time together."

"Yes," he replied, and she could see his gaze searching them out.

"You don't mind?" she ventured.

He glanced back at her, a slight frown furrowing his brow. "Mind? Why should I mind? I'm the one who told Charlie to ask her for this dance."

"You did?" She began to smile. "I thought you liked Annalise."

"Why does everyone try to pair me off with Annalise?" The annoyance was clear in his tone this time.

"Well, you wanted me to befriend her, for one thing."

He looked at her in astonishment. "I just wanted you to behave in the kind, decent way you usually do. That's all. It doesn't mean I'm sweet on the girl."

"Oh." She stopped talking after that and fixed her gaze on the lapel of Silas's jacket, her touch tightening imperceptibly on his shoulder.

A deep joy welled up inside her, threatening to overflow. *Well, well, what do you know? He isn't sweet on Annalise. And he was looking at me as if he cared about me....*

When the dance ended, Cherish looked up at Silas with her sweetest smile and asked him for one more. That one turned into another.

By the time Silas got his wits back together, he realized he had danced exclusively with Cherish for more than half the dances.

# ❧ Chapter Ten ❧

For the next few days it rained. Cherish's initial euphoria that she would be able to spend every day with Silas working on the Whitehall diminished as she realized all the men from the shipyard had to spend those days in the boat shop along with the two of them, working on the various small boat hulls.

"You still interested in boats, Cherish?" Ezra asked. "Thought after becoming such a fine lady, you wouldn't want to get your hands dirty with this kind of work."

She laughed, looking down at her hands. Gone were the long, buffed fingernails. "What, don't you think I'm still a fine lady, even in my work clothes?" She glanced toward Silas as she asked Ezra the question.

Silas was studiously bent over the hull, transferring markings with a pencil onto a small scrap of paper, and didn't seem to notice Cherish's attention.

"Oh, you'd be a fine lady even if you were dressed in rags," the other workman answered with a chuckle.

Cherish had noticed in the days following the dance that Silas seemed more distant than ever. He treated her with courtesy, but never uttered the least playful or teasing remark. Not by a mere hint in his eyes did he reveal that she was anything more than a fellow employee of her father's.

But her heart danced all the same. She kept going over the naked look she'd caught in his eyes and repeated to herself, "He *does* care!"

The question was, how much? She tried everything to discover this, without using the blatant tactics of before. Whenever the opportunity arose, which was often, she would ask for his assistance. But never by a glance or gesture could she discover that her proximity affected him at all.

"Silas, how does this look?" she asked him from the other side of the hull.

"Hmm?" he asked, his attention still on the numbers he copied down.

"Do you think I've beveled it enough?"

He came around to her side and crouched beside her. They looked at the plank she'd placed temporarily against the ribbing and observed how flush its surface lay against the vertical ribs. His finger indicated a slight gap. "I think it could use a little more bevel here."

"Yes, I see."

"How's young Mr. Townsend?"

Cherish looked up at Ezra's question. "He's fine, I suppose."

"Now, there's a fine young gentleman. I bet he appreciates all that education you got overseas," William put in from across the shop.

"The Townsends have a pretty operation over there in Hatsfield," Ezra added. "I hear they're going to expand their lumber shipments and need some more schooners. I wouldn't mind hearing we got some orders from them." He adjusted the pencil in back of his ear.

"I hear the shipyard up by the brickyard is closing down after this summer." William shook his head sadly.

"Yep. Sad to see them go." Ezra sighed deeply.

Silas didn't participate in the conversation. He'd taken his figures over to the long piece of cedar that lay on a worktable.

She knew it was critical that the curve of the hull be transferred accurately to the plank of wood.

Just then her father entered the boat shop. "Gentlemen, if you want to step into the office before you break for dinner, I'll have your wages for you."

"We'll be right there!" came a chorus from the workers. Silas acted as if he hadn't even heard. He continued working on the plank he was measuring for the hull.

Cherish removed the frame and took it to the workbench to sand out the curve some more on its inner side. As her hand worked back and forth over the smooth wood, her mind continued pondering the impasse with Silas. He'd been so elusive since the dance, she sometimes wondered if he was avoiding her.

But then why had he danced exclusively with her?

After he'd collected his wages, Silas pried up one of the wallboards in his room. He reached all the way down into the dark space and pulled up a metal box. Using a key on a string around his neck, he unlocked it and lifted the lid. Inside lay tightly bound bundles of greenbacks and other paper currency and stacks of gold and silver coins.

Carefully he loosened the string around one bundle and added the bills he'd just been paid by Winslow, then retied it and set it back in with the others. He sat looking at his hoard a few minutes longer, thinking of the years of toil it had taken to accumulate what filled the box.

He had very few expenses. Winslow provided him with room and board, and Mrs. Sullivan kept his shirts and trousers usable until she could literally mend them no more, and only then did he outlay the money to replace them. He didn't drink, didn't gamble, as the men in the yard did on a Friday night. He didn't court, and had put all thoughts of marriage aside until such a time as he had his own shipyard.

Now, inexplicably, a wave of despair gripped him as he measured his pile of savings against his years of sacrifice. It occurred to him that just one of Cherish's gowns from Paris cost more than all the money he had in his tin box.

He rubbed a hand across his forehead, trying to stave off the doubts. What did he have to show for all his years of saving? A pitifully small pile of coins and bills. He remembered the young men and women at the grange dance. Young men and women he'd grown up with, now beginning to court, making plans to marry, start families of their own, setting up in business or working their family farms, building their fishing boats. For the first time in his life he began to envy them.

Never had anything tempted him to stray from his single-minded efforts until now.

He couldn't—*mustn't*—let an insane, wild, impossible longing for his employer's daughter cause him to shift his focus from his goal. Silas relocked his box and replaced it in its hiding place, his precise movements in jarring contrast to his disorderly thoughts.

Saturday proved warm and sunny. Cherish knew things would be quiet down in the boat shop, as the men had gone back down to work on the yard. Although she normally didn't work in the shop on Saturdays, she had asked Silas to spend a few hours there in the afternoon to work on the Whitehall.

He was already there when she arrived. He was fitting a plank onto the hull. Cherish looked with satisfaction at the Whitehall. It was coming along nicely, planked almost halfway.

"Hi, there," she said, advancing toward the hull. "Need a hand?"

He glanced at her briefly before returning to the job. "You can hold that end down."

She complied, content to watch as he concentrated on fitting the plank against the one on top of it and determine if its angle fit snugly enough against it. Judging that it didn't, he straightened.

"Okay, you can let go. I'm going to bevel this one a bit more," he said, indicating the angle with his fingertips.

Cherish got to work on the opposite side of the hull with a plank of her own. They worked together steadily. She would look across at Silas from time to time, hoping to catch him looking at her again as he had during the dance, but her efforts were in vain.

"Any plans to go over to Hatsfield anytime soon?" he surprised her by asking.

"No. Why, do you?"

He glanced at her then. "No."

They had worked some more when he asked, "No plans for the weekend?"

"None at all," she replied, clamping down one end of her plank.

"That's not like you."

"Why shouldn't I spend a quiet weekend at home?"

He shrugged. "No reason. It's just you've had something going every weekend since arriving home. Last week Annalise came here. I thought you might be going there this weekend."

"No. I didn't receive an invitation."

"If you had, would you have gone?"

She looked up, wondering why he was being so persistent. "I don't know. I kind of like how this weekend has turned out. We've gotten to do more work on the Whitehall, for one thing. Haven't you liked that?"

He shrugged. "Sure."

She suppressed her irritation. He could be annoyingly casual at times. So casual one hadn't the least idea what he really thought.

He bent over a plank, directly across the keel from her. A thick wave of golden hair fell over his forehead. On impulse Cherish reached over and pushed it upward with her fingertips.

He flinched, dropping the pencil he held. "Please don't do that, Cherish," he said in a quiet, firm voice.

She drew her hand back as if it had been slapped. Was this the boy she'd grown up with, who'd been her best friend, the person she most admired, the one who was patient, kind and teasing? Her eyes welled up with tears.

She wouldn't let him see that he'd hurt her. As he bent to pick up the pencil, she backed away from the boat hull. She'd taken only two steps backward when Silas looked up and noticed her tear-filled eyes. Quickly she turned.

"I'm sorry, Cherish. I didn't mean to talk to you that way."

She kept walking, needing to get out of the room.

"Please, Cherish." The first note of entreaty she'd heard all week sounded in his voice. "Don't go. I didn't mean to upset you."

She'd reached the door and held the doorknob. "You didn't upset me," she said in her most controlled voice. She would turn the knob and walk out.

Instead, she said, "You know, the other night at the grange dance you behaved almost like your old self. I was just standing there looking at everyone dancing and having a good time, and I realized they'd all grown up and gotten on with their lives while I'd been away. Most young men and women were paired off. I was beginning to feel a little like a freak. Despite all of Papa's good intentions, he might have given me a little too much education, and now I don't fit in anymore. I sometimes think he's given me so much polish, I cause a glare." She gave a bitter chuckle.

"When you walked over and asked me to dance, you were like a hero coming to my rescue." She sighed and continued addressing the doorknob. "I don't know, Silas, since I've been home I've felt as if I can't do anything right around you anymore.

"I give up, Silas. If you're too blind, too unfeeling to notice that I—I care about you…" Here she faltered, but plowed on resolutely. "Well, I'll have you know, Silas van der Zee, I don't need your affections."

As the seconds dragged by and he said nothing, she began to feel stupid. Abruptly she turned the doorknob.

In the still second before she pulled the door open, he began to speak. "You say I'm unfeeling." A low laugh reached her ears. "Is it unfeeling to say how much I've wanted to kiss you since that day my lips accidentally touched yours? That I've been thinking of little else but that since?"

Cherish turned slowly, mesmerized by his quiet confession, her hand still on the doorknob behind her. Silas stood the way she'd left him, on the far side of the upended hull, the compass and pencil in his hand.

"You say I haven't noticed you've become a woman. Oh, Cherish, how can I help but notice it? Every time you pass near me and I smell the lilacs in your hair, I've got to hold myself from reaching for you—

"Every time your arm brushes against mine it sends a current through me.

"Every time you innocently put your hand in mine like in the olden days, I want to hold you to me."

Cherish released the breath she hadn't realized she'd been holding. "Oh, Silas, I never dreamed…" She took a step toward him. When she was halfway across the room, he shook his head and said only one word. "Cherish." It came out sounding like an anguished plea.

The tone encouraged her to keep walking. She skirted the hull that separated them. They stood only inches from each other. His Adam's apple moved as he swallowed, but before he could say anything, she took the pencil and compass from his unresisting hands and dropped them onto the floor behind her. The dull clank of metal on wood was the only sound in the room.

"Show me," she whispered softly.

It seemed to take an eternity, but slowly his face neared hers, his eyes closing, until finally his lips made contact once again with hers. She leaned into his lips, placing her hands against his chest to steady herself on her tiptoes. His heartbeat thudded under her palm. She grabbed his shirt, afraid of losing her balance.

His lips pressed against hers as his hands cupped her shoulders. Their bodies touched nowhere else. At that moment Cherish was fused with him in time forever. This was what she'd waited for, dreamed of, prayed for—all her preparation and obedience over the years coming to fruition in that single contact of hands and lips.

In the next instant she discovered that whatever had held Silas in control, whatever had made her suspect him of being unfeeling, had snapped. He kissed her as she'd never dreamed of being kissed. Kissed her as she'd never heard of being kissed by her flirtatious friends. His was no gentlemanly peck on the cheek, or soft brushing of lips as the first one had been. This was more intimate than anything she'd ever imagined. After her initial shock, Cherish yielded to him, determined to destroy every barrier that existed between them.

As soon as his lips touched hers, Silas knew he should stop. He should have withdrawn after a gentle and chaste kiss. But he couldn't. One touch of her, one whiff of the sweet scent of her, one look into the wide-eyed innocence of those smoky-blue eyes, and he could no longer contain himself. Like a piece of dry wood hitting the fire, his feelings ignited and Silas felt himself being consumed in a conflagration that he couldn't understand, that hadn't been of his own making, and that he certainly didn't know how he'd come out of alive—but none of it mattered in those moments as his mouth sought hers.

She was springtime—newness of life, hope, warmth and light all rolled into one earth-shattering sensation.

She whispered his name, as her small hands flattened themselves against his cheeks. He opened his eyes. She was like a blind person reading someone's face as she touched his cheeks and jaw and temples, grazing his skin with her fingertips.

When her fingers reached his eyelids, he closed them again, whispering against her ear, "Tell me about all the suitors you've left scattered across the Continent…the princes and counts…there must have been dozens."

"What suitors?" she responded dreamily. "They're all forgotten."

Silas chuckled, hardly daring to believe in the reality of the two of them. Was this truly Cherish standing here in his arms? His lips found hers once more.

"*Cherish!* What in thunder!" Tom Winslow's roar threw them apart.

Before Silas could draw back any farther, Winslow crossed the space between them. The next thing Silas knew, Cherish's father grabbed him by the shirt collar and hauled him away from his daughter.

Winslow's fist flew into his jaw and Silas's head snapped back.

"Papa!" Cherish shouted as she grabbed his arm with both her hands. "No, Papa!"

Her father's fist came at him again, this time smashing against the corner of his mouth, jamming his lips against his teeth.

"Silas, do something!" screamed Cherish behind her father. "Papa, stop it!"

Finally Winslow flung Silas from him, sending him flying across the floor to land several feet away.

Cherish sobbed, not letting go of her father's arm.

"Get away from me," he shouted, shaking her off.

Silas stood, ready to protect Cherish, but Winslow's attention went back to him.

"Papa, you don't understand! What's gotten into you?" Tears streamed down her face as her hands went out to her father.

"Don't push me, child. Get on home, while I deal with this—this—" Not finding a word sufficiently strong to express his disgust, he gave Silas a look full of loathing. "Go home, Cherish."

Cherish stood her ground.

"Go, Cherish," Silas said gently, wiping the blood he felt against the side of his mouth.

Her father turned to him. "You shut up!"

Silas fell silent with a final nod to Cherish. She turned once more to her father and back to Silas. Seeing no further encouragement from either, she finally backed slowly out of the room.

When the two men were alone, Silas faced Winslow, knowing deep inside that it was over.

"I could kill you! I would run you out of Haven's End if I could. But I can only get you off my property. I want you out of here. *Now!*" He brought his fists up in impotent rage. "Don't ever cross my path again."

Suddenly he turned his hate-filled eyes away from Silas and brought his hands up to his face, his voice incredulous, seeking understanding. "I *trusted* you! I trusted you with my Cherish…my sweet baby…" His voice broke, and Silas felt his own heart twist at the man's anguish.

Winslow turned back to face him, his arm sweeping across the boat shop. "I trusted you with everything. Everything! Do you understand? And how do you reward me? Stab me in the back! Steal my only child! My innocent girl!" The thought re-kindled his anger and he turned murderous eyes once again on Silas.

"I told you to get out! *Get out! Get out!*" Like a man pos-sessed, he advanced toward Silas and lunged at him. Silas didn't wait further. He knew he would get nowhere with Cherish's fa-ther, so he turned toward the door.

He'd known it would be like this.

He walked out the door without looking back at the place that had been his home for the past fourteen years of his life.

Silas walked blindly down to the shipyard, knowing only one place to go—his boat. The only thing that belonged to him.

"Hey, Silas, thought you were up to the boathouse," Ezra called to him from the schooner hull. "Are you all right? What happened to you?"

Silas averted his face. Suddenly he felt ashamed. He didn't want anyone to know he'd just been thrown out on his rump like a stray dog.

He hurried past the men to his skiff. "Just going out for a sail."

Ezra glanced at the sky. "Sky looks a mite growly. I wouldn't take her out too far."

Silas confirmed the man's assessment. The clouds had thick-ened while he'd been inside. "No, I won't go far." Where in-deed could he go, with no money, no gear? Too late to think about that now. He certainly wouldn't attempt to go up to his room now. *His* room, what a delusion, he thought as he pulled the boat seaward and pushed it into the tide.

He rowed out to his yawl and climbed aboard. Once he was clear of the port and out on the ocean, his mind was free to re-act to the scene in the boat shop.

What had possessed him? Why couldn't he have controlled himself? He'd known Cherish for fourteen years. Why this feeling that overwhelmed him at her mere presence? He'd been fighting it for weeks now. How had it developed? When had he first noticed every womanly curve of her? Every feminine wile?

For she *had* been flirting with him, he could be certain of that.

Perhaps she wasn't scared of her father. She probably underestimated his disapproval toward Silas as a suitor. She was so used to having her way with Winslow that it wouldn't occur to her that he might not condone her pursuit of Silas.

But Silas could claim no such excuse. He'd known. If Winslow hadn't considered him to replace his nephew Henry in the shipyard, why would he ever give Silas a blessing with his only daughter? Knowing this, Silas had insisted on playing with fire. He should have put a stop to it much earlier. He'd tried, he argued with himself, remembering his "talk" with Cherish. She'd reacted like a spoiled child.

Well, isn't that what she was? And he was a fool. A stupid fool who should have known better. He certainly didn't deserve any better than what he'd gotten.

If he'd wanted female companionship, there were certainly comely enough girls in the village. Why did it have to be the one who was off-limits that drew him?

His boat skimmed across the leaden gray water, the spray hitting him in the face, the wind whipping his hair back. He drove the boat harder, needing the action, the elements as a release to the anger, the frustration, the utter despair that rose from inside him.

*Oh, God! Why now? Why this? I didn't ask for this! Why did she have to come home now and suddenly develop some imagined fancy for me?*

When he'd spent his energies, if not his anger, he pulled up his centerboard and beached his boat in a sheltered cove. The clouds, which had threatened, began to send down the first drops as he secured the boat up above the high-water mark. He realized he would probably be spending the night with it as his only shelter, a tarpaulin as his cover.

He could have bedded down with Ezra or William, but something had held him back from asking. A sense of humiliation engulfed him. He didn't want his emotions examined by one and all. He had a horror of having his most private feelings the talk of the town.

*Did you hear about that Silas van der Zee? Kissing Winslow's daughter! Can you imagine? The apple of his eye. Who did he think he was, anyway?* The town matrons would cluck their tongues and shake their heads. *Shows what happens when you open your house to some stranger. What do you get for your effort and sacrifice? A slap in the face! Oh, for shame, Silas!* The accusing eyes would stare at him in the street, from the church pews, across the store counter.

Silas, his stomach growling from hunger, his body shivering through his thin shirt, huddled in the cuddy of his boat, wrapped himself in the tarpaulin and bedded down for the night under the steady patter of cold rain.

## Chapter Eleven

Cherish spent the rest of the afternoon alternately crying and marveling in wonder at Silas's kiss. She touched her lips afresh, unable to believe what she had experienced.

She cried at the injustice of her father's reaction, sickened by his treatment of Silas. How she longed to run to Silas, nurse his bruised jaw, but she knew her father wouldn't let her within sight of him. She had to give her father time to cool down. Then she could talk to him reasonably and tell him of her love for Silas. She could explain that it wasn't an overnight infatuation, but a devotion spanning years.

She'd felt each blow to Silas as if it had been directed against her own body. She cried into the pillow once again, wanting to hold Silas and tend to him.

*Dear Lord, You know our hearts. I pray for Your mercy. Please soften Papa's heart. Make him see reason. Oh, please take care of Silas until I can go to him.*

She continued praying, but found it hard to concentrate as she began to relive Silas's kisses. Was this the quiet, reserved, gently teasing Silas she knew? Was this her Silas? The man who'd held her close, as if he would crush her? The same man who'd given her a lecture about flirting just days ago?

She hugged the pillow to herself, rolling across her bed, wanting nothing more than to be in his arms again.

The only thing that marred her discovery of this new Silas was her memory of his reaction to her father. She had to stifle her sense of disappointment at Silas, who'd done nothing to defend himself against her father, but had just stood there passively receiving her father's blows.

Was this the same man who'd displayed such emotion just moments before?

How could the two men be one and the same?

Cherish got up from her bed when she heard the front door open, knowing her father was home. She washed her face with cold water and brushed her hair. With a final smoothing down of her gown and apron, she made her way downstairs.

Her father was seated in his chair in the front parlor. Uncharacteristically he was doing nothing but staring into space. His newspaper lay ignored on the table beside his chair.

"Papa?" she began softly, entering the room.

He stared at her unsmilingly. "Close the door, Cherish."

She complied and came into the room and stood before him.

"Sit down."

She took the chair beside him and clasped her hands.

He rubbed his face as if finding it difficult to begin.

"Papa—" She decided to help him by explaining her feelings for Silas.

He held up a hand. "Don't say anything, Cherish." After a few moments of silence, he began again. "Cherish, you don't know how disappointed I am in you today."

Tears stung her eyes afresh. He sounded so disillusioned.

Again he rubbed his jaw, and suddenly she saw him as gray and haggard.

"Are you all right, Papa?"

He gave her a look. "No, Cherish, I'm not." He looked away from her as if he couldn't bear to look at her anymore. "I can't tell you what seeing you like that has done to me."

"But, Papa, Silas—"

At that her father showed signs of life again. "Don't even *speak* that name in this house again!"

Cherish stood, her own frustration rising. "Papa, how can you say that? Aren't you going to give me a chance to tell you how much I love him?"

He stood, too. "Love him? Love him?" he roared. "Are you going to have the effrontery to stand there and tell me some story about your attachment to a good-for-nothing boy who works on my shipyard..."

Her voice rose to match her father's. "A good-for-nothing boy! How can you say that about Silas? He's worked—slaved— for you for years. What has he gotten in return? Has he ever had a good word from you? A promotion? A chance at learning to design ships?"

He didn't let her go on. "What has he gotten from me?" He raked a hand through his dark hair and turned away with a bitter laugh. "You dare ask me what he's had the gall to take from me? I could kill him, I swear I could. If I ever see him skulking around you again— If he so much as dares look at you again—"

"Papa! I love him. Can't you see that?"

"Love!" His voice thundered at her, his brown eyes black in their fury. "Don't you dare utter that word!

"After all I did for him," he muttered. "All I did for *you!* I'm not going to have you waste all the education, all the manners you've been taught—to throw it all away on some barely literate ship's carpenter." He turned to her. "You must promise me you'll have no more to do with Silas."

When she said nothing, it seemed to infuriate him anew. "I'll send you away, Cherish, I swear I will. I'll send you back to your cousin Penelope. I'll send you as far as it takes."

"Papa. You wouldn't! You wouldn't do anything so cruel."

"Don't push me, Cherish. Now, you get your silly notions about Silas out of your head. Do you hear me?"

The two were shouting at each other by then, though neither noticed how loudly until they heard a banging on the door. Aunt Phoebe poked her head in. "If you don't want everyone in Haven's End to know what you're quarreling about, you'd better keep your voices down."

Winslow scowled at his sister and fell silent, but only for a moment.

Cherish turned to her aunt. "Aunt Phoebe, you must make Papa see reason. He can't forbid me to see Silas."

"I can and I will! I've already kicked him out of the ship-yard and promised that if he so much as steps inside, he'll be accused of breaking and entering."

"How could you? This is his home. All his belongings are at the boat shop. Where's he going to go?"

"He can go to perdition for all I care!" he roared.

Even Phoebe felt compelled to intervene at that. "Thomas Winslow, you get a hold of yourself. Cherish, you'd better go. I'll talk to your father."

Cherish left the house, running to the boat shop. She had to find Silas. No one was in the workshop. It looked exactly as they'd left it. She went up the steps to Silas's room.

She paused on the threshold. She had never been in his room. Nothing looked moved. A narrow cot stood along one wall, neatly made up. A few garments hung on hooks. She stepped in cautiously. On the chest of drawers were a few boat models, a comb and brush. She slowly opened the top drawer. Everything neatly folded. She opened the second one and found the same.

Her father hadn't given him a chance to take anything with him! She brought a fist to her mouth. The extent of her father's prejudice against Silas was becoming clearer to her.

Still hoping she was wrong, she walked to the only window in the room and scanned the activity down below. The men were working as if nothing had occurred. There was no sign of Silas.

She searched for his boat, but it wasn't there.

Perhaps he'd left it moored in the harbor. She had to know. She'd go down and ask the men below. If they knew nothing, she'd walk to the harbor and look for his boat.

Feeling better for having made a concrete decision, Cherish headed out the door. She took one last glance around the room, a part of her wishing she could linger, to breathe in the scent of him from his pillow, his clothes, touch the things he'd touched that morning....

Tom Winslow spent an uneasy night and woke up feeling battered. The vision of that young upstart presuming—daring—to take his daughter in his calloused hands threatened to resurrect the rage all over again, a rage that overwhelmed him and made him feel physically ill.

After a meager breakfast, his stomach feeling queasy, Winslow stood on his front veranda, staring at the inlet beyond the front yard. Why couldn't his daughter—his only child, the light of his life since his dear Isabel had passed away—have fallen for someone like that handsome Warren Townsend? Good English stock, well educated, with the kind of wealth to give Cherish the life he had raised her for.

How he needed his wife, his Isabel, now. She would understand. Why did she have to be taken away from him?

His thoughts returned to Silas. Who was he? Nothing but the son of immigrants, with not a penny to his name, no formal education, no roots in Haven's End. Why, his own—and the Townsend—family went back to pre-Revolutionary days. They each had ancestors who had fought on the *Margaretta*, in the first naval battle of the war against the English.

Winslow shook his head. He'd never experienced the anger he'd felt yesterday. Not when a competitor outbid him on a contract. Not when he was frustrated with all the setbacks that life had to offer. The bile rose in his throat and he decided to put his ire to constructive use before it flooded him.

Such rage was having an effect on his body. He must be getting old, he thought. He felt a vague malaise and a pain in his chest, which he attributed to heartburn.

He turned his attention to the day ahead. He would go into Hatsfield. Yes, he had people to see. If he could do anything in his power to see that Silas found no employment in any shipyard, he could force Silas to leave the area for good.

He'd thought long and hard all night over what he could tell his competitors about Silas and why he was undesirable. It had to be convincing. They all knew Silas's work and would hire him in a flash if they knew he was seeking employment.

A hint, a mere hint was all, something to taint his character...that was all it would take.

Tom Winslow left the house, a man with a mission.

Silas's neck and back groaned in protest when he finally stretched himself out of his cramped sleeping quarters. His jaw hurt and his lips felt tender where they'd connected with Winslow's fist.

Although it had stopped raining sometime in the night, the day looked as dismal as the dirty water pooling around him.

He picked up a can and began bailing it out. He had nothing better to do at the moment. He felt chilled to the bone and his hunger had turned to a dull gnaw in his stomach.

Ignoring both, he returned to bailing.

At least the action served to warm him up. After some moments of steady work he stopped to stretch the kinks out of his back. As soon as he did, he heard a raspy voice behind him.

"Ahoy there! Some rain we got last night."

The man who spoke looked ancient. He was hunched over and wore a captain's cap atop a scrawny head of gray hair and about three days' growth of gray beard. He scratched this as he approached Silas's boat.

He wore an old seaman's jersey that was frayed at the edges and had a few holes at the elbows. His dungarees were held up by a rope belt. A pair of mud-encrusted boots crunched across the pebbles as he neared.

Silas recognized him, though he'd never addressed him personally. No one knew the origins of Tobias Tibbetts, the village drunk. No one remembered just when he'd settled in Haven's End after a life at sea. They knew only that he was never quite sober and tended to ramble on about his days at sea if spoken to.

"Good morning," Silas answered.

"Fine day it be."

Silas didn't find he could agree, so he remained silent.

The man contemplated the boat, his hand continuing to scrape at his grizzled jaw. "Fine yawl she looks."

"Yes." There he could agree.

The man suddenly stared up at him, his bleary blue gaze taking on a sharpness. "You slept in 'er?"

"Yes," he answered without thinking.

The man sniffed. "Want some chow?"

Before Silas could think how to refuse, the man turned and shuffled up the pebbly cove. "Come along and have yourself a cup o' coffee. Looks like you can use it."

Silas slowly let the can drop. Jumping down from the boat, he followed the man up a path almost hidden by the high grasses covering the steep cliff that led up from the beach.

Tibbetts led him through the meadow to a little tar-paper shack set in a grove of evergreen trees overlooking the cove.

When Silas stepped into the one-room shanty, the odor made him stop. He wondered how such a small space set amidst the fresh-scented spruce and sea could smell so fetid.

The answer came to him as his eyes roamed the cramped quarters. The room looked as if it had never been cleaned or set in order since it had been built. Bundles lay everywhere.

Odd bits of metal, old, broken furniture, oily rags, dirty dishes, opened cans of food, heaps of clothes—there wasn't a space not taken up with something old and dirty. To intensify the smell, the room had the hot, overstuffed atmosphere of a woodstove burning in summer. Amidst the disorder Silas spied at least three cats silently prowling through the mess.

He had to breathe through his mouth for a few moments as he followed the old man into the room. Tobias cleared off some old newspapers from a wooden chair. "Here, have a seat. I'll get us both some coffee." Leaving Silas to make himself comfortable, he shuffled over to the iron stove and took off the enamel coffeepot. "Just go fill this up with water," he muttered as he exited the shack.

When the water began to boil, Tobias rummaged around the crowded countertop against one wall, shooing off a couple of cats. He examined an iron frying pan, took a dish towel from the counter, wiped the insides of the pan and set it on the stove top. "I'll fry ya up some bacon. Know it's here somewheres 'cause I bought a pound yesterday, that and some eggs. Couldn't have gone far, unless'n those cats got at it. That's probably why I stashed it somewhere." As he prepared breakfast, he continued talking.

"You're the boatbuilder, ain't ya? Seen you working down on Winslow's yard."

"Yes, sir."

"You build the yawl?"

"Yes. Finished her last summer."

The bubbling coffee and frying bacon began to overcome the other smells. When the plate was set before Silas along with the cup of steaming coffee, he temporarily forgot his surroundings and dug in hungrily.

"Here's some toast. The bread was a mite stale, but I put it on the stove to toast and it ain't bad this way."

Tobias sat across from him, pushing another cat off a chair. The cat, unfazed, climbed back onto his bony legs and curled up after a few attempts to find a comfortable spot.

They ate in silence. When they'd finished, Tobias sat back and gave a long, satisfied burp. "Nothing like bacon and eggs after—" He didn't finish his sentence. Instead, he got up and rummaged around in another part of the room. He came back with a bottle in one hand and a plug of tobacco in the other. He offered both to Silas, who shook his head.

Tobias poured the rum into his half-filled coffee cup. "Top it off. Gets the blood going," he explained, settling himself back in his chair and taking a satisfied sip.

Silas got up, the plate held uncertainly in his hand. "Mind if I wash things up?"

The old man waved a hand. "Not at all. Make yourself at home. You can bunk with me if you need a berth."

Silas hesitated. "Thank you. I—I no longer work at the shipyard."

"Don't have to explain nothin' to me. Many a time I've found myself in port, my money stole outta my pocket, waking in a gutter after a night o' this." He lifted the bottle and shook his head. "It's got me, boy. Can't live without it." This time he took a swig directly from the bottle.

Silas wanted to explain he hadn't been sleeping off a night of drinking and brawling, but he turned away, realizing it didn't matter what the old man thought. He walked through the clutter on the floor to the counter he took to be the kitchen. The sight that greeted his eyes made him want to stop and give up before starting. Dirty dishes and pans were stacked everywhere. Suddenly the food that had tasted so good moments before threatened to be cast up as he wondered what kind of plate he'd eaten from. He set his plate down gingerly atop some others. Immediately the cat who'd been nosing around came and sniffed it. Judging it appetizing, it lapped up the remaining egg yolk and bacon rind.

"You hungry?" Silas asked, idly petting the skinny cat. He gave the cat more scraps of bacon and set a plate down on the floor. The cat jumped down agilely and continued eating. It was soon joined by two others. Silas gave them some more food.

He found a pot large enough to hold a good quantity of water and took it outside to look for the well. Hot water, he decided. He would start with hot water.

After two days thinking about things as he set about cleaning up the dishes and clearing up a space for himself in the shack, Silas settled on a course of action. He would just have to find work in another shipyard.

It took him a while to accept that, after having been so many years with Winslow. But no matter how he analyzed the situation, Silas could not see Winslow taking him back. Cherish was just too precious to her father.

No, he would just have to start over somewhere else. Silas worked this over in his mind as he cleaned out his boat and put it in order. He came to accept the fact that it was time to move on from Haven's End and Winslow's Shipyard as he scrubbed pots and pans and scoured plates and cutlery in hot water. He fought down images of Cherish and thoughts of her in his arms as he washed dirty linen and hung smelly blankets up on a line in the whipping breeze.

Finally he was able to sleep in fresh sheets and at least know his food was served on clean plates. As for the rest of the shack, he shrugged, surveying the room from the sofa he'd made up as his bed. The sofa had a few holes, where no doubt mice had made their nests at one time. He needn't fear mice now, as Tobias had at least four cats roaming around the place, and as far as Silas could tell, they lived on whatever they could hunt for themselves.

Tobias's snores came across the room to Silas. Tobias slept on his back, his nose thrown back as if groping for air. Silas had come to figure out the man's routine. He rose after a drunken sleep, rummaged around for enough food to sustain him, washed it down with some rum, then after puttering around among his "things" he'd eventually head down to the cove, depending on the time of the tide, and dig some clams, which he'd sell in the village. He'd come back with a fresh bottle of rum and spend the evening nursing it. Silas offered to cook, but Tobias wasn't too interested in food.

Silas turned over, away from the snoring figure, and faced the grimy sofa. He wondered where it had come from. Once it had been a fine piece of furniture. Silas ran a finger along the curl of a fleur-de-lis pattern on its brocaded surface. Tobias was a scavenger, rarely coming home without something he had "picked up" somewhere, probably out of someone's rubbish.

Once again Silas fought down the memory of his last moment with Cherish. Where was she now? What had she been doing since he'd left? Had she thought of him at all?

He told himself tomorrow would be different. He'd sail into Hatsfield and begin looking for work. Perhaps some day in the far-off distance, if he managed to earn enough, he could see her again. Better forget that train of thought, he admonished himself. By then she'd be married to Townsend.

He'd left his life savings in his old room, but he figured they were safe for now. He didn't think anyone would find them, and perhaps he could ask someone he trusted, maybe Cherish—

no, he had to stay away from her—to get them for him some day. Some day. Everything seemed in the far distant future now.

Fighting despair, he turned his mind to a ship's design. He knew at length it would bring the oblivion of sleep as he calculated length and breadth and sharpness of a hull.

"How'd it go?" Tobias asked from his rickety rocking chair on an equally rickety porch. He held a week-old paper in his hands and worked a plug of tobacco placidly between his gums.

Silas sat on the wooden steps in front of him and faced the cove. "Nothing available."

"Aw, that's a shame." The paper rustled behind Silas. "Well, you can stay as long as you like, you know. Maybe somethin'll turn up."

There was silence as he went back to his paper. Silas watched the gulls fly overhead, circling the mudflats in search of carrion. Two days searching for work. He couldn't understand it. He thought he'd acquired some reputation in all his years with Winslow.

The rocker creaked as Tobias got up. "Well, guess I'll be goin' down to do some clammin'. Hey! Why don't you come along? I got an extra rake here somewheres," he muttered, going to the back of the porch, where assorted old equipment and tools were heaped up.

Silas was going to refuse, but then reconsidered. Why not earn some money instead of sitting around thinking?

The work proved hard and backbreaking—bending over at a ninety-degree angle for several hours, shoving the rake into the hard clay mud without gouging the clams, then heaving it forward to search for clams while avoiding the razor-sharp broken shells and mud worms.

He straightened to ease his sore back and spotted Tobias off in the distance. He marveled how the scrawny man could do this almost every day sustained on rum and a few victuals. There were a few other clammers along the cove at a good distance from him.

He turned his eyes shoreward. Suddenly he squinted. It couldn't be. Cherish! His heart began to thump at the mere sight of her, the way she shaded her eyes and surveyed the shoreline from above and her light-colored skirt blew against her legs in the breeze. He could tell the moment she spotted him and began heading down from the shack, making her way onto the beach.

He fought down the longing to see her. It would be futile and only lead to more frustration. He stood motionless, hoping she'd give up and go home. But no, she began walking resolutely toward him, lugging a satchel in one hand.

Disgusted for feeling weak-kneed at the very sight of her—wasn't she the cause of all his present problems?—he bent back to digging.

He could feel her eyes on him, but he refused to look up.

Finally she reached him. "Hello, Silas."

He straightened. She was beautiful, as fresh as a sea breeze with her white dress sprinkled with a pattern of forget-me-nots. Her two hands clutched the satchel in front of her.

"What do you have there?" he asked, indicating the bag with a jut of his chin.

Her smile disappeared at his lack of greeting. "I brought some of your things. I—I…" She swallowed. "I asked Ezra to pack up what he thought you'd need."

Silas felt ashamed at his rudeness. "Thanks. You shouldn't have carried it all the way out here." He glanced down at his muddy hands. "Let me rinse off my hands."

She shook her head. "That's all right. I'll take it back up to the beach."

"You shouldn't have come out here."

She swallowed. "I was worried about you."

"It's a little late for that."

"I'm sorry about Papa. He shouldn't have treated you so."

He smiled mirthlessly. "You mean *we* shouldn't have behaved the way we did."

"I'm not ashamed of our kiss. Are you?"

He looked away from her, afraid he'd lose his resolution in those smoky-blue eyes. He fixed his gaze on the gray mud covering his boots, reminding himself that he was bending over these flats and not working on boats because he'd forgotten everything but his feelings for her.

"It was a foolish thing to do."

"Silas, how can you say that?" Her voice was breathless.

"Because I'm standing here, knee-deep in mud, and my life—" he waved the clam rake shoreward, unable to speak for a moment "—is over there in a shipyard. And because of one instant of—of—insanity, I lost it all!" He glared at her, as angry at her as at himself.

Her eyes beseeched him. He wanted to reach for her and reassure her that everything was going to be all right, but he couldn't. Too much of his dream had been destroyed, and whether she liked it or not, she was the cause of it.

"Is that what you think our kiss was? Insanity?"

"What else was it? Are you satisfied your little experiment proved true? Just dangle the prize in front of Silas and see how he'll react?" He wanted to hurt her, hating himself for finding her irresistible even now, in her summer frock, her lips pressed together as if to keep from crying. But he couldn't stop himself. "Well, you proved it. I'm a man like all those others you left strewn across Europe. I'm not immune to your charms. You had to prove you could jerk my string and I'd react. You snapped your finger and Silas came to heel, just like your father.

"Except he's not so easy as you imagined. He's not going to give in to your whims this time, is he?"

She shook her head at him as she backed away. "That's not fair!" she whispered. "I was so worried about you when I found out Papa had dismissed you. I looked everywhere for you, but no one knew where you'd gone. Why didn't you let me know?"

He kicked at a barnacle-encrusted stone at his feet, not wanting her worry or concern. He didn't want to know about her feelings. He wanted to hold on to his anger at her thoughtlessness. "Let you know? You mean, go up to your house and knock on your door like any proper young suitor? Like Warren Townsend?"

She shook her head. "You could have let Ezra know."

"As if I knew where I was going. Do you think I had a plan all mapped out? If Winslow fires you, you can go to old drunk Tobias and beg a room. Give me that," he said impatiently, reaching for the bag. "You shouldn't be carrying that heavy thing. You're getting yourself all muddy out here."

Without bothering to give her a backward glance, he headed back to the beach, despising himself for his deliberately long stride, but all his instincts for self-preservation told him to get away from her. Make her hate you, he told himself. Get her over her infatuation. Let her see who you really are.

She ran to catch up with him. "What do I care about a bit of mud? It'll wash off."

He glanced back at her. She had her skirts hiked up in one hand. It was a long walk back to the beach over the slippery, pockmarked mud strewn with broken shells and sea-filled holes left by the clam diggers.

They finally reached the pebbly shoreline. He set the satchel down and stood waiting for Cherish to reach him. "Look, thanks for my things, but you shouldn't have come. Your father made it plain he doesn't want me anywhere near you."

"Papa will get over his silly notions."

"Will he?"

"Of course he will. You let me worry about Papa." When he said nothing, but continued looking at her skeptically, she asked curiously, "What's it like at Tobias's?"

"Let's just say it's not your aunt Phoebe's."

She giggled. "I've missed you."

He wanted to reach for her. His hand curled on the clam rake. Hadn't he done enough damage? But still the hunger gnawed at him and he felt engulfed by a deeper, greater, more terrifying need—to be held and cherished by her.

He looked away. "I—I better get back to the flats."

"What will you do now?"

He knew what she meant—the future. "Look for work."

"In another shipyard?"

He grimaced. "No one is hiring. I'll have to try farther than Hatsfield." The thought only intensified his gloom. The cold reception he'd gotten at the Hatsfield shipyards had made him feel worthless.

"Then I shall have to find a way there, as well," she said quietly. "Perhaps as a schoolteacher or shop clerk."

"Don't be silly. You can't just leave your father, your home…."

"Can't I?" She took a step toward him. Before he could stop her, she had leaned forward, placing her hands on his shoulders.

"Cherish." He motioned with his hands. "You'll get yourself full of mud."

"I told you, Silas, it'll wash off." She placed a quick, soft kiss on his lips.

"Don't, Cherish. This isn't a game."

She pulled away from him, her eyes frosty. "How dare you? I'm not playing a game!"

When he said nothing, but stood there with jaw and fists clenched, fighting the desire that rose up in him, she told him in a quiet, sure voice, "Some day you're going to kiss me back, Silas van der Zee." Then she turned and left him.

*If I kiss you back, I won't be able to stop,* he told her departing back.

# ❧ Chapter Twelve ❧

Cherish had no sooner walked in the front door than Celia came running out to meet her.

"Where have you been? Your aunt's been looking for you everywhere. Your father—" The woman clutched Cherish's arm.

"What is it? What's wrong with Papa?"

"He's collapsed."

"No! What happened?" Cherish grabbed Celia as if she could shake the information out of her.

"We don't know. He'd just had his dinner and gone to read his paper when we both heard it, your aunt and I—a big crash, like something had fallen. We ran into the parlor and there he lay on the floor, the potted plant and its stand knocked over. We got Jacob to ride over to get Doc Turner. He's up there with him now. You'd better go up to him. He's been asking for you."

Cherish didn't wait for any more. She took the stairs two at a time and stopped only when she got to her father's room. Then she hesitated, afraid of what she'd find on the other side of the door. She gave a tentative knock.

Her aunt opened the door. "Oh, I'm so glad you're back. Celia's told you what happened?" As she spoke she ushered Cherish into the room, motioning with a finger for quiet. "Your father seems very agitated. Try to calm him. The doctor says he mustn't be disturbed on any account."

Before her aunt could explain any further, Cherish reached her father's large four-poster bed. He lay in the middle, seeming shrunken in its midst. Cherish closed her eyes. *Oh, dear God, let him be all right. Don't take him from us. Help me, help me, Jesus, to be strong.*

Dr. Turner turned from where he had been bending over her father. "Good, there you are, Cherish. Your father wants you. Come." Seeing her hesitation, he gave her a smile and took one hand in his, giving it a pat. "That's a girl. Just let your papa know you're here."

He moved away from the bed, leaving space for Cherish. She bent forward, reaching for her father's hand, which lay on the coverlet. "Papa."

He opened his eyes and seeing her, blinked at her a few times. "Cherish… I don't know how much time I have." The words came out in a hoarse whisper.

"Shh, Papa, don't talk like that."

Her attempts to soothe him only agitated him. "You've got to find Silas for me." His dark eyes implored her. "Promise me you'll bring him here as soon as you find him."

"Of course, Papa." She felt her heart lift, thinking her father meant to make everything right with Silas once again. "I'll find him for you right away. How are you feeling, Papa?"

Dr. Turner touched her lightly on the shoulder. "He mustn't exert himself talking anymore. Come, child. Let him sleep. I've given him a sedative."

As she was turning away, her father called out one last time, "Don't forget. Bring me Silas…must talk to him."

"I will, Papa. I'll be right back with him. I promise."

Once in the corridor, she turned to the doctor. "What happened? Papa was fine."

"By all indications he's suffered an infarction of the heart, caused by a thrombosis." At her look of utter incomprehension, he clarified. "His heart hasn't received sufficient air, due to a blockage somewhere. It's very serious, resulting in damage to his heart. It's very weak right now."

"But how? Why?" whispered Cherish, unable to understand what the doctor was telling her.

"We don't know. All we know is it's not uncommon in a man your father's age. He needs complete bed rest and absolutely no agitation. His heart must be given time to heal. It will never regain what it has lost, but can, God willing, with rest and quiet, continue functioning.

"He seems overwrought about something. He keeps asking for Silas. We must reassure your father in this or he'll work himself up to another—"

"No!" Cherish refused to have the doctor even say it. "I'm going to get Silas."

"Where is he?" Aunt Phoebe asked her sharply. "No one seems to have seen him for a few days."

"He's staying with Tobias Tibbetts."

"What?" She stared at Cherish.

"That's right. He had nowhere else to go. I spoke to him today. I'm going to fetch him now."

"Let Jacob go. You're too distraught."

She shook her head, already walking away. "No, I'm going. I'll take the horse and buggy."

She rode over the rutted, dusty roads until she once again reached the cove. It was a couple of miles out of the village, an isolated, lonely spot. Silas and Tobias had just returned from the beach and were washing off at the well.

Silas saw her and immediately came to her. "Cherish, what are you doing here? I thought I made it clear—"

Before he could admonish her further, she said, "It's Papa! He's collapsed. It's his heart. Dr. Turner has been to see him. But he's asking for you. Papa has been asking for *you*. Please come, Silas! He needs to say something to you. He thinks he might—" Her voice broke. "He thinks he might d-die."

Silas didn't wait for any more explanation. "I'll come with you. Don't worry, Cherish. He'll be all right."

She sniffed. "How do you know?"

He gave her a reassuring smile. "He's too angry at me, for one thing. You'll see."

She smiled through her tears.

He took her by the hand and led her to the buggy. During the ride back she told him everything she knew. He reassured her again as she alternated between despair at the memory of her father lying in the bed and comfort at the feel of Silas's arm against hers and his soft voice encouraging her.

When they returned to the house, the doctor had left. Aunt Phoebe led them up to the bedroom. "He's still restless. Keeps asking for you, Silas. You'd better make your peace with him."

She paused at the door before opening it. "Whatever you do, don't say anything to disturb him further."

She held Cherish back when she began to follow Silas. "This is between the two of them. You'd best let them be."

"But I must know. Maybe Papa will ask Silas's forgiveness for what he did to him."

The door clicked shut firmly behind Silas. "If so, you'll find out soon enough. Come along and clean yourself up. You can sit with your father a while when Silas comes out."

Silas entered the dim room and headed immediately for the bed that dominated it. He stood for a moment silently observing the man whose eyes remained closed, wondering what he should do. Winslow looked deathly pale.

Silas cleared his throat softly. Winslow stirred immediately. "Cherish, did you find him?" he asked, but stopped as soon as he opened his eyes.

"Silas" was all he said for a long time.

"Yes, sir," Silas answered, shifting from one leg to the other, feeling awkward before this man who had known him since he was an adolescent and who had witnessed his strong feelings toward his daughter.

"Come here, boy." His words came out with an effort. Silas immediately edged closer. The older man's breathing was the only sound in the room. It was heavy going in and let out in an exhausted gust as if it was too much effort to keep it in his lungs. "Come closer."

Silas sat on the chair set next to the bed. "What is it, sir? I came as soon as I heard."

Winslow had closed his eyes again. Now he tapped at his chest. "The old heart is giving way at last."

"You'll get better. You'll see. You just have to rest." He felt he was mouthing a bunch of platitudes he didn't know whether he believed himself.

"I don't know…it's up to my Maker." Another moment of labored breathing passed. "All I know is I don't want to face Him without making a clean breast of things."

Silas waited, wondering what the older man had to say to him. Was he going to apologize for throwing him out? But the man's next words surprised him.

"You try to…get any work at another shipyard?"

He flushed, remembering the humiliating experience. "Yes."

"Any luck?"

"No, sir."

"I didn't think so."

Silas frowned. "Why not?"

Winslow opened his eyes, regarding him silently. "I went…to see the owners in Hatsfield after…I threw you out. I wanted to make sure you…couldn't find any work there."

Silas stared at him, too shocked to be outraged.

"I made enough insinuations about your character to…convince…you weren't trustworthy." He reclosed his eyes as if gathering strength. "I didn't bring Cherish into it at all. Just dropped…enough hints…unscrupulous character, out to steal a person's designs and…customers…start your own business…moment person's back was turned." The effort to speak had cost him and he fell silent.

Silas could feel the blood pounding between his ears. After all those years of giving Winslow his best—this was how the man repaid him. He wanted to get up and leave—leave his presence, his house, Haven's End altogether.

As if reading his mind, Winslow said, his words more labored, "Don't know…how long…got on this earth. Want to ask…pardon. Know I did wrong. Can…you…forgive me?"

Silas looked away from the man's pale face. He couldn't shut his ears, however, to his slow, ponderous breathing, or keep the sight of the man's searching hand from the edge of his vision.

Winslow's hand finally found his arm and clutched it. "You've got…to forgive me. I wronged you. I repent of it, do you hear? If God gives me leave…make it good. I'll go to those shipyards and take back everything I said."

Silas felt the bitterness tighten his heart. Empty promises, he thought. By the looks of it, Winslow wouldn't last the night. And if he did by chance recover, what good would his recanting do? The damage had been done. Those shipyard owners would be more suspicious than ever, asking themselves why Winslow would get rid of him and then be trying to get a competitor to hire him.

Even more telling was the fact that Winslow—even on his deathbed—was not ready to take him back.

Silas stood, unable to sit near the man a minute longer, but the man's hand was wrapped around his wrist.

Winslow's agitation increased. "Silas, please, so sorry. Shouldn't have done it…."

Silas was moved, despite himself, by the man's condition. Winslow would most likely be facing eternity soon. Silas leaned over the bed and said as convincingly as he could, "It's all right, Mr. Winslow. I—I—" The words stuck in his throat. "I forgive you."

Strangely enough, once he uttered the words, Silas felt a release. He straightened again and repeated, "Don't trouble yourself. It's all right. I forgive you."

"Thank you, Silas. Thank you." The man relaxed. His fingers fell still.

When Silas exited the bedroom, the first person he saw was Cherish. His heart twisted within him at the sight of her pale face, waiting for an encouraging verdict from him. One hand of hers clutched a handkerchief, which must have been sodden, judging by her tear-filled eyes.

She was too hesitant to approach him, too afraid of what he might say about her father's condition. Hope warred with fear in her eyes. He tried to smile as he stepped toward her.

As he neared her, it was as if she couldn't hold back any longer. "I did this to him, didn't I?" she whimpered.

He thought of nothing else then but of comforting her. He took another step toward her, bridging the space between them, and took her in his arms. "No, no, you didn't," he murmured against her hair as she cried into his chest. He cradled her, one hand cupped against her hair.

"It's going to be all right. Everything's going to be all right," he whispered softly against her hair, his hand smoothing it. A part of him noted that he'd come full circle, back to his old role of big brother, adviser, friend—the one who bore the ultimate responsibility.

Silas breathed in the lilac scent of her hair, knowing it would haunt him that night and for the nights to come.

"Did Papa…did Papa say anything about us?" she managed to ask between sniffles.

He swallowed, finally answering, "No. He just wanted to ask my forgiveness for having fired me. That's all."

He could feel her slump against him. "Oh. I'm glad about that. But…you don't think it means he might have reconsidered things about us?"

Silas gently drew Cherish from him, although he kept hold of her. He peered into her eyes, knowing he must make her understand, without hurting her further. "I don't know. What I do know is that he mustn't be disturbed in any way. As the doctor said, he needs absolute peace and quiet."

She nodded like an obedient child. He drew her into his arms again, unable to stop himself from indulging one more time in the very feel and scent of her, before he had to leave her.

## Chapter Thirteen

Silas sat in the middle of the church, far enough away from the Winslow pew to be separated from them, but close enough to afford him a good view of Cherish. He had come in after the service had started and would probably escape before the pastor had a chance to station himself in the doorway to greet parishioners. The pastor announced Winslow's collapse and led the entire congregation in prayer for Cherish's father.

When the sermon began, Silas saw that it attempted to address the situation confronting Winslow.

"The title of my message this morning is 'Trials and Tribulations,'" Pastor McDuffie told them after the last hymn had been sung and the collection plate passed around. His gaze seemed to include each and every one of them.

"Jesus said, 'In the world ye shall have tribulation.' We sorrow and wonder when a fellow brother is struck down by a trial, such as our dear friend and neighbor Thomas Winslow. Our hearts go out to his family." He gave Cherish and her aunt a compassionate smile.

"But how many of us don't secretly feel a tiny measure of relief that it wasn't one of us this time?" His gaze drew them all back in again. "We know it has to come some time, but aren't we glad it passed us by this time?

"How are we supposed to view trials and tribulations?" Here he asked them to turn to the book of Job. "'But he knoweth the way that I take: when he hath tried me, I shall come forth as gold.'

"None of us likes to be tested, do we? None of us likes to pass through the 'fiery furnace.' It's nice to talk about it afterward. It's somewhat romantic to describe it, once one has graduated to a higher plane of spirituality, isn't that so?

"I remember when I was in Bible school, full of zeal and ready to evangelize the world." He chuckled, looking down at his podium a second. "It didn't take long to bring me down a few pegs and shake up some of my assumptions once I entered the realities of pastoring, where one's flock doesn't necessarily want to be led where one is convinced they ought to go."

The pastor continued giving examples of his own life and trials in taking on the commission God had ordained for him. Silas found it hard to relate in many ways to what he was saying, since he'd never felt himself particularly called of the Lord to do anything. He assumed everyone around him was a Christian, and he felt it his duty only to support missionaries on foreign fields, to try to keep the Ten Commandments and treat others the way he wanted them to treat him.

Pastor McDuffie's message, on the other hand, caused him a certain discomfort. Perhaps he was feeling particularly sensitive since he'd had his life turned topsy-turvy by Winslow. His glance strayed to the back of Cherish's head. She wore a pretty bonnet, her dark hair cascading down the back of her gown in a simple ponytail. All it took was a look and he felt a longing sweep through him. He fixed his attention on McDuffie at the pulpit.

If this message was meant to comfort Cherish and her aunt, he thought it was a strange way to go about it.

McDuffie exhorted his congregation to use every situation, every circumstance to learn from the Lord. Silas rubbed the back of his neck, feeling only impatience at such advice.

"Please turn to the first verse in Romans 12." Silas picked up the black Bible at his side, hearing the rustle of pages turning all around him. It took him a while to locate the book, which he knew only was somewhere in the New Testament.

"'I beseech you therefore, brethren, by the mercies of God, that ye present your bodies a living sacrifice....'"

The rest of the verse faded out. He had stopped listening after the word *sacrifice.* It sounded almost pagan, presenting one's body as a sacrifice to God. It conjured up images of Abraham offering up his son to be burned on an altar to please God in some strange, barbaric fashion. This was not the God Silas could imagine as the Christian God.

He preferred to think of God as the good shepherd. Jesus, in a white robe, surrounded by children, holding out His hands to them to bless them.

As the sermon wound down, Pastor McDuffie urged the people to come up to the altar to recommit their lives to God— to present themselves indeed as "living sacrifices" to Him.

Silas sat in his pew as he watched a good number of people, though by no means all, file up to the altar, where the pastor and his wife and the deacons prayed for them.

The impromptu prayer service put a hitch in Silas's plans to escape quietly from the service before the others. By the time the pastor dismissed the congregation, Silas was stuck in the middle of all those standing, moving like sheep through the pews and into the crowded aisle.

At the doorway McDuffie shook his hand, his other gripping his arm. "Hello, Silas. How have you been keeping? I'm sorry about Mr. Winslow. It must be terrible for you. I know he must be like a father to you. We have all of you in our prayers. Please let me know if there's anything I can do for you."

Silas disengaged his hand, murmuring his assent and turning away. He felt like a fraud. Winslow's son? Did people assume he was holding down the fort at the shipyard? What was he supposed to say? That he was camping out at a drunkard's shack?

"You and Cherish must come over for dinner this week."

Silas looked back over his shoulder at the pastor. "We'll see," he muttered, stepping quickly down the steps. There he was stopped by another man, who wanted to know about his dory.

What should he tell people? That he no longer worked at the shipyard? He felt in limbo since Winslow's collapse. It was one thing for the man to ask his pardon; it was another thing to know that Winslow wanted to rehire him. And if he did, did Silas even want to come back? The question stumped him.

"I know the dory's about ready," he told the man. "Why don't you check in at the shop tomorrow?" he suggested.

Before he had a chance to make a getaway, Cherish reached him. "Silas, why didn't you sit with us?" She looked beautiful in her deep-rose-and-white gown, ladylike in every detail from the dainty white gloves to the ruffled hem.

"I'm not part of your household anymore," he answered quietly, not wishing anyone to overhear their conversation. Before she could reply, he asked, "How is your father?"

"Very weak, but at least he made it through the night. I must get right back."

He nodded.

"I thought Papa…" She floundered. "Didn't Papa say he was sorry to you?"

He toyed with the hat brim in his hands. "But he didn't ask me to come back."

She closed her eyes a moment. "Why?" she asked simply.

"You'll have to ask him that," he answered, knowing full well she wouldn't be able to do so as long as her father's health was so precarious.

"What did he tell you?"

"It doesn't matter. What matters is that Dr. Turner doesn't want him to be upset by anything right now. And I think that includes me."

"I see." She looked away a moment, answering someone's greeting with a smile that didn't let on that she was feeling anything more than good Sunday cheer.

Two women accosted her, inquiring solicitously after her father.

"Dr. Turner says his condition has stabilized, but he will have to maintain bed rest for some time."

"Oh, thank the good Lord that he's better," said one, her white gloves clasped together in an attitude of prayer.

"What a shame," the other one clucked, shaking her head. "He was so healthy…such a vigorous man, your father…."

"Yes, I think he was working too hard. Dr. Turner told him he must slow down."

Silas watched Cherish, hardly listening to the conversation. She gave all her attention to the older women, hiding her own feelings. No one watching her could guess what she had been through in the past twenty-four hours.

He knew how much she loved her father. He realized as he observed her that she always put on a good face. She was truly a lady, he admitted, with a kind, polite word for whoever crossed her path. Only those closest to her were privileged to see her moments of crossness, her tears, her bad moments. He'd been one of the few, he realized.

When the women left, Cherish turned back to him. "Won't you be coming back to the boat shop?"

He shook his head. "Your father even told me he would give me a good recommendation to any other shipyard."

Again she was interrupted by some people leaving the churchyard.

When she gave him her attention once more, all she said was "Let me know…if you find anything away from here. Will you do that?"

He could promise her that. He nodded. "I will." He put out his hand. "Goodbye, Cherish."

Her hand met his and he clasped it. She turned from him before he could make a move away.

As he took his road homeward, he wished for things as they had been. Wouldn't it be nice now to go home with the Winslows for Sunday dinner and afterward sit on the front porch on the swing and discuss things with Cherish—perhaps the morning's sermon? He could ask her how it had affected her. Had she, like him, found it a bit extreme? No, for she had gone up to the altar. Did that mean she had accepted the pastor's challenge, or simply that she needed prayer today?

He sighed and trudged the long, dusty road to Lupine Cove to break bread with Tobias Tibbetts. He wouldn't know now.

That week neighbors brought covered dishes to the Winslow household. After a dinner of a mixture of foods, Cherish sat upstairs with her father, reading to him from the Bible.

"Cherish?"

"Yes, Papa, can I get you anything?"

"Did you see Silas today?"

"Not since Sunday."

"He hasn't come back to the shipyard?" His tone betrayed only mild interest.

"No."

"I'd like to see him again. Could you have Jacob fetch him?"

Her heartbeat quickened. Maybe he had relented. "Yes, Papa" was all she said.

Tom Winslow was sitting up in bed, propped up against pillows, when Silas was shown into his room. "Hello, Silas."

"Hello, Mr. Winslow," he replied, having come as soon as he'd been summoned. "You're looking better."

"Thank you. I didn't think I was going to make it the other day. Sit down…please."

Silas complied, wondering what Winslow wanted. Hadn't Silas given him enough?

He was quiet some moments longer. Finally Winslow said, "You know how angry I was at you."

"Yes, sir."

"That's the only reason I did what I did. I…I didn't want you finding work anywhere near Cherish."

"Forget it. It's over and done," he said, realizing how weak Winslow's condition still was.

The man's mouth worked silently as he struggled to express himself. While Silas was figuring out how to calm him, Winslow continued. "Cherish…she can have the best man in the county…. Don't keep her back, Silas."

"I wouldn't do that, sir."

He continued as if Silas hadn't spoken. "I gave her the best of everything…education, the best that money could buy…exposure to the world…she's had the *best* of everything…. Don't hold her back, Silas. Please!"

"I didn't set out to court her, Mr. Winslow. I didn't do anything to pursue her, I swear it! Believe me, I fought it as hard as I could."

Winslow regarded him and finally nodded his head with an effort. "I believe you, son. But you have fallen for her, haven't you? I can see it in your eyes, hear it in your voice. You couldn't help yourself, could you? She's special.

"I know…she's headstrong and impetuous. When she makes up her mind she wants something, she'll pursue it with all her will. I don't blame you, son. She's like her mother. I fell for her, fell hard, the first time I laid eyes on her." He smiled in reminiscence.

"She was beautiful, not just on the outside, but through and through, like Cherish. It just shines out of her. I know how irresistible Cherish must have been to you, waltzing in from abroad. She probably took your breath away, like her mother did mine."

Then he sobered, his eyes narrowing at Silas. "But you're older than she is. You bear the burden of responsibility."

Silas shifted in his chair at the last words. They echoed too closely what his own conscience had been telling him.

"You and I, Silas, we're just simple boatbuilders." He lifted his hand from the bedspread and turned it around. "Nothing but carpenters, deep down. Our needs are simple. Give us a boat plan and some wood and we'll be happy.

"But Cherish, she's special. She's seen the world. She's beautiful, intelligent, lively. She can have her heart's desire. She thinks she'd be happy working in the boat shop for the rest of her days. Would you limit her to that life—the only one you can offer her?"

Silas felt himself growing smaller with each sentence. They pounded into his soul, finding confirmation there.

"If you really care about her, don't you wish more for her— the things a fine gentleman can give her? The kind of life she deserves? I've done all in my power to prepare her. Now it's time for her to live it. Would you truly shackle Cherish to your narrow world? Would you, son?"

The word hit Silas on the raw. How could Winslow call him son—a term he'd never before used with him—and ask what he was asking of him?

They gazed hard at one another, Silas wrestling with yearnings so deep, he'd never had the chance to give voice to them. Winslow's gaze was understanding but uncompromising.

"No, sir," Silas answered finally, wondering why he found it so hard to utter two simple words. Nothing Winslow had said came as a surprise. They were the same words he'd told himself—if not in such clear detail. Certainly deep in his subconscious he'd been telling himself these same things since the day Cherish had walked into the boat shop after her two-year absence.

Why were they so difficult to receive as he heard them spoken aloud by someone who loved Cherish and wanted only the best for her?

As soon as he left Winslow's room, Cherish came to him.

"What did my father want?"

He looked straight into her eyes, knowing he'd have to be candid with her, for the sake of her father's health. "He doesn't want us to see each other anymore."

After Silas had left, Cherish sat with her father until he fell asleep. She didn't let on that she knew anything of his conversation with Silas.

Softly she exited the room and made her way outside to the veranda. The trees were lush and green, interspersed with the lacy white blossoms of the wild pear trees. It seemed that everything bloomed at once in June, from roses to lilacs, as if they knew how fleeting the season would be.

Loneliness engulfed her. It saddened her to see her father brought so low. Only a few days before, he had been hale and hearty. Now he seemed pathetically weak. Worse than his physical weakness was his spiritual and emotional weakness. He seemed so lost.

Her sorrow fought with her frustration at her father's attitude toward Silas. How could her father be so unreasonable? Every instinct screamed out to do something, even as her common sense reminded her of her father's delicate condition.

Deciding she needed to talk to someone, she grabbed up her parasol and told Aunt Phoebe she was going out.

She walked to the parsonage. It was doubtful she would find Pastor McDuffie and his wife alone, so she prepared herself mentally to smile and greet whoever else might be visiting. But the house seemed quiet as she knocked on the screen door.

"Hello there, Cherish." Carrie McDuffie gave her a wide smile as she opened the door and drew her into the house.

"I'm sorry to come unannounced."

"Nonsense. We've been meaning to have you over since you returned home. How is your father? Arlo will walk down later and pay him another short call."

"He'll like that. I told him about Sunday's sermon, and he seemed to enjoy hearing it."

"That's good." Carrie led her down the corridor to the back porch. "We were just sitting out here, digesting our dinner and admiring the flowers."

"How nice and peaceful it seems," Cherish told her as they emerged onto the shaded porch.

"Hello, Cherish," Pastor McDuffie greeted her, getting up from a wicker rocker.

"Don't get up. I just stopped by to say hello."

Pastor McDuffie didn't heed her, but came over and gave her a warm handclasp. "We've been praying for you. Don't despair."

She smiled and took the rocker Carrie indicated for her. "Say hello to Miss Cherish, Janey."

Cherish smiled at their five-year-old daughter, who sat on the steps with a doll. "Hello, Janey."

"Hello, Miss Cherish," she said, turning to her and holding up her doll. "See Miss Eliza?"

"Hello, Miss Eliza." She took her porcelain hand. "How do you do?"

"Fine, thank you, Miss Cherish. I hope you enjoy your visit to the parsonage."

"Why, thank you. I'm sure I shall."

"Come, Janey, let's give Miss Cherish a chance to talk to your papa."

"But Mama, I want to visit with Miss Cherish."

Her mother took the girl by the hand. "I'm sure you do. But we'll come back and talk with her later and maybe have some lemonade together. How about that?"

Cherish watched the two walk away together. She could tell by Mrs. McDuffie's thickened waistline that there would soon be another McDuffie added to the household. How blessed she must be, with a loving husband and daughter and now another child on the way, living in this beautiful house surrounded by flowers.

"How are you holding up, my dear?" The pastor's soft question intruded into her thoughts.

She sighed and turned to him with a sad smile. She had meant to be brave and give him a shining example of someone facing her trials with the kind of trusting faithfulness he had spoken about in his sermon.

Now, looking into his sympathetic eyes, she found her own filling with tears. She pressed her lips together and looked toward the garden. The flower beds, coming alive with blossoms, became a blurry green-and-pink-and-lavender landscape.

"That's all right. Let it out," he said softly. After a while he handed her a clean white handkerchief.

She took it gratefully. "I didn't mean to come here and bawl. It's too fine a day for that."

"You're welcome to come here any day and bawl. I'll make sure to have a handkerchief ready."

She gave a watery laugh. With a final wipe of her eyes and nose, she said, "All right, I'm finished feeling sorry for myself."

"Care to tell me about it?"

"Oh, Pastor McDuffie, where do I begin?"

"I suppose you're worried about your father."

She bit her lip. "It's more than that." She looked down at her hands clasped around the handkerchief. "It's my fault his heart gave out."

"Why do you say that?" he asked quietly.

"I upset him frightfully."

"What did you do that was so terrible? You've hardly been home long enough to get into too much trouble."

"You would think so, wouldn't you? 'Cherish always does what she is supposed to. She is such a credit to her family,'" she mimicked. "It seems as if all I've discovered since I've come home is how black my soul really is."

Then it came out. She told him all she'd been feeling for Silas for as long as she could remember, Silas's reticence and his final capitulation, and her father's violent reaction.

"I never dreamed Papa would be so against anything between Silas and me." She sniffed. "I mean, in many ways it would be a natural thing, wouldn't it? I've practically grown up around him and the boat shop. Silas is perfectly able to take things over when Papa…when Papa gets too old." Tears threatened again at the thought, which seemed all too real now.

"Instead, here he's run Silas off the yard. Now he's laid up for who knows how long. He'll need constant attention for some weeks at least, and who is supposed to run the shop?" She looked at McDuffie's gentle face, not expecting an answer.

He seemed to sense that, since he didn't reply right away. Instead he picked up his large, worn Bible and opened it. He began to read from Matthew, a passage familiar to Cherish about the lilies of the field. He ended with "'Take therefore no thought for the morrow: for the morrow shall take thought for the things of itself.'" He closed the book.

"Let's pray, shall we?" He laid the book down, took both her hands in his and bowed his head, shutting his eyes. His voice continued gently, and gradually Cherish's heart felt peace. He prayed for her father, for his recovery, for reconciliation between him and Silas. He prayed for Silas, that he would find the road chosen for him of God. And finally he prayed for Cherish herself.

"Grant her Your grace, Lord, to see this through. We know You have a purpose in all this, that all things 'work together for good to those that love You, to those who are the called according to Your purpose.'"

When he'd finished praying he sat back and regarded her for a few moments. "It's tough falling in love, isn't it?"

She nodded. "I never thought it would be. It seems I've always loved Silas. Since the first day I met him. Can a five-year-old fall in love?"

"A five-year-old can love."

"The more I read First Corinthians thirteen, the worse I feel. My love seems to fall so short. It seems since I got back all I've been doing is trip over myself trying to get Silas to notice me—to notice the woman I've become—and the more I strive to do so, the more childishly I behave, until…this. I know you'll probably say, like Silas, that I had nothing to do with my father's condition, but you didn't see him that day in the boat shop. I've never seen him in such a rage. It can't have done his heart any good."

"You know the Bible says that Christ's love has already been poured out into our spirits by His Holy Spirit."

She nodded, again recognizing the verse.

"When you begin meditating on that, you'll begin to see how you can have the charity described in First Corinthians. Let me ask you something else." He held up a hand. "Don't answer me right away. It won't have an easy answer."

"What is it?" she asked, feeling her heart accelerate at the steady way he was looking at her. She knew that look. It meant a spiritual question was coming that she wouldn't like.

"Would you be willing—truly willing—to accept God's will in this situation between you and Silas and your father?"

She licked her lips. "You mean, would I accept it gracefully if I knew it wasn't God's will for Silas and me to be together?"

"That's right."

"I have asked the Lord to have His perfect way in my—our—lives. But it seems ever since I did, I've been receiving crossed signals. Sometimes it seems so clear that the Lord is showing me that Silas returns my feelings, and other times it seems I'm 'kicking against the pricks,' as Saul was," she ended ruefully.

He smiled in understanding. "If you've truly given it over to the Lord, He will show you the way. He understands your frame, your weaknesses, and He'll work through them. You just wait on Him now and have patience."

She wrinkled her nose. "I think I'm going to come to hate that word."

"Don't. It's a beautiful word. 'But they that wait upon the Lord shall renew their strength; they shall mount up with wings as eagles; they shall run, and not be weary; and they shall walk, and not faint.'"

By the time she left the parsonage, Cherish felt strengthened in her spirit. The Scriptures had reminded her that the real battle was a spiritual one—that it would be won only on her knees, waiting patiently for the Lord to do His perfect work.

# ❧ *Chapter Fourteen* ❧

Silas woke in a sweat. He flung off his sheets and blankets, feeling stifled in the closed, smelly shack. Across it he could hear Tobias's breathing, each intake of oxygen sounding as if it could hardly make the journey up his nostrils.

Silas turned away from the noise, placing the pillow over his ears to stifle the sound.

His dream was still too vivid to his senses. He'd been dreaming of Cherish, of holding her in his arms. He tried to blot out the image. He had to forget her. He must. Look at your plight, he told himself sternly.

Each day he'd been looking for work unsuccessfully. It suddenly seemed as if he was a pariah. He was starting to get desperate. He'd always earned his keep, never been beholden to anyone.

Once thoughts of work got into his mind, the feverish worries began, and he knew the rest of the night would be spent tossing and turning, trying to recapture that blessed oblivion of sleep.

The next morning, leaving Tobias snoring blissfully, Silas, not bothering with even a cup of coffee, let the cats out and set out for the village. He'd been avoiding it, preferring to look for work in the neighboring towns. But whenever he'd passed it, the looming cannery along the wharf beckoned him.

The last thing he wanted was to lower himself to apply for work in that barnlike warehouse. From shipwright to cannery worker. He kicked at the rocks in the rutted road. Familiar anger built inside him at the injustice. But it had no outlet, nor ever would. Whom could he be angry at but himself?

He glanced up at the sky, the promise of a gloriously warm day in its pale blue expanse above the evergreen trees. Already at six in the morning it was fully light.

He could be mad at God, Who'd made him, Who'd taken his parents away from him at an early age, his home…but he couldn't even work up anger at Him. Somewhere, deep down, Silas felt he deserved everything he was getting. He'd done something wrong and now he was being punished.

He walked resolutely down the main street. Already fishermen were about, walking onto the docks, preparing to set off, calling to each other in a friendly manner.

"Hey, Silas, what're you doing down to the wharf so early?"

He lifted a hand in greeting, but didn't stop to chat.

"How's Winslow?" another asked.

"Better," he answered, keeping his pace steady, straight to the cannery. There was only one cannery in Haven's End, which had opened just last year, as had many others along the coastal towns. It packed herring for the sardine industry.

As Silas entered the long building set over a wharf, the smell of fish hit even more intensely than along the docks themselves. The interior was a large, damp, cavernous space. Already it was filling with workers, many of them Portuguese and Irish immigrants.

Well, he was only one generation removed from immigrants himself, he told himself, thinking of his Frisian parents as he crossed the wet floor. He asked someone for the manager and was pointed to a side door leading to an office.

Five minutes later he donned a full-length black waterproof apron and was pointed to a long table to stand between others dressed similarly, and set to work to clean and cut herring at a third of the salary he'd been making at Winslow's.

He shut out all thoughts from his mind but the job before him. He would survive this, just as he'd survived leaving home at the age of twelve, just as he'd survived being kicked out by Winslow. He'd achieve his dream yet. It might take longer, but he would achieve it.

By the time Silas arrived at Tobias's shack, his legs felt like rubber from standing so long, his fingers were stiff from holding the herring with one hand and wielding the knife with the other, the skin of his hands was red and puckered from hours in salt water, nicked here and there from the sharp knife, and he smelled as fishy as the warehouse.

He went immediately to the well and began hauling water for a bath. Tobias was nowhere to be seen. The fire had gone out, so Silas rekindled it. He kicked off his filthy boots, and as soon as the water was barely tepid, he filled a tin tub that had been hanging on a hook on the exterior wall of the shanty, ignoring the cats, which came whining and rubbing against his legs.

"Sorry, I've got no fish for you. I might smell as if I do, but I left it all in the steaming vats."

As he shed his clothes, he saw with disgust a shower of tiny silvery scales fall from them. The apron hadn't been enough to protect him from the millions of scales he'd scraped off the fish.

Quickly he stepped into the tub and scrubbed himself from scalp to toes. As he was dunking his head into the water to rinse away any remaining scales, the door banged opened. He lifted his head.

"Hey, Silas, that you?" Tobias's slurred voice came across the room as he leaned his scrawny neck forward to peer at him.

"Yes," he answered shortly, annoyed by the interruption of his privacy. He was used to the solitary boat shop where he had the place to himself in the evenings.

"Don't mind me." The old man waved a hand in his direction as he weaved across the room to his rocker. "You just go ahead with your bath. I'll just set myself down here. Feeling a little woozy...."

The rocker creaked under his weight. With a sigh Silas finished his bath, giving himself a final rinse with the remaining water. He gritted his teeth, seeing a few tiny scales still fall from his hair into the used bathwater.

He wrapped himself in a threadbare towel and dragged the tub toward the door. On an impulse he looked across at Tobias, who sat rocking, looking out the window toward the bay. "Would you care to have me fix you a bath?" It would certainly improve the air quality in the little room.

"Oh, no, thanks, boy. Much obliged. Never take one."

"No, I didn't suppose you did."

Silas began to feel a little like his old self once he was dressed in clean clothes, his wet hair combed back. He sliced some bacon from a slab he'd bought on his way home and set it on a frying pan, putting the scraps in a dish for the cats. They immediately swarmed around it.

"Hungry?" he asked Tobias.

"Naw." The man mumbled something and felt around in his pocket for his tobacco. Soon the smell of pipe smoke began to mingle with that of the frying bacon.

Silas tended the bacon and cracked a couple of eggs into the pan. As they cooked, he set his work clothes in the tub and rinsed them out. He hung them on the line outside, where they flapped in the ever-present sea breeze, and he hoped they'd be dry by morning.

He sliced some bread from the loaf he'd bought and sat down to eat. He didn't feel any real appetite, but knew he had to eat to keep his strength up. As thoughts of the morrow emerged, he pushed them back. He knew from experience that it was better to deal with only one day at a time. He dug in to his food.

After a few moments Tobias got up from the rocker and came shuffling over to the table. "Reminds me of the smell aboard a Grand Banks schooner, coming into the galley for a good hot breakfast 'fore going out in our dories."

"You were on the Grand Banks?"

"Yep." He screwed up one eye as he scratched the gray stubble on his jaw. "Let's see, that was in the summers of sixty-one and sixty-two. Fleets were down, most of the young men gone to the Great War."

"My dad was on the Grand Banks."

Tobias eyed him appraisingly. "Was he now? Mebbe I knew him."

Silas shook his head. "I don't think so. His vessel went down in '61. The *Laurie Ann*."

Tobias nodded slowly. "Seem to recall that name. What a shame. Lot o' good men went down on those banks."

"Yes." His father had been one of them.

"So you never fished the banks yourself?"

"No. Came up here to apprentice at Winslow's yard."

"I set out to sea when I was a lad. Worked up to able seaman." Tobias leaned back in the wooden chair, a faraway look in his eyes. "That was the life—a rough one, make no mistake, but a good one. Ah, well." He took a puff from his pipe.

"You sail on any clippers?" Silas asked with interest. He wished in many ways to have been old enough to have worked on those great, sleek sailing vessels.

"Did I sail on the clippers! I sailed on the *Flying Cloud* in '53 during the great race 'tween us and the *Hornet*." He chuckled. "The *Hornet* had left New York two days 'fore us, but we caught up. We never reefed sail nor furled the spanker in all hundred and five days it took us to reach 'Frisco. The *Hornet* beat us by about forty minutes, but it took her a hundred and six days to make the trip." Tobias cackled at the memory, slapping a palm down on the table. "There were a lot of wagers placed on those two ships.

"We didn't stop in 'Frisco long, just enough to unload our cargo, load her with ballast and off we went to the south Chiny coast to pick up tea."

Silas pushed his empty plate aside and sat back to listen.

"On another trip 'round the Horn, she did eighty-nine days and twenty-one hours. Our captain believed the only way to sail a ship was to pile on as much sail as he could and keep it there as long as possible. Sometimes we had as much as six thousand square yards o' canvas above us."

"You must have seen some rough weather around the Horn."

"Wicked gales. One time our ship was dismasted, and we had to put up in Valparaiso for a few days. Still made it to 'Frisco in a hundred and thirteen days." He grinned. "Only to lose most of our crew to the gold fields."

"You weren't interested in panning yourself?"

The old man worked his lips in the gap where his front teeth used to be. "Naw. I found after a few days ashore I got homesick for the sea. It was a hard life. Climbing up that rigging in all kinds o' weather. I never made more than fifteen dollars a month." He grinned. "Pretty much spent it all after a few days in port. Wine and women."

"You never married?"

He shook his head slowly. "I was married to the sea. Besides, there wuz plenty o' willing women in port. I've known women across the globe, from Chiny women to Portugee and everything in between." He scratched the edge of his jaw with the end of his pipe. "Naw, a sailor's life and a wife don't mix."

The older man's conversation soon returned to the ships. "Those were the days. Ships were sharp and their captains knew how to get the most out o' their sail." He cleared his throat in disgust. "Before these great hulking cargo ships that look more like washtubs—no royals, a stumpy topgallant and an engine to raise steam in port. Nothing like the clippers."

Silas rose, taking his plate to the dishpan. The momentary euphoria of hearing about the great days of the clippers had evaporated, leaving a vague depression. Had the days of sail truly passed, and with it the days of the great ship designers—the McKays and Webbs, those celebrated names of shipbuilding?

Had Silas simply been born too late?

* * *

Cherish came in to check on her father. The doctor still had him on sedatives much of the time to keep him resting quietly. He was awake at the moment and smiled when he saw Cherish. "I'm glad you've come, my dear."

"Anything you need, Papa?" she asked with a cheerful smile as she came to sit at the edge of the bed.

"Your smile is more help to me than all these pills and potions Doc Turner leaves me," he said, with a motion toward the bottles on his bedside table.

"He just wants to see you better."

"I feel better already."

"Well, you need to rest a while longer," she said, smoothing the coverlet under her hand.

"I don't know how long I can leave the shipyard unattended. How long have I been sleeping away the days, anyway?"

"Only a few days. But Dr. Turner was adamant. You mustn't strain yourself for many weeks yet."

He grimaced. "And what about the shipyard? Am I supposed to lie abed and watch it fall to pieces in the meantime?"

"Papa, you know I can take care of things until you're well enough to come down yourself."

He pressed his lips together, looking away from her. "If only Henry had had the decency to stay. I don't suppose we could summon him back for a while. Maybe I should talk to Phoebe about it…."

"Papa! Haven't you heard anything I said? What about me? Don't you think I know something about the work that goes on there? Don't you think I could manage for a few weeks? After all, you're right here. I could ask you anything I'm not sure about, and I could report everything at the end of each day."

He still made no answer, but she could see by the drumming of his fingertips on the coverlet that he was becoming agitated.

"Papa," she pleaded softly. "The most important thing is that you get well. You know you mustn't worry about things down at the yard. Who can watch over things better than your own daughter?"

"Are you sure Henry wouldn't come?"

"Papa, he has a job. He can't just drop everything and come back here."

"If only…"

"If only what?"

"If only you were already married to someone like Warren Townsend, then he could look after things until I recuperate fully."

"Papa! What does he know about shipbuilding?"

"He knows about business. He's a good, honorable man. His father is interested in expanding into shipbuilding. What could be better than an alliance between our two families?"

She refrained from answering, remembering the doctor's strong admonition against upsetting her father. "Well, Papa, I'm not married to Mr. Townsend, so can you make do in the meantime with my sole expertise?"

He turned to her at last with a smile. "I know you're trying to help. All right, then, you go down to the yard and see what the men are doing. The dories should be finished up by now. They can be delivered. We need to collect the payment. There are some bills outstanding that must be paid. Others can wait. I'm sure if we explain things to the bank, to our creditors, about my being laid up, extensions will be made…"

She could see once again her father's worry building. "All right, Papa. I'll see to everything. I'll be back this afternoon to report to you. Now, can I bring you anything before I go?"

"No, thank you, dear. You've eased my mind greatly with your encouraging words about the Townsends."

She frowned. "What words?"

"You haven't married into them *yet*. Let's hope it won't be too long, eh?"

He closed his eyes, and she again bit back what she wanted to say. As much as she loved her father and would do anything for him, at the moment she felt he was building an unfair case against her. In his present condition, she couldn't fight back.

Cherish found only half the crew at work down on the shipyard.

"Well, no one knows rightly what to do. Is the yard closed for now, or does Mr. Winslow want us to keep working?" Ezra sounded unsure and apologetic as he glanced toward the schooner hull behind him. "I've tried to direct the men, but everyone's uncertain of his future."

"I understand," she told him with a reassuring smile. "Well, I have good news. Papa has put me in charge until he gets back on his feet." Before he could express his surprise, she continued in a brisker tone. "Could you please call the men together and I'll say a few words to them?"

She prayed silently for the necessary authority as she watched Ezra lumber back to the schooner and give the order. A few minutes later the group of weathered, hard-looking men stood around her.

"Good morning, gentlemen," she began, using her best boarding-school elocution, although she was trembling within. "I want to thank all of you for your patience and dedication in these few days while my father has been bedridden.

"I know there has been a lot of uncertainty, but first of all, I want to let you know that Dr. Turner says there is every chance for a good recovery for Papa, but he must have complete bed rest for a few weeks.

"In the meantime, he has put me in charge of things down here. I shall report to him every day, and he will give me the day's orders." She smiled at the assembled men's serious faces, in which she could read nothing. Before she could begin with the day's assignment, one of them asked, "What about Silas?"

She swallowed, caught short. Whatever would she say?

"When's he coming back?"

Another put in, "Where'd he go?"

The others began to mumble. She caught "Why isn't he put in charge?"

She cleared her throat. "Silas…and my father had a—a disagreement last week, but let me assure you it has all been sorted out now."

"So, when's he coming back?" the first man persisted.

She looked down at the toes of her feet. "As soon as possible." She looked up at them with a bright smile. "In the meantime, let us get to work and make sure everything proceeds on schedule. Ezra, why don't you show me what you have been doing this morning?" With that she dismissed the gathering and walked with Ezra around the hull taking shape on the stocks.

Later that morning she sat in her father's office and began opening ledgers and deciphering columns of figures. The more time she spent going over them, the more her disquiet grew. To her eye, it looked as if more was going out than coming in. She didn't dare speak to her father about it, but she needed to find out for herself just what the monthly expenses of running the shipyard came to.

How she wished Silas were there. Even the men felt lost without him. How much more did she, she wanted to tell them. But she mustn't show any sign of weakness or let on that anything was wrong.

She bowed her head over the desk and prayed for grace.

*I don't understand any of this. Why did Papa have to fall ill? Why can't Silas be here to take over in the meantime? Why doesn't Papa understand how good that would be? Why does he have such a blind spot where Silas is concerned? Why can't Papa see that Silas and I belong together?*

*Help me be strong. Oh, please, let me just talk to Silas, visit with him a little while, have his eyes look into mine, his reassuring presence near me.*

She must stop that train of thought or she'd break down again. She focused on the ledgers, although the spidery numbers and entries threatened to waver under her gaze. Before she could regain her concentration, a knock sounded on the doorpost.

"Hello, may I come in?"

"Warren!" She looked up in surprise at the handsome man peering into the shop. "What are you doing here?" She quickly rubbed at the edge of her eye with the corner of her handkerchief.

"I came to see you. I just heard about your father." He entered and came to the desk. "How is he?"

Cherish rose. "He's better, though he must still keep to his bed a while."

"Please, don't get up on my account. I wanted to tell you how sorry I was and to offer any help. Whatever my family or I can do, please let us know."

She motioned to a chair. "Please, have a seat," she told him as she retook her own. "Thank you, that's most generous of you. Everyone has been wonderful. Neighbors have brought food. People have stopped by to visit Papa."

"How did it happen?"

She looked down at the open ledger and told the same story she'd gotten used to reciting to friends and neighbors, although telling it to Warren made her once again conscious that it wasn't strictly the truth. What was it that had been taught her in Sunday school? Lying by omission. She still carried around a burden of guilt, although common sense told her she wasn't responsible.

"Papa has been working too hard. Dr. Turner says he must just slow down," she ended lamely, her mind picturing again her father's fury when he'd caught her and Silas.

Warren shook his head. "I tell my father the same thing, but he doesn't listen." An awkward silence fell between them, and Cherish had the sense he wanted to say more. Instead, he said, "Annalise sends her regards."

"Thank you. Tell her…" What? That she hoped to see her soon? That was certainly not true. "Tell her everything will be back to normal soon." Would it?

"She wanted to come with me today. Perhaps the next time."

"Yes, that would be lovely. Would you like to stay for dinner?" She glanced at her watch. "Goodness, it's about that time. I was going to go earlier to help Aunt Phoebe, but the time has flown by this morning."

"I would love to stay, if it wouldn't be too much trouble. I'd like to say hello to your father, if you think he can see me."

"He'd enjoy seeing you." Cherish's heart sank. He'd be thrilled to see her come in with Warren.

By the time Warren left, it was midafternoon. All day the

longing in Cherish to see Silas had been growing, and now as she waved goodbye to Warren, the feeling overwhelmed her.

She put on her hat and grabbed up her parasol, calling out to her aunt, "I'm going down to the village. I won't be long."

Her aunt looked up from her sewing. "All right. You've been shut in here too much these last few days. The sunshine will do you good."

Cherish fairly flew down the road, feeling as if she'd received a momentary reprieve. The day was a glorious one, the sun bleaching the sky pale blue, the apple blossoms beginning to open their pink buds, the wild strawberries creating a white carpet of blossoms on the grass. She breathed deeply of these sweet scents mixed with the ever-present tang of the sea.

Her thoughts turned to Silas. She had heard from Celia that he was working at the sardine factory! She could scarcely credit the story and hoped it was mere gossip.

Should she visit the factory or take the long walk past the village to old Tobias's place?

She smiled in greeting at the acquaintances she passed. Her footsteps slowed as she passed by the wharves and neared the last one, where the factory stood. She arrived at the weathered gray, shingled building with its tall, slim brick chimney spewing out white billowing steam. A row of seagulls sat on the ridgepole of the roof. Several men, women and children moved about, each involved in some stage of production.

The reek of fish, which permeated the whole harbor area, intensified as she neared the building. The workers eyed her warily as she approached the building. She lifted her skirts off the slimy wharf boards and opened the door.

The interior was hot and damp from the cooking vats at one end. At the near end stood long tables lined with men and boys, piles of fish in front of them. The workers wore long aprons and wielded knives, scraping the scales off the fish and cutting off their heads. She hesitated, uncertain what to do next, the heat and smell stifling. Before she could take a step, a man separated himself from the others and came toward her.

"What can I do to help you, miss?"

"I—I'm looking for…" What if her information was wrong? "For Mr. Silas van der Zee."

The man turned his head toward the tables. "Van der Zee!" he bellowed. All eyes turned to her. "You're wanted." He jerked his head in Cherish's direction when Silas looked up from his knife.

Cherish waited, her heart thudding as she met Silas's eyes. He looked at her a long second before putting down his knife and stepping back from the table.

"You've got one minute," the man told him when he neared them.

Silas nodded his head. As soon as the man had left them, Silas said, "Let's step outside."

Glancing down at his slime-coated hands and finding nowhere to wipe them, he gingerly held the door open for her.

Once outside, he dipped his bloody hands into a water-filled barrel and dried them off on a rag hanging on a nail.

He turned his full attention on her. "What's wrong?" he asked with no other greeting. "Is it your father?"

Cherish swallowed her disappointment. She shouldn't have come. She hated seeing Silas like this—a factory worker, his time totally at the mercy of someone else.

"Look, you heard the foreman. I don't have much time," he said.

"I know. I'm sorry. No, it's not Papa. He's all right."

"What is it, then?" His voice was so unfeeling, it cut Cherish to the quick.

"I—I just wanted to see you."

He looked away from her. She heard the sharp exhalation of his breath. "Well, you saw me. Are you satisfied?"

The bitterness in his tone was stronger than the revolting stench filling her nostrils.

"No." *I need you,* she longed to tell him. Her lower lip trembled, as she felt only hostility emanating from every inch of him.

"Well, you'd better get used to it. It's my new occupation… until I find something better."

"I'm sorry, Silas. I wish…I wish you could come back to the shipyard."

Something flickered in his gray eyes. "Did your father send you?"

She couldn't lie to him. "No. But the shipyard needs you."

He gave a bitter laugh. "Well, I guess it's going to have to do without me."

"Silas."

His gray eyes met hers again. When she said nothing he finally asked, "What?"

"Give me time. I know I can convince Papa to ask you back."

"I'm thinking of applying to the shipyard up in Calais. They're still building square-riggers. Maybe they'll have room for one more carpenter." She recognized that look of determination in his eyes. Nothing she could say would move him.

He wasn't going to see the despair his words filled her with. She squared her shoulders and lifted her chin. "Then I'll just have to find a way to Calais."

He shook his head. "I think you've got to wake up from your dreams and face reality."

"No, Silas. It's you who has to face reality."

"Oh, I'm facing it, all right."

She could say nothing to that.

"Go home, Cherish. Take care of your father." His tone sounded utterly weary. She hated the sound of defeat in it.

She began to back away from him. When he made no motion to detain her, she turned with a half wave of her hand. "Goodbye, Silas. I'm sorry to have bothered you."

"Cherish."

She turned hopefully.

"Is everything all right?" His tone was the old Silas's—caring, tender, soft.

*No!* she wanted to scream. "Nothing's been right since you left," she murmured, sure he couldn't distinguish her words above the sudden cry of gulls above them.

Silas watched her make her way off the wharf. His body strained to go after her. Then he caught sight of the workers eyeing him curiously. He glanced down at his filthy wet apron and clenched his fists. What could he offer her?

He thought he'd heard her say nothing had been right since he'd left. What had she meant? Were there problems at the shipyard? Was she all right? Who was overseeing things now?

Telling himself it no longer concerned him, he still stood, uncertainty warring in him as Cherish's figure grew to a tiny speck on the dusty road leading out of the village.

"Van der Zee! Get to work!"

"Yes, sir," he muttered, heading back to the building.

The tears that had been threatening the entire time Cherish had seen and talked to Silas came forth once she'd arrived home and gone up to her room. She didn't bother removing her bonnet. She didn't care about removing her pretty summer frock. She flung herself across the bed and wept.

After a while she heard someone knock.

"Cherish, that you in there?" Aunt Phoebe asked.

Cherish didn't answer, but lay with her wet cheek against the pillow.

She heard her aunt open the door and enter. She didn't look up, even when she felt her aunt stand over her. Finally she felt the bed sink beside her.

"What's happened, dear?"

"*Everything!* Oh, Aunt Phoebe, why did Papa have to fire Silas? Why can't I love him? I—I just…just went to—to see him and he acts like he ha-hates me…that it's all my fault. I feel sometimes that it is. Why can't Papa accept Silas?" She began to cry anew, hiccuping and stammering out her misery.

Her aunt listened in silence until Cherish finally fell silent. When she sat up enough to grope for her handkerchief, her aunt handed her one from her apron pocket.

Cherish blew her nose and pushed the hair from her face. She removed the hat pins from her hat and took the bonnet from her head.

"Why does Papa have to be so stubborn? I don't know what he told Silas that afternoon he called for him, but ever since then Silas acts as if he never wants to see me again. What am I going to do?" she ended, flinging her hat away.

"You've always gotten your way with your father, between smiles and tears. Neither will move him this time—even if you were allowed to use them. But as Doc Turner said, he mustn't be upset about anything."

Her aunt rose from the bed and smoothed the counterpane. "Now, I suggest you wash your face and comb your hair and begin acting like the sensible young lady you were brought up to be. I know you have it in you somewhere. If you want to do something useful, come to the kitchen and help me with supper.

"I have to go into Hatsfield tomorrow. My cousin Miriam isn't doing at all well since Patrick passed away. And with Celia's husband sick, I'll need you to see to dinner tomorrow morning. Do you think you've learned enough to manage that?"

Her aunt's words acted like a splash of cold water on her flushed face. She rose and walked over to the dresser. "Yes, Aunt Phoebe. I'll manage perfectly," she said through gritted teeth. If she'd wanted sympathy, she should have known better than to talk to her aunt.

After Aunt Phoebe left her room, however, Cherish followed her advice. With her face washed and hair brushed, she felt somewhat better. Perhaps the crying had done her good. As she gave her face a final inspection in the mirror, she suddenly squared her shoulders and lifted her chin.

She would do as Aunt Phoebe asked and prepare the finest Sunday dinner Haven's End had ever seen. She'd make her aunt proud.

And some day, no matter how long it took, she'd make Silas proud.

## ∽ Chapter Fifteen ∽

That evening, after leaving the sardine factory, Silas felt too tired to wash or eat, discouragement bowing him down more strongly than the heaviest ship's timber. He sat for a long time in the grassy meadow behind Tobias's shack.

*God, what do You want of me?* he asked. The words of Pastor McDuffie's sermon came back to him. *Present your bodies a living sacrifice.*

In the days following the sermon, the verse had stayed in his thoughts. *Present your bodies a living sacrifice, present your bodies a living sacrifice* had beaten a refrain, which matched the rhythm of his knife against the slippery, scaly sides of the fish.

After the first days of clumsily trying to grasp the tiny fish and getting frequently nicked by his knife, Silas had caught on. Though not as fast as some of the veteran workers, nor even some of the boys, at least he put in a good quota by day's end.

He couldn't escape the annoying repetition of the Bible verse. It slithered into his thoughts like the tide filling every nook and cranny of rock and mud and marsh grass.

*God, what do You want of me?* he asked again. *I'm no missionary, no eloquent speaker. I have no gifts…except to take wood and*

*shape it and mold it. It's all I know how to do. It's all I'm good for.*
He looked down at his hands. *What good is that gift now?*

That evening as he turned from emptying his dirty bathwater, his body feeling exhausted, the thought of preparing himself a meal too much to cope with, he saw Pastor McDuffie coming through the long uncut grass of the yard. He groaned inwardly. He felt too weary to fight on both the physical and spiritual fronts together.

He set the washtub back on its hook and stood, waiting.

"Good evening, young man."

"Evening, Pastor."

McDuffie came up and shook his hand firmly, his baby-blue eyes peering at him all the while. "I've missed you in church."

Silas looked away. "There've been a few changes in my life."

He nodded. "So I see. You know, usually when one's life takes a turn, either for better or worse, that's when we most need to stay close to the Lord. Many times our inclination is to do the opposite."

Silas shrugged, having no answer.

"May I come in and visit for a while?"

"I don't know if I'd recommend coming inside."

McDuffie smiled. "Where is old Tobias anyway?"

"Sleeping."

He nodded. "I haven't been by to see him in a while. The last time he shooed me off with his shotgun. The time before that he wasn't quite coherent."

"He's all right." Silas would always feel grateful to the old man, who'd offered him everything he had.

"He is." McDuffie turned away from the shack. "It's a fine evening. Why don't we just visit out here?"

"Sure." Silas looked around and finally settled on a couple of old crates. "Come on, if we set these by the water, the blackflies won't be so bad, with the breeze coming in."

Pastor McDuffie swatted at one of the tiny black gnatlike bugs with a chuckle. "Excellent suggestion." He took one of the crates.

"Watch your step. These floorboards aren't all intact."

"Thanks for the warning." McDuffie stepped over a caved-in board on the porch as he followed Silas to the meadow overlooking the cove.

"Lovely time of day, isn't it?" he asked as the two set down their crates by the cliff. With a satisfied sigh he sat down on the dirty crate as if it were a damask-silk armchair.

"I suppose so," Silas answered, observing the milky-blue sky, which melded with the silvery gray of the sea, almost obliterating the line of the horizon.

"So, young man, you want to marry Cherish Winslow?"

Silas's jaw dropped as he turned to find Pastor McDuffie's twinkling blue gaze on him.

Suddenly Silas found he couldn't answer. He turned his gaze back toward the sea. What *did* he want?

"How can I want anything? I've lost my job—my profession. Winslow forbids me to cross his path, let alone his daughter's." How could he tell McDuffie that what he wanted, more than life itself, was his own shipyard? It was a modest dream; he didn't want a large one, just a small boatbuilding yard was enough. But now that dream seemed further away than ever.

McDuffie only chuckled, which made Silas all the angrier. "It's fine to laugh. You aren't living in a stinking hovel, working in a stinking factory, getting covered with fish guts every day." He jabbed his hand through his hair. "I come home with scales everywhere, even in my hair, under my fingernails! I wash, thinking I've gotten rid of every last one of them, and I find some more."

"Why don't you come and stay with us for a while?" McDuffie's eyes had lost their twinkle, and he looked in deadly earnest.

"What?"

"Come and live with Sister McDuffie and myself until you decide what course to take."

"I—I couldn't do that."

"Why not?"

Silas was stumped. "Well, because…you've got your own family…you've got your own obligations…I'm nothing to you…." He struggled to find more reasons. The pastor sat placidly watching him. "Besides, how do you know you could trust me?" he ended bitterly.

McDuffie said simply, "You're my brother in Christ. There's no closer relation than that."

"I don't feel like your brother in Christ." Silas answered him honestly. "In fact, at the moment I don't even feel like a very good Christian."

McDuffie only chuckled. "I'm curious. What is a 'good' Christian in your book?"

Again Silas found himself at a loss for words. "I don't know," he began impatiently, rubbing his palms along his trouser legs. "Someone who does good to others, keeps the Ten Commandments, goes to church every Sunday."

McDuffie laughed out loud. Silas looked at him irritably, wondering what the big joke was about.

"How about, a good Christian is one who has accepted the atoning work of his Lord and Savior Jesus Christ on his behalf?"

The words sounded too complicated for Silas. "Look, Pastor, I don't mean any offense, but I've had a long day, and my mind doesn't seem able to think beyond fish scales and what I'm going to prepare myself for supper."

The pastor, rather than take offense, seemed in complete harmony. He reached over and patted Silas on the shoulder. "Let me ask you one thing before I leave."

Silas looked at him in suspicion. "What's that?"

"Have you ever made Jesus the Lord and Savior of your life?"

"Well, I know He's our Savior. I've gone to Sunday school all my life. I've read the Bible. I understand He was sent by God to die on the cross for the sins of mankind."

"Yes, that's true. Do you know Him as *your* Savior, Silas? Have you received Him and accepted that He's paid the price for *your* sins? Have you made Him the Lord of your life? Is

He sovereign over every decision you make? Do you commit your day to Him when you leave here in the morning and head for the factory? Do you submit to Him when you'd like to give up?"

Not giving Silas a chance to reply, the pastor rose from his crate and took it up again in his hand. "I'll leave you to your supper now. Think about what I said. The invitation to stay at the parsonage is open. Come any time of the day or night." He held out his hand, and the two men shook hands.

Silas walked back with him silently to the shack, where they set down the crates along the side of the rickety porch amidst all the variety of rusty and dilapidated objects sitting there.

"See you at church tomorrow" were the pastor's last words as he gave a final wave and turned down the grassy path.

Silas remained standing until the pastor was out of sight.

*Lord of his life?* The phrase had too uncomfortably close a ring to offering up his body as a living sacrifice.

It sounded too ominously like something that, once accepted, gave a person no maneuvering room. Silas wasn't sure it was something he wanted to think about.

Cherish blew the wisps of hair away from her face. She felt hot and sticky and dangerously close to crying again.

She bent over the chicken carcass she was filling with a cracker stuffing. Her hands were greasy from the salt pork and raw egg mixed through it. She glanced once again at the scrap of paper in her aunt's handwriting. All it said was "Stuff the chicken and put it in the oven to bake."

She drew her forearm impatiently across her forehead, driven mad by the hair that threatened to fall across it again. Wiping her hands against the apron that had started out brilliantly white that morning, she tried to think back to all the chickens she had seen Aunt Phoebe prepare for roasting. Why hadn't she paid more attention?

Oh, yes! String, that was it. She had to tie up the carcass before putting it into the oven. She rummaged in a drawer for string and a pair of scissors, then went back to work on the chicken. The kitchen clock ticked on, reminding her she hadn't much more time to tidy up before church.

"There, you'll have to do," she said to the lumpy-looking, trussed-up bird. She set it in the roasting pan and took it over to the oven.

Now for the potatoes. She'd leave them boiled and mash them when she came home from church, she decided. Then for some biscuit batter. That she felt confident of, having assisted Aunt Phoebe several times with them now.

She had peeled the potatoes and set them on the stove to boil, along with some of last winter's carrots, and was cutting butter into the flour when a knock sounded on the kitchen door.

Who on earth could be coming by so early on a Sunday morning? Jacob wouldn't knock. She glanced down at her soiled apron and flour-covered hands before calling out, "Come in!"

Silas had woken up once again with a dream about Cherish. The last image he had of her was the expression he had seen on her face when she'd stood on the wharf. A little lost but trying to be brave. What had she been trying to tell him?

He'd felt uneasy as he dressed and fixed Tobias and himself some breakfast. He regretted his harsh attitude yesterday, but the last thing he'd wanted was for her to see him there. What must the villagers, among whom he'd built a sort of reputation as a gifted shipwright, be thinking at seeing him reduced to taking work at the factory?

But the thought of Cherish wouldn't leave him, and after he'd eaten and cleaned up—as much as he could amidst the clutter—he'd set out early, intending to stop quickly at Cherish's.

He'd pay a call on her father—if Winslow would see him. He would do nothing underhanded with his daughter. He wouldn't get between Winslow and his daughter, but in passing, he could at least apologize to her.

His heart pounded through his clean, though unpressed, shirt and jacket as he entered the door into the long shed that led to the kitchen door. He knocked loudly to drown it out.

Expecting to hear Celia or Mrs. Sullivan's voice, he started when he heard Cherish call out, and he turned the knob.

The sight that greeted him took him aback. Instead of the usually tidy kitchen, it seemed as if a legion of cooks had been through it. All the countertops were filled with pots, crocks, canisters and bowls. Cherish turned startled eyes on him from the worktable in the middle of the kitchen. She looked the antithesis of her usual fashionable Sunday-morning-attired self. Her hair, in a disheveled braid down her back, had traces of flour in it. Her face looked shiny with perspiration. Her sleeves were rolled up past her elbows, and her hands were covered in white.

"Silas, what are you doing here?"

He stood in the doorway, fighting with himself. Why *had* he come?

"I—I came to see your father…to see how he's doing."

"Oh." Did she sound disappointed? She rubbed the back of her hand against her forehead and turned her attention back to the bowl before her. "He is doing better. It was nice of you to come see him," she said stiffly.

Seeing he was going to get no invitation to come in, he hesitated before stepping into the hot kitchen. He fiddled with the hat in his hand, wondering what to do next. Was she angry at him? She certainly had a right to be.

"Can I help you with anything?" he asked finally.

She looked up again, with that same startled expression. "No. I'm fine. Why don't you go up and see Papa? He's awake."

"Where's your aunt?"

"She had to see a cousin in Hatsfield whose son just passed away."

"And Celia?" he asked, glancing around the disorderly kitchen.

"Her husband is ailing."

He nodded. Just then a hissing came from the woodstove. Both turned to the noise as a pot lid began clacking against the pot and foaming water started to spill over the edge.

They sprang toward the stove. Silas reached it before Cherish, and he grabbed the pot by its handle. He let it go a second later. "Ouch!"

Cherish clutched it with a pot holder and took it off the heat. She removed the lid and replaced the pot onto the iron stove top.

"Did you burn yourself?" she asked solicitously, looking at his reddened palm.

"No, it's okay." He felt embarrassed at his stupidity. He sensed her eyes on him and finally met her gaze. He could see the amusement begin in those smoky-blue irises before the smile reached her lips. The humor touched him and he could feel the tug on his lips. Suddenly both of them were laughing.

When their laughter subsided, she wiped the edge of her eyes with the hem of her apron.

"Careful, you'll get flour in your eyes."

She realized how dusty her apron was and burst into fresh peals of laughter. He joined her as he handed her a clean handkerchief. "Tha-thank you," she gasped, this time managing to wipe her eyes dry.

"Do I have any flour on my face?" she asked when she could speak.

Before he could stop himself, he took her chin in his fingertips and examined her face closely. It was flushed, her eyes sparkling, her lips like a succulent fruit. He remembered his boyhood name for her. "Cherry." He spoke aloud without thinking.

He saw the smile die on her lips. She moved her face away and he let his hand drop. "No, you're all clean."

"Thank you," she said in a husky tone.

In the distance they could hear the church bells pealing.

Her eyes grew round. "Oh, no! I've got to get dressed and I'm still not half done here." She looked down at her soiled apron and then around at the kitchen.

"What still needs to be done?"

"I've got to make the biscuits—and—and set the table…and leave a refreshment for Papa."

He took her by the elbow and led her toward the doorway as she was speaking. "Why don't you go get dressed and I'll— I'll—" He tried to figure out how he could help. "I'll set the table and see what your father needs." He glanced at the tabletop. "I don't know if I can help you with the biscuits…."

She giggled. "I suppose I can finish them when I get back from church."

Before they parted at the dining-room door, she turned to him. "Thank you, Silas. *Thank you.*"

He only nodded, feeling his throat tighten at the grateful look in her eyes. He turned away then, remembering Winslow's words about his responsibility.

They walked to the service together, along with Jacob. Silas addressed his conversation to the older man, although he was conscious of Cherish all the while at his other side, her hand resting in the crook of his elbow.

She had gotten ready in record time, and still emerged looking as if it had taken all morning instead of ten minutes. All traces of the kitchen were gone. In their place, her skin looked like a porcelain doll's, her gown spotless and pressed, her hands in their dainty lace gloves as if they'd never been in contact with pastry dough.

He hesitated at the back of the church, intending to sit there, but Cherish tugged gently at his arm and he didn't have the will to fight her. He argued that with Jacob seated at his other side, it wouldn't appear quite so much as if he and Cherish were a couple.

When Pastor McDuffie began to preach, Silas forgot all other considerations, his attention riveted by the sermon.

"Some of you may wonder about the circumstances in your life. You may rail at God, or you may simply look up to heaven and despair, wondering why God seems so silent. What is He doing to you? you may wonder. But I'm here to tell you that God does speak to you.

"Job 33:14 tells us 'For God speaketh once, yea twice, yet man perceiveth it not.'"

The pastor continued his explanation, sometimes exhorting, other times persuasive, using verses to build his case. Suddenly something he said caused Silas to sit up.

"Is God, perchance, trying to root out the idols in your life?" He smiled around the congregation. "'Who, me? Idols? I'm not a heathen. I don't bow down to Balaam.'

"You may sit back smugly, thinking you've conquered those evils that enslave your neighbor. You don't drink, you don't smoke, you don't beat your wife, you may answer. What idols, indeed? What secret sin? We're all God-fearing people in this hamlet.

"'Little children, keep yourselves from idols,' the apostle John tells us. He was talking to the saints here, to you and me." He paused to let it sink in, and once again Silas heard the words *present your bodies a living sacrifice* ringing in his ears.

With crystal clarity it came to him. Was his love of boat-building an idol?

No! came the immediate internal cry. He refused to even consider it.

The next instant the pastor was talking about Jesus dying on the cross for each and every member of that congregation—and what had they done with that gift?

As Silas left the service, he put the notions the sermon had raised out of his head and greeted people. He thought he'd have an awkward time explaining to people why he was no longer at the shipyard and was working instead at a sardine factory, but Cherish preempted him, telling all those they greeted, as she clung to his arm, "Silas left us just before my father's attack. Little did he know how much we'd need him. But he's decided to try greener pastures, just like my cousin Henry." She looked up at him in admiration. "He's just waiting for word from Calais. Soon, I have no doubts, we'll be hearing of his innovative designs coming out of there."

Whatever people thought of this explanation, they accepted it. They could do little else before Cherish's charming, ladylike manner. Silas marveled at her social skills, expertly navigating the waters, knowing just how to bring up the subject before anyone else did and when to change it after she'd given her explanation, whether it satisfied her listeners or not.

With her airy laugh and cheery remarks, she waved goodbye to all and led the way out of the churchyard, Jacob on one side of her and Silas on the other. "Our Sunday dinner will get cold. Aunt Phoebe's away and I have three hungry men to feed, so I mustn't linger."

"I'd better get back to Tobias," Silas began when they reached the Winslow gate.

Jacob looked at him in surprise. "Ain't you stayin' for dinner, Silas?"

He looked helplessly at Jacob and then Cherish, who didn't say anything, but whose expression reminded him afresh of his dream of her. He wanted to say yes, but he knew he was putting himself in an untenable position if he did.

"You can visit some more with Papa," Cherish suggested quietly.

He nodded. "I suppose I could stay a while longer."

The three walked up the path toward the house.

Cherish immediately left them to finish her biscuits and check on her roast.

She called them about three-quarters of an hour later. The table, which he had set that morning, looked inviting. Cherish had added a bouquet of lilacs. The chicken smelled delicious. A mound of mashed potatoes in a silver dish was set beside it, with another bowl of steaming carrots farther down the table. A snowy-white linen napkin covered the biscuits. A dish of preserves added a deep crimson.

Jacob carried up a tray for Mr. Winslow, and then they sat down to eat.

"Would you say grace, Silas?" Cherish asked him.

They bowed their heads and he gave thanks for the food.

"Silas, you may carve and pass me the dishes to serve the vegetables."

He took up the silver-handled cutting knife, reminded sharply that this was Mr. Winslow's task. He felt like a usurper. He passed each plate to Cherish.

Despite the appetizing appearance of the food, the contents didn't live up to Mrs. Sullivan's table. The chicken was dry, the mashed potatoes lumpy and the biscuits hard. The carrots had a slightly scorched taste to them.

Silas said nothing, but continued eating, grateful for the change from his own fare of fried eggs, bacon and canned beans.

He heard Cherish drop her fork. "I'm sorry. I guess it's pretty awful."

"Aw, no, Miss Cherish. It's right good," Jacob piped up immediately.

She smiled sadly. "No, it isn't." She got up from the table, her plate only half-empty. "Well, I'm happy to tell you that dessert is Aunt Phoebe's. There's some pie left from yesterday. I'll bring you each a piece, if you'll excuse me."

Silas made sure he cleaned his plate, and he noticed Jacob did the same.

"Poor thing," Jacob muttered. "She's been trying to do the best she can since ol' Winslow fell ill. He's put her in charge of the shipyard, and her only a young slip of a thing." He shook his head. "Why did you leave, Silas, just when you're most needed?"

Silas swallowed down the last piece of stringy chicken meat, which threatened to stick in his throat. He coughed and took a sip of tea before answering. "I guess Winslow and I just didn't see eye to eye on some things." *One* thing.

"Well, can't you smooth things out, even if it's only till he's well enough to take over again? Though I don't know as he'll ever be able to run things the way he used to. Doc Turner thinks he's got a weak ticker and the thing could stop at any moment. The fellow could drop dead before our very eyes."

It was a sobering thought, and Silas remembered Winslow's ashy demeanor in bed that morning. Not wanting to dwell on such a thought—or what it would do to Cherish—Silas pushed back his chair and stood, his plate in his hand.

"Let me take these things out to the kitchen," he told Jacob.

Jacob, accustomed to being served at the table by women-
folk, made no move to join Silas. Silas stacked the older man's
plate atop his own and left the dining room.

The kitchen still looked as if a whirlwind had passed
through it. Cherish stood in the midst of the chaos, a neatly
ordered tray in front of her, with its pie plates and china coffeepot and matching cups and saucers. She looked up with a
rueful smile. "I hope this makes up for dinner. Although I
don't know about the coffee. I hope I didn't burn it."

"Dinner was fine," Silas said quietly. "It sure beats my cooking," he added.

She returned his smile. "If you care—or dare—to try my
cooking again, you can come anytime. You'll probably get Aunt
Phoebe's fare next time."

He cleared off the dishes and set them in the sink.

"You don't have to do that," she told him. "Go on in and have
your pie."

"I'll be right there," he answered, ignoring her request.
When he returned to the dining room and noticed her begin
to clear off the table rather than sit with them, he told her, "Sit
down. I'll help you clear after."

"Nonsense. I didn't invite you here to clean up after yourself."

"If you don't sit down, I'll get up and help you clear up
right now."

She looked at him sharply and, judging that he meant it,
took her seat. "Very well."

"This coffee is excellent," Jacob said, smacking his lips and
sitting back in his chair.

"Well, one item out of five is a start, I suppose," she replied
with a small laugh.

After dessert, while Silas and Cherish cleared the table, Jacob went up to retrieve Winslow's tray. Ignoring Cherish's pro-
tests, Silas rolled up his sleeves and poured hot water into the
dishpan to begin washing the dishes.

"Don't worry," he told her. "I'm developing quite a knack
for this."

Seeing she would get nowhere with him, she tackled the mess in the kitchen, bringing him all the bowls and pans that needed to be washed, putting away the leftover food and shaking out the tablecloth from the dining-room table. When she finally came to stand beside him, she took up a dish towel and began drying the stacked dishes.

"How are things at the boat shop?" he asked casually, swishing his rag into a cup and then dunking the soapy cup into the rinse water before setting it upside down to drain.

"All right," she answered.

He looked across at her, but she didn't meet his gaze, concentrating on polishing the glass in her hand.

"The dories delivered?"

"They're coming for them tomorrow."

He nodded and turned back to the next cup in the sink.

"The schooner?"

"I spoke to the men and Ezra will try to keep them on schedule." She set the glass on the table and took up another. "I promised Papa I'd report to him every afternoon, and he'll give me the orders for the next day." She hesitated. "I don't know how much to tell him and how much to keep back. Dr. Turner was adamant that he mustn't be disturbed."

"Look, Cherish, if I go up and see your father now, and if he agrees to it, I could stop by after my shift and help the men for a few hours on the schooner."

She met his gaze over the glass and dish towel in her hand. "Why should you do that after how Papa has treated you?"

He swallowed, realizing he would be doing it for her, and her alone. He shrugged, turning to take a pot caked with mashed potato and dunking it into the water. "I've been at the boat shop so long, I guess I find it hard to leave it all behind."

"It sure misses you."

He glanced at her again. She hadn't referred to herself. "Do you want me to talk to your father?"

After a second she gave him a tentative smile. "I'll pray for you when you go upstairs."

The word *pray* brought back reminders of church and Silas frowned.

"What's the matter?" she asked immediately.

He turned back to the pot, scrubbing at its insides. "This morning's sermon—didn't you find it a bit extreme?"

She considered. "No-o. I think Pastor McDuffie is a true man of God. I think he desires with all his heart to see his flock discipled in the things of the Lord."

Silas concentrated on the pot, dissatisfied with her answer.

"Do you feel you're doing all you're supposed to be doing when it comes to serving God?" he asked as he rinsed out the pot.

"No," she answered, humor evident in her tone. "There was a time I did. Right after Mama died and I genuinely began to seek God. He made Himself very real to me one night. I prayed with all my heart that He would show me that He was real, and I felt His presence, right in my bedroom. I knew then that He indeed was and that He'd never 'leave me nor forsake me,' as He promises us in the Bible. I also had the comfort and assurance of knowing Mama was with Him and that I'd see her again.

"It was after this that I began to take a real interest in things in church and to listen to what Pastor McDuffie preached and taught. He was new here then. I began to understand how someone could give himself heart and soul to his calling."

Silas looked at her curiously. "Why didn't you ever tell me about this?"

She shrugged, her face reddening. "I don't know. You seemed so wrapped up in things at the boatyard, and I went away to school. I found it hard to imagine that I could get you to understand. I think I was a little afraid that if you weren't impressed by what I'd experienced that it would diminish it in some way. So I kept it to myself—I only shared it with Pastor McDuffie and his wife."

"And now?"

"Now?"

"You know, are you still so…so devoted?"

She fixed her gaze on the handful of silverware she was drying. "I thought I was...until this summer, that is. This summer has taught me that somewhere I left my 'first love' and things became unbalanced in my life. I don't know how or when it started—somewhere between the rigors of boarding school, trying to shine at Cousin Penelope's social gatherings and then holding my own in Europe."

"But you're a good person. You're an example to the community. Everyone admires how you've come back such a lady." He flushed as he said the words, but she didn't seem to notice.

"Why then do I sometimes have the sneaking suspicion all my 'accomplishments' are, as Isaiah said, 'filthy rags'?"

They continued washing and drying in silence. Silas would never have supposed Cherish would have doubts about her Christian walk.

As he set the last pot facedown to dry, he said with a laugh, "I never realized what a Sunday dinner entailed for four people. I thought these dishes would never end." He glanced at the cleared-off counters and tabletops. "It seemed as if you used every dish in the pantry."

"It certainly looked liked it, especially when you first walked in this morning." Her expression fell. "So much work for such a poor result. I'm sorry for the quality of the cooking."

She stood so close he could have touched her. "Don't be. Believe me, it rated far better than what I make for myself when I come home in the evenings and face Tobias's kitchen. Compared to that, this was the best chicken and mashed potatoes I've tasted in my life. And let's not forget the coffee. You heard Jacob. Best coffee he ever drank, and he wouldn't lie to you."

"Don't, Silas, or you'll make me do something stupid like cry. It seems all I do these days." Before he could determine if she really meant that, she reached across him and took the soapy dishrag from his hand. "Give me that," she said in a no-nonsense tone, wringing out the rag. "I've got to wipe off the table."

She turned from him and began scrubbing off the worktable in the center of the kitchen.

Silas watched her vigorous movements as she leaned across the table. Something was different in her attitude toward him. Something had changed subtly, although he wasn't quite sure what it was. It was as if she had taken a step back and there was a small gulf between them. This wasn't the same girl who had teased him with her proximity, who had approached him and given herself to him fearlessly and wholeheartedly.

He tried to dismiss the sense of disappointment that hit him, and turned back to the dishpan. If she had withdrawn, it was for the best. There could be no other way.

Silas carried the dishpan out to the backyard to empty it. When he returned to the kitchen, Cherish was hanging out the towels to dry. The kitchen looked as shipshape as when Mrs. Sullivan was home.

"Your aunt Phoebe will approve," he told her.

She smiled. "I believe so. She'll be back this evening."

"Well, I guess I'll go up and see your father."

"Maybe I should go up first and tell him you're here."

"No, that's all right. I'll face him alone," he said with a slight grin.

There was understanding in her eyes. "Let me know what he says."

"Sure."

Although there was nothing more to say, neither seemed inclined to move out of the kitchen. Finally Silas took a deep breath and headed toward the opposite doorway. "If I'm not down in an hour, you can send a search party."

"I'll come myself."

They regarded each other one last time, she standing in the middle of the kitchen, he on the threshold of the dining room. He remembered his dream afresh, how much she'd needed him.

He half raised a hand. "I'll see you in a bit."

He left her nodding.

Silas knocked softly on the doorjamb. Winslow, who was sitting up in his bed, looked toward him. An expression of surprise crossed his features, but then to Silas's relief, they softened into a smile.

"Come in, Silas, come in. Draw up a chair. Come to chat with an old invalid?"

Silas set the chair beside the bed and sat down. "Hello, Mr. Winslow. I just wanted to stop by and visit a bit. I didn't have much of a chance to this morning."

"I'm glad you came by. I'm getting fed up with being cooped up in here. Old Doc Turner has confined me here like a prisoner, but he's promised if I follow his orders I may be up by the Fourth."

"I'm glad to hear it," Silas told him. "You're looking better than you did the other day."

He grinned in understanding. "Had one foot in the grave the day you saw me. I feel the Lord has spared me, but not without a warning." He tapped his chest. "We're all just a heartbeat away from death, and I don't think I'm going to forget that too easily."

"No, sir."

They fell silent. Silas didn't know how to bring up the shipyard. Would Winslow think he was after his old job? Would he think he was trying to insinuate himself into his good graces…and thereby into his daughter's? Silas didn't want anyone questioning his motives—he was questioning them too much himself. He had half a mind to say nothing and head to Calais, leaving Haven's End for good.

But something kept him rooted to the chair.

"I've had you on my mind."

Winslow's words startled Silas. "You have?"

The older man nodded. "That's why I'm glad you came by. I've been meaning to send Jacob to fetch you. Nobody has given me news of you. What have you been doing," he asked, looking away from Silas and focusing on the bedspread, "since I asked you to leave the shipyard?"

"This and that." Why didn't he tell him where he was? Shame once again stilled his tongue.

"You must have a little saved up." Winslow's tone revealed relief that things were all right with Silas.

"Yes, sir. A little."

"That's good, that's good." He worked at a thread in the bed-spread with his fingertips. "I wanted to apologize once again for...losing my temper with you the other day. I shouldn't have gone to Hatsfield to the shipyards the way I did. I told you I'd make it up to you...as soon as I'm up from this confounded bed." His hands gripped the bedclothes in fists.

"Don't upset yourself, Mr. Winslow. I told you I'm fine for now. I've got some savings, as you imagined." Silas sat forward in his chair, clearing his throat. "I—I came by today to see if you needed any help at the shipyard...just until you're up and about again."

Instead of taking offense at his suggestion, Mr. Winslow's face broke into a smile. "You don't know how relieved I am to hear you. It's precisely what I wanted to see you about."

Silas felt hope spring in his breast. "It is?"

"Yes. I know I have no right to ask you this, but would you consider coming by for a few hours a day and seeing how the men are doing on the schooner? I'd pay you for your services."

Winslow wasn't asking to take him back on a full-time ba-sis. Silas swallowed his disappointment. Wasn't this part-time arrangement precisely what he'd come to offer himself? "Yes, I'd be glad to. I'd come by after supper. You don't have to pay me," he added. He would take no more of Winslow's money. Whatever he was doing was for Cherish's sake alone.

"Oh, Silas, of course I'll pay you. You need to be earning something. You can't live on air." He gave a nervous chuckle as if all the talk of money were making him uncomfortable.

Silas cleared his throat, deciding he might as well be frank about everything. "I've gotten a job down in the harbor in the meantime, so I'm getting by all right. That's why I can't spare any time on the shipyard until the evenings."

"Yes, I understand. Where are you working, if you don't mind my asking?"

Silas felt his ears reddening. He kept his gaze fixed on Wins-low's hands, which had ceased their restless movement over the bedspread. "At the cannery."

"I see."

"It's just temporary," put in Silas hastily. "I just didn't want to use up my savings. I'm...I'm thinking of applying at the shipyard up in Calais." There, he'd voiced it aloud, committing himself to that course of action.

Winslow nodded in satisfaction. "They've got quite a big operation up there. Much bigger than ours here."

Once again Silas had to swallow a bitter sense of how little his years of service meant to Winslow. "Well, I haven't gone up there yet. I don't have a lot of free time now."

"No, of course not." Winslow coughed. "But I'll give you a good recommendation when you get ready to go." He had the grace to look embarrassed as he spoke the words.

"I won't leave until you're back on your feet."

"I appreciate that. I'd hate to lose you...but I understand." He cracked a smile. "Like my nephew Henry. You're young and ambitious...you've got talent."

The words hit Silas like a fresh blow. Winslow no longer even spoke as if he'd fired him. He seemed to have convinced himself Silas had gone of his own free will. All traces of his fourteen years of service at Winslow's Shipyard were absorbed into the past like an incoming wave onto the sand.

## ❧ Chapter Sixteen ❧

After a busy afternoon putting things to rights at the boat shop, Cherish returned to the house to a second visit from Warren Townsend.

After Cherish showed him up to her father's room, the three sat around as Tom Winslow told Warren all the particulars of his heart failure. "I've always been as strong as a horse. Just goes to show you, you never know what's around the corner." He sighed. "Makes me all the more eager to see my only child married and settled down with someone who can take better care of her than I can."

"Oh, Papa, I don't need anyone to take care of me!" she said, mortified at the turn in the conversation.

"Your father's right. It's only natural he wants to see you settled down."

"Well, for the moment I'm not going anywhere, since I'm his nurse," she said with a false laugh, wanting to steer the conversation elsewhere.

"How's your father, Warren?" her father asked.

"He's fine, sir. He wanted to come by himself, but didn't want to overwhelm you with visitors. He asked to let him know how soon he can come by to visit you himself."

"Tell him to come at his earliest convenience. I'm feeling fitter every day, and the doctor says I'll soon be sitting up in a chair, and walking around by the Fourth if I continue as I have been."

"That's wonderful news. I'm sure my father will come by tomorrow."

"You must stay for supper." He turned to Cherish. "Mustn't he? We can't let him return all the way to Hatsfield without at least a simple meal, can we, my dear?"

"No, Papa, of course not," she replied, trying to muster up her enthusiasm. She knew what her father was doing, and yet she felt less and less able to counter his maneuverings. The doctor's warnings rang too forcefully in her ears. What could she do to keep from giving Warren a false impression? She didn't want to lead him on.

Warren sat with her on the front veranda afterward.

"You know, your father is right. You need someone to look after you."

"I have my father and my aunt Phoebe. Besides, as I said, I'm too old to need looking after."

"I didn't mean to imply you couldn't look after yourself." He leaned forward in the wicker chair. "I guess I think most women your age want to settle down and have a home of their own. I know my own sister would like that."

"Forgive me if I snapped at you. I don't mean I don't want that some day. It just seems as if my father has been trying to marry me off as soon as I came home this summer."

"I understand. It reminds me of my father and all the advice he gives me about running the business."

They smiled at each other. She raised her glass of lemonade to him. "Here's to overly officious fathers—good health and long life to them."

He joined her in the toast.

"By the way, I was thinking of stopping by the boatyard to see Silas."

Oh, no. What was she going to tell him?

"My father was quite impressed with him." He looked down at his lemonade. "I know my sister was, too."

"Annalise?" she asked, her voice faltering. She had hoped absence, in this case, didn't make the heart grow fonder.

"Yes," he answered. "I know I shouldn't say anything about this. I respect her feelings, but I sense I can confide in you. She considers you a friend. I know in the short time they spent together, Annalise grew fond of Mr. van der Zee. I've never seen her form any sort of attachment to any young gentleman. She's been too much afraid of them to do so."

He cleared his throat, as if the subject embarrassed him. "I just wanted to give my sister an opportunity to meet this young man again to see if her first impressions have held. She'd never put herself forward in any way."

Cherish cringed, remembering her own behavior. She pressed her lips together, trying to figure out what to say.

"Please forgive me if I sound like some matchmaker. I've never spoken so on my sister's behalf. I was just impressed with the young man myself, and well, I love my sister…." His voice trailed off.

Her heart went out to Annalise. How could she explain to her brother that perhaps Silas's heart was not free? Even though Silas had rejected her, Cherish felt the moment had come to be honest with Warren about her own love for Silas. She cleared her throat, ready to begin.

Warren interrupted her with a chuckle. "I know my father was impressed with him. If he ever decides to leave the shipyard, he could get a job at our company. You know Father is thinking of opening his own shipyard."

Cherish stared at him, the words dying on her lips.

"Silas is no longer at Papa's shipyard," she said softly, watching Warren's reaction.

"He's not? Why ever not?"

She moistened her lips. "Papa and he had a—misunderstanding. Silas left," she ended, leaving the details deliberately vague.

"It must have been pretty serious to cause Silas to leave. Hasn't he been with your father since he apprenticed with him?"

"Yes, but Papa has never given him the credit he deserves.

He could go far…at another shipyard," she ended, watching to see if Warren would take the hint.

He nodded. "I know Father would snatch him up if he knew."

"Silas van der Zee is a fine man. Your father would be privileged to have him. And…any woman would be blessed to have his regard." She looked down at her lemonade, astonished at the calmness of her tone. They little reflected what it cost her to say the words. "He's still in Haven's End, although I don't know for how much longer. He has spoken of getting work up at the Calais shipyard."

"Well, I'm sure I should see him before he does that. Your father won't mind?"

"No, Papa has a high regard for him, despite their differences." She hesitated. How could she deny Silas the opportunity that might present itself through the Townsends? She fingered the sweat beads on her glass, deliberating. She would *not* expose Silas to Warren at the cannery. Memories of her own visit still pained her. She didn't know if Silas would be at the boat shop that evening. Would Silas be angry if she sent Warren over to see him at Tobias's?

"You may find him after supper at a little place beyond the harbor, where he is staying temporarily," she finally said, and explained the way to Tobias's shack.

When Warren left, Cherish stood, hugging herself as she looked across the lawn. The scent of lilacs drifted on the warm breeze.

How it hurt her to see Silas as he was now, his dream shattered, and know she was at fault. She hoped her words to Warren today would begin to make up for all the misfortune she had brought to Silas.

Tobias and Silas had just finished their supper when they heard a knock.

"Wonder who in tarnation is coming by now?" mumbled Tobias, rising to make his slow way to the door.

"Who're you?" he asked the tall gentleman standing at the door.

"I'm Warren Townsend. I was wondering if this is where Mr. Silas van der Zee resides."

Silas turned his head quickly from the dirty dishes in the sink. Wiping his hands on a rag, he made his way to the door.

"Hello. You're looking for me?" he asked doubtfully.

"Yes," he answered with a relieved smile, and held out his hand. "I must say, I feel I've ridden the full length of Haven's End in search of you."

"You know this young fellow?" Tobias asked.

"Yes. He's a…friend of Tom Winslow's. Warren, may I present Tobias Tibbetts?"

"Much obliged," Tobias mumbled, taking the young man's smooth hand in his gnarled brown one. "Well, I got to see about something. I'll leave you two to whatever it is you want," he added, heading out the door.

After he'd left, Silas stood awkwardly. Should he invite Townsend in, or should he step outside with him? He looked at the young man's clean, pressed suit and hesitated. Before he could decide, Warren asked, "May I come in?"

"Yes, of course."

The place looked even worse as Silas imagined it through Townsend's eyes. He followed him to the only upright chairs in the room, the ones he and Tobias had just vacated.

"Have a seat," Silas offered, then too late noticed the chair held a filthy rag dropped by Tobias.

Before Silas could remove it, Townsend picked it off the chair. Silas reached over and took it from him. "Sorry about that." He threw it atop a pile of old newspapers. "Can I offer you some coffee?"

"No, thank you."

"I heard you were no longer with Winslow," Townsend began after they both sat down.

Silas looked down at the paint-chipped table. "No."

"Miss Winslow has spoken very highly of you."

At the name Silas looked up immediately, but seeing nothing personal in the other man's reference, he averted his gaze once again.

"My father, too, had a very favorable impression of you."

"Well, I appreciate the praise, but—"

"Please don't take offense." After a moment he said, "My sister sends you her best regards."

Silas could feel the heat stealing into his face and felt immediately on the defensive. "Give her my best," he answered stiffly.

Warren cleared his throat. "She has missed you."

Silas shifted in his chair, growing more and more uncomfortable on the wooden seat. What was Townsend driving at? "Miss Townsend is a very nice person," he said quietly.

"Annalise is a very special person. You might not have been in her company long enough to appreciate this, but she is very kindhearted. She has a great sense of humor, and she has received a very good education."

"Yes, I could see that. Please give her my very best regards," he repeated, and felt foolish that he could think of nothing else to say.

Townsend gave a wry laugh. "I guess I'm here sort of as the protective older brother, trying to gauge if perhaps you reciprocate any of my sister's sentiments."

Silas looked at the other man, his mind reeling. What had been said or done by him to give this man the idea that he was interested in his sister? "Excuse me, but I think you're under a false impression. I scarcely know your sister. We met a few times. Your family was gracious enough to have me over for a weekend. I think your sister is a fine young lady—I think very highly of her—but I don't feel the kind of things I imagine a man should feel toward a woman he is thinking of courting." Did he himself know what they were? Were they the fireworks going off in his heart at the mere touch of Cherish's fingers on his skin?

"I'm sorry to hear that," Warren said. "I know my sister will be even sorrier." He stood. "Forgive my having taken up your time."

Silas waved away the apology. "There's no need to. Miss Townsend is fortunate to have a brother like you."

"I don't know about that."

Silas rose, as well. "I'm sorry you wasted your time coming all the way out here."

He grinned faintly. "I never call it a waste of time to come out to Haven's End."

Silas felt a pang, knowing what brought Townsend to Haven's End. Had he already been to see Cherish? Of course he had; how else would he have known where to find him? Silas had heard from Jacob how solicitous Warren Townsend had been since Winslow's illness, how he'd dined with the Winslow family. The knowledge was just another bitter reminder of the world Cherish belonged to.

"My father has a high regard for you," Townsend said as Silas walked him to the door. "Even though he only talked with you that weekend, he is a good judge of character and ability. He thinks you have a bright future under the right employer."

Silas said nothing.

"When he puts his eye on someone, to get them he'll give them whatever they want." His green eyes met Silas's.

"You can write your own ticket, Silas, if you ever decide your feelings for Annalise are more than just friendly. My father would set you up in your own shipyard." He paused. "I wouldn't be telling you these things if I didn't regard you highly myself. I love my sister too much."

Silas stood still. Townsend would give Silas his own shipyard in exchange for wooing and wedding his daughter.

His dream was being dangled right there before his eyes. For a crazy moment he had an inkling of what Jesus had gone through when the devil had offered Him the world if only He'd bow down and worship him, but he dismissed the image, feeling blasphemous to compare himself to the Son of God.

But the image persisted. What was the price of this tempting offer?

His soul. The word flashed quickly into his mind before he again waved away the thought.

"Did you hear me? What do you think?" Townsend asked him quietly.

Silas shook his head as if to wake himself from a dream. "Your father is very generous."

"My father would do anything for his children. My sister is very special."

"I know she is," Silas replied.

"You don't have to give me an answer right this minute."

"Mr. Townsend," he said formally, knowing the answer was going to cause pain to them both, "I'm sorry. I wish I did feel something more than respect and admiration for your sister."

"Those are noble feelings. In time they could deepen."

*Not when the image of another one is engraved on your very soul.* Aloud he said, "But not enough. Please tell your father that I appreciate his offer, but I'm fine where I am for now."

"Fine being a mere hand on a shipyard?" he asked ironically. "But you don't even have that now, do you?"

Silas's jaw tightened at the pitying look in the other man's eyes.

"My father investigates those he takes an interest in. He knows your fine reputation among builders. He's talked with people who own the ships you've labored over.

"How long do you want to keep building the ships others design? Follow orders, cut and nail and sand and paint? Don't you have a dream of putting your own ideas on paper and seeing them take shape?"

The gentleman's soft words drove into him like spikes into planks, each one hitting its mark.

"As I said, you don't have to make a decision right away." Townsend set the low bowler hat back on his head. "But don't wait too long. Once you say no, my father won't renew the offer."

Silas swallowed and nodded.

The other, as if understanding his turmoil, said, "You're a good man, Silas, an honorable one. I'll be sorry if you turn my father down. But if you do, will you do me a personal favor? Will you come by and see Annalise some day? Sort of as a goodbye? She'll never know I spoke with you," he added.

"All right."

As he watched Townsend walk down the overgrown path, he reflected on the offer just made to him.

Why now? Just when he was beginning to question whether he'd put his love of boats and boatbuilding before his love for the Lord. *Why, Lord?* his heart cried out.

He heard Townsend's words again. *You're a good man, Silas. An honorable one.*

Honorable? Good?

Or was he just a mediocre, quixotic fool?

# Chapter Seventeen

Cherish looked up when she heard a knock on the boat-shop door. She got up, curious at seeing a man's silhouette through the glass panes.

"Good afternoon," the man said, lifting his hat. "Stanley Morrow from the Hatsfield Bank."

"Come in, Mr. Morrow," she said, opening the door wider. "How can I help you?"

"I'm here to see Mr. Winslow."

"I'm sorry, but Mr. Winslow is bedridden at present." Briefly she explained what had happened.

"Oh, I'm so sorry to hear that."

"He is recuperating nicely. We hope to see him here again soon," she hastened to add. Something about the man's frozen smile and formal manner gave her a queer feeling.

"Whom, may I ask, am I addressing?" he asked her after a pause in the conversation.

"I am his daughter, Cherish Winslow."

"Pleased to meet you, Miss Winslow. Who is—" he cleared his throat softly "—in charge of the shipyard while your father is incapacitated?"

"My father is not incapacitated. I bring him reports daily."

"I see. So he is still in charge of operations here?"

"He has placed me in charge for the time being," she answered with more confidence than she felt.

"Ah." He drew out a leather portfolio. "The reason I came by from Hatsfield today was to talk about the loan your father took out from us some time past."

"A loan?"

"Yes. He needed some extra cash at that time, and we arranged for it, on the understanding of future profits, at which time he would repay the loan." As he spoke he removed some papers from the portfolio and spread them out before her. "You'll see everything here."

She looked at the documents closely. The thing that stood out was the sum of two thousand dollars and the date—June 30, 1875.

"What does this mean?" She looked up at the black-suited man.

"It means the note is due at the end of this month."

"But surely, in light of my father's illness, you can give him an extension." All the while she was thinking wildly that there was no such sum of money in her father's bank account. Already what she'd seen were expenses exceeding income and the difference was being taken out of her father's savings, which seemed meager now in light of the amount of this loan.

"A bank is not in the habit of making exceptions because of illness. If we did, we would soon be out of business ourselves." He ended with another straight-lipped smile.

"Yes. I understand."

Mr. Morrow rose. "I shall leave this with you," he said, indicating one of the papers and collecting everything else into his portfolio. "You may discuss it with your father and come in at your earliest convenience if you or your father should have any further questions. I wish you good day, Miss Winslow."

"Good day, Mr. Morrow." She spoke distractedly, going to the door and seeing him out. When he had left, she sat at the desk and pondered the paper in front of her.

What could it mean?

She had a thought, but dismissed it before it could take root. The date of the loan coincided with her trip to Europe. No, it couldn't be.

Finally she bowed her head and began to pray, asking the Lord for wisdom. What was she to do about this information that had come to her?

The next day she sat with her father a while after his breakfast. They chatted about inconsequential things as she waited to broach the subject uppermost on her mind.

"Papa?"

"Yes, dear?" he asked with a smile.

"Do you owe money to the Hatsfield Bank?"

He looked away. "Well, every business owes money somewhere."

"Yes, but do you have an outstanding loan from the bank?"

"Those aren't things for you to worry your head about. I don't want to have you down at the shipyard if it means you're going to have to be dealing with numbers and finances."

"Papa, I know something about bookkeeping. I can see from the accounts that we've been a little short lately. But, well, yesterday I had a visit from a banker. He said you also took out a loan a little more than a year ago."

Her father's fingers began to rove restlessly across the bedspread. "Yes, well, what of it? It isn't due yet. They shouldn't have come by and burdened a young lady with such things. What were they thinking? I've a good mind to write that bank and ask to have that clerk reprimanded. Did you get his name?"

"Papa, don't fret. I wouldn't have brought it up if I thought I'd upset you. Mr. Morrow said we had until the end of the month to settle this." She looked down at her hands clasped tightly in her lap. "I just thought I would get a little more information about it from you."

"It's precisely because of things like this that I find myself lying awake here at night. I can't afford to be abed right now.

I need to be out, looking for new contracts. This loan could be paid in a snap, once we get more orders in."

"I understand, Papa," she soothed.

They fell silent. After a while Cherish gathered her courage once again. "Papa, what did you need that money for?" When he said nothing, she asked, "Did it have to do with my trip to Europe?"

He looked away from her and still did not answer.

"I thought Cousin Penelope paid for my trip."

He snorted. "Cousin Penelope? Do something for someone else? I had to convince her that you'd be a companion to her, promising you'd see to her comforts, before she even agreed to act as your chaperone."

"I see." She looked back down at her hands. "You didn't have to go borrowing money to give me a trip abroad. I would have been perfectly happy staying here at home."

"Nonsense. It was part of your education, so you could enter society with your head held high."

"I would never be ashamed of who I am. I didn't need any European polish to achieve that."

"I wanted you to be able to hold your own among people like the Townsends, the Aarons, the Bradshaws and all the best families of Hatsfield. Why, look at young Warren. He's had the benefit of a Grand Tour. I want you to be able to move in their society and some day marry into them." He gave a deep, mournful sigh. "I was so hoping you and Warren would get along well enough to formalize things."

"Oh, Papa, I told you I…I like him, but he's not, I mean, he's very nice, but…" Her voice trailed off.

He smiled bitterly. "But you have your heart set on Silas van der Zee at present."

"I can't help whom I love."

He turned sad eyes on her. "You're very young, my dear. Marriage can be very difficult. When there are financial straits, things are made harder. When there are differences in upbringing and education, a person might seem very attractive when one is young, but a few years down the line, things that seemed so attractive will begin to grate. You're a bright, vivacious young lady. You've been given the advantages and privileges few girls around here ever dream of. You are curious about life, you enjoy people."

He shrugged helplessly. "Silas is a good man. He's a hard worker. He's very dedicated and talented in one area alone. And he's penniless. He has no family, no heritage. He's single-minded in his boatbuilding to the exclusion of everything else around him. I shudder to think of you shackled to him for life.

"Oh, Cherish, I've withheld nothing from you. Can't you accept my wisdom on this, this once?"

Her heart felt stretched in pain. She could understand what her father was saying. She wanted to cry out that it wasn't so. He didn't truly know Silas as she did. No better man, no truer man had she ever met. But her love for her father restrained her. There was an irrefutable logic to his words. Her father had always been the man she'd striven to please, the one whose wisdom she'd always looked up to, and now she found herself mute against his arguments.

He didn't realize how he was tearing her up inside, asking her to forget Silas and consider someone like Warren Townsend.

The sum of two thousand dollars rose before her like an insurmountable obstacle between her and happiness.

Cherish sat in church on Sunday with her aunt and Jacob. She'd looked around for Silas, but he wasn't there. She'd so hoped to catch a glimpse of him today. She would ask him to Sunday dinner to make up for the previous one. There could be no harm in that. But he was nowhere to be seen. She knew he'd begun coming to the shipyard after hours, but she hadn't been able to go down then. She had to be home helping her aunt with supper and taking care of her father.

Swallowing her disappointment that she hadn't seen Silas since last Sunday, she turned her attention to Pastor McDuffie.

"My message today addresses the most important fruit of the Holy Spirit," Pastor McDuffie began. He paused to get everyone's attention. "It is the fruit that receives the most attention at the hands of poets and artists when addressing its romantic manifestation, but few come to truly know and live God's definition of it.

"I am speaking of love. *Agape.*" Pastor McDuffie's eyes scanned the congregation and came to rest on Cherish. His gaze lingered on her, a smile on his cherubic face as if he could discern the feelings she'd harbored for Silas over the years and was now going to hold them up for public examination.

By the time Cherish left the service she felt as if she'd been examined, not by McDuffie or the congregation, but by God Himself. She'd felt His convicting power like a light thrust into her very heart, which forced her to take an unvarnished look at her comportment since she'd returned home.

She was silent over dinner, only answering questions directed to her and escaping to the kitchen to wash up as soon as it was over. Then she took up a shawl and headed toward the back door. "I'm going for a walk," she told Aunt Phoebe.

"It's not such a nice day. Might be damp with this fog."

"That's all right. I'm not going far. Just up the hill."

The hill meant the rise behind the house where the forest began. Cherish crossed the backyard, passing the sheds, barn and sprouting garden beds, and began to climb the narrow rocky pastureland that led to the forest.

She entered by a fir-needle-laden path, using the jutting rocks as footholds as she climbed upward, her spirit quieted by the scent of balsam and spruce. The path continued climbing. Cherish took a fork that led back to the edge of the trees to her favorite perch. It was a large, moss-covered boulder, with a hollow almost like a seat, which faced the land down below. From its vantage, Cherish could see the house and the road. Beyond lay the harbor surrounded by white houses with steep black roofs. The wharves jutted out into the water, the tall warehouses edging them.

The still water, what was visible through the mist, was a gray-green, the color of Silas's eyes. She could hear the foghorn sounding every few minutes.

She sat atop the granite stone, its roughness softened by the moss, drawing her knees up and pulling the shawl closer. She thought long and hard on the morning's message. She felt ashamed to call the feelings she harbored for Silas love when compared to that divine love, *agape*, which was described as "suffering long." It "was kind, it didn't envy, it didn't vaunt itself nor was puffed up."

She cringed, remembering her anger toward poor Annalise. It didn't "behave itself unseemly." Cherish huddled farther into her shawl, thinking how she had been throwing herself at Silas ever since she'd been home.

Love *sought not her own, was not easily provoked, thought no evil....*

The pastor had gone over each one of these points and drawn it all back to Christ's love for His church. He'd described the capacity of this love to endure being mocked and scourged, and to be poured out to demonstrate the Father's love.

Her own childish feelings paled in comparison and she questioned whether what she felt for Silas was indeed true love. It seemed she'd loved him so long with everything she possessed and had waited patiently for the day she'd be a woman to offer herself to him, and now she wondered whether her feelings were even worthy of being called love. Were they nothing more than a desire to have her own will above all? Had she done nothing since she'd been home but manipulate circumstances to her will? Had it taken her father's near death to make her see how far she'd grown from allowing the Lord to take charge of her life?

Her father's words came back to her. Her own girlish feelings couldn't withstand their logic and common sense. How could she know what love was? How could she know that her love would pass the test of time? Hadn't her father sacrificed all these years for love of her? Even this awful debt looming over them had been out of love for her.

*Dear Lord,* she prayed, resting her head against her knees, *forgive me. I gave myself to You a long time ago, but it seems that in these last few years I've lost touch with Your will. I've been so intent on achieving my goals—come home, prove to Father that I can form a partnership with him, prove to him that Silas should be his right hand, and show Silas my love.* She shook her head against the fabric of her gown. *Now I don't know. It all seems so petty and selfish—all me, me, me, when Your Word tells us to take up our cross and follow You. What would You have me do, Lord?*

She uttered the words with trepidation, not sure she wanted to hear the reply, but then she proceeded, knowing she couldn't turn back. *Show me Your will, Lord.* She remained silent a long time, waiting.

She kept sensing the reply, although she tried to ignore it and tell herself it was her own voice.

*Do You want me to give up Silas? God, I don't think I can do that. These feelings have been with me far too long.* Another verse came back to her. Grace. *My grace is sufficient for thee....*

She pictured an altar with Abraham laying Isaac there, and a story that had never made sense to her was suddenly filled with meaning. It didn't have to do with a sadistic god forcing a person to give to him what he loved. It had to do with trusting a God who was love itself.

She spoke the words aloud, though they came out muffled against her skirt. "Very well, Lord, I give You Silas. I lay my feelings for him on the altar. Take them, Lord, they're Yours, in Jesus' precious name."

Tears rolled down her cheeks as she felt a pain more acute than any physical pain she'd ever experienced. But she felt a release in saying the words, as if because they had been spoken aloud, with only the witness of the trees, they could not be taken back.

Silas climbed the steps to the shack's porch, feeling bone weary, a bag containing a loaf of bread and a wedge of cheese in his hand. If he hadn't felt so filthy, he would have had neither the will nor the energy to wash himself. After spending the day at the factory, he'd put in a few hours on the shipyard.

The men had been happy to see him back. He'd explained how he wasn't coming back permanently, only until Mr. Winslow was up and about again. He'd told them he was just waiting until then to pull up stakes and head for a bigger shipyard—letting them believe it was his ambition that had led to his rift with Winslow. After all, didn't Winslow himself believe it now? Maybe it was true. Maybe all along he'd wanted Winslow to give him credit and treat him as an heir apparent.

The work on the schooner had soon occupied the men and left little time for personal conversation. Even though Silas had been tired when he'd arrived on the stocks, the work had invigorated him. He'd felt like a human being again, someone worthy of something.

But now, after half-past eight in the evening, he felt he could fall asleep in his clothes, fish scales, sawdust and all. He didn't know how long he would be able to keep up this pace. He was eating poorly, and every morning before the rising of the sun he felt as if he could use a few more hours' sleep.

"Hey, there, Silas, you back?" came Tobias's slurred voice from the darkened porch.

"Yes."

"Still working at the shipyard?"

"Yes, I will be every night this week, as I told you." Since the weather had been hot and sunny, he'd filled the washtub from the well before he'd left in the morning and left it sitting in the sun. It was still tepid from the day's heat.

He began stripping off his clothes in the dusk.

"Yes, so you did," Tobias said reflectively, drawing on his cold pipe.

Silas, used to the old man's presence by now, turned his back on him and proceeded with his bathing.

"We used to wash with salt water aboard ship. Yep, and our clothes, too. They never felt clean, just stiff." He chuckled.

Silas, having heard the same thing every evening, knew no reply was necessary. After his bath he went inside to fix supper. Tobias shuffled in after a while. Theirs had become a ritual. Tobias would sit at the table, rambling on about various things, mostly events that had taken place in the past, while Silas set about preparing a simple meal. Tobias would accept whatever he served him and usually ate very little. Silas wondered what kept him alive.

Afterward, the two sat awhile, the kerosene lamp between them, and Silas listened until weariness finally overcame him and he excused himself to lie on the sofa. He drifted off to sleep to the sound of Tobias's unsteady hand pouring himself another nightcap.

"I remember sailing on the square-rigger *Emerald Seas.* She was a beauty, built right down in Belfast…sixteen hundred tons, two hundred and two feet long…Boston to 'Frisco with a cargo worth more than forty thousand dollars. She was lost in a hurricane in '49." His lips smacked after taking a sip from his bottle. "Clipper *Red Jacket*…handsomest vessel I ever laid eyes on…extreme clipper she was…"

Silas was continuously amazed at the old man's memory when it came to ship specifications, dates and sailing times. He probably had no idea what day it was, but he was a compendium of information on the sailing vessels he'd signed aboard.

As the old man went on about sailing times, ship length and beam, crews and their hard-driving captains, Silas felt a deep gloom come over him. To hear the days of Tobias's youth and manhood was to hear of the glory days of sailing ships built on the down east coast. He argued with himself that there were still good ships being built in these parts, but it was hard to compare the cargo horses of his day with those sharp-hulled, sail-laden vessels of the forties and fifties.

The next morning he rose to face the dirty dishes of the evening before, in addition to the raucous snores of Tobias lying faceup, a dirty quilt covering him, and the general dirt and decay of the one-room shack, which the evening had managed to dim.

He put on his other set of work clothes, drew up the threadbare quilt over his sofa and placed the remaining bread and cheese in his dinner pail for his noon meal. Finally he opened a can of beans and sat and ate directly from the can as he watched the sky lighten the horizon.

McDuffie's invitation came back to him again, as it had every day since the pastor had issued it. Silas didn't know why he didn't accept it. All he knew was that he'd fought the pastor's hand of friendship.

But he also knew he couldn't live the way Tobias lived much longer.

Cherish had Ezra sail her over to Hatsfield on Tuesday. June was nearly over, and she knew she must do something about the note coming due. She'd spent many a night agonizing over it. There seemed only one thing to do—go to her father's other creditors and ask for extensions on bills due, pleading her father's incapacitation. She also thought about visiting some of the other businesses and seeing what she could do about interesting them in future shipbuilding.

The Townsends came to mind, but she shied away from approaching them about business. Her father's wishes were too apparent. She wondered how much her father and Warren had discussed relations between their two families.

Several hours later she left a lumberyard. She felt only half-successful. Most of the businesses had been sympathetic when she'd told them about her father's condition. They had been generous with giving Winslow more time to pay his bills. But as far as securing more business was concerned, the well for ships seemed to have dried up. The Townsend company seemed to be the only firm interested in building new schooners for the coastal trade.

She walked along Main Street, remembering how much she used to like to come to this bustling town to shop in the emporiums and dry goods stores. She stopped before a millinery, admiring the display of new hats. She hadn't thought about her attire in an age, she realized. This morning she had dressed with care, choosing her most sober outfit, but only because she wanted to be taken seriously by the businessmen she would see.

With a sigh she turned away from the display. The day was hot. Her feet were beginning to ache, her corset to pinch and her high collar to chafe at her neck. How she longed to sail back to Haven's End. To take her hair down from its tight chignon and braid it simply down the back, to put on her old calico and perhaps spend a few hours working on the Whitehall. Ezra and Will had taken turns working on it with her, but how she missed the partnership she'd had with Silas those afternoons.

Silas took advantage of a lull in their evening conversation to tell Tobias about his decision.

"I'm moving into the parsonage tomorrow. Pastor McDuffie has invited me to live with him, until I decide where I'm going."

Tobias didn't say anything, his toothless mouth moving silently. Finally he took a swig from his bottle. "Well, good luck to you. I'll miss the chow."

"I'll be by to see you."

"Sure. Anytime. I'm always here," he said, then cackled at the observation.

"Thanks—" Silas cleared his throat. "Thanks for having me."

Tobias waved a hand groggily in the air. "Don't mention it, boy. Any time, any time." He belched, then wiped his mouth with the back of his hand. "We seamen have to help each other out. I remember back in fifty-two…" His voice rambled on and Silas tried to stifle the pity he felt for the shell of the able seaman.

Would he end up like Tobias some day, telling some young fellow about all the ships and schooners he'd built anonymously? He shook aside the gloomy thought and focused instead on his upcoming move. Maybe it would be the first step in pulling up stakes and making a truly new beginning.

## ⌘ Chapter Eighteen ⌘

The next evening Silas knocked at the door of the parsonage, seeing a light still on through the lace-covered window.

The parsonage lay across from Haven's End harbor. From its porch, Silas could see the fishing boats moored for the evening. The sky was dusk, the lights beginning to twinkle from the white clapboard houses across the harbor.

The sound of the door opening brought him back to his reason for standing there.

"Silas!" Pastor McDuffie greeted him heartily. "Come in. Let me take that for you."

Silas didn't relinquish his satchel. "I hope I'm not disturbing you so late. I've been putting in a few hours down on the shipyard after my shift at the factory. I didn't want to waste the daylight hours."

"Of course not. Come on in," he said, ushering him into the front hallway. "Look who finally came by," he told his wife, who had come into the hall.

"Hello, Silas." Mrs. McDuffie greeted him with a smile as she held out her hand to him. "Welcome. I hope this means you've decided to take my husband up on his invitation."

Silas looked down, still feeling uncomfortable with the notion. "Yes, if you're sure it's no trouble."

Mrs. McDuffie's smile deepened. "No trouble at all. Have you eaten?"

Silas was about to say yes, when she turned toward the interior of the house. "Come along. I'll make you a snack. My husband will take your bag upstairs."

He looked at the pastor. "I really should wash up first. I didn't have time after leaving the cannery."

"Certainly. Come along."

When he was cleaned up, he entered the kitchen. Mrs. McDuffie turned to him with a smile and indicated a seat. "Come, have your food."

"I'm sorry to put you to so much trouble."

"If I hear one more thing about 'trouble' I shall become seriously offended."

He pulled out the chair and sat down. Suddenly the food looked very good—a simple chicken sandwich, a dish of stewed rhubarb and a glass of milk.

He bowed his head and gave thanks, realizing he had more than just the food for which to be thankful.

Mrs. McDuffie worked on a basket of mending at the other end of the table. Silas ate hungrily, realizing how food had lost its taste for him since he had left the Winslows, but tonight it held its full savor.

Mrs. McDuffie didn't engage him in conversation, yet he felt a serenity about her presence. When he was nearly finished eating, her husband came in and sat down across from Silas.

"I'm glad you've come to stay with us, Silas," he told him. "Do you have any other plans right now?"

Silas stacked the empty bowl onto the plate and sat back on his chair. Mrs. McDuffie stood to remove the dirty dishes. Immediately Silas began to rise, but she stayed him with a light touch on his shoulder. "Sit," she told him with a soft smile.

He turned his attention back to McDuffie. "I was thinking about applying to a shipyard farther afield, Calais, or farther down the coast—Rockland or Belfast."

The pastor nodded but said nothing. When his wife came back to the table, he turned to her. "Let's pray for Silas and ask the Lord's direction for his life."

Before Silas knew what he was about, McDuffie reached across the table offering his hands to both his wife and Silas. Silas laid his own in the pastor's warm one, which immediately clasped it firmly.

"Dear Lord, We come before You by the precious blood of Your Son, Jesus. You see Silas here. You know the desires of his heart. You know his destiny, the plan You have for his life, and the call You have upon it. We ask for Your illumination and guidance for him. Clarify things for him. Grant him the 'knowledge of Your will in all wisdom and understanding.' Grant him the grace to conform to Your perfect will that he might walk worthy of You, Lord, unto 'all pleasing, being fruitful in every good work, always increasing in the knowledge of You.' We ask these things in Your dear Son's name."

Pastor McDuffie released his hand and smiled at him as if everything were already taken care of. There was nothing Silas need concern himself with further.

That night, Silas slept between lilac-scented sheets. He lay, resting his head on his hands, looking up at the ceiling, feeling clean for the first time since he began working in the factory.

He didn't understand why the pastor and his wife had put themselves out on his account. He certainly didn't feel deserving of their hospitality. He still felt a twinge of regret at having left Tobias, almost as if he'd abandoned him. But he knew it was nonsense. The old man was deep into his cups by now and would soon notice nothing around him. He decided to visit him on the weekend when he had a little more time.

Silas turned finally and buried himself in the pillow. The scent reminded him of Cherish, and he had to fight the urge to indulge in thoughts of her. He'd managed to avoid her at the shipyard and hadn't seen her since the Sunday dinner she'd prepared.

It was best this way. The recollection of their kiss would fade in time. Soon he would be moving away to a place where sailing ships were still being built. Tobias's stories had inspired him to seek a place where he could learn more about building better and faster craft.

On Sunday morning Jacob hitched up the buggy. Dr. Turner had pronounced Mr. Winslow well enough to attend church as long as he didn't walk there.

Cherish waved to him and Aunt Phoebe as they set off. Then she turned to Annalise, whom she had invited down for the weekend. Taking her by the arm, the two set off walking to the church. They had sat up the evening before in her bedroom talking a good long time. Once Annalise had asked about Silas. Cherish could tell by her demeanor that she was smitten.

Although it pained her as before, since her prayer she had felt a curious sort of release. Determined not to let jealousy get the best of her, she would see how Silas reacted to Annalise. Surely he would be in church this Sunday!

He was not only in church, but he was acting as usher. Cherish's eyes widened as she saw him escort an elderly couple to their pew.

"Good morning, Cherish," McDuffie greeted her cheerfully. "Whom have you brought along with you?"

"Good morning, Pastor McDuffie. This is my friend Annalise Townsend from Hatsfield. She has come to spend the weekend with me."

"Welcome, Miss Townsend." Pastor McDuffie shook her hand.

"Is Silas ushering?" Cherish ventured before the pastor had a chance to move on to greet others.

"Yes, indeed. I asked him to this morning." Seeing her gaze following him, he added, "He's come to stay with Mrs. McDuffie and myself."

"He has?" she asked in surprise. Then she smiled. "I'm so glad."

"Yes, I thought you might be. We invited him a while ago, but he didn't accept the invitation until the other night. He seems to have grown fond of old Tobias. He even went out to see him yesterday."

Cherish nodded, her gaze going back to Silas. Yes, Silas would do that, she thought, all the love she thought she'd settled into the deep recesses of her heart welling up once again, threatening to overwhelm her reason.

"Why don't you stop by the parsonage this afternoon for a visit? We haven't seen you for a while. Come have a good chat with Carrie."

"Yes, I should love to," Cherish answered with a smile. "Annalise has made Silas's acquaintance, and it will be nice for her to see him again, as well."

The two turned to Annalise, who began to blush furiously. Cherish, taking pity on her, took her by the arm. "We'd best find our seats. Papa is already in the pew. We shall see you this afternoon, then."

"So long," McDuffie said with a smile.

As they sat through the service, Cherish didn't get a chance to see Silas. The church was full, and she surmised he must be at the back. She saw him once again when the collection was taken up. He passed the plate down their half of the pews. Cherish's glance crossed his when he came to their row, although they were too far apart for either of them to say anything to each other. She noticed his glance going to Annalise, and she wondered what he thought of seeing her again.

Was there any chance he might come to care for Annalise?

Her mind went back to the verses she'd been reading every day since giving her love over to the Lord. Charity bears all things. Would she be able to bear it if Silas fell in love with Annalise? She remembered Warren's words. Perhaps Silas's future lay with the Townsends.

Could Cherish think more highly of Annalise than she did of herself, as her Lord commanded her to?

She prayed for His grace, remembering what Jesus had promised: My grace is sufficient for thee. If Jesus had said it, it must be so. She must receive it by faith.

In the afternoon Cherish and Annalise rode to the parsonage on the other side of the bay. Hoping to see Silas, and yet fearing the encounter, Cherish got down from the buggy and relinquished the reins to Pastor McDuffie.

"Glad you could stop by. Carrie is out on the back veranda. Come along."

Cherish had to bite back her desire to ask where Silas was. She breathed a sigh of relief when she saw him sitting on the veranda steps playing cat's cradle with Janey.

"Hello, Cherish, Annalise," Mrs. McDuffie greeted them.

"Hello, Silas." Cherish turned to him as he rose.

"Hello, Cherish," he answered. "Good to see you again, Annalise."

Cherish looked from one to another, but she could read nothing from Silas's features, although Annalise was looking as if she'd met her hero in person.

They took the wicker chairs, and Silas went back to his seat with Janey. Cherish felt a pang hearing the murmur of their two voices, remembering herself at Janey's age when she'd first met Silas. He had always been patient and kind with her.

She sighed and turned her attention to the conversation between the McDuffies and Annalise. The day was beautiful. She gazed at the garden, which was full of blooming lilacs and purple lupines and pink phlox.

Her glance strayed to Silas, although she'd fought the urge to do so countless times. He was watching her, but immediately turned his attention back to the string in Janey's hand.

Why hadn't he come by the house at all? She knew he came to the shipyard in the evenings and his contribution was evident, not only in the work on the schooner but also in the uplifted spirits of the workmen. They seemed to have a renewed confidence in the operation of the shipyard since he'd been back.

The burden of the debt weighed upon her. Its weight would come upon her in sudden bursts, when she'd thought she'd managed to put it out of her mind. She still had no idea what to do.

"Let me get some refreshment," Mrs. McDuffie said.

Cherish got up. "I'll help you. No, you stay here," she quickly reassured Annalise. "Why don't you show her around,

Silas?" she suggested on impulse. "You two must have some catching up to do." She turned to the pastor. "They were dance partners a few weeks back at my house," she explained with a smile. Pastor McDuffie merely raised an eyebrow.

She hurried after Mrs. McDuffie before either of them could refuse her suggestion, not quite sure why she had made it. She certainly didn't want them to advance their acquaintance. Why had she made such a silly suggestion, then? Another ugly thought entered her mind. Was she trying to prove how saintly she was?

In the kitchen Cherish peered out the lace curtain at Silas walking around the garden, Janey skipping along on one side and Annalise walking more sedately on his other side.

They could have been a married couple with their child beside them. Cherish's hand twisted the edge of the curtain.

"They make a nice couple, don't they?" she blurted out when Carrie McDuffie came to stand by her a moment.

"Yes," she ventured slowly. "Excuse me if I'm prying, but I was under the impression you cared about Silas and he about you. Has something changed?"

Cherish looked down. "Yes. I'm letting him go, I suppose." She looked up with a sad smile. "What I mean is I'm giving up my dream of having him. I guess the Lord helped me see how obsessed I was becoming with the notion."

Carrie touched her cheek. "Praise the Lord, then. Don't worry, if it's of God, you and Silas will be together."

"I don't think so." Her gaze followed the couple in the garden. "It's becoming less and less likely."

"Is that why you brought your friend out to visit? Is she a sort of consolation prize for Silas?"

Her eyes turned to Carrie in shock. But seeing only sympathy, she tried to explain. "No. I think Annalise is sweet on him. And for a while I even thought Silas might like her, too. Now I don't know. Maybe I was hoping to see today. I don't know," she ended miserably.

"It's not for us to play matchmaker. I think that's more safely left in God's hands," Carrie told her gently.

"But Silas—he's so reserved. He might miss an opportunity. He certainly doesn't want me. He's made it very clear." She couldn't help the bitterness creeping into her tone and was instantly ashamed of it. "Besides, the Townsends think highly of Silas. Think of the future he'd have with them."

Carrie's hand rested on her belly a moment and a look of wonder crossed her face.

"What is it?" Cherish asked. "Are you all right?"

Carrie didn't speak for a few seconds, then she smiled. "Yes, I'm fine. It was just the first time I've felt him move."

"Felt him move?" What was she talking about? Cherish looked down at the soft mound of Carrie's abdomen.

"The baby." At Cherish's look of amazement, Carrie laughed. "Come, feel." She took Cherish's hand and placed it over her apron.

Cherish could feel nothing, and felt awkward with her hand on Carrie. But suddenly there was a shifting under her palm. Her eyes widened and she smiled. "Yes! I felt the baby!"

"Now, Cherish," Carrie said, taking up the thread of their previous conversation, her voice brisker, "don't fret about Silas. It's not for you to try to figure out his future for him. Give him time to find his own way. Give your father time to see the kind of man he is."

"He's had fourteen years!" she cried in anguish, turning back for a last look at Silas. "And he's dead set against anything between Silas and me. And now—and now—" She wrung her hands, thinking of the debt that hung over Winslow's Shipyard.

"Now what?" Carrie asked.

Too ashamed to mention the financial situation, Cherish looked down. "Nothing. It just seems more hopeless than ever."

Carrie enfolded her in her arms. "You know what I suggest?"

"No, what?" she asked, her voice muffled against Carrie's shoulder.

"That you go out there and join those two instead of trying to throw them together. Be Silas's friend as you always have, and be Annalise's friend."

"What if they don't want me?"

"Oh," she crooned, a smile in her voice, "remember Who you have living on the inside of you. If Silas doesn't love you in the way you dream about, he still cares for you very much. Otherwise he wouldn't be trekking over there to the shipyard every evening after putting in a hard day at the cannery."

Cherish acknowledged the truth of what the pastor's wife was saying and felt doubly ashamed. Had she ever done anything like that for Silas?

As if reading her thoughts, Carrie told her, "Just love him with the love of the Lord, and you'll find fulfillment beyond anything you ever imagined."

Cherish straightened. "Yes, you're right. The Lord has been showing me that. Thank you for reminding me."

"Now, go."

When she came back outside, Silas and Annalise were returning from their stroll around the garden. Cherish, feeling nervous, walked down the steps to meet them. She felt Silas's gaze on her, and she met it squarely. She turned to Annalise, who had her eyes upon Silas. Cherish took hold of a lilac spray at the edge of the veranda and inhaled deeply. "I think this is my favorite scent."

Silas reached over, broke it off and presented it to her. "It smells like you."

She took the branch from him and brought it to her nostrils. "Does it?" In that instant it was as if the two of them were alone in the garden. Annalise ceased to exist; Pastor McDuffie's voice behind her faded away. She wanted to reach out and touch Silas's brow and brush back the shock of hair. Instead she gave him a wobbly smile and looked down at the flowers held to her nose.

At the end of his shift Silas left the cannery, took the small skiff he'd left tied to the wharf and rowed back across the harbor to the parsonage. The McDuffies had insisted he return there first, wash and eat supper before putting in his time at the shipyard.

When he entered the parsonage kitchen, Mrs. McDuffie greeted him from the stove. "Hello, there. Your bathwater is ready." Before he could react, she had stooped and was dragging the full tub forward.

He moved immediately. "You shouldn't be doing that."

She straightened and pushed the damp tendrils away from her face. "You and Arlo are the same, thinking I'm a fragile butterfly."

"I hope you didn't go and fill this tub by yourself."

She smiled. "Put your worries at rest. Arlo did it for me. Now I'll leave you to your bath. I've laid out your clean clothes there." She indicated the neatly draped clothes over the chair back. "Leave your dirty ones here. I'll wash them out later. We'll eat supper when you're ready."

Before he could argue with her, she was gone. As he sat in the tin tub, he reflected on what had just happened. The pastor had prepared a bath for him; his wife had washed and pressed his clothes and had an appetizing dinner ready at his convenience.

He finished his bath, dressed and combed his hair—Mrs. McDuffie had even laid out his comb and handkerchief for him. He emptied out the dirty bathwater in the yard. Then he called Mrs. McDuffie back into the kitchen.

"You smell good, Silas," Janey told him, coming over to stand beside him.

"Thank you."

"Will you play with me?"

"First let me see what I can do to help your mother."

"Janey will set the table for us," her mother told them. "Supper is just about ready. Why don't you call Arlo in?"

"Where is he?"

She laughed. "Oh, at this time most likely you'll find him down on the beach."

Silas walked across the lawn, past the barn and outbuildings, to the crushed-clamshell path leading to the pebbly beach. This side of the yard looked seaward. The open surf washed up pieces of driftwood, old buoys and broken lobster pots onto the dark, slate-colored stones. He spied the pastor down the narrow stretch of beach. His hands folded behind his back, he was pacing up and down, talking to himself in a loud voice.

Silas began walking toward him, hoping he'd be spotted and not embarrass the pastor in his soliloquy.

His wish was not granted. As he neared McDuffie, the pastor still had his back to him. His speech had turned to lusty singing.

"'A mighty fortress is our God…'"

Just then he turned, and the words died on his lips. His mouth broke into a smile, and he didn't seem at all disconcerted at finding Silas there.

"Good evening, Silas."

"I didn't mean to interrupt you."

"You're no interruption." He turned and stood facing the surf. "Beautiful day, isn't it? He has truly given us 'His wonders to behold,' wouldn't you say?"

When Silas didn't answer, he continued. "This is where I come to talk with God—worship Him, give Him thanks—"

"Do you ever…get mad at God?" The words were out before he could stop them.

McDuffie only smiled. "Oh, yes. I've had my times of railing against circumstances. I don't always like what the Lord shows me—least of all about myself. I don't always want to do what He wants me to do."

Silas gazed at his calm face. "What do you do at those times?"

"After haranguing and arguing, you mean? Oh, the Lord lets me get it out of my system. And then His presence is there—still, unsearchable, uncompromising, steady.

"I'm always reminded of the words He gave His servant Job. 'Who is this that darkeneth counsel by words without knowledge? Gird up now thy loins like a man.'" He turned his face to Silas. "You know what never ceases to amaze me?"

Silas shook his head.

"He never recognized Job's right to self-pity." McDuffie leaned down, picked up a smooth stone and threw it into the sea. "Yet we humans would love nothing better than to wallow in it. That and bitterness—twin evils, I call them."

"I can't imagine you indulging in self-pity."

He gestured with his head upward. "He wouldn't permit it. There's too much work to be done. You know I came here to Haven's End a young man on fire for God and found myself in a spiritual wasteland, you might say, as stagnant as a marsh. People here, although good, God-fearing folk, wouldn't move. They didn't want any more of God than they already had, thank you very much. They'd receive my Sunday sermon, the Sunday-school lesson, read the sermon in the paper on Sunday afternoon, and that was it until the following Sunday.

"I would exhort them. They could have so much more of the fullness of God, to walk in that 'life more abundantly' that Jesus promised us, to receive the 'inner court' blessings, to enter in the Holiest of Holies!" His voice had risen, his demeanor reflecting all the enthusiasm he felt. He broke off with a smile. "Be careful or you'll have me preaching.

"I suppose you've been sent to call me in to supper."

"Yes."

"Come, then," he said, directing him back to the house.

"How did you reconcile your situation here?" asked Silas, feeling curious after seeing the fire, now banked, in McDuffie, and realizing it was not present just during Sunday sermons.

"I spent many hours down here, pounding the sand, you might say," he said. "Eventually the Lord showed me that if I could reach—truly reach—one or two individuals during a period, I should count myself blessed indeed."

"What do you mean, truly reach? Are all the rest of us sinners?"

Pastor McDuffie took his question seriously.

"To truly reach someone is to have the chance to disciple that individual, to watch him grow into the deeper truths of the Word. To go from the milk to the meat of the Word." He shook his head thoughtfully. "After all, how many did our Lord choose out as disciples but twelve?"

As they neared the farmhouse, McDuffie said, "Cherish was one of those the Lord gave me. How hungry she was to know God," he recalled. "She'd devour the Scriptures."

"You speak in the past tense," Silas observed.

"So I do. The truth is she's been away quite a bit since those days. I've been remiss since she's come home, busy with so many things that I've had little time to talk with her and find out the state of her spirit. Carrie has been after me about it. I know it's been difficult for Cherish these last couple of weeks with her father's illness. Sometimes the good Lord allows certain things we might perceive as calamities to remind us of Who He is and what our real purpose on this earth is."

As they washed their hands at the pump, McDuffie began talking about how he and his wife met. "Carrie was the daughter of one of my professors at seminary. A great man of God, he was. He went to his final homecoming a few years back.

"Carrie and I fancied each other from the first time we met, and we sought the Lord's will for our future. He confirmed it more than once that she and I were to be man and wife."

When Silas made no comment, McDuffie turned to him as they entered the kitchen door. "It's a great comfort to a man, you know, to have a helpmate. God gave us each a partner, and there's no closer relationship than that between a man and woman. He has made us one when we're joined by Him."

Silas followed him to the table, wondering at his words. Did he guess what was in Silas's heart? As Silas watched Pastor McDuffie and his wife at the table, listened to their conversation, observed their understanding and their interaction with their daughter, he felt a pang of envy.

There was only one woman with whom he could imagine such a union as the pastor spoke of. That woman was denied to him.

## ✦ Chapter Nineteen ✦

Silas stood at the kitchen door to the Winslow house. He told himself he was going to see Winslow and report on the progress of the schooner. He swallowed his disappointment when Aunt Phoebe answered his knock on the door.

"Oh, it's you, Silas. I've missed you so. Come in, don't stand there." Mrs. Sullivan shooed him inside. "I hear you're at Pastor McDuffie's."

"Yes, they invited me to stay a while."

"I'm glad. They're good people." She gave him a look of understanding. "I wish…well, it doesn't much matter what I wish. I'm just sorry you're not here anymore."

"Thank you, Mrs. Sullivan."

"Well, I assume you've come to see Cherish or Tom. They're both up in his bedroom. Why don't you go on up?"

Silas took the stairs slowly, wondering whether he shouldn't just turn back. He didn't know how Mr. Winslow would react if he just showed up when Cherish was there with him.

At Mr. Winslow's bedroom he hesitated again. The door was closed, although not quite all the way. He heard Cherish's voice coming through. He stopped, his hand lifted to knock.

"Why is the sum so large?" he heard Cherish ask her father.

"Your trip abroad came at a bad time at the shipyard. Things had been slowing gradually, and I kept telling myself all it would take was one good month and I'd pay everything off."

Silas knew he should back away, but he stood motionless.

"Why would the bank lend you such a sum knowing how things were? Didn't they want to be paid back?"

"As long as I had the collateral, they were willing to advance me the money."

"The collateral?"

"I put up the shipyard as a guarantee."

"You mean…if you couldn't pay back the loan, they could take the shipyard?"

"But I knew that would never happen! I mean…since you came home and I saw how well you and Warren Townsend were getting along, I just hoped…well, if the two of you should decide on formalizing things, there would be no problem. Old Townsend could have an interest in the shipyard."

"Oh, Papa." Cherish's voice sounded defeated, as if she had been over this argument before. "Is that why you've been pushing me to be friends with Warren?"

"Of course not! It's just you two seem so right for each other. I really wish you'd give him a chance, for my sake."

Their voices grew lower and Silas turned around then, one thought uppermost in his mind—to get away before either of them knew he had overheard their conversation.

He let himself out of the now deserted kitchen and walked briskly toward the boat shop. He went immediately to work with the other men on the interior hull of the schooner. They were now laying the decks and caulking the hull.

After he'd worked for more than an hour, he felt calm enough in his thoughts to know how to proceed. He made up his mind to go back and visit Winslow, alone, and find out exactly the sum of money he owed.

This time it was Cherish who opened the front door to him. He knew that probably no one would be in the kitchen at that hour, so he had walked up to the front veranda this time.

Now he wished Mrs. Sullivan had answered his knock.

"Silas! Good evening." Cherish opened the door wider. "Won't you come in? Is something the matter?"

He stepped into the corridor as Cherish closed the door behind him. "I don't want to let the june bugs in," she said with a nervous laugh as they turned to each other.

He peered at her face. It looked pale. Her eyes, their pupils wide, looked dark. His dream came back to him, and he realized he should have heeded it. If he hadn't been so busy lately with his own misery, he would have discerned sooner the changes in her manner toward him. But he realized, looking at her now, watching her hands knot in front of her, that she was indeed uneasy around him.

Did it have to do with her father's heart attack? Or with the financial situation?

He cleared his throat. "I came by to see your father. I hope it's not too late in the evening."

"No, he's still up. He'd like a visitor, I'm sure. Come, I'll take you up."

She made no effort to make small talk with him, and he didn't know whether to be relieved or disappointed. He followed her silently up the stairs he'd just recently descended.

"Papa, look who's here to visit you."

"Oh, Silas, good evening. Come on in."

"Can I get you anything?" Cherish asked him, and he felt a pang at the formality of her tone, as if he were a guest and she the mistress inquiring politely.

"No, thank you," he said, holding his hat in his hands.

"Well, have a seat, Silas, and tell me about the schooner."

Cherish excused herself and closed the door behind her.

After talking about the activities down on the stocks, Silas fell silent, wondering how to bring up what was uppermost in his mind.

"Mr. Winslow?"

"Yes, what is it?"

He cleared his throat. There was no help for it but to plunge in. "Is it true you owe some money to the bank?"

He could see the other man's immediate agitation in the way his hands moved over the bedcovers. "Who told you about that?"

Silas cleared his throat again. "I just overheard something. I don't mean to pry, but I thought maybe…there was something I could do…help in some way." He leaned forward, regretting already that he'd come. What could he do?

But Winslow, rather than be offended or find it humorous, patted his hand. "I appreciate your concern, my boy." He sighed deeply, leaning his head back against his pillows. "I guess I've made quite a mess of things."

"How much do you owe?"

"Two thousand dollars," he said, giving him a sidelong glance that said more eloquently than words that such a quantity was beyond Silas's noble offer of help.

The words reverberated in Silas's mind. It was an enormous sum. He didn't know anyone in Haven's End who could easily lay hands on that amount.

"When is it due?" he finally asked.

"End of the month," Winslow said with a twist of his lips. End of the month? That left scarcely a week more.

When he left Winslow's house, he scarcely noticed his walk home. All he could think of was the sum of two thousand dollars. What was Winslow to do? What would become of the boatyard? What would become of Cherish?

Cherish spent the next day pondering her course of action. Since the night before with her father, she knew she must face what must be done.

She slumped over the papers in front of her on her father's desk. The numbers, no matter how many times added, continued to tell her the same thing—there simply was not enough money coming in.

Her head snapped up at the sound of the door.

"Hello, Cherish. What are you looking so dejected about?"

"Oh, nothing!" she answered immediately, and put on her brightest smile. "Hello, Warren. What brings you to Haven's End?"

"I thought I'd come see you in your place of employment this time. I'll ride over to see your father in a little while."

She smiled. "Well, here you see me."

He took a seat across the desk from her and she admired once again what a good-looking gentleman he was. He was wearing a lightweight tweed jacket and fawn-colored trousers.

They chatted a while about things in Hatsfield.

"Cherish." Warren's gentle tones made her raise her eyes.

"Yes?"

"We've been seeing each other quite a few weeks now. I'd say we get along pretty well, wouldn't you?"

"Yes, we do." Oh, no, she thought, it couldn't be. Was he going to? Suddenly she found she wasn't prepared for the thing she'd been thinking about so much. What would she say?

He leaned forward in his chair and gave a small cough into his hand. Then he looked earnestly at her. "Would you ever consider…that is, would you do me the honor of…becoming my wife?"

She found she didn't know what to say. She should be honored, relieved. This is what her father wanted. This would solve everything. Warren was the most eligible bachelor in the county, and here she sat mute as a mouse.

He gave a rueful smile. "You don't have to look so astonished. Does this come as a complete surprise?"

She had to smile at that. "No, not if I'm completely honest." She became serious. "Warren, you've flattered me deeply with your proposal."

"Why do I hear a 'but' coming?"

She blushed, again wishing…

"You don't have to give me an answer today."

She would almost say he looked relieved. Was Warren truly in love with her?

"I—I'll think about it," she promised him.

She invited him to dinner, and the conversation turned to other things. Gradually she was able to relax again in his company and almost forget the proposal she'd just received. Warren seemed in no hurry for an answer.

She felt as if she'd been given a reprieve. Even though the June 30 deadline loomed.

Silas took out his sailboat at twilight, needing a place to think. He left the harbor behind and sailed beyond the last point of land, beyond the small islands skirting the coast, until he came to a large bay. It was past eight o'clock and the sky was still light, although the sun was sinking low.

The sails luffed as the wind suddenly stilled, then they, too, fell silent. The sea was a perfectly calm expanse. He looked toward the horizon of sea and sky. It came to him that God's grace was something like that—a vast, incalculable gift.

Pastor McDuffie had told him, "You've treated Winslow better than he's deserved. You did this for his daughter's sake, didn't you?"

Silas hadn't been able to deny that, although he hadn't said anything in reply.

"What if you did it for love of Jesus?" the pastor had challenged him, explaining to him about being a blessing to Winslow. "'Therefore if thine enemy hunger, feed him; if he thirst, give him drink.'"

Silas remembered the sermon about offering his body a living sacrifice. He had gone back and read the verse in his Bible. "I beseech you therefore, brethren, by the mercies of God, that ye present your bodies a living sacrifice, holy, acceptable unto God, which is your reasonable service." The words that had sounded so extreme to him when he'd first heard them from the pulpit now jolted him by their last five words. *Which is your reasonable service.* What God was asking was something He considered merely reasonable.

Silas thought of the piles of bills and coins hidden away in his old room above the boat shop.

He had it in his power to hand it all over to Winslow.

He could give up his dream. All those years of working and saving. Had they been in vain? Had he been fooling himself? Was the day of the sailing ship over? Silas spied the Eastport steamer trudging past him on the far horizon on its way south to Portland. Had he been born twenty years too late? Is that what shipbuilding was becoming—turning out big, ugly, barge-like vessels? He was a man of wood and sail. Would there be no place for him and his craft in this world?

When the steamer had disappeared and everything lay once again still and calm, his thoughts turned to Cherish.

It would be easy to hand over his life's savings to Winslow if he thought of it as a gift to Cherish. It came to him that he would give his life for Cherish. The fact sank in as he realized how much he loved her. Without her, the money meant nothing.

He turned his face westward toward the coastline. The sun was a fiery phosphorescent orange ball, only half visible, the other half already below the hilly line of trees.

Suddenly a still, small voice came to him. Would he give his life for his Savior?

*Your reasonable service.*

Is that what his Christian service came to—giving up his life for his Savior?

He thought long and hard about his Christian walk. He'd always gone to church because he was made to; he'd brought his offerings, he'd tried to do right by his fellow man—look how he'd submitted to Winslow. Wasn't all that enough?

Suddenly all those efforts seemed just that—efforts. Not things done out of love, but obligations fulfilled in order to feel right. He'd satisfied Pastor McDuffie with his Sunday attendance; he'd satisfied Cherish by accompanying her to choir practice; he'd satisfied his employer and Mrs. Sullivan by living a clean, upright life.

In that moment all his service appeared "as filthy rags," as Cherish had remarked. What was it Jesus had called the Pharisees? Whitewashed sepulchres? Silas found himself comparing himself to them. He'd always listened to those Sunday-school lessons and thought how hypocritical those Pharisees were with their external worship. They were the ones who'd ended up crucifying Jesus.

Silas saw himself covered with the same filth—his behavior outwardly holy, when his heart had never been engaged.

He stared at the skyline where the sun had sunk and dusk was beginning to penetrate. *But who are You, Lord? How do I get to know You?*

When he returned to the parsonage, he asked Pastor McDuffie where he should begin reading his Bible. McDuffie showed no surprise at the question, but immediately turned to the book of John and handed the Bible back to him.

"In the beginning was the Word, and the Word was with God, and the Word was God...."

The following night after dinner Tom Winslow told Cherish he wanted to talk to her. She looked across the table in alarm. "Is something wrong, Papa?"

"No. In fact, it's good news I want to share with you."

What could it be? She rose from the table and began to help Aunt Phoebe clear the dishes.

"You go on with your father. It's important."

More and more intrigued, Cherish followed her father to his large cherrywood desk.

Her father handed her a bulky envelope. He waited as she turned it over, trying to figure out what it contained.

"Fifteen hundred dollars," he told her. "Open it and see."

She undid the clasp. She could hear the sound of coins rattling inside, but still couldn't help gasping when she peeked inside. A thick pile of bills was stuffed into it, with gold and silver coins jammed in alongside.

"That should satisfy the bank to give us an extension at least until we can get the final five hundred."

"Fifteen hundred dollars? How, Papa, how?"

"A friend has given me twelve hundred, and your aunt Phoebe put in her nest egg of three hundred."

Cherish could feel the tears welling in her eyes. Dear Aunt Phoebe. She had to concentrate to catch the rest of what her father was saying.

"He's given me all the time I need to repay him. Didn't even *want* to be repaid, except that I insisted, of course."

"But who, Papa? Who has that kind of money?"

"No need to trouble yourself about that. Just trust me that it's all right." Her father turned to the papers on his desk as if anxious to get on to something else. "We'll figure out a way to get the final five hundred. We'll take it from the earnings from the schooner. It's nearing completion." He rubbed his chin. "Perhaps I could put a bug into Warren Townsend's ear. His father sits on the bank board…."

"Oh, Papa, no!" She'd die of shame to think they were begging favors of him. And she'd feel under further obligation.

"Don't worry, my dear. I know how to do it. You needn't fret."

Cherish left her father's presence in a daze. The sudden lifting of her heaviest burden left her thoroughly confused. Who could have given her father such a sum? She had never beheld such a vast quantity of money. It was true her father had many friends and many who admired him in the business community. They had all been to see him since he'd suffered his collapse. Could he have spoken of his troubles to one of them?

Cherish still found it hard to accept. If her father hadn't told her until forced to, what would compel him to confide in someone else? Could it have been to ease her mind? She conceded that most likely that was the motive.

She went up to her room, knelt by her bed and thanked God for the reprieve. It was true that the debt still remained, no matter what her father had said about the mysterious benefactor giving them all the time needed to repay it. It was true they were still five hundred dollars short. But for the moment, all Cherish could feel was relief and gratitude.

Most of all, she felt an overwhelming lifting of a burden. She would be able to turn Warren down in good conscience.

Warren Townsend sat across the desk from his father.

"You've been going over to Haven's End quite a bit recently. Still interested in the Winslow girl?"

He reddened, not liking the direct way his father put it. "I've been by to see her father."

"How's he doing?"

"He's on the mend. The doctor warns him he can't put any stress on his heart."

"His days of running the shipyard are over."

"I don't know. His daughter has been managing quite capably in the interim."

The older Townsend snorted. "I'm sure she won't be able to weather things in a few days."

"Why is that?" He didn't like it when his father got that knowing tone.

"Winslow's Shipyard owes quite a tidy sum to Hatsfield Bank. The note comes due tomorrow."

"How did you find that out?" he asked to hide his shock, although he shouldn't have been surprised. His father made it his business to find out what went on at the bank.

"I don't sit on their board of directors for nothing." He eased back in his chair and crossed the legs of his pressed trousers. "The timing couldn't be better. I've had my eye on that shipyard for some time. Now that we've acquired the sawmill, and we have the emporium going, what's more natural than to supply our companies with their own fleet of schooners?"

"Is that why you encouraged my friendship with Miss Winslow?" Warren asked, although again he knew the answer before it came.

His father shrugged, looking at the ends of his buffed nails. "She's a pretty gal, smart by the sounds of it. Winslow's given her every advantage. Do you fancy her?"

Warren felt uncomfortable under his father's direct scrutiny. Did he fancy Cherish? He admired her, respected her, thought her the prettiest, most ladylike young woman in the area. "I've asked her to marry me."

His father nodded. "She'll soon be a pauper, but you'll have more than enough for the both of you. Make her a more amenable wife, I'd say. At any rate, I give you my blessing."

Warren didn't tell him she hadn't given him an answer yet. "How much does Winslow owe the bank?"

"Something to the tune of two thousand dollars."

Warren couldn't help whistling softly. That was a lot of money for the small businesses around here. Even Warren didn't have that kind of money. His father kept him on a short rein.

"And you say it's due tomorrow? Do you think he'll be able to pay it?"

"I hardly think he'll come up with the sum. He's been abed practically a month." His father waved his hand dismissively. "Winslow has overextended, and now it's time to pay the piper. That's all there is to it."

Warren was thinking fast, but knew he couldn't get his hands on that kind of money so quickly. All he knew was that he felt a compelling desire to offer Cherish a way out. He didn't want her forced to accept his proposal.

The more he saw of business, the less he liked it. It seemed everything depended on finding a competitor's weakness and exploiting it.

"I want you to go over to Haven's End—that should be no hardship to you," his father added with a chuckle. "Keep close to the situation. It's to your advantage."

Warren felt sick. He liked Cherish, but he didn't want her that way. Even though he should be relieved to have his father's blessing, instead he felt repulsed.

Somewhere he had a yearning for a kind of love that swept a person off his feet. A love that faced every kind of challenge and triumphed. He didn't feel this kind of love, nor did he think he inspired it in Cherish. All he felt was a desire to do what little he could to help her out of her predicament.

# Chapter Twenty

Silas had a day off from the cannery on the Fourth of July. The whole village was closed, and everyone turned out for the festivities.

But he was in no mood to celebrate as he sailed to Hatsfield, preparing to meet Annalise. Warren had arranged everything, knowing his parents were busy with official functions.

Now he stood, hat in hand, in the Townsend parlor, where Warren had left him with Annalise for a few moments. The house was dim and quiet, in contrast to the bright hot sun outside.

"Hello, Annalise. I haven't seen you in a while," he began.

"Hello, Silas. Won't you have a seat?" She indicated a chair beside the settee where she was seated with her hands folded primly in her lap.

He sat down with his hat in his lap. What now? What was he supposed to say to make things all right? Annalise was a lovely person. He could see the shy expectancy in her eyes before she fixed her attention on her clasped hands.

"Have you been busy working?"

"Yes, yes, I have," he answered rapidly, then stopped. No, he would be honest. "Annalise, the reason I stopped by today was to tell you goodbye."

Her eyes flashed up at him quickly before looking down again. "Goodbye?"

He cleared his throat. "Yes. You see, I'm going away soon. I don't know exactly when. It depends on Mr. Winslow, when he's feeling fully recuperated. Then I intend to head farther north or south and look for work in another—bigger—shipyard."

"Why can't you continue working where you are?"

Her eyes, magnified by the spectacles, were very direct.

He was the one to shift his gaze this time. He concentrated on the band of his hat. "Shipbuilding is dying in this area. I thought about looking down around Rockland, even Portland, where I hear a lot of ships are still being built."

"Oh, I see. You wouldn't consider any other sort of work?"

"No." He thought of his present work at the cannery. "That is, I hope I can find something in shipbuilding. You see, it's what I do best. Work with my hands. I don't think I'm much good for anything else."

"I'm sure there are lots of things you are good at."

He smiled slightly. "Thank you." Suddenly he wished he did love her and that he wouldn't hurt her too much with his words or with his goodbye. "Annalise."

"Yes?" She blinked, the hopeful look returning.

"Some day you'll meet some fine gentleman worthy of you—someone who's well educated like you and can offer you the kind of home you deserve." The wild thought occurred to him that he could just as well be making the same speech to Cherish. In her case, that "someone" was already in the picture—Warren Townsend.

Annalise was shaking her head at his words.

"You will, you'll see. Your family is well connected. You'll probably end up traveling quite a bit the way your brother has, or Cher—Miss Winslow." He was searching desperately for words of encouragement. Her muteness alarmed him. Even more did the silent tears that began filling her large eyes.

He swallowed, feeling like the lowest scoundrel. "Please don't cry. I'm certainly not worth it."

She sniffed. He could see her fingernails white as she clutched her hands together.

"Please, Annalise, don't cry," he repeated. "Do you want me to get your brother?"

She shook her head. "Please go," she whispered, turning her head away and wiping at the wet trail down her cheek.

He finally stood, his hat still in his hand, seeing his words only made things worse.

With sadness and self-contempt, but no regret at the decision he had taken, he left the room. Once he was outside, Warren came to him. "Well?" he asked.

"You probably ought to go to her," Silas answered quietly. "I'll see myself out."

Warren hesitated. "You told her?"

"I told her goodbye."

"You're making a mistake, van der Zee. A big mistake."

At the front door Townsend said to him, "If you see Miss Winslow today, please send her my best regards. Tell her I'm sorry to miss the festivities over at Haven's End, but duty calls here at Hatsfield. There are a lot of official functions my father and I must preside over." He hesitated once again. "Please tell her I'll be by to see her tomorrow."

For a man who had courted no women since his childhood sweetheart had died, Silas had just lost two women vastly superior to himself in just the first half of summer.

He shoved the hat onto his head as he walked down the flagstone path. He was doing the right thing, he told himself, feeling at the moment as if he didn't have a clue what that was.

Cherish had walked down to the village on the morning of the Fourth to watch the parade. She'd anticipated the day, hoping things would appear a bit like old times—she and Silas and their childhood friends having a good time together.

She had looked for him, but in vain. She stood now with some girlhood friends, waiting for the parade to begin.

"Oh, look at Captain Phelps and his wife." Julie nudged her with an elbow.

Cherish turned curious eyes across the street. The crowd parted for a tall, elegant couple walking arm in arm. She knew who Captain Caleb Phelps was from his business at the shipyard, but she had never addressed him personally. She'd been a mere girl, and he an important client who came up from Boston occasionally to oversee his father's shipping concerns on the down east coast.

Captain Phelps's bride was another story. Cherish drew in her breath, seeing her. Although the woman, known locally as Geneva, was a few years older than Cherish, Cherish had known her all her life. Now she scarcely recognized her.

"Can you believe that's 'Salt Fish Ginny'?" Julie asked with a giggle. Cherish shook her head, her eyes fixed on the dark-haired woman who had lived until recently on her own, dressing like a man and fishing cod.

Now she appeared more elegant than Cherish herself. She walked tall and straight, carrying a frilly parasol. Her dress, a cool-looking cream-and-blue-striped silk, contrasted well with her deep ebony hair. Cherish knew Geneva had been considered an oddity and about as devoid of natural feeling as the rocky coast. Now Cherish looked in amazement as she greeted everyone warmly and was well received in turn.

"Don't they make a handsome couple?" Lucy on her other side asked.

"Yes," breathed Cherish, watching how Captain Phelps turned to his bride, patting the hand that was tucked into the crook of his elbow and saying something to her. She responded with a smiling answer. Cherish remembered how she'd scared little Cherish with her dark, scowling looks. "However did they meet?" she asked curiously, finding it hard to imagine such a couple from the Geneva she'd known.

"Oh, it's the most romantic story," Julie told her eagerly. "Captain Phelps spent the summer before last out in that beautiful house on the Point that he had built for his bride. She'd jilted him because of some scandal. Well, lo and behold, he and

Geneva ended up falling in love. Can you imagine anything so improbable?"

"She looks nothing like she used to."

"Because she's had all kinds of lessons in deportment. Mama told me that old Mrs. Bradford took a liking to her. At the end of the summer, after Captain Phelps left Haven's End for Boston, Mrs. Bradford invited Geneva to go to Boston with her as her companion. By then Captain Phelps had sailed out to New Orleans. By the time he returned, Geneva had undergone the transformation you see now."

"They married last year in Boston, I heard," Lucy added. "They've just come up to spend the summer out on Ferguson Point."

"It sounds very romantic," Cherish said, still viewing the couple.

"You needn't feel any envy," Julie said with a laugh. "Your Mr. Townsend is certainly a handsome fellow, and his father, if not as wealthy as Captain Phelps, is the richest one around here."

Cherish looked at her friend. Were they already pairing her off with Warren? And was that how they viewed him—as a good match because of his looks and family wealth? Wasn't that how her father viewed him? Was that how she viewed him?

What would she think of him if he were not so handsome and didn't have a penny to his name? Would she have looked twice at him?

Her gaze scanned the crowd once more, but the golden hair she sought was nowhere to be seen.

As if reading her mind, Lucy said, "I wouldn't mind a dance or two with your father's apprentice. I think he's even more handsome than your Mr. Townsend."

Cherish glanced at her sharply. "Who, Silas? He's no longer an apprentice. He's a shipwright."

"All the better," her friend answered calmly, ignoring her tone. "Maybe I can convince Papa to have a boat built. Then I could hang around the boat shop like you!"

"Silas is no longer working with us," she said quietly.

"Why not?"

"He's going to work at a larger shipyard."

"Oh, what a shame."

"I thought I saw him leave the cannery the other day!" Julie exclaimed. "I could scarcely credit it."

"Oh, he's just working there temporarily," Cherish hastened to explain. "He's helping Papa out in the evenings until Papa is able to take over things in the shipyard once again. That—that time is fast approaching."

The conversation turned to her father, then the parade started and they were distracted by the sound of trumpets, horns and drums. Cherish watched, remembering her excitement as a girl whenever the parade marched by on the Fourth.

The two young men who were walking out with Julie and Lucy came by to stand with them during the parade. Watching them, Cherish wondered what her future would be like in Haven's End. She knew despite the sudden appearance of the fifteen hundred dollars, it was only a temporary reprieve. The bank had granted a two-week extension for them to come up with the final five hundred dollars. And what then? She and her father would still have to repay their benefactor, which in turn would reduce the profits from the schooner. Would they even be able to keep the boat shop open during the winter months?

Would Cherish have to seek employment? She had heard that one of the village schools was in need of a teacher. She could offer her services. Would she and her father be forced to live in reduced circumstances and would she become an old-maid schoolteacher? From her pinnacle atop Haven's End society, would she now be relegated to the fringes at its base?

After the parade, Cherish walked with the two couples to watch them join in the games—the three-legged race, the egg-and-spoon race, the burlap sack race. She joined them in horseshoes. All the while her eyes roamed the area looking for the only person who would make her feel at home again in her native village.

She might as well be back in Europe for all she saw of him.

She went home to have dinner with her father, and in the afternoon they hitched up the buggy to go back to the harbor to watch the annual boat race. Any kind of craft was eligible to race—both working boat and pleasure craft.

She was certain she would see Silas at the races. He had always represented Winslow's Shipyard, and for the past five years had taken first prize. This year she knew he would be racing his own yawl.

But there was no sign of Silas. She couldn't understand where he could be. To her knowledge he had never missed a Fourth.

She watched the beautiful yacht owned by Captain Phelps. She knew Silas had been the principal builder and designer on it last summer. It beat all the other boats by a healthy length.

She clapped vigorously when it sailed past the finish line, feeling joy that in a sense the victory was one for Silas. It was his craft that had won, even if it hadn't been the one registered in his name.

By the time Silas sailed back to Haven's End the sky had darkened and the fireworks were in full swing over the harbor. Silas secured his line to its mooring and rowed to the wharf. It was crowded with people "oohing and aahing" over the bright display in the black sky overhead.

He answered a few greetings as he passed them by, his eyes scanning the faces for Cherish. With a scant glance at the brilliant red, white and blue lights above, Silas turned his back on the crowd and walked up the road leading out of town.

He could have crossed the harbor to the parsonage in the skiff, but he walked the longer way, past Cherish's house. He'd fought so hard to stay away from her, but that night his legs drew him in her direction.

When he reached her house, it was dark except for a dim light visible through the front door. He stood for a moment at her gate. What had she done to him since she'd come back?

She'd twisted him around so much he no longer knew what was up or down, right or wrong.

He entered the gate and began walking up the path to the veranda, not knowing what he was about. Clearly everyone was abed. It was late and he should be headed to his own bed. Tomorrow was another workday.

He stood at the foot of the steps leading up the porch, staring upward. Before he could will himself to turn back, he heard her voice.

"Silas?" It was soft, questioning. It was too late for him to back out now.

"I didn't see you at the fireworks," he answered. He could barely make her out at the far end of the veranda, on the swing. He could hear its creak as she set it in motion.

"I didn't go. I watched them from here." Her tone was matter-of-fact.

"Is your father all right?"

"Yes."

Silas hesitated, torn between going and staying. He finally compromised by sitting on the steps, not trusting himself to take a seat beside her on the swing. He truly didn't know what her proximity would do to him this evening.

"You missed the boat race."

"I had to go to Hatsfield and couldn't get back in time" was all he could think to say.

"I thought you wanted to try your boat out this year."

"Yes, I did."

"Why didn't you?"

"I had to see someone in Hatsfield."

"Oh."

Before she could ask him whom he said, "I ran into Warren Townsend. He sends you his best regards."

"You did?" Her voice brightened. "That was nice of him. What else did he say?"

The question cut through him. He leaned against the balustrade and tried to remember. "He asked me to apologize to you for not being able to attend the festivities here in Haven's End.

It sounds as if he had a lot of official duties in town with his father."

"Yes, I imagine he had."

Silas said nothing about Annalise. Even the thought of her made him feel disloyal toward Cherish.

"Do you have any idea when you might be leaving Haven's End?"

Cherish's question caught him by surprise. Was he already relegated to her past? A brief flirtation like the ones she'd described by her friends, but now it was time to settle down to a serious prospect like Warren Townsend?

"No, I haven't thought about it yet."

"There's nothing keeping you here."

Was she telling him not to think about her anymore?

"No, I suppose there isn't. I was waiting for the schooner to be launched."

The two fell silent. The only sound breaking the stillness was the lapping of the high tide in the inlet across the street. The sound of the fireworks was dying down as the last rocket was shot off.

Finally Silas rose, feeling old in every limb. "I'd better get to the McDuffies. They're probably in bed by now."

"Captain Phelps won the race."

He turned toward her, joy mingled with regret. "Did he? In the sandbagger?"

"Yes. Isn't that the one you worked on?"

"Yes, the one I wrote you about."

"It's a beautiful boat. You should have seen her skim the water."

"Maybe I'll still be able to. He's up for the summer?"

"Yes, with Geneva."

Cherish didn't move from her seat. Silas hesitated, but finally turned away from her. "Good night, Cherish."

"Good night," her voice called softly after him.

As she heard his soft footfalls die away on the gravel, Cherish sighed, feeling as if with them went the vital part of her.

Silas hadn't told her where he'd been all day. What had been so important to make him miss the boat race?

It could only be about seeking work at another shipyard. She could think of nothing else that would be more important to Silas.

Did it mean he had received an offer somewhere?

He seemed so distant lately. She thought sadly of her great expectations on returning to Haven's End. All her hopes and dreams of a lifetime so quickly brought to nothing. Had Silas adjusted to life without her in the two years she had been absent from home? It certainly appeared so. And what of their kiss? Had he kissed her only to demonstrate his warnings to her about the nature of a man toward a flirtatious woman? She touched her lips. Had there been no love for her in that kiss, merely masculine desire?

*Dear Lord, show me what is the right way. Would You have me marry Warren? It seems right. It would make Papa so happy. It would solve our financial problems. It would ensure Papa's peace of mind. If I didn't marry him, where would we be? Would I be precipitating Papa's ill health if I turn Warren down?*

*Silas doesn't seem to care for me at all. Perhaps as a sister, but nothing more.* She attempted to suppress the wave of despair that swept over her. *Oh, Lord, I gave my love for him over to You. I know I have no rights to him. What is best for him? Should he go away from Haven's End? Is his future somewhere else? Grant me grace to accept Your will for Silas.*

Silas arrived at the parsonage expecting to find all dark and quiet. As he walked up to the house, he heard the pastor's and Mrs. McDuffie's voices coming to him over the yard. They were seated on a bench overlooking the harbor.

"Good evening, Silas. You saw the fireworks from the other side? Weren't they grand?" McDuffie asked.

"Uh—yes. I didn't see too much of them. I was just getting back from Hatsfield."

"Oh, they were beautiful," Mrs. McDuffie told him. "We had a perfect night for them. No fog."

"A minor miracle, I would call that, for July," McDuffie added with a chuckle. "We've just been sitting here, not wanting the evening to end."

"Don't let me disturb you," Silas said quickly. "I'm going to turn in."

Mrs. McDuffie rose from the bench. "Just my thoughts exactly. Why don't you stay out and keep my husband company a little while?"

"Yes, come have a seat, Silas." Pastor McDuffie patted the bench beside him. "I'm reluctant to get up and call it a night."

"All right." Suddenly Silas desired the company. He didn't want to face his own thoughts. Most likely they would only point to what a stupid fool he had been to throw away every chance that had come his way. First his hard-earned savings and now the offer of his own shipyard.

After Mrs. McDuffie wished them both good-night, the pastor and Silas sat quietly for a few minutes, listening to the rippling sound of the waves upon the pebbles of the beach.

Slowly Silas began to tell McDuffie of his day.

"What do you think?" he asked as he finished. "I turned down the offer to court a decent young lady whose father would open every door for me. Opportunity's only supposed to knock once." He contemplated the black expanse of sky and water in front of them, their presence evident only by the sound of the waves and twinkle of the stars. "I missed the boat race today. You know how much I wanted to race my own boat? I've raced boats I've built for Winslow for the last several years and won the last five. This time I wanted the chance to sail my own boat."

As he sat silent, he realized how good it felt to unburden himself and how much he desired to hear this man's opinion.

"Well, you've had yourself quite a day…quite a day, I would say."

"I feel like…like…" Silas groped for words. "Like God's taken it all—my sense of worth, my dreams, plans, even any…any hopes I had about Cherish—and now I'm just adrift. I'm surrounded by sea with no thought which is north, south, east or west. What should I do now? I keep asking myself, but I get no sense of direction."

"Have you never heard of 'waiting on the Lord'?"

Silas rubbed the back of his neck. "I suppose so. It just never struck a chord with me. I always had a goal, a purpose to my life. It's what kept me going through the bad times."

"The Lord tells us to seek His kingdom and righteousness and all the rest will be added to us. You need to take Him at His Word."

"But what does that mean, 'seek His kingdom'? They sound like words that have very little meaning for a boatbuilder."

"What about starting with getting to know your Savior? Have you been reading the Bible?"

"Yes."

"And?"

"Well, I've enjoyed it."

"But?"

"I don't know. I guess I still haven't gotten to the point where I see the connection with my own life, here and now. How can I serve the Lord? What can I do?"

"Well, as I see it, the Lord has already given you a perfect opportunity."

Silas glanced at him in surprise. "Yeah? How so?"

"Well, old Tobias, for one. You can minister to him."

Silas let out a breath. The thought hadn't even occurred to him. "You mean, tell him about Jesus?"

"Do as you've been doing. Be his friend. Share the light of Jesus through that friendship. The Word says not to despise small beginnings. I would say this qualifies." Silas could hear the humor in McDuffie's voice.

"You know, Silas, if you learn the secret to obedience, God will take you places you never dreamed. You say you want to build boats. God will open doors you never imagined possible, that His name might be glorified through you—that name that is above every name." McDuffie's voice rose in the sheer excitement of it. Then his voice sank. "But you've got to be a willing vessel. There's only one way to be a vessel. Empty yourself out on the altar, that He may fill you.

"Become the clay in the potter's hands, and you'll see, Silas, what the Lord will do."

Well, from high-flown dreams of designing fast ships to visiting the village drunk was quite a shift in purpose. Silas rose and stretched.

He had nothing else to offer. All that was left was to be obedient.

# Chapter Twenty-One

"Hello, Warren." Cherish greeted him at the front door the day after the Fourth.

He apologized for not being able to come out the day before, but she put him at ease. After the initial pleasantries, he asked if he could see her father. He seemed quite serious, and she wondered what it was about.

"Certainly. I believe he's in the parlor." When she had taken him to her father, she left the two men.

By the time she came back to them a quarter of an hour later, her father's face was wreathed in smiles.

"Cherish, I have some wonderful news."

She looked from one man to the other. Warren no longer seemed embarrassed or serious. He was smiling, as well. "What is it?"

"Warren, our good friend, and I hope soon to be something more," he added with an eager look in her direction, "has been so generous as to offer me five hundred dollars to help us out at the shipyard until I can get fully back on my feet."

She looked at Warren in stupefaction. "How did you know? Did you tell him?" She could scarcely believe her father would request money from a man who was no relation to them.

"Of course not! Warren knew from his father, who is on the bank board. He was aware of our temporary difficulties." His attention turned back to Warren. "You don't know how grateful we are for your friendship." The two men shook hands warmly.

Later her father excused himself and left her to visit with Warren. She didn't know what to say. She felt overwhelmed by the gift.

"Oh, Warren, you can't imagine how much we needed this. We will repay you some day, I promise," she added fervently.

"You don't have to repay me, you know," he said quietly. "I wanted to help you out." He grinned. "I didn't really have much money stored away. I had to scrape it together."

She felt doubly under obligation. "You didn't have to give us this money."

"Yes, I did," he answered grimly. "I didn't tell your father— I didn't want to upset or worry him—but my father has been waiting for an opportunity like this. He's looking to take over a shipyard, and this was ideal."

She listened in shock as he told her his father's role at the bank.

Warren got up to pace the room. "So you see, I had to come up with the cash somehow. I don't have much of my own. But I didn't want you to be under any pressure to accept my proposal. If you decide to marry me, I want you to do it because you want to, not to save your father."

She could feel her face heat up, seeing that he had guessed her turmoil. Tears welled in her eyes as she realized what a true friend he was. "Oh, Warren, how can we ever thank you?" She rose then and embraced him. He held her, though he didn't use the moment to his own advantage.

She eased out of the embrace and sought her handkerchief from her pocket. "I'll—I'll give you my answer soon, I promise," she told him fervently, wiping her eyes, and not meeting his gaze.

Later that afternoon, when Cherish was in the boat shop office, the door opened. She looked up in surprise to see Captain Phelps entering.

"Good afternoon," he said with a smile that crinkled the corners of his deep blue eyes. She was struck by what a handsome man he was, and she thought again of what a striking couple he and his wife made.

"Good afternoon, Captain Phelps," she said, returning his smile. "How may I help you?"

"Are you Tom Winslow's daughter?" he asked, narrowing his eyes.

"Yes."

"My, but you're a young lady now. I remember you as a little thing peeking out at me from around a boat frame."

She laughed. "Yes, that sounds like me."

"Is your father around?"

She sobered. "No, my father has suffered some ill health this summer. The doctor still hasn't given him permission to return to the shipyard."

"Oh, I'm so sorry to hear that. How is he now?"

"He's better. It was his heart."

Captain Phelps shook his head. "What a shame. So, you are here covering for your father?" he asked with a smile.

"I'm trying my best. It's not easy to fill his shoes."

"No, it never is," he replied with understanding, and she remembered that he, too, worked for his father's company.

"I'd like to congratulate you on your win yesterday. It was a wonderful race."

"Thank you. You know the boat was built at this shipyard?"

She smiled. "Yes, I know. Even though I've been away, I have kept up-to-date with the goings-on here. That's why I can congratulate you sincerely—I know the win is just as much a triumph for us!"

"Indeed it is. That's one of the reasons I stopped by today. I wanted to talk to the young man who built it for me. Could you tell me if Silas van der Zee is around?"

Her face grew serious. What would she tell him? "He's not around right now," she began. "You can find him after four down at the parsonage," she suggested with sudden inspiration, glad she didn't have to mention the cannery. She wondered what Captain Phelps wanted to talk to Silas about. Commissioning a new boat perhaps? That seemed unlikely, seeing as he had just had one built. Still, one could only hope.

"Oh." The captain seemed disappointed. "He's a fine builder."

"Yes, he is," Cherish answered immediately. "The best."

He smiled at her as if amused by her enthusiasm.

He placed his hat back on his head. "Well, you can tell him I stopped by if you see him. Otherwise, I shall make my way to Pastor McDuffie's this afternoon."

"Captain Phelps?"

"Yes?" He turned back to her.

"I wanted to congratulate you also on your marriage."

He smiled again. "Thank you. I am a very blessed man."

She nodded, wondering again at the transformation in the woman who used to be known in Haven's End as "Salt Fish Ginny."

"We'll stop by and call on your father this week."

"He would enjoy that," she told him.


Silas had scarcely had time to wash and change into clean clothes when he was visited by Captain Phelps.

He and Mrs. McDuffie exchanged greetings before she left the two of them on the porch to talk. Silas was surprised that the captain had come to see him, but the reason for his visit surprised him even more.

"I have a friend in Boston who would like to commission you to build him a yacht. A racing yacht."

Silas stared at him, hardly believing what he was hearing.

"I don't know if you saw the race yesterday."

"No, I missed it."

"That's a shame. The boat you built me won hands down. But that's not all. I raced her down in Boston before coming up here, and she won." He grinned at him. "My friend was impressed enough to want one himself."

Silas blew out a breath. "I don't know. I—I'm not working at the shipyard, for one thing."

Captain Phelps pierced him with those sharp blue eyes. "You're not? Why not?"

Silas looked away. "I…it's a long story," he answered finally. "Let's just say Mr. Winslow and I had a disagreement. So I have no workshop, nor any tools to work with."

Captain Phelps considered a moment. "You could work in my barn. We could convert it into a workshop."

Silas felt himself floundering. He stared past Captain Phelps to the inky-blue sea beyond. *What would You have me do, Lord? Is this of You?*

It was a dream come true, and yet, Silas realized, for the first time in his life he knew there was something more important than mere boatbuilding.

"Can I give you my answer tomorrow?"

"Of course. You think about it."

"I've committed myself to helping out at Winslow's Shipyard just until the schooner they're building is launched. But that's only in the evenings that I put in a few hours."

"This shouldn't interfere with that."

Silas cleared his throat. "I'm spending my days at the cannery in town."

Captain Phelps merely nodded at the information. "That wouldn't leave you enough time for this project. Would you consider quitting that job to take on this short-term one?" He paused. "If this boat is as fast as the one you built for me, your reputation would spread. I'd make sure of it."

Before Silas could absorb this, the captain continued, his enthusiasm growing. "Did you hear about the race that was just held in England? A yacht named *Jullanar* won. They say it had some interesting innovations—the builder cut away all the deadwood in both stem and stern and rigged it as a yawl instead of a schooner. I'm awaiting the particulars. But the interesting thing is these innovations were designed by someone who was unknown—he wasn't even a shipwright."

Silas could feel his excitement growing as Caleb talked to him about yachts and yacht racing, a heretofore unknown aspect of sailing to Silas.

"The yachts introduced in the fifties have a raking sternpost and sharp lines like a clipper. The canvas is set flatter. In the sixties, designers began combining an iron framework with the wooden skin. Now you begin to see a clipperlike bow.

"I think if we put our heads together and study the design of *Jullanar,* we could come up with some innovations of our own," the captain told him as he shook his hand in farewell.

Silas stood watching the captain's buggy as it left the lane. His mind was so full of possibilities, he could hardly form a coherent thought. All he knew was he needed to find a quiet place to commune with God.

The moment Cherish had been dreading arrived. Warren Townsend visited her again, and she knew she must give him an answer.

They sat across from each other in the boat-shop office.

"Have you had a chance to think about my proposal?" Warren asked after they'd chatted a while.

"Yes." She looked down at the letter opener on her desk. "Warren, I care about you deeply, and I can never tell you how much your help has meant to me. It has come at a very timely moment. I promise you, my father and I will repay you."

"Forget about the money. I told you that wasn't the reason I gave it to you."

"You're very kind. I wish—" She bit her lip, wondering even now if she had the courage to face her future in Haven's End without the security Warren Townsend offered.

"I know you don't love me," he surprised her by saying, "but we get along well."

"Well, you don't love me either!" she found herself blurting back to him.

He didn't seem fazed by her remark. Instead he seemed relieved. "But I think an awful lot of you. You're the nicest, prettiest girl I know. I'd do anything to help you out."

She took his hand across the desk. "Oh, Warren, you're too good. You'll never know how you've touched me."

He squeezed her hand. "You still don't have to give me an answer right now. I'm in no hurry—to my parents' exasperation."

She looked at him in sympathy and patted his hand. "Thank you, but I won't string you along." She looked down at their joined hands. "The answer must be no." In her heart she knew she had made the right choice, though she didn't yet know how she was going to tell her father. "I wish sometimes that we were in love. It would make things easier, don't you think?"

"It sure would," he said with a laugh. Then his eyes grew somber. "Sometimes I feel as if we're born with this loose noose around our necks and as we grow older, it slowly tightens and there's less and less slack in which to wiggle."

"Oh, Warren, no! Is it so bad…being the son of Warren Townsend the Second?"

He ran a finger inside his stiff collar as if illustrating the point. "I feel right now that between taking over more and more of the business for Father and getting married to 'the right young lady,' my life is being stifled to the point that I have no breathing room left. I mean that as no offense to you."

She laughed. "No offense taken. Poor Warren." She reached across both hands this time and clasped his. "I feel I, too, shall greatly disappoint my father by refusing your proposal."

They sat smiling sadly at one another.


Silas had prayed through the night after telling the McDuffies briefly about Captain Phelps's offer.

Now he wanted to tell the only person who would truly understand. He left the cannery on his lunch break, knowing he had very little time. He walked up the road toward the boat shop and made his way toward the office, figuring she would be there if she hadn't yet left for her dinner. Peering in the window, he stopped short when he saw Townsend and Cherish, eyeing each other warmly and clasping each other by the hands.

All the pleasure and anticipation died within him in those seconds he stood watching them. He thought back to the time Cherish had told him she behaved with that informality only with him, Silas. His mouth pressed into a grim line as he watched Cherish smile at Warren. Then he turned and left the area, trying to smother the bitterness that threatened to quench the excitement he had felt since Captain Phelps had visited him.

The day had been hot and steamy. At seven in the evening the tide was out, there wasn't a cloud in the sky, the sun was still high on the horizon and the mudflats seemed to radiate the heat of the afternoon sun. Cherish made her way up the ramp to the deserted schooner.

It was nearly completed, lacking only masts, which would be stepped later, after the ship was launched. She hiked up her skirts and climbed onto the deck. It smelled of turpentine.

Silas stood with his back to her, a bucket in one hand and a brush in the other. She remained where she was, watching him. She hadn't seen him in days. He could almost have gone off to live in another town for all she saw of him now.

"Hello, Silas," she said finally.

He jumped around at the sound of her voice, the bucket sloshing its contents. He held his brush as if fending her off.

"Hello, Cherish." His tone was serious, the look in his eyes wary.

His shirt hung open. He brought a hand up to his chest to clutch the two edges of it together.

"What smells so bad up here?" she asked.

He indicated the linseed oil and kerosene mixture used to prevent dry rot on the exposed wooden surfaces. He set down the bucket and brush and turned his back on her as he began buttoning up his shirt. When he faced her again, working on the last button, he seemed more composed.

Ignoring her further, he took up the brush again, dipped it into the bucket and began brushing the floor planks. Since he didn't seem inclined to talk with her, she found a perch upon the gunwale and watched quietly.

He dipped the brush into the bucket again and brushed it over the planks. He shoved away a lock of hair that kept fall-

ing over his forehead as he knelt on the wood and continued
to paint the boards. After a while he took up a stained rag. With
it he began rubbing the area soaked in the linseed oil.

She could see the back of his shirt sticking to him with perspiration. "Silas, why don't you ever come up to the house anymore? Papa's not angry with you. He's grateful for all you've
done for him down on the yard while he's been laid up."

He didn't answer, and Cherish tried to stifle the annoyance
that rose in her. Why didn't he talk to her?

"Silas?"

He finally looked at her from his kneeling position on the
floorboards, his arm resting against his knee, the rag suspended
in his hand.

She longed to go over to him and push away that lock of hair
that had fallen across his forehead again.

"Do you think it's a good idea to be here with me so late in
the day?"

She stared at him. "What do you mean?"

He turned the rag over in his hand. "Is it something your
friend Mr. Townsend would approve of?"

"Warren? What does he have to do with my talking with
you?"

His gray eyes scanned her. "Is it customary for the young ladies of Boston or the Continent to speak privately with other
men when their suitors are not around?"

Was he…perhaps…a little jealous? "Do you think Warren
is my suitor?"

"Isn't he?" His eyes held hers captive.

She didn't look away. "He *could* have been."

He glanced back down. "What do you mean?"

"He asked me to marry him."

"Isn't that what you and your father wanted?"

"It's what Papa wanted, yes." Glad and relieved that she
would finally have the opportunity to talk with him about it,
she explained, "It would have made Papa happy. It would have
solved a lot of problems." She met his eyes, which didn't waver from their steady perusal of her face. "Warren has been very

good to us. I don't know if you realize this, but…well, Papa has had some financial troubles. With his heart illness, everything just seemed to come to a head." She sighed. "But thanks to God's grace, Papa received the help he needed. Warren Townsend is one of those who stepped in just when we needed it most. He just did it as a friend."

"Or because he loves you."

She could feel herself coloring.

"He said he didn't want me to feel…under any obligation of that sort."

Silas began rubbing the woodwork with the rag again. "What did you tell him?" he asked her, his attention back on the deck boards. Cherish swallowed her disappointment.

"I told him I was deeply honored that he would consider me for his wife, but that I couldn't marry him."

He stopped his rubbing. "Why not?"

What could she say? For a moment she wanted to toy with him, because he acted so cool and aloof. But just as quickly the impulse died. What she felt for Silas was too important for coy games. "Because I'm in love with somebody else."

His eyelids shuttered over his eyes, so she had no idea how the information affected him. "You'd be better off with him."

"How could I be if I'm not in love with him?"

"Aren't you?" His hand began to move the rag back and forth again vigorously.

"How can I love him when I love you?"

He stopped the motion and they looked long moments into each other's eyes. Her heart thudded at her boldness, but she refused to back down. She didn't understand the barrier between them and wanted to get to the bottom of it.

"Didn't you hear what I said?" she whispered.

He stood and turned away from her. "I heard you."

"Silas, what's happened to us this summer? I used to be able to come and talk to you. Now you act as if—as if either I'm your enemy or I don't exist!"

When he didn't reply, but kept looking down at the rag in his hands, she composed her tone. "My father shouldn't have behaved the way he did to you. He must learn that I'm a grown woman capable of making my own decisions."

"Cherish, maybe your father is right. You're very young. How do you know what you feel is love and not some—some youthful fancy that you'll grow out of?"

This wasn't going at all the way she had dreamed. How could he doubt her love?

"You think it's an infatuation I'm feeling? Do you have any idea how long I've loved you?

"Did you think Warren Townsend was my first suitor and that my head would be turned by his attentions? If I behaved indecisively at all it was because I was feeling so desperate with Papa ill and the threat of the bankruptcy hanging over us. Yes, that's right, bankruptcy! I had no one to turn to. I wanted to tell you, but Papa had treated you so unforgivably and I knew you had opportunities elsewhere." Her lip trembled, but she kept on, the words rushing out of her.

"But I knew even then, I couldn't accept Warren's proposal, even if Papa and I ended up on the street."

"I'm sorry about the financial situation," Silas began and hesitated, as if not knowing what else to say.

"I thank the Lord Warren was a good friend, who didn't expect any recompense for his generous action. He took of his meager savings just to help us out. I've promised to repay him someday…somehow."

Silas had turned away from her again as she described Warren's generosity. Too late she realized how bad he might feel, not having been able to do the same.

"Oh, Silas, you've helped us, too, by coming here every evening after putting in a full day's work. And after how my father treated you! No one could ask for a better friend."

"Stop it, Cherish. I did no more than Ezra or Will," he said sharply, as if her words had offended him somehow. "Listen, I want you to forget your feelings for me. You're only nineteen. You think they're real, but you're young. You'll meet someone else. Maybe not Warren, but there'll be someone…."

She stared at him, feeling as if he'd taken her love and trampled all over it. "You haven't heard a word I've said, have you? I've had my share of suitors—better, more eligible than even Warren Townsend himself!" she said frigidly. "I left a whole string of them across Europe. I knew what Papa's intentions were for my Grand Tour!

"Oh, I did my duty to Papa while I was there. I went inside every cathedral, viewed every monument, trod every cobbled street, viewed every scenic vista recommended to me.

"I did everything with enthusiasm, with a smile on my face, no matter how forced it felt at times because I was so far away from here—so far away from *you!*

"All the while I would think, *I wish Silas were here.* Every scene I viewed, I pictured through your eyes. What would Silas have thought looking up at the Sistine Chapel ceiling? Dining al fresco on the hills of Fiesole? Walking the halls of the Louvre?" She shook her head ruefully. "I wrote you about them, but all I received in return were a few skimpy postcards that I would pore over for weeks until the next one."

She gave a dry laugh. "I knew what you'd have thought. You might humor me, accompany me all over, but you'd truly only have eyes for the sea. That and your precious boats, not all those man-made things of grandeur."

Silas threw down the rag and dragged a hand through his hair. "Don't you see? With everything you're telling me, you're only making it more clear that I'm the wrong man for you. I've never been anywhere, barely even to school! As you said—I know nothing about anything except boats. Your father is right—"

"Silas, don't say those things!" She took a step toward him. "Don't put me on some sort of pedestal. I'm a woman, not some goddess."

He held a hand out. "Don't come closer, Cherish. Don't make it more difficult."

"What are you so afraid of? Sometimes I think you care more about my father than you do about me. You didn't even try to defend yourself the day he saw us together. You acted ashamed. Is that what it is? Are you ashamed of feeling something for me?

"Is your precious boatbuilding more important than us? My father already fired you. What more can he do to you?"

He didn't say anything. All she could see was how set his jaw was. She wanted to goad him until he told her what he really felt.

"You're a coward, Silas. Or are you just waiting to leave for greener pastures?" She turned away from him, not wanting him to see the tears that threatened to spill.

"Cherish…" His tone was hesitant, unsure. She didn't even know if he would say anything more. But finally he spoke again, softly. "Maybe you're right. Maybe I don't know how to love. Maybe I'm afraid of the kind of love I see in your eyes."

She turned around slowly. Now, just as she had done, he held out a hand before dropping it in a gesture of futility.

"I can't live up to your ideals, Cherish. Sometimes I think everything died inside me a long time ago."

Cherish swallowed, tasting defeat for the first time since she'd come home. She knew the fear in his eyes, in his voice, in his every gesture was genuine. She didn't understand it, or where it came from, but she felt it as surely as the sturdy oak planks between them.

She knew in that moment she could have faced down her father's disappointment, could face a life of reduced circumstances, the loss of the shipyard and her privileged position in Haven's End, but she couldn't fight the fear she saw in Silas's eyes. She realized it was probably older than her acquaintance with him. It had probably been with him since before she'd set eyes on him in her father's boat shop.

She had no weapons against that kind of fear.

"I'm sorry, Silas. I'm so sorry for you."

As she made her way back down the ramp onto the beach, she didn't expect him to call her back and he didn't.

*Oh, Father, only You can set Silas free. I've tried to break through, but I can't. I don't want to cause him more pain. I can see he feels something for me, but not enough.*

The tears ran down her cheeks as she continued walking away from the shipyard and boat shop.

## ❧ Chapter Twenty-Two ❧

Cherish sat at the breakfast table with her father and Aunt Phoebe.

Her aunt looked over at her brother. "Well, Cousin Penelope has finally answered my letter, but I must say her reply makes up for her tardiness."

"How is she?" Winslow grunted, taking a forkful of baked beans.

"She's fine. I wrote her as soon as you had your collapse, asking her advice about a specialist in Boston."

"What?" Winslow threw down his fork.

"You heard me. If anyone knows about heart specialists it's Penelope. She's been suffering from palpitations for decades. She writes here that she's made an appointment for you with the best doctor in Boston. We're to stay with her, and afterward she graciously extends her invitation to her place on the lake in New Hampshire for your continued recuperation."

Tom Winslow sat back, his mouth grim. "You didn't think to inform me you were writing to Penelope about my condition?"

"Considering what condition you were in, frankly no," Aunt Phoebe replied. "Pass me the biscuits, would you, Cherish?"

"Certainly." The news from Penelope surprised Cherish as much as it had her father. "When would Papa have to leave?"

"As soon as possible. The appointment is for…let's see—" she perused the letter "—the eighteenth, a week from today. We would take the overnight steamer to Boston. Afterward, she suggests taking the train to the White Mountains."

"She thinks I can pack up and leave everything in a matter of days? Obviously she has no idea about running a business."

"Papa, you haven't been spending but an hour or two down at the shipyard," Cherish reminded him gently. "I think it's a good idea for you to see a specialist and get some real rest, away from everything here."

"And who's going to run things down on the yard?"

"I can see to things. It's rather slow right now, anyhow," she ended quietly.

"Nonsense, you're to go with us!" Without waiting for her reply, Phoebe turned to her brother. "Look at your daughter. She's paler than a ghost! If you don't accept Penelope's invitation for your own sake, then do it for Cherish's."

Her father took a long enough look at her as to make Cherish grow uncomfortable. She knew well the shadows under her eyes that refused to go away. He nodded slowly. "Very well, we'll cable her that we'll be down in a couple of days."

The first few days after Cherish and her father had left for Boston seemed to go as usual for Silas. He'd thrown himself into his new work for Captain Phelps. Going over design plans with him kept Silas distracted. He'd had time for only a few words with Winslow before his departure, and Silas had agreed to work at the boat shop the month they would be away. He had agreed to only half days, reserving the other half to work at the captain's.

It had been a deeply satisfying moment when Silas had been able to hand in his resignation at the cannery. Although he'd come to admire the people working there, he would be happy never to have to handle another raw sardine in his life.

He walked away from the job thanking God for the door that was opening with the captain, but also for the time spent at the cannery. He realized now that the Lord had taught him things, and he was grateful for the lessons.

On the surface his life seemed complete. He spent his free time in Pastor McDuffie's company. In his conversations with him, in Bible studies with him and his wife, Silas was beginning to learn that every answer he ever needed was found in the Word.

He realized that as he developed a habit of reading the Bible daily, a love and a hunger for it grew in him. If he skipped a day, he began to miss the spiritual nourishment it gave him.

The most important lesson he was learning was that boat-building was not the beginning or end of his life. He had learned that he *could* live without it. He still loved it, and it gave him a sense of accomplishment more than any other task, but his life did not consist of that, but in doing his Father's will. He continued visiting Tobias, and experienced a new type of joy the evening the Lord gave him an opportunity to tell Tobias about Jesus. As he talked of his own personal experiences, Silas had a sense of accomplishing something with eternal value such as his shipbuilding had never given him.

He was content with the mere fact that Tobias had listened, and he remembered the parable of the sower sowing seed.

Silas avoided thinking of Cherish. He instinctively knew that way lay pain. He hoped he had managed to convince her he was no good for her.

But as the week passed, and the silence and emptiness of the boat shop and office grew oppressive, as he scanned the church congregation for her elegant silhouette and realized a second later she wouldn't be there, as he missed her standing beside him at choir practice, or seeing her in the village, he began to realize what life would truly be like without her.

When the Whitehall was finished, and the boat shop stood empty, Silas wandered through it, running his hand through the cedar shavings, their pungent scent bringing back images of Cherish working side by side with him.

One early evening, as he was sailing back from a trip to Hatsfield, Silas meditated on the things Pastor McDuffie had been teaching him about the cross of Christ.

The verse about presenting his body a living sacrifice unto God found a parallel command in each of the gospels he'd pored over. Jesus told all his disciples to deny themselves and take up their cross if they wished to follow him.

Pastor McDuffie had tried to get Silas to see the positive side of what on the surface seemed an impossibly demanding requisite.

"Silas, when you come to understand the kingdom of heaven, you'll come to know that it is we who receive much more than God gains by demanding our very lives. In His Son, we have everything—every desire fulfilled, every need met, complete freedom from our old, weak nature, and on top of everything else, everlasting life. Think on it, Silas! We have all that by God's grace! His free gift!" he'd said, his eyes shining with the excitement of the merchant who'd sold everything he had to possess that one pearl of value beyond measure.

Now, as Silas contemplated the early-evening sky and sea, a verse he'd read that morning that had puzzled him, but which he hadn't lingered over, came back to him. *I do not frustrate the grace of God....*

Paul had written those words. Paul, as Silas was coming to learn, was the paragon of the Christian faith. How could Paul think such a thought?

Now meditating on those words of Scripture as he gazed out at the horizon, Silas saw that all his efforts to be "good" had been merely frustrating God's grace, for they had all been ways to try to please God without doing the one thing God demanded: accept His Son's life, in place of his own. One life for another. The only condition was that the former life must go.

As long as he had kept hold of one shred of the old Silas van der Zee, he could still have a modicum of his own will in the equation.

Cherish's love for him came to him. He tried to dodge it, but it refused to leave his mind. Was she part of this?

He'd done everything in his power—of his own will—to convince himself what Cherish felt for him wasn't true love. A childish passion, a young girl's infatuation, nothing more.

What was he so afraid of in admitting that it was a woman's love? Cherish had called him a coward. The words hurt now as much as they had then. He'd persuaded himself he was doing the right thing by pushing her away.

Now he admitted she was right. He was a coward. What was he afraid of? The light of truth probed deeper, and he flinched at its relentless invasion.

Why had he avoided thinking of the true reason he was denying himself Cherish's love, when he knew what he felt for her was love? He'd argued that it was because of his background and because of her father's prejudice—all external, temporal reasons, he admitted now as he gazed at the flat horizon. The broad expanse of ocean meeting sky brought a sudden clarity to his spirit that he couldn't hide from.

Had he been frustrating the grace of God by refusing to accept Cherish's love and give her his own?

Was this refusal rooted in fear of giving God the power to hurt him again? By having a woman to love and open his heart to, Silas was at risk. Because love to him meant pain, he admitted. His heart felt suddenly naked and exposed even as he acknowledged it. Love meant a pain buried for so long, so deeply, he hadn't even realized he still carried it.

On the wave of that revelation came the knowledge of how vulnerable God had made Himself to man through His Son, Jesus.

Jesus had told His disciples near the end of His sojourn with them, "Henceforth I call you not servants; for the servant knoweth not what his lord doeth: but I have called you friends; for all things that I have heard of My Father I have made known unto you." To befriend someone meant knowing him and being known of him. God was allowing man the opportunity to know Him.

McDuffie had shown Silas Paul's cry: "That I may know Him, and the power of His resurrection…"

If the apostle Paul had had that driving ambition, the converse must be true: God had a desire to *be* known. What was the Bible about but a message to man? What had Jesus come to earth for but to reveal the Father to man? Didn't that mean God wanted man to know Him? God in effect was giving humanity the opportunity to hurt Him.

Once again, Silas received a mental image of Jesus' agony on the cross. But this time he saw himself pounding one more nail into the flesh of his Savior.

By refusing to acknowledge his love for Cherish and hers for him, Silas was in effect pounding that nail of distrust into his Savior's hand.

It all came down to trust. Did Silas trust the keeping of his heart to the Lord, Who had paid so high a price for him?

Wasn't it enough what Christ had already suffered for Silas's sake? Must Silas crucify his Savior afresh?

*I do not frustrate the grace of God....*

Silas had to trust in the love that took Jesus to the cross. That God's love was big enough, true enough, to see him through any eventuality—even perhaps someday losing Cherish if he allowed her to have his heart.

The answer was the cross...Silas must relinquish that last stronghold of fear and see it nailed there.

"For God so loved the world that He gave His only begotten Son..."

God had given Silas His best, the best He had to give, His beloved, His very Self in Jesus. Was that not enough for Silas?

In refusing to love again, Silas was demanding more. He was demanding more than what Jesus had purchased for him on the cross. What more guarantee than Jesus' death on the cross? As the full import of Silas's behavior hit him, he knew repentance.

His knees slid onto the floorboards of his boat and tears filled his eyes.

*No, Lord, I don't want to crucify You afresh. Forgive me, Lord, for my unbelief...my anger...my fear...forgive me for frustrating Your grace.*

# ◈ Chapter Twenty-Three ◈

*One month later*
*August 1875*

Silas hadn't been able to concentrate all morning on the work on the schooner. The Winslows were due back that day and all he could think of was seeing Cherish once again. He was aware just when the schooner from Eastport lowered anchor in the harbor. He calculated the time of their disembarking, knowing Jacob was meeting them with the wagon and bringing them home.

He wondered if they would come to the boat shop at all today. He couldn't imagine Mr. Winslow not making an appearance.

Silas came up from the shipyard and looked over the shop one more time. The wood shavings had been swept up, the tools neatly hung on their hooks or placed into the toolbox. No new work had begun, and if the cavernous room had a vacant look, at least it looked neat and clean.

When the afternoon waned and no one from the Winslow house came, Silas swallowed his disappointment. He toyed with the idea of going there and reporting on things in the past month, but then changed his mind. They were probably weary from their journey. Maybe Winslow even had taken to his bed.

He hadn't had news from any of them in the month they'd been away. He'd known from Celia only that they'd spent most of the month on a lake resort somewhere in the White Mountains with a cousin, the same one who'd escorted Cherish all over Europe.

Cherish hadn't written to him at all, not even a postcard.

He sighed and closed the shop in the late afternoon. No use keeping it open. He headed to the point to work on the yacht in Caleb's workshop.

The following morning he came down to the shipyard without bothering to stop at either the boat shop or office, not thinking anyone would be there so early. But when he arrived at the schooner, Will hailed him.

"The boss is back," he said with a grin. "Wants to see you as soon as you're in."

"Thanks," Silas replied, turning and heading back up the beach to the buildings, neither his tone nor features betraying what he was feeling inside. Would she be with her father? Would Winslow be satisfied with Silas's stewardship during the time he'd been away?

He knocked on the office door and opened it. His eyes went immediately to Cherish, who sat in front of her father's desk, studying a ledger. She glanced up as he entered, but said nothing.

His eyes lingered on her. She wore a simple navy blue skirt and white blouse, her hair in a knot at the nape of her neck. She looked older, more subdued than he was accustomed to seeing her.

"Silas! There you are!" Tom Winslow called out, standing and coming around the desk, his hand stretched out.

"Welcome back, sir," Silas responded, dragging his eyes from Cherish and taking the proffered hand. Winslow took his in a firm grip. "You're looking very well," he told Cherish's father, noting the man's tanned features and cheery demeanor.

"I feel like a new man. How have you been, son? Everything looks wonderful. You did a fine job holding down the fort, didn't he, Cherish?" He turned toward his daughter.

"Yes," she answered quietly.

Silas wondered at her reserved manner. Was it her father's health? Was it the fact that no new orders had come into the shipyard? Why then did Winslow seem so exuberant?

Winslow kept a hand on his arm and led him toward a window overlooking the shipyard below. They saw the schooner hull, which the men were painting.

"She's about ready to launch. Have you set a date?"

Silas glanced at Winslow. He wanted *Silas* to set a date? He felt the pressure of Winslow's hand on his arm. He couldn't recall Winslow ever touching him like the son he was calling him. "No. I thought I'd wait until you got back."

"So, what do you estimate?"

He shrugged. "Another week, ten days. We're just painting the hull with the copper paint. The rest of the interior work can be done after she's launched."

Winslow nodded. "Good, then. Let's look at the calendar."

They walked back to the desk and leaned over a desk calendar. This time Cherish didn't look up. Silas gazed at the top of her head.

Having no reason to linger, although Winslow seemed in no hurry to dismiss him, Silas said, "Well, I'll get back down to the yard."

"Oh, sure. Didn't mean to keep you. Say, why don't you come up to the house for dinner?"

Silas glanced from father to daughter, who seemed not to have heard, although he noticed her pencil had stopped writing.

"Thank you, but Mrs. McDuffie is expecting me at the parsonage."

"Oh, of course. Well, what about tomorrow? That way you can let her know you won't be home. I want to speak to you about a few things."

"All right," he answered slowly, wondering what was coming. The termination of their temporary arrangement?

He nodded to Cherish, who looked up only when he was saying goodbye to her father.

"I'll be seeing you, Cherish."

"Goodbye, Silas."

The next morning Silas entered the boat shop hoping to see Cherish before going down to the shipyard. He breathed a sigh of relief upon seeing her sitting on a high stool, looking at a lines drawing, like old times.

He cleared his throat. "Good morning."

"Good morning."

Again she was a vision to his hungry eyes, dressed this morning in a pretty calico print, her hair in a ponytail. He approached the worktable. "Are you glad to be back home?" he asked, wondering how to get past the formality that was between them.

"Yes."

"How was Boston?"

"Very nice, thank you."

She was studying the plan, and he couldn't help the disappointment he felt at her dismissive though polite replies.

"Did you see many friends?"

"Yes. What do you think of this plan for a schooner?" she asked. "On our trip back George Henderson asked Papa for his opinion. He's thinking of having it built."

Silas drew the paper closer to him and looked at it, but his eyes didn't really see it. Instead, the hint of lilacs reached his nostrils and he noticed the sheen of the dark brown hair cascading from its yellow ribbon down Cherish's back.

He remembered the feel of her soft lips against his in this very room. It seemed an eternity ago.

"Well?" Cherish asked him, seemingly unaware of where his thoughts had wandered. Her own tone was businesslike.

He focused on the lines drawing and saw it held the three views for a forty-foot fishing smack. He made the proper replies, all the while realizing that his harsh words to her had been as effective as he'd hoped. Cherish acted like a polite acquaintance, and he didn't blame her. He'd treated her rather cavalierly and now he was reaping the rewards.

At the noon hour he quickly washed up at the water pump and put on the clean shirt he had brought. He managed to enter the office before Cherish had left.

Her father looked up with a smile. "Are you ready to join us? The Boston doctor said I had to do a lot of walking."

They walked three abreast, Cherish between them. Winslow asked him about the McDuffies. "I ran into Captain Phelps. He said you were doing some work for him. Tell me about it."

His tone did not seem accusatory in the least. "Well, he wanted to commission a yacht. Actually it's for an acquaintance of his in Boston. We worked on some plans and models and have laid the keel. His friend wants it built mainly for speed."

Winslow nodded and asked him some more questions about it. He seemed genuinely interested. Although Cherish had given him a startled glance at the first mention of Caleb, she did not participate in the conversation at all. Silas swallowed his disappointment, remembering all the times Cherish and he had discussed different aspects of boat design.

Soon they arrived at the house, where Silas was greeted warmly by Mrs. Sullivan.

Although the meal proceeded pleasantly enough, he soon noticed that it was Mrs. Sullivan and Mr. Winslow carrying the conversation. Cherish answered cheerfully enough when spoken to, but did not contribute of her own accord. He keenly missed her interest in his boatbuilding activities.

As soon as the meal was over, she disappeared into the kitchen to help her aunt and Celia with washing up. Silas felt frustrated in his desire to see her alone and ask her about her month away. What had it done to her? What had *he* done to her?

But Mr. Winslow called him into the parlor. "The doctor forbade my accustomed cigar," he told him as he settled himself in his armchair. "Have a seat, Silas."

Winslow sat regarding him a moment when the two were seated. Silas began to feel uncomfortable. He wasn't used to Mr. Winslow's new manner—half jovial, half amused. It was almost as if the two of them—father and daughter—had undergone some sort of transformation during their time away, more so than in the two years Cherish had spent away from Haven's End.

"So you've found favor with Caleb Phelps."

"For the time being. There's no knowing how the vessel will sail until it's launched."

"That's true, that's true. But you've got a track record, Silas. I have all the confidence that she'll be a beauty."

Silas shifted on his seat. "Well, it's only one yacht. I still need to find full-time work at a shipyard. I was just waiting…until you came back." He cleared his throat. "And now, until the yacht is completed."

"Yes, of course." Winslow fell silent again, though he continued to regard Silas keenly, until Silas felt as if there must be something unusual about his face.

"I'm selling the shipyard," he said abruptly.

Silas stared at Winslow. "Excuse me?"

"I said I'm selling the shipyard. I've given it a lot of thought this past month. The heart specialist put it to me bluntly." He tapped his chest. "It isn't what it used to be. It sustained a lot of damage, and who knows when it'll decide to stop on me again. So no matter how much I might have wanted to protest, the fact was that I could either accept it and make my peace with God and enjoy the few years I have left—if in fact they are years—or I could squander the remaining time with a lot of worries."

He nodded his head at Silas. "I may be a pigheaded fool at times, but this time the good Lord managed to get my attention long enough for me to see what has been staring me in the face for a long time."

Silas still didn't understand where the conversation was leading. He felt shocked over Winslow's revelations about his health and decision to sell the shipyard. He thought about something else. "What about Cherish? She loves the shipyard."

He nodded. "Yes, that's so. It's going to be hard on her."

He stared at the older man. "You haven't told her?"

"Not yet. As I said, I've been mulling things around in my own head these past few weeks." He tapped the arms of his chair with his hands. "So, young man, do you want to buy it?"

"Me?"

He nodded calmly, as if he had said the most natural thing in the world.

Silas sat forward. "But that would be impossible."

"Would it? As I see it, you've already paid for it. Twelve hundred dollars cash."

Silas wiped a hand across his mouth, trying to absorb what Winslow was telling him.

"Silas, the Lord opened my eyes to the truth. You're like the son I never had, the one I always wished for. I'm sorry for not seeing that sooner, for treating you like a hired hand for so many years instead of the most talented boatbuilder I've ever seen at work in all my years in the business.

"My daughter tried to tell me many a time. She'd get angry at me, but that only made me more adamant in not seeing the talent in you."

Silas stood, unable to sit any longer. He couldn't fathom the words coming out of Winslow's mouth. "I'm sorry, sir, I don't understand. I can't—"

"I know this is probably a little abrupt for you." The older man's tone was gentle. "You think about it. I know the shipyard needs someone with a fresh vision. I think you're that man. Maybe it will no longer be a yard for building sailing ships. Maybe you'll make a name for yourself building yachts for speed and pleasure. In any case, I leave the decision up to you. If you decide you'd rather find work in a bigger yard, I'll still sell this and repay you your money."

"But what will you do?"

He shrugged. "I told you. I'm about useless now as far as work goes. Cherish has talked about getting a job teaching in the fall, perhaps. We have this place. We'll get by."

Silas shook his head. He couldn't see Cherish away from her beloved shipyard, much less forced to seek employment.

"Anyway, you give it some thought. If you still want to seek your fortune elsewhere, I'll understand perfectly. Your savings will see you on your way to fulfilling that dream you had of owning your own yard. You'll never know how grateful I am for your help when I most needed it."

"You don't have to repay me."

"I do and I will." His tone was firm. He rose from his chair. "Anyway, take all the time you need. Now, let's talk about more agreeable things. Are you going to invite me down to view this yacht you're building?"

"Of course. Whenever you wish."

Winslow escorted him to the door. As he stood holding the knob, he focused his keen gaze once more on Silas. "If you still care for that daughter of mine the way you gave evidence to that day I caught the two of you, you have my blessing."

Of all that he had heard that afternoon, this statement astounded him the most. "Does that mean you wouldn't object to my asking her to marry me?" He wanted it clearly spelled out.

"I certainly don't mean anything less."

"Yes, sir." The older man held out his hand and slowly Silas took it.

Having Winslow's blessing and putting his intentions into action proved to be two different things. Cherish appeared as aloof and evasive as a fawn. Whenever he did manage to be in her company, she rarely made eye contact with him—which was so contrary to those clear, direct gazes that used to make him so uncomfortable. Now he craved those looks. What a fool he had been.

Was he too late? Had she met someone in the past month? Had she finally gotten over her girlish infatuation as he'd kept insisting it was?

It certainly wasn't Winslow's fault if Silas seemed to make no headway with Cherish. When he wasn't inviting Silas to dinner, he was asking him to come calling in the evening.

Cherish would then spend half her time in the kitchen. When she did finally sit down in the parlor with them, it was usually to bend over some stitching and not contribute to the conversation at all. After a while she would rise and disappear into another room.

The second time she did this, Silas decided to go in search of her. He bid Mr. Winslow and Mrs. Sullivan good-night and headed toward the kitchen to exit by the back way. Sure enough, Cherish sat at the kitchen table reading by a kerosene lamp.

He came and stood across from her. "What are you reading?"

"Oh, just a book." She shut it, but didn't offer to show it to him.

"Do you mind if I sit down a moment?"

"No, of course not." But her tone conveyed only perfunctory politeness.

"Your father seems a very different man since his return," he began, not really knowing how to proceed.

She placed her chin in her hand and looked out the window. "Does he? I suppose he does to you, since you've only just seen him. To me, it seems a more gradual change—ever since his collapse, really."

"Does the specialist really give him so little hope?"

She nodded and began picking at a thread in the tablecloth.

"I'm sorry, Cherish." How he longed to take her in his arms and comfort her, but she didn't seem to want anything from him. He remembered when she was a little girl and would run to him for solace.

"We've grown closer to each other in the past month, but in a different way. I was always Papa's little girl, but now I feel he sees me as a person in my own right."

Cherish stared out at the waning light. She turned as she finished speaking and was caught by the intent way Silas was looking at her.

*Don't look at me that way! You'll destroy all the equilibrium I've managed to build up in the weeks I've been away.*

She dragged her gaze away.

Before she could compose herself, he spoke, his voice as calm as always, which told her he was the same. Nothing had changed with him.

*Not what I will, but Thy will be done,* she reminded herself.

"You know there's a grange dance tomorrow night. Are you planning on going?"

He'd caught her off guard. "No."

"Why not? I thought you enjoyed those dances."

"I enjoy sitting at home just as well."

"I'm sure your father doesn't want you sitting here every evening. He'd want you to get out and be around young people."

She smiled sadly. "You sound like an elderly aunt."

He rubbed the back of his neck. "Well, that wasn't my intention. I just mean you should—"

She cut him off before he could pursue the topic. "Tell me more about the project with Captain Phelps."

He eyed her warily a few seconds, then proceeded to tell her how the captain had approached him. She didn't really listen to his words, but let them wash over her like a balm. She preferred to drink in his features as she made the appropriate movements to indicate she was listening.

His greenish-gray eyes looked somber, although he was speaking about something he loved. He was blessed with that smooth, deep golden skin that some blond people of northern European extraction had. His dark golden hair was bleached lighter at the ends. He still pushed back the shock that insisted on falling forward.

Soon he would leave for good. In the month she'd been away she'd come to accept that. She was prepared for whatever life the Lord had for her without Silas.

She smiled in encouragement at what he was saying, and was rewarded by seeing the light touch his eyes as he described the way he envisioned the yacht.

When he rose to leave, she congratulated herself on her casual way of bidding him good-night, not even giving him her hand. Soon she bent back over her book. Who knew that the words merely stared back at her, their meaning as impenetrable as a rock wall?

* * *

Silas didn't know what more to do. Cherish was unreachable, more so than when it seemed she was on the brink of marrying Warren Townsend.

He finally confided his doubts to Mrs. McDuffie.

She smiled at him as she wiped the dishes dry. "Have you told her what you're telling me?"

"How can I? She doesn't seem to want to be around me."

"This doesn't sound like the Cherish I know." She laid the plate on a stack and took up another. "Sometimes a woman needs to be courted. You have her father's approval. Why don't you take advantage of that?"

He thought over her advice, wondering how to go about courting a young woman who, by her own admission, had been courted by the best in Europe. She'd certainly had her choice of the best in Hatsfield, and they had not impressed her.

What could one semiemployed boatbuilder, whom she'd known practically all her life, do to impress her?

He remembered when she'd first come home—her enthusiasm, her joyfulness whenever they were together. He remembered her pride in her cooking ability. He thought about the day she'd insisted he accompany her on a picnic.

A picnic. The image of that day alone with her in the meadow took hold.

He asked Mrs. McDuffie's advice.

"That's a wonderful idea. The days have been so warm—you must enjoy the good summer weather while it lasts. I can prepare a picnic basket for you."

"I appreciate that, but...I'd like to do this myself."

She nodded in understanding. "I'll show you where everything is."

Convincing Cherish to accompany him was another story.

"A picnic?" She looked as if he'd suggested taking cod-liver oil. "Oh, that's sweet of you, but I really must go home. Papa and Aunt Phoebe are expecting me for dinner."

"It's all right. I told them."

"You told them?" Her eyes widened. Then she glanced out the window. "But the weather. Aren't we supposed to get fog?"

"It's a perfectly fine day."

"I don't know. I'm not prepared—"

"What's to prepare for?" He was beginning to wish he'd never proposed the idea. "It's just a picnic. Who knows when we'll have another opportunity? You used to like picnics."

She met his gaze a second, and he wondered if she was remembering their picnic at the beginning of the summer.

Then she looked away. The next second she'd stood and was brushing off her apron. "Oh, all right, if you insist." Her tone was ungracious—something he'd never heard from Cherish Winslow.

They were silent on the sail over. When she noticed he was heading out to sea instead of to the next bay, she turned to him. "Where are we going?"

"I thought we'd try McKinnon Island. We can get a view of the puffins."

She nodded and turned away again. He was content to watch her profile, the way the tendrils of hair flew away from her face.

When they landed at the island, which housed only a lighthouse, he rowed them to the small dock in the skiff. Before he had a chance to help her out, she jumped out herself.

She ran ahead of him up the pebbly path as he followed more slowly with the picnic hamper.

They climbed up a slope through tall grass to the top of the island. The lighthouse keeper walked toward them and they waved. When he neared, they chatted a few moments, then headed beyond the lighthouse to find a spot for their picnic.

They chose a sheltered spot where they could look at the sea all around them and keep an eye on the grassy slope and rocky shore before them to watch out for the puffins. Silas laid the simple food out diffidently, noticing the unevenly cut bread.

"I hope I remembered everything. Here are some pickles," he said, removing a jar. "And lemonade. Mrs. McDuffie gave me some slices of cake for afterward."

"Everything looks delicious," she said, taking a sandwich from him, her fingers not touching his.

They bowed their heads and said a blessing. Afterward they ate in silence, the sound of the waves sufficient. When they'd finished eating, they watched the puffins, which had reemerged after a while, since Cherish and Silas had sat so still. He handed her a pair of binoculars and she took them wordlessly.

The puffins were like miniature penguins, with the exception of their thicker, more colorful beaks. Cherish pointed to one and they watched as he dived off a rock and emerged from the water with a fish in his beak.

Cherish handed the binoculars back to him. "Thank you." Her eyes, for the first time since her return, glowed with something of their old enthusiasm. "Thank you for bringing me here today."

He knew it was now or never that he had to talk to her. But it was harder than he'd expected. He looked down at the emerald grass between his knees and began to pluck it absently.

"You know, when I first arrived in Haven's End, to be apprenticed to your father, it was the first time in my life I'd been away from home, away from everything I knew…those I loved and who loved me. I didn't understand why I had to be sent so far away. All I knew was that Papa had died and life would never be the same again."

He drew a deep breath, not liking to recall those days. "The nights were the worst. Your father would close up the shop. I'd hear that last turn of the key, and I'd know I was alone for the night. Then the sounds would come, the creak here, the sudden gust of wind, the ceaseless drone of the waves, closing in on me.

"I knew I had to behave like a man. I was twelve. I was no longer a baby, I knew that full well. Yet I can't count the number of nights I cried myself to sleep."

He glanced across at her, his arm propped against his knees. She hadn't made a sound, but sat watching him, listening. He gave a lopsided grin. "You were the only friendly face in those first days, the only one who seemed to sense how homesick I was. You remember what you gave me that first day?"

"I remember," she answered softly. "Annie. She was my favorite doll. I must have really felt sorry for you that day to give up Annie."

He eyed her. "I still have her."

She looked at him in amazement.

"Do you know how many nights I fell asleep crying over that rag doll? Quite a few, as your childish mind supposed."

"I'm glad you had Annie."

"She got pretty sodden that first month, though I wouldn't have admitted that to anyone, least of all to such a self-assured five-year-old."

She smiled. "I was pretty cocky back then, wasn't I? I'm sorry you were so lonely."

He looked seaward. "I learned to concentrate on the reason I'd come here—to learn to build boats, and maybe some day even to design them. I knew I was being given a rare opportunity for a boy whose life would probably have followed his father's as a fisherman if he had lived." He sighed. "So I learned to put aside self-pity and loneliness and concentrate on what I loved best.

"Somewhere along the way I forgot how to love anyone or anything else."

Cherish's heart sank. It was as she had feared. She scarcely heard his next words as the numbness threatened to envelop her.

"It took a beautiful young woman of the same fearlessness and single-mindedness of that five-year-old to show me what I had missed."

Her eyes turned to him in wonder. *Could it be?*

"Cherish…" His voice faltered. "I wish you could understand how deeply I care about you."

She finished for him, her tone flat, "It's just not *love*."

"It *is* love. It's the kind of love that rips a man apart with longing. You don't know how hard this summer has been for me ever since you came home, so much a lady. I never dreamed you cared the least bit for me, much less aspired to win you—my feelings were buried too deep. I would never have discovered them on my own. But as you came to make me see how much I did care, I realized I hadn't even known they were there."

He gave a dry laugh. "I guess maybe that's why I never looked at another woman after losing Emma. I think I've always been in love with you."

His hands tore at the grass. "I never wanted to hurt you. I never wanted to separate you from your father—I never wanted you to go through what I'd been through.

"It's why I didn't let myself even dream of having you."

"Oh, Silas, why didn't you tell me? You made me think you didn't care."

"I didn't want you to have to go against your father's wishes if all you felt was a girlish fancy."

"Silas! Do you think that's all I felt?"

He answered slowly, as if groping for the explanation. "I didn't want you to defy your father just to get something you couldn't have, and once you got it, decide it wasn't worth having. You know, I haven't the education you've had, been to the places you've been to…"

Tears smarted her eyes. There was nothing to say against that. If he thought so little of her.

"Don't cry, Cherish. I don't ever want to hurt you. I'm sorry if it causes you pain to hear this, but I wanted to explain what I've been going through.

"It wasn't until you went away this past month that I realized—" he swallowed, looking straight ahead at the ocean, his hair falling over his forehead "—I realized how bleak life would be without you…how much I'd been fooling myself to think I could give you up."

"Oh, Silas," she whispered.

"And when you did come back—after I pleaded with God to at least let me have your friendship—you've been so distant. I didn't think life could get any worse." He sighed deeply. "I guess what I brought you out here today to say is that I love you with all my heart, and I'll take any little part of yours that you're able to spare me—"

She laid a hand gently on his forearm. He looked down at her hand, but otherwise remained motionless.

"Silas, do you think you'll ever come to believe that my heart is yours—that it's been yours for the last fourteen years? The only reason I didn't show you this before was because I was being the dutiful daughter. I was learning patience. I was waiting, dreaming, for the day I could come to you as a woman and offer it to you."

He turned to her as she spoke, his eyes taking on hope as she revealed her heart to him. He reached his hand upward to cup her cheek. "Forgive me, Cherish, for doubting that love. I never will again."

She smiled.

Slowly he leaned closer, his fingers touching her temple lightly, his eyes gazing at her in wonder. "You are so beautiful," he breathed. His fingers stroked her cheek.

"Am I finally going to get kissed properly?" she asked with a giggle.

He smiled at her. "I don't know about properly…but I shall do my best."

"Why don't you let me be the judge of your efforts?"

"Yes, Miss Winslow."

"Much obliged, Mr. van der Zee," she answered demurely.

No more words were necessary as his face neared hers and he grazed her lips with his.

She drew in her breath at the first contact. Her hands curved around his neck to bring his head closer to hers. This time his kiss was sweet and gentle.

When he finished kissing her, they looked into each other's eyes. "How did I do?" he asked, a smile lighting the depths of his greenish-gray eyes.

"I think I shall need a lifetime of repeat performances before I can give you a proper evaluation."

She touched the lock of hair falling over his forehead. "Do you know how many times I've wanted to do that?" she murmured.

"You may do it whenever you wish."

"May I?" She touched her finger to his face and ran it along his jawline. "How very gracious of you."

"Do you know how many times I've wanted to kiss you?" he asked in turn.

"No, how many?"

"Innumerable."

She giggled. "Well, you may do so any time you wish."

"May I? How very amiable of you."

A few moments later she asked him. "Don't you think we were meant for each other? Or do you think that's an excessively romantic notion?"

"I do believe it's a very sensible observation," he replied.

Her finger traced the edge of his collar. "I'm glad to see you're sporting the shirt I made you. I took great pleasure in sewing it."

His eyes glanced downward to what they could see of it. "Did you indeed? No wonder it's become my favorite shirt."

When they rose to go, Silas gave Cherish his hand. "Come, there's something still to be done."

She followed him curiously as he led her to a large boulder, where he seated her.

"Let's see…how would Count—or was it Prince?—Leopold do this?"

"I'm not interested in Count Leopold."

They looked at each other in acknowledgment. "All right, how would Silas van der Zee go about proposing?" As he spoke, he got down on one knee and took her hand. "Cherish Elizabeth Winslow, will you be my wife?"

"With great pleasure, Silas Todd van der Zee."

He brought her hand up to his lips and kissed it.

"Do you think we could be married soon?" he asked as he helped her up.

"As soon as you'd like," she replied.

"That would be this instant."

"Although it would be nice to be courted by you, Silas…as I was today," she demurred.

"I shall court you every day until our wedding day…and beyond."

Abruptly her face clouded.

"What is it?" he asked immediately.

"Silas, are you still going to leave Haven's End?"

"Your father has offered to sell me the shipyard."

Her eyes widened. "He has?" She sobered. "Is he asking a lot…?"

"Not more than what he owes me," he answered with a grin.

Her eyes grew even wider. "He owes you? What do you mean?"

He told her about the twelve hundred dollars.

"It was you!" she whispered in awe. "Of course! How could I not have known? I knew you were saving for your own boat-yard. I guess that's why it never occurred to me you'd be able to part with your savings—especially not to my father."

"I wasn't thinking of him. I would have done it for you in an instant, I realized."

"Oh, Silas." Her eyes filled with tears. "After how my father has treated you all these years…"

"I told you, I didn't do it for him. Don't cry," he begged softly, wiping a tear that fell down her cheek. "I would do it again gladly. God used it to set me free."

"Oh, Silas, Papa's changed toward you. I don't know what happened while we were away, but he's been so nice to you since we returned. He's treating you now the way he always should have."

"He gave me his blessing to propose to you."

She smiled. "Did he now? When was that?"

"The first chance he got."

They laughed happily, linking arms and walking toward the boat. She thought of something else. "So what did you tell my father about buying the shipyard?"

"I haven't given him my answer yet."

"Why not?" she asked slowly.

"I haven't decided yet whether to accept his generous offer or not."

She waited.

"It depends on you."

"I leave the decision to you," she replied. "As Ruth said, 'Whithersoever thou goest, I will go….'"

He smiled in reply. "Then we'll stay in Haven's End for the time being. I have a feeling the Lord will take us places we've never dreamed possible."

\* \* \* \* \*

### *Lilac Spring* book club discussion questions:

1) Apart from the courtship of Silas and Cherish, what would you say is the main theme of *Lilac Spring*?

2) At the beginning of the story, Cherish returns home after a trip to Europe. Do you think her travels abroad help or hurt her ability to fit in with the small town of Haven's End?

3) Silas lost his father at an early age and was sent to Haven's End soon thereafter. How did this separation from his family affect his ability to love?

4) How does Cherish's adoration of her father affect her relationship with Silas?

5) Neither a servant nor part of the Winslow family, Silas is somewhere in between. How does this affect him and his relationship with the Winslows?

6) Why must Silas give up his dream, and in doing so, give up his sense of self-worth?

7) After Mr. Winslow throws Silas out of the shipyard in anger, is it believable that he would ask for Silas's forgiveness so soon afterward?

8) Despite his outward respect for Mr. Winslow, one might say Silas's attitude isn't one of true humility. Why is it important for him to give his life savings to Mr. Winslow?

9) Why is it important for Cherish to face losing everything before getting Silas?

10) *Romans* 12:1 is the verse that converts Silas. Can you explain the verse? And how is it a turning point in his life?

11) In relation to question number 10, what is "wrong" with Silas's Christianity?

12) Both Cherish and Silas are forced to face a situation alone, and are subject to everyone's scrutiny. Have you ever found yourself in the same situation? How did you find your way out of it?

13) Some might call Cherish a spoiled young woman. Is it important to you as a reader that the heroine be likable? Why or why not?

14) What was your favorite scene in the book? Why?

15) *Lilac Spring* is set in nineteenth-century Maine. Was the author's description of the landscape and the community a good one? How was the setting important to the story? Could it have been set somewhere else?

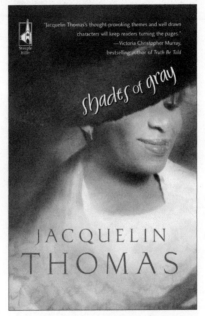

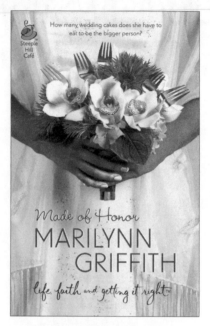

# YULETIDE PERIL

## by Irene Brand

Hoping to start a new life for herself and her younger sister, Janice Reid moves to Stanton, West Virginia, to take possession of a house her uncle left her. But Janice soon becomes the target of harassment and threats, which threaten both her newfound security and her developing relationship with Lance Gordon.

"Irene Brand pens a heartwarming romance with a strong message."
—*Romantic Times BOOKclub*

Steeple Hill®

**Don't miss *Yuletide Peril***
**On sale December 2005**
**Available at your favorite retail outlet.**

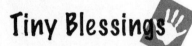

THE

# Tiny Blessings

SERIES CONCLUDES WITH

# PAST SECRETS, PRESENT LOVE

BY

## LOIS RICHER

The missing now-adult child's identity is finally
revealed by private investigator Ross Van Zandt,
complicating several lives. Ross has more than a
professional interest in Kelly Young, the lovely
director of Tiny Blessings adoption agency. But will
the secrets Ross has promised to keep destroy the
relationship before it begins?

**TINY BLESSINGS: Giving thanks for the neediest of
God's children, and the families who take them in!**

**Don't miss PAST SECRETS, PRESENT LOVE**

**On sale December 2005**

*Available at your favorite retail outlet.*

**www.SteepleHill.com**

# *Love Inspired*™®

## SUGAR PLUMS FOR DRY CREEK

### BY

### JANET TRONSTAD

Judd Bowman wanted to give his young cousins, whom he was raising, a Christmas to remember. Being part of Dry Creek's first *Nutcracker* production was the one thing they wanted. Yet when Judd met Lizette Baker, the ballet teacher, he discovered he had a wish of his own: to have Lizette by his side for the rest of their lives....

**Don't miss SUGAR PLUMS FOR DRY CREEK**
**On sale December 2005**

*Available at your favorite retail outlet.*